John Greenleaf Whittier, Oliver Johnson

William Lloyd Garrison and his Times

Or, Sketches of the anti-slavery movement in America, and of the man who was its

founder and moral leader

John Greenleaf Whittier, Oliver Johnson

William Lloyd Garrison and his Times
Or, Sketches of the anti-slavery movement in America, and of the man who was its founder and moral leader

ISBN/EAN: 9783744726405

Printed in Europe, USA, Canada, Australia, Japan

Cover: Foto ©Andreas Hilbeck / pixelio.de

More available books at **www.hansebooks.com**

WILLIAM LLOYD GARRISON

AND HIS TIMES;

OR,

SKETCHES OF THE ANTI-SLAVERY MOVEMENT
IN AMERICA,

AND OF

THE MAN WHO WAS ITS FOUNDER AND MORAL LEADER.

By OLIVER JOHNSON.

WITH AN INTRODUCTION BY
JOHN G. WHITTIER.

O, my brethren! I have told
Most bitter truth, but without bitterness. — COLERIDGE.

BOSTON:

B. B. RUSSELL & CO., No. 57 CORNHILL.

SAN FRANCISCO: A. L. BANCROFT & CO. PORTLAND: JOHN RUSSELL.
PHILADELPHIA: QUAKER CITY PUBLISHING HOUSE.
NEW YORK: CHARLES DREW. CHICAGO: ANDREWS & DORMAN.
INDIANAPOLIS, IND.: FRED L. HORTON & CO.

1880.

To the

SURVIVING HEROES

OF THE

AMERICAN ANTI-SLAVERY STRUGGLE,

IN WHATEVER FIELD OR BY WHATEVER INSTRUMENTALITIES
THEY CONSCIENTIOUSLY LABORED

FOR THE

DELIVERANCE OF THE LAND FROM THE CRIME AND CURSE
OF HUMAN BONDAGE,

This Volume

IS FRATERNALLY INSCRIBED BY

THE AUTHOR.

PREFACE.

SOME months since the writer of these pages was invited to contribute to the " New York Tribune " a short series of papers, embracing some of his recollections of the American Anti-Slavery Movement, and of the persons most prominently connected therewith. His attempt to fulfil this task was received with so much favor in various quarters, that he was induced, the Editor of the " Tribune " kindly consenting, to go far beyond his original intention, and take a rapid survey of the whole movement, which, beginning in the labors of WILLIAM LLOYD GARRISON, in 1829, finally led to the abolition of slavery by the exercise of the powers of war, as a means of putting down the Rebellion. The sketches thus written are now gathered, with some slight revision, and with large additions, into a volume, at the suggestion of many of the writer's old friends, and in the belief that in this form they will meet a public want.

The writer desires it to be understood that this volume does not claim to be a complete history of the Anti-Slavery Movement, either in its moral or political aspects. His purpose is simply to make a contribution, which he hopes will be of some value, to the materials for such a history, which may be written by another hand, when the prejudices and passions engendered by the conflict have passed away. The author has attempted, in a series of brief sketches, to present an outline, first, of the action of the Abolitionists up to the divisions of 1839–40; and, secondly, after stating as impartially as he is able the circumstances and causes of those divisions, to follow the course of the American Anti-Slavery Society, and those who co-operated with it, under the lead of Mr. Garrison, to the close of the conflict. This plan, it will be seen, does not embrace a history, however brief, of the anti-slavery political parties, or of the labors of those who worked through these instrumentalities to prevent the extension of slavery, and to resist its encroachments upon the institutions of freedom. Without intending to disparage, in any degree, the action of those parties, or of the men who labored in and through them, but, on the contrary, while gratefully acknowledging the importance and value of what they accomplished, the writer has chosen to confine himself mainly to an account of the MORAL AGITATION, which was the original cause and constant stimulus of political action; and this because, while the progress of the movement, in a political sense, was necessarily conspicuous, and is therefore certain to attract the attention of the historian, — indeed has already been treated with great fullness and ample justice by the Hon. Henry Wilson, in his "History of the Rise and Fall of the Slave Power,"— the distinctively MORAL FORCES, which were so powerful in moulding public sentiment, are far less likely to receive the attention they deserve.

Mr. Garrison is the central figure in these pages, which contain an outline of his life and public career as the founder and leader of the Anti-Slavery Movement. He will be forever honored, not, indeed, as the first American to denounce slavery as a sin and seek its abolition, — for in this a multitude of honorable and eminent men were before him, — but the first to unfurl the banner of IMMEDIATE AND UNCONDITIONAL EMANCIPATION, and to organize upon that principle a movement which, under God, proved mighty enough to accomplish its object. The laurel will be the more willingly placed upon his brow because he never claimed it for himself, or in any way sought to win the applause of his countrymen. In his speech at the Breakfast given in his honor in London, in 1867, he said :—

" I must here disclaim, with all sincerity of soul, any special praise for anything that I have done. I have simply tried to maintain the integrity of my soul before God, and to do my duty. I have refused to go with the multitude to do evil. I have endeavored to save my country from ruin. I have sought to liberate such as were held captive in the house of bondage. But all this I ought to have done."

Having been associated with Mr. Garrison from the beginning, and served the cause at times not only as a lecturer, but as temporary Editor of " The Liberator," and later, at different periods, as Editor of the Ohio " Anti-Slavery Bugle," the " Pennsylvania Freeman," and the " National Anti-Slavery Standard," the writer has enjoyed unusual opportunities for observing the progress of the cause, for studying its principles and the nature and character of the opposition arrayed against it, as well as for becoming acquainted with the men and women by whose toils and sacrifices it was carried forward, through great difficulties, to a successful issue. With Mr. Garrison himself he was on terms of the closest intimacy, from the founding of " The Liberator " to the day of his death, and is therefore entitled to speak of his character, his aims, purposes and spirit, with something like authority. In doing so, however, he has aimed to speak not as a partisan, but as a conscientious if not a quite impartial observer. He has written of matters and things, " all of which he saw, and part of which he was " ; and yet, writing sometimes in haste and without opportunity to consult original documents, it will be strange if he has not fallen into some minor errors, which, however, it is believed, will not impair the integrity of his narrative.

Of one deficiency the author is deeply sensible. He has done but scant justice to many noble workers in the cause, whose zeal, devotion, and unswerving loyalty entitle them to the gratitude of mankind. Most of these, indeed, limited as he was for space, he has not been able so much as to name. But their " record is on high," and they have their reward in the remembrance of what they did to open the way for the emancipation of four millions of slaves. Let me here record, and make my own, the tribute paid to them by Mr. Garrison, himself, in London, in 1867 :

"Here allow me to pay a brief tribute to the American Abolitionists. Putting myself entirely out of the question, I believe that in no land, at any time, was there ever a more devoted, self-sacrificing, and uncompromising band of men and women. Nothing can be said to their credit which they do not deserve. With apostolic zeal, they counted nothing dear to them for the sake of the slave, and him dehumanized. But whatever has been achieved through them is all of God, to whom alone is the glory due. Thankful are we all that we have been permitted to live to see this day, for our country's sake, and for the good of mankind. Of course we are glad that our reproach is at last taken away ; for it is ever desirable, if possible, to have the good opinions of our fellow-men ; but if, to secure these, we must sell our manhood, and sully our souls, then their bad opinions of us are to be coveted instead."

If this volume shall serve to give to the people of this and future generations a clearer apprehension of the instrumentalities and influences by which American slavery was overthrown, the writer's highest ambition will be fulfilled.

81 COLUMBIA HEIGHTS, BROOKLYN, N. Y.

INTRODUCTION.

I DO not know that any word of mine can give additional interest to this memorial of William Lloyd Garrison, from the pen of one of his earliest and most devoted friends, whose privilege it has been to share his confidence and his labors for nearly half a century; but I cannot well forego the opportunity afforded me to add briefly my testimony to the tribute of the following pages to the memory of the great Reformer, whose friendship I have shared, and with whom I have been associated in a common cause from youth to age.

My acquaintance with him commenced in boyhood. My father was a subscriber to his first paper, the "Free Press," and the humanitarian tone of his editorials awakened a deep interest in our little household, which was increased by a visit which he made us. When he afterwards edited the "Journal of the Times," at Bennington, Vt., I ventured to write him a letter of encouragement and sympathy, urging him to continue his labors against slavery, and assuring him that he could "do great things," an unconscious prophecy which has been fulfilled beyond the dream of my boyish enthusiasm. The friendship thus commenced has remained unbroken through half a century, confirming my early confidence in his zeal and devotion, and in the great intellectual and moral strength which he brought to the cause with which his name is identified.

During the long and hard struggle in which the Abolitionists were engaged, and amidst the new and difficult questions and side-issues which presented themselves, it could scarcely be otherwise than that differences of opinion and action should arise among them. The leader and his disciples could not always see alike. My friend, the author of this book, I think, generally found himself in full accord with him, while I often decidedly dissented. I felt it my duty to use my right of citizenship at the ballot-box in the cause of liberty, while Garrison, with equal sincerity, judged and counselled otherwise. Each acted under a sense of individual duty and responsibility, and our personal relations were undisturbed. If, at times, the great anti-slavery leader failed to do justice to the motives of those who, while in hearty sympathy with his hatred of slavery, did not agree with some of his opinions and methods, it was but the pardonable and not unnatural result of his intensity of purpose, and his self-identification with the cause he advocated; and, while compelled to dissent, in some particulars, from his judgment of men and measures, the great mass of the anti-slavery people recognized his moral leadership. The controversies of Old and New organization, Non-Resistance and Political action, may now be looked upon by the parties to them, who still survive, with the philosophic calmness which follows the subsidence of prejudice and passion. We were but fallible men, and doubtless often erred in feeling, speech and action. Ours was but the common experience of Reformers in all ages.

> " Never in Custom's oiled grooves
> The world to a higher level moves,
> But grates and grinds with friction hard
> On granite bowlder and flinty shard.
> Ever the Virtues blush to find
> The Vices wearing their badge behind,
> And Graces and Charities feel the fire
> Wherein the sins of the age expire."

It is too late now to dwell on these differences. I choose rather, with a feeling of gratitude to God, to recall the great happiness of laboring with the noble company of whom Garrison was the central figure. I love to think of him as he seemed to me, when in the fresh dawn of manhood he sat with me in the old Haverhill farm-house, revolving even then schemes of benevolence ; or, with cheery smile, welcoming me to his frugal meal of bread and milk in the dingy Boston printing-room ; or, as I found him in the gray December morning in the small attic of a colored man, in Philadelphia, finishing his night-long task of drafting his immortal " Declaration of Sentiments " of the American Anti-Slavery Society ; or, as I saw him in the jail of Leverett Street, after his almost miraculous escape from the mob, playfully inviting me to share the safe lodgings which the State had provided for him ; and in all the varied scenes and situations where we acted together our parts in the great endeavor and success of Freedom.

The verdict of posterity in his case may be safely anticipated. With the true Reformers and Benefactors of his race he occupies a place inferior to none other. The private lives of many who fought well the battles of humanity have not been without spot or blemish. But his private character, like his public, knew no dishonor. No shadow of suspicion rests upon the white statue of a life, the fitting garland of which should be the Alpine flower that symbolizes Noble Purity.

JOHN G. WHITTIER.

10TH Mo. 3, 1879.

CONTENTS.

XV.

XVI.

XVII.

XVIII.

XIX.

ILLUSTRATIONS.

GARRISON AND HIS TIMES.

I.

Preliminary — The Revolutionary Period — The Quakers — Benjamin Lundy — The Hour and the Man — Birth and Boyhood of Garrison — He Learns the Trade of a Printer — Becomes a Writer and an Editor — In Boston and Benuington — Joins Lundy in Baltimore — His Imprisonment.

THE abolition of slavery in the United States is an event of the past, and the generation now coming upon the stage will know no more of the struggles it cost, or of the men and women by whose toils and sacrifices it was brought about than can be found in a chapter of history but imperfectly written as yet, or than they may be able to gather from the private recollections of the now venerable actors who are rapidly disappearing from the field on which their triumphs were won. The war in which the great conflict was brought to its final culmination, and in which such mighty moral and material forces were engaged, will be duly celebrated in history; but the moral and political agitations that preceded and led up to that event, and the men and women who took a conspicuous and honorable part therein, are not so likely to receive from posterity the tribute due to their courageous devotion to the cause of justice and liberty. The lines of this picture are growing fainter day by day, and soon every hand that can retouch them will be mouldering in the dust. As one who took a constant, though modest part in those agitations, from

their feeble beginning to their triumphant conclusion,
I have undertaken to give the public the benefit of
some of my recollections of the events of that time,
and of the actors therein.

All great changes in human affairs spring from
causes whose workings may be traced, with more or less
distinctness, to a remote past. Slavery being a very
ancient institution, it was not left to America to make
the first protest against it. There was not, and there
could not be any originality in the American Anti-
Slavery movement. The principles involved were as
old as humanity itself, and had their champions and
martyrs long before the discovery of the New World.
During the colonial period of our history, and for some
years after the adoption of the Constitution, there was
a strong current of opposition to slavery. The discussions that preceded the Revolutionary War, involving
as they did the fundamental principles of human
liberty, could not but remind all thoughtful persons of
the guilt and shame of slaveholding. The Declaration
of Independence, though adopted for no such purpose,
virtually set the seal of condemnation upon slavery as
a system at war with human nature and the law of God.
In lifting up that beacon-light before the world, the
American people challenged the judgment of mankind
upon their shameful inconsistency in making merchandise of human flesh. The sting of " the world's
reproach around them burning " was keenly felt by
many of the most eminent statesmen, divines and philanthropists of that day. Franklin, Rush, Hamilton and
Jay ; Hopkins, Edwards and Stiles ; and Woolman,
Lay and Benezet, among the Quakers, deserve honorable mention for their sturdy and unyielding hostility
to slavery. To the credit of the Quakers as a body it
should be said, that as early as 1780, after a long and
serious contest, they emancipated all their slaves,
which were very numerous in Maryland, New Jersey

and Pennsylvania, one monthly meeting setting free
eleven hundred. They also refused to hire slave-labor
of the masters.

In a certain sense the Abolitionists of a later period
entered into and completed the labors of these noble
and far-seeing men. But I am not to write a history
of the introduction of slavery into this country, nor to
record the efforts of some of the founders of the
Republic to resist its encroachments. I set my stake
at the beginning of the later movement against slavery,
which, dating from 1829, went forward with constantly
increasing momentum until the fetters of the slave
were melted in the hot flames of war. At the date
above mentioned there was hardly a ripple of excitement about slavery in any part of the nation. The
fathers of the Republic had fallen asleep; the Anti-
Slavery sentiment of the country, defeated in the spas-
modic Missouri struggle in 1821, had become too feeble
to utter even a whisper. From one year's end to
another there was scarcely a newspaper in all the land
that made the slightest allusion to the subject. The
Abolition societies in which Franklin and Rush and Jay
were once so active were either dead or sleeping. One
voice there was, and one only. Need I say that was
the voice of a Quaker? It was Benjamin Lundy, who,
in his little paper with a great name, — "The Genius
of Universal Emancipation," — lifted up that "voice
crying in the wilderness," first in Ohio, next in Ten-
nessee, and subsequently in Baltimore, then a mart of
the domestic traffic in slaves. It was a brave and an
earnest voice, but it was scarcely heard outside of the
Quaker body, to which Mr. Lundy belonged, and which
was fast becoming almost as torpid as other religious
bodies on this question. There was a time, as some
one has said, when one Quaker was enough to shake
the country for twenty miles around; but the time
came at length when it required the whole country for

twenty miles around to shake one Quaker ! The cotton
traffic had become immensely profitable, and Quakers
in the great cities loved its gains as well as others.
The still, small voice of conscience was overwhelmed
by the hoarse clamors of avarice. It was a universally
accepted proverb that slavery was absolutely necessary
to the production of a staple that was filling the coffers
of Northern merchants and manufacturers with untold
wealth. The moral sense of the people of the North
became paralyzed. Pulpit and press were generally
silent. If they spoke at all it was only to say that
slavery was too dangerous a subject to be discussed —
that the Union would not long survive its agitation.
To Benjamin Lundy chiefly belongs the honor of keeping the flame of Anti-Slavery sentiment from utterly
dying out in those dark days, and putting the burning
torch of liberty into the hands of the man raised up
by Providence to lead the new crusade against the
Slave Power.

No careful student of history can fail to be struck
by the fact that in every crisis of human affairs men
have been raised up with special qualifications for the
work that needed to be done at that particular time.
The hour strikes for the achievement of a great reform,
and lo ! a man appears upon the stage, commissioned
and equipped of God for the task. He gives the key-
note for rallying thousands; he sounds the charge
against an iniquitous institution, mighty in aspect, but
ripening for destruction. He calls a nation to repentance for its crimes against humanity, and warns it of
the Divine retributions for sin. Such men are the
prophets of God in their generation — misrepresented,
persecuted, maligned, and sometimes slain ; but always
honored of God, and sure at last to be honored of
men. What a catalogue of such men, " of whom the
world was not worthy," might be culled from the pages
of history — men whose bloody footsteps are the way-

marks of human progress, and to whom, under God, we owe what is most valuable in our civilization, and most beneficent in the application of Christianity to society and its institutions.

One of the greatest of all this host, the prophet of one of the grandest reforms that the world has ever witnessed, was the man whose labors and achievements will find a partial record in these pages. It is not any clearer to me that Moses was commissioned to lead the children of Israel out of the house of bondage, that Elijah was sent of God to rebuke the iniquity of Ahab, or that Jesus of Nazareth (I speak with reverence) came into the world to "bear witness unto the truth," than it is that Mr. Garrison was raised up by Divine Providence to deliver this Republic from the sin and crime of slavery. The circumstances of his appearance were remarkable. The nation was fast asleep, and heard not the rumblings of the earthquake that threatened her destruction. The state was morally paralyzed; the pulpit was dumb; the church heeded not the cry of the slave. Commerce, greedy of gain, piled her hoards by the unpaid toil of the bondman. Judgment was turned away backward; Justice stood afar off; Truth was fallen in the street, and Equity could not enter. The hands of the people were defiled with blood, their fingers with iniquity; their lips spoke lies, their tongues muttered perverseness. Men talked of slavery in that day (when they talked at all) with an incoherency like that of Bedlam, with a moral blindness and perverseness like that of Sodom and Gomorrah. That in this hour of thick darkness a voice was heard pleading, trumpet-tongued, for immediate emancipation, as the duty of every master and the right of every slave, seems to us now one of the most signal illustrations of the immanence of God in human affairs. I must believe that that voice, crying in the wilderness and calling the people to repentance, was

divinely inspired — not, indeed, in a miraculous, but
certainly in a providential sense.   It spoke for God's
outraged law of justice and love.   It pleaded for the
inalienable rights of man.   It rebuked a sin that was
preying upon the nation's life.

WILLIAM LLOYD GARRISON was born in Newburyport, Mass., in a house still standing in close prox-
imity to the church, under whose pulpit repose the
remains of George Whitefield, on the 10th of December, 1805.   His father was a sea-captain from
New Brunswick, and a man of some literary ability
and ambition.   His mother was a deeply religious
woman — a Baptist, when to be such required no
small amount of moral courage.   The son inherited
the mother's intuitive reverence for God and for human
nature as his image, her fine moral and spiritual sensitiveness, and her abhorrence of oppression in all its
forms.   As a boy he was responsive to those sentiments of liberty and patriotism which pervaded the
political and social atmosphere of the time.   His
opinions upon every question affecting the public welfare rested upon the solid basis of the Divine Law.
Ethical considerations in his mind outweighed all
others, and any compromise with an unjust or oppressive institution was, in his eyes, a sin to be rebuked
and denounced.   His clear moral vision, penetrating
at once all the subterfuges of the champions and apologists of slavery, enabled him to discern the true
character of the system, and to depict it in language
that stirred the consciences and moved the hearts of
those who read or listened.

Mrs. Garrison, while her son was yet too small to
support comfortably the weight of the lapstone, set
him to learning the trade of a shoemaker.   As he was
unhappy in this occupation, she next apprenticed him

BIRTHPLACE OF WILLIAM LLOYD GARRISON, NEWBURYPORT, MASS.

to a cabinet-maker. But he was still discontented, yearning continually for an occupation more congenial to his feelings and tastes, and his articles of apprenticeship were cancelled at his own earnest request. He found, at length, his right place in a printing-office in his native place. This proved for him both high school and college, from which he graduated with honor after a long and faithful apprenticeship. During the period of his minority he became deeply interested in current moral and political questions, upon which he wrote frequently and acceptably for the newspaper on which he daily worked as a printer, "The Newburyport Herald." He also contributed to a Boston paper a series of political essays, which, being anonymous, were by many attributed to the Hon. Timothy Pickering, then one of the most eminent citizens of Massachusetts. At the end of his apprenticeship he became the editor of a new paper, "The Free Press," in his native place. It was distinguished for its high moral tone, but proved unremunerative, as such papers generally do. He was next heard of as editor of "The National Philanthropist," in Boston, the first paper ever established to support the doctrine of total abstinence from intoxicating drinks. The theme was congenial to him, and he discussed it with great earnestness and ability. The motto of the paper was his own. It expressed a great truth in these words: "Moderate drinking is the down-hill road to drunkenness." This was in 1827–28. While engaged upon this paper he made the acquaintance of Benjamin Lundy, who came to Boston for the purpose of interesting some of the people of that city in the question of slavery.

Sometime in 1828 Mr. Garrison accepted an invitation to go to Bennington, Vt., to establish a paper for the support of John Quincy Adams for the Presidency. The title of this paper was "The Journal

of the Times." As a boy, I had greatly admired
"The National Philanthropist," and had tried my own
'prentice hand as a writer in its columns. But I found
new cause for admiring "The Journal of the Times"
in the fact that it was published in my native State.
How eagerly did I read and file away for preservation
every number as it came to the office in which I was
serving my own apprenticeship — "The Watchman"
office in Montpelier. It was to me the ideal newspaper, and it stirred in me that ambition of editorship
which springs up in the breast of every boy who learns
to handle a composing-stick. Mr. Garrison did not
neglect the purpose for which his paper was established.
He supported Mr. Adams with zeal and ability, but he
also discussed questions of reform which were quite
distasteful to some of his readers. He was the champion of temperance and peace, and Lundy's "Genius of
Universal Emancipation," which was among his ex-
changes, fanned his instinctive hatred of slavery to an
intense heat. He wrote a petition for the abolition of
slavery in the District of Columbia, which he sent to
all the postmasters in the State of Vermont, begging
them to procure signatures thereto. In that day postmasters enjoyed the privilege of receiving and sending
letters free of postage, and Mr. Garrison succeeded in
getting a large number of signatures to his petition,
which caused quite a flutter in Congress.

Mr. Lundy's paper was a small sheet, published but
once a month. He spent the greater portion of his
time in travelling from place to place procuring subscribers and endeavoring to excite an interest in the
subject by conversation and lecturing. In some instances he carried the head-rules, column-rules and
subscription book of his paper with him, and when he
came to a town where he found a printing-office, he
would stop long enough to print and mail a number of
"The Genius." He travelled for the most part on

foot, carrying a heavy pack. He was a man of slight figure, though of a wiry temperament, and these exertions no doubt overtaxed his strength. In his boyhood he had seen coffles of Virginia slaves going down the Ohio on their way to the far South, and his Quaker education had so intensified his hatred of the slave system that he counted no labor or sacrifice on his part too great to be endured in efforts for its suppression. No apostle of the Christian faith ever exhibited a more ardent and unselfish devotion to his work than that which characterized the anti-slavery labors of this devoted but simple-minded Quaker, who obeyed the rule of his sect in "minding the light" of the Divine Spirit in his own soul. The torch of liberty which Mr. Garrison was holding aloft in the Green Mountains of Vermont naturally attracted his attention and kindled a new hope in his bosom. His heart yearned toward the young champion of freedom, and he longed to enlist him more fully in the cause — to make him, if it were possible, his coadjutor. After making the journey to Boston by stage, he walked, staff in hand and pack on back, in the winter snow, all the long and weary way from that city to Bennington. The meeting of these two men under the shadow of the Green Mountains, whose winds were ever the swift messengers of freedom, may be regarded as the beginning of a movement that was destined, under God, to work the overthrow of American slavery. In this fresh mountain-spring originated the moral influences which, feeble at the first, became at length too mighty to be resisted. The two men took sweet and solemn counsel together, and formed a resolution whose final results were seen in the deliverance of their country from slavery, and proclaimed in the exultant shouts of millions of emancipated bondmen. The immediate result of the conference was that Mr. Garrison agreed to join Mr. Lundy in Baltimore. He went there accordingly in the fall of 1829, and took the principal charge of "The Genius of Universal Emancipation," which was enlarged, and from that time issued weekly. Mr. Lundy, it was understood, would contribute to the editorial columns so far as he could while spending most of his time in lecturing and soliciting subscriptions. Never was a partnership entered upon for a holier purpose or in a more fraternal spirit. And yet, from the outset, there was between the two men a wide difference of opinion upon one fundamental point. Mr. Lundy's conviction of the wrong, and sinfulness of slavery was as deep and earnest as that of Mr. Garrison, but he was an advocate of gradual emancipation, while his mind was preoccupied with schemes for colonizing the slaves as fast as they should be set free. Mr. Garrison, on the other hand, from the moment of setting himself to the serious consideration of the subject, saw clearly that gradualism was a delusion and a snare. Slavery was either right or wrong in principle, as well as in practice. If it was right even for an hour, it might be so for a year, for a century, or to the end of time; and, therefore, any effort for its abolition would be a war upon Divine Providence. If it was wrong, it was so upon the instant and in the nature of things; and, therefore, there could be no excuse for its continuance for a day or even an hour. All this seemed as clear to him as any mathematical axiom, and as fundamental as the law of Divine justice. His experience in the temperance cause had taught him that any movement against a wrong custom or an unrighteous institution, if it was to be of much avail, must rest upon some clearly defined moral principle which would commend itself instantly to the popular apprehension as a self-evident truth.

It was this clear moral perception of Mr. Garrison, which, penetrating through all the subterfuges in which slavery had become intrenched, qualified him to

lead the great movement to which he was henceforth to
be devoted. It was only in being himself lifted up to
this high plane of moral principle, that he could hope
to draw his fellow-countrymen into sympathy with the
movement, or even to arrest their attention for more
than a fleeting hour. To spend his time in depicting
the cruelties of the slave system, while tacitly consenting to the casuistry by which its existence for the time
was excused, would be such a process of self-stultifica-
tion as inevitably to defeat the object he had in view.

Mr. Garrison explained his views to Mr. Lundy
with the utmost frankness, and they talked the matter
over without coming to an agreement. How were the
two men in the face of this difference to walk together?
Mr. Lundy, in his sweet Quaker way, solved the difficulty. He said to Mr. Garrison : " Well, thee may put
thy initials to thy articles, and I will put my initials to
mine, and each will bear his own burden." And so
the two men struck hands, and "The Genius of Universal Emancipation" was a paper with two voices,
but one was a voice of thunder, while the other sunk
almost to a whisper. Up to this time the paper had
made little impression upon public sentiment. Its
readers wept over the wrongs and cruelties of slavery,
but they thought that a sudden emancipation would be
attended with still worse evils; and so, while they
pitied the slave, they excused the masters, and made
no intelligent and well directed assault upon the system. The chief sin of slavery they assigned to its
guilty originators; the duty of repentance and emancipation was postponed to an indefinite future. In
the nature of things the holders of slaves could see
little ground for alarm in an anti-slavery sentiment so
unintelligent and blind as this. But when Mr. Garrison lifted up the standard of Immediate Emancipation,
the ears of the slaveholders of Maryland and Virginia
began to tingle. Under Mr. Lundy's exposures of the

cruelties of the system they had indeed been annoyed
and angry; but the sight of that banner of Immediate
Emancipation filled them with alarm for the safety of
their system.   For the first time they heard their right
to keep even one slave in bondage for a single hour
disputed.   They were told that by every principle of
justice and by the law of God it was their duty to
"break every yoke and let the oppressed go free."
All the excuses and subterfuges by which they had
stifled the voice of conscience were swept away by an
invincible logic, and they saw themselves arraigned
before the Nation as a body of oppressors.

Baltimore was not only a slave-holding city, but one
of the chief marts of the domestic traffic in slaves.
Slave-pens flaunted their signs in open day upon the
principal streets, and their wealthy owners moved in
the best society and occupied pews in Christian
churches.   Vessels loaded with slaves, torn from their
kindred and friends in Maryland and Virginia, were
constantly departing for Mobile, Savannah, New
Orleans and other Southern ports; and coffles of
slaves, chained together, often moved in sad procession, sometimes to mocking strains of music, through
the streets out into the open country, on their way to
the National Capital.   The state of society in which
scenes like these were tolerated need not be described.
And yet it was in this seat of the domestic slave-trade
that Lundy and Garrison set up their anti-slavery
banner. . Their friends, of course, were few and very
timid, and ready to run under cover at the first alarm.
Slavery was indeed acknowledged to be a bad system,
leading to many gross wrongs and cruelties.   Even
the slaveholders, generally admitted as much as this.
But emancipation was held even by the sincere opponents of slavery to be impracticable.   The holder of
slaves was declared to be in the position of a man
having a wolf by the ears — he must hold on to save

his own life. The slaves, if emancipated, would take revenge for past wrongs by cutting the throats of the masters, burning their houses and ravaging the land. They could not take care of themselves in a state of freedom, and in fact did not desire to be free. In this sort of sophistry and falsehood the common-sense and the conscience of the whole community were enmeshed. Emancipation in any shape, however gradual, was held to be an impossibility; the very thought of immediate emancipation the wildest fanatical dream; and even the discussion of the subject was dreaded as a knell of doom to the Republic itself.

We need not wonder, therefore, if "The Genius of Universal Emancipation," which as a small monthly under Mr. Lundy's mild management had been barely tolerated, was now, in its enlarged form and issued every week, absolutely intolerable to the people of Baltimore and the surrounding region. The slave power, entrenched in church and state, began to growl like a wild beast at bay. The air was thick with fierce denunciation of "that madcap Garrison," and men in places of power and influence began to look each other in the face and ask whereunto this new crusade against slavery would grow if some means of crushing it out were not speedily found. The slaveholders hardly dared then to make open war upon the freedom of the press, lest in doing so they should arouse an enemy too strong to be successfully resisted. They contented themselves, therefore, with exciting a popular clamor against the obnoxious paper, under which the more timid of its subscribers fell away. Mr. Garrison himself says: "My doctrine of immediate emancipation so alarmed and excited the people everywhere, that where friend Lundy would get one new subscriber I would knock a dozen off. It was the old experiment of the frog in the well, that went up two feet and fell back three at every jump." Men who could see only

half-truths and lacked courage to maintain even those
with firmness, said: "How foolish to throw away all
chance of doing any good by such ultraism." But
Wisdom then, as always, was justified of her children.
The excitement by which the slaveholders hoped to
extinguish the rising tide of anti-slavery sentiment
only served to fan it to an intense flame, and more was
done in a single month to prepare the way for the new
crusade than could have been accomplished by years
of timid, half-way effort. It was no confused or uncertain sound that the new tocsin rang out upon the
air. It proclaimed slavery a sin and shame, and demanded that ·every yoke should be broken, every
fetter sundered, every captive set free. It startled
and aroused thousands who would have been deaf to
any more equivocal message, and kindled in the hearts
of a noble few a fixed determination to cry aloud and
spare not until slavery should be utterly abolished.

It was not long, however, before the slaveholders of
Baltimore found what they thought was an opportunity
to crush out the new movement and the paper that
represented it. Mr. Garrison, of course, did not fail
to denounce the domestic slave-trade, of which Baltimore was one of the principal marts. There came to
that port a vessel owned by Mr. Francis Todd of
Newburyport, Mr. Garrison's native place, and commanded by one of her citizens, named Brown. The
vessel took from Baltimore to New Orleans a cargo of
eighty slaves. Here was a case of Northern complicity
with the infamous traffic which stirred Mr. Garrison's
deepest indignation, and he denounced the transaction
as in no respect different in principle from taking a
cargo of human flesh on the coast of Africa and carrying it across the ocean to a market. The law denounced
the foreign slave-trade as piracy ; the·domestic slave-
trade, in the sight of God and according to every principle of justice, was no whit better, nor in any respect

different in quality. Mr. Todd, stung to the quick by
Mr. Garrison's denunciations, brought suit against him
for libel. A trial in a slaveholding court and before
a slaveholding jury could have but one result. Mr.
Garrison was found guilty and fined in the sum of fifty
dollars and costs of court. If he had been a rich man
he probably would not have consented to pay a single
cent of the sum demanded of him. But he was too
poor to pay, and so of necessity went to jail. There
was no effort on the part of the patrons of "The Genius"
to avert his fate. The excitement in Baltimore was
almost as intense as that in Jerusalem when Jesus was
led away to be crucified. "And they all forsook him
and fled" was hardly more true in the one case than in
the other of those who before had professed to be
friendly to the cause and its champion. But the young
Abolitionist was neither cast down nor dismayed, nor
did he for a moment waver in his adherence to the
principles he had avowed. He would make no apology,
nor retract a single word. He knew that the ultimate
effect of his imprisonment would be to arouse popular
hostility to slavery, and promote the cause of emancipation. His undaunted spirit found utterance in two
sonnets, which he inscribed with a pencil on the walls
of his cell, as follows : —

THE GUILTLESS PRISONER.

Prisoner! within these gloomy walls close pent,
　Guiltless of horrid crime or venal wrong—
Bear nobly up against thy punishment,
　And in thy innocence be great and strong!
Perchance thy fault was love to all mankind;
　Thou didst oppose some vile, oppressive law;
Or strive all human fetters to unbind;
　Or wouldst not bear the implements of war:—
What then? Dost thou so soon repent the deed?
　A martyr's crown is richer than a king's!
Think it an honor with thy Lord to bleed,
　And glory midst intensest sufferings!
Though beat, imprisoned, put to open shame,
Time shall embalm and magnify thy name!

FREEDOM OF THE MIND.

High walls and huge the BODY may confine,
   And iron grates obstruct the prisoner's gaze,
And massive bolts may baffle his design,
   And vigilant keepers watch his devious ways :
Yet scorns th' immortal MIND this base control!
   No chains can bind it and no cell inclose :
Swifter than light, it flies from pole to pole,
   And, in a flash, from earth to heaven it goes !
It leaps from mount to mount—from vale to vale
   It wanders, plucking honeyed fruits and flowers;
It visits home, to hear the fireside tale,
   Or in sweet converse pass the joyous hours :
'Tis up before the sun, roaming afar,
And, in its watches, wearies every star !

II.

Garrison's Imprisonment, and Its Effects at the North—The Release
—Whittier, Clay, Tappan—Partnership of Lundy and Garrison
Dissolved—Tribute of the Latter to the Former—Founding of
"The Liberator" in Boston rather than in Washington—Garrison
on a Lecturing Tour—Boston and the Cotton Traffic—Garrison
Appeals in Vain to the Clergy—Dr. Lyman Beecher and Jere-
miah Evarts—"The Liberator" Born in a Dark Time—Purposes
and Hopes of its Founder—Responsibility of the Church.

THE news of Mr. Garrison's imprisonment was received with fierce exultation at the South, while many
Northern people openly said: "It is just what he
deserves; a man so reckless of the public welfare as to
attempt to stir up an excitement on the slavery question ought to be brought up with a round turn." The
expressions of mild indignation and sympathy that
found utterance here and there were qualified by regrets that a man engaged in so good a cause should be
so wild and fanatical as to demand the instant emancipation of the slaves. "The Boston Courier," edited
by that famous journalist, Joseph T. Buckingham, a
man of singular independence of spirit, while not
approving Mr. Garrison's views and methods, did yet
appreciate his unselfish devotion to liberty and his
willingness to suffer in a good cause. It published
the sonnets which he inscribed on the walls of his cell,
and, if my recollection is not at fault, printed one or
two letters from him, written during his imprisonment.
I was then in Boston, and full of a boy's enthusiasm
for my hero, whom I had never seen, but had admired
from the time of his connection with "The National
Philanthropist." I was often a visitor at a Cornhill
book-store, which was a place of resort for the ortho-

dox clergymen of Boston, including my own pastor, the Rev. Dr. Lyman Beecher. Newspapers, religious and secular, were on file there for the accommodation of visitors, and at times conversation was free upon topics of public interest. Well do I remember the discussions in that circle of Mr. Garrison's imprisonment, and how few of all those who took part in them expressed more than a qualified sympathy for the prisoner, while most of them spoke of him as a visionary and a fanatic. Indeed, the whole community seemed to be far more deeply impressed by what they thought the fanaticism of the new champion of the slave than by the injustice and shame of imprisoning a man for a too ardent devotion to liberty.

But the discussion thus excited in different parts of the country, though lacking in a true appreciation of the crisis, exerted a wholesome influence, and prepared the way for the growth of a more enlightened public sentiment. Expediency was a very popular word in those days, being held to embody the very highest wisdom in all things relating to slavery. Everybody was ready to affirm that "slavery in the abstract" was something dreadful, the very acme, indeed, of human wickedness; but for slavery in the United States every man's mouth was full of apologies. Texts of Scripture were cited for its defence as freely as if it had been the very corner-stone of the Christian faith, and the Constitution of the United States was appealed to as the very charter and bulwark of the hateful system. At the bottom of all the wretched casuistry by which men silenced the demands of justice in their hearts, was this one fact — the slaves were black; or, to use the word more deeply freighted with atheistic contempt of human nature than any other, "niggers." If, by a miracle, the slaves had been made white, all excuses for slavery would have been overthrown, and the whole people would have risen up as one man to demand its instant abolition. Gradualism in that case would have become intolerable, and immediate emancipation the popular cry. Mr. Garrison's primary fault was his belief in the absolute humanity of the negro ; but this was just what fitted him for the work to which he was called of God, and that made his appeals to the consciences of men so powerful.

The story of his release, after an imprisonment of forty-nine days, is of almost romantic interest. John G. Whittier, then unknown to fame, was the editor of "The New England Review," at Hartford, having succeeded the late George D. Prentice, who was called by the friends of Henry Clay to become the editor of "The Louisville Daily Journal." Whittier and Garrison were not unknown to each other. When the latter was editing "The Free Press," at Newburyport, the former had sent to him for publication several of his earliest poems, in which Mr. Garrison saw indications of the genius now universally recognized. Educated in all the best principles and traditions of Quakerism, there was even then burning in his heart that love of freedom which subsequently burst forth in impassioned verse. He was deeply moved by the imprisonment of his friend, and naturally anxious to do what he could for his deliverance. He was a great admirer of Henry Clay, and cherished the hope that he might one day become President. Of course, he knew that Mr. Clay was a slaveholder, but he had faith in him as at heart a true friend of freedom, for he had observed his efforts to provide for the ultimate abolition of slavery in Kentucky, and admired his eloquent defence of the Greeks in their struggle for freedom. He wrote to the Kentucky statesman, asking his interposition in behalf of the "guiltless prisoner" at Baltimore, and begging him to open his prison-door by paying his fine. Mr. Clay responded promptly, making some preliminary inquiries which indicated a purpose to comply with

Whittier's request.   This appears all the more creditable to him when it is remembered that Mr. Garrison
was an opponent of the scheme of African colonization,
of which Mr. Clay was then the foremost champion,
and had sharply criticised some of his speeches on that
subject.   The Kentucky statesman, though he doubtless had little patience with Mr. Garrison's doctrine of
immediate emancipation, was not then wholly devoid
of a noble though blind ambition to connect his name
in some way with the deliverance of his country from
slavery.   If he had been told at that moment what he
would do, ere the lapse of many years, as a candidate
for the Presidency, to promote the schemes of the Slave
Power, he would doubtless have said : " Is thy servant
a dog that he should do this thing ? "   While Mr. Clay
was probably getting ready to do what Mr. Whittier
had recommended, another stepped in before him, paid
the prisoner's fine and bill of costs, and thus opened
his prison-door.   It was Arthur Tappan, then a prosperous merchant of New York, who seized the laurel
that might otherwise have adorned the brow of the
great Compromiser of Kentucky.   Mr. Tappan was a
reader of "The Genius of Universal Emancipation,"
and thus familiar with Mr. Garrison's views.   Like
Mr. Clay, he was a Colonizationist, and little inclined
to sanction what was then regarded as ultraism in dealing with slavery.   He did, however, admire Mr. Garrison's independence and courage, his loyalty to God
and his devotion to freedom, and was willing to take
upon himself the odium of setting the "fanatic" at
liberty.

The partnership between Mr. Lundy and Mr. Garrison, which had been interrupted by the imprisonment
of the latter, was now formally dissolved by mutual
consent, and with the most fraternal feelings on both
sides.   "The Genius" fell back from a weekly to a
monthly publication, under Mr. Lundy's exclusive con-

trol, while Mr. Garrison took measures to establish a journal of his own, in which, upon his sole responsibility, he could deal with the slavery question according to his own convictions and his matured judgment. Never, however, did he cease to admire the indomitable courage and devotion of Lundy, or forget to be grateful to him as the man who first called his attention to the wrongs and woes of slavery. It was not long afterward that his admiration and gratitude found utterance in the following lines : —

TO BENJAMIN LUNDY.

Self-taught, unaided, poor, reviled, contemned,
  Beset with enemies, by friends betrayed;
As madman and fanatic oft condemned,
  Yet in thy noble cause still undismayed!
Leonidas could not thy courage boast;
  Less numerous were his foes, his band more strong:
Alone, unto a more than Persian host,
  Thou hast undauntedly given battle long.
Nor shalt thou singly wage the unequal strife;
  Unto thy aid, with spear and shield, I rush,
And freely do I offer up my life,
  And bid my heart's-blood find a wound to gush!
New volunteers are trooping to the field;
To die we are prepared, BUT NOT AN INCH TO YIELD!

For several years Mr. Lundy went on in his old way, exposing the wrongs of slavery, advocating gradual emancipation, and busying himself, with small success, in various schemes for colonizing the negroes, until the moral agitation created by the more uncompromising efforts of Garrison drew him with thousands of others into its mighty wake.

Mr. Garrison at first resolved to unfurl the standard of Immediate Emancipation at the National Capital, the seat of the domestic slave-trade and of those mighty political influences by means of which the Slave Power dominated over the Republic. In August, 1830, he issued the prospectus of a weekly paper to be published in Washington, and called " The

Liberator." The proposition was as natural as it was
bold. Certainly it was most appropriate that a public
journal intended to promote the deliverance of the
nation from the crime and curse of human bondage
should be published in Washington, and sent forth
from that centre to every part of the United States.
It was then supposed that emancipation would find at
least a few firm friends at the South, and that it would
be possible to organize there a movement, which,
appealing to the consciences of the slaveholders,
would soon become formidable enough to work the
overthrow of slavery. Such thoughts and expectations, however, were founded in a mistaken estimate
of the power as well as the purposes of the supporters
of slavery, who were ready, if necessary for the
defence of their system, to deny the freedom of speech,
and establish a reign of terror throughout the South.

Having issued his prospectus, Mr. Garrison soon
left Baltimore for the North, where he hoped to find
sympathy and support among his old friends, and in
the community generally. Of course, he had no capital of his own on which to found the proposed paper.
His only possessions were his indomitable courage and
will, his ardent love of liberty, his faith in human
nature, and his trust in God. But these were enough,
and without a doubt of the goodness of his cause and
of its early triumph, he went forth to battle in its
behalf. During his imprisonment he had prepared
several lectures on the subject of slavery and the
delusive scheme of African colonization, and these he
proposed to deliver in Northern cities and towns where
he could gain a hearing. He first visited Philadelphia,
where he was warmly received by the free people of
color and by a few others, mostly Quakers; but he was
unable to make any wide or deep impression upon the
citizens generally, for Philadelphia then, and for many
years afterwards, was intensely Southern in her inter-

ests and sympathies. His experiences in New York
were hardly more favorable. Here, however, he met
for the first time his benefactor, the man who had
opened his prison-door, Mr. Arthur Tappan, who from
that hour became his warm friend and supporter.
The colored people of the city welcomed him as a
hero, but the white people for the most part were
hostile or apathetic. From New York he went on to
New England — to New Haven, Hartford, Providence,
Boston — where his reception was hardly more encouraging than it had been in places further south. In
view of such a state of public sentiment in the free
States, he soon became convinced that Boston rather
than Washington was the place where "The Liberator"
should be established, and he changed his plans accordingly. To fight slavery at the South while the North
was hostile would be like going into battle in an
enemy's country with no base for re-enforcements or
supplies. It would be in vain to appeal against
slavery to Richmond, Charleston and New Orleans,
while Boston, New York and Philadelphia were apolo-
gizing for the system; in vain to seek the support of
Southern statesmen while those of the North were
hostile; in vain to look for sympathy to the Southern
churches while those of the North were either apathetic
or lending an open support to the evil. Writing on
this subject, he said : —

" During my recent tour for the purpose of exciting the
minds of the people by a series of discourses on the subject
of slavery, every place that I visited gave fresh evidence of
the fact that a greater revolution in public sentiment was to
be effected in the free States — and particularly in New England — than at the South. I found contempt more bitter,
opposition more active, detraction more relentless, prejudice
more stubborn and apathy more frozen than among slave-
owners themselves. Of course there were individual exceptions to the contrary. This state of things afflicted, but did

not dishearten me.   I determined, at every hazard, to lift
up the standard of emancipation in the eyes of the nation,
within sight of Bunker Hill, and in the birth-place of Liberty."

The resolution thus formed was an illustration of the
hard common-sense for which he was ever afterwards
distinguished. He saw that Washington was too near
the fulcrum to afford the requisite purchase — he must
throw his weight upon the end of the lever.   A battle
must first be fought to establish the right to *discuss*
the subject of slavery, and this contest, in the then
inflammable condition of the Southern mind, could not
be successfully waged upon slave soil.   The slaveholders would be certain to take alarm from the establishment of an uncompromising anti-slavery journal at the
National Capital, and to suppress it with a strong
hand ; while the people of the North, in their indifference and blindness, would be almost sure to say,
" Served him right ; if he had not been a mad-cap, he
would no more have established his incendiary sheet
on slave soil than he would have walked into a powder
magazine with a lighted torch."   And yet the very
people who would have said this, when they saw the
first number of "The Liberator" with a Boston imprint,
exclaimed : " Coward ! Why does he not go to the
South, instead of assailing slavery at this safe distance?   The people of New England are not slaveholders, and this fanatic has no right to pester us with
this perplexing question."   But Mr. Garrison's clear-
sightedness enabled him to discern, even at that early
day, that the influences which chiefly sustained slavery
were supplied by the people of the North.   He clearly
saw that all efforts to redeem the South would be vain
so long as the Northern people, through ecclesiastical,
political, commercial and social channels, supplied the
moral power by which the slave system was upheld.

Boston was then the heart of New England, and

spoke for it far more emphatically than she does now. The cotton traffic had grown to gigantic proportions there, and by it men gained vast wealth. Cotton factories were springing up on every side, giving profitable employment to large numbers of men, women and children, and by opening extensive markets for agricultural produce, enabling the farmers to pay off their mortgages and redeem themselves from the slavery of debt. The cotton traffic, in short, was regarded as the chief source of New England's prosperity, and the people were impatient of everything that seemed likely to disturb it. It was almost universally believed that cotton could be raised only by the labor of slaves, as no freeman would submit to the hardships necessarily involved in its culture. The appearance of "The Liberator" consequently set the whole cotton interest into a fever of excitement. Southern planters, filled with rage, wrote to their Northern customers protesting against such a paper, as calculated to excite the slaves to insurrection and deluge the South in blood. Northern merchants, yielding readily to such appeals to their cupidity and their fears, cried out against the anti-slavery movement as a wicked and inexcusable conspiracy. The press was their willing servant, and so to a great extent was the pulpit, especially in the cities and larger towns. These merchants occupied the most prominent pews in the churches, and contributed largely and liberally for the support of the ministry and for those missionary and other benevolent organizations that enjoyed the favor of the churches. The pulpit was thus sorely tempted to swerve from the laws of humanity and rectitude and become the apologist if not the defender of slavery. When I say that it often yielded to this temptation, or, where it did not fully yield, was seduced into a scarcely less guilty silence, I set down naught in malice, but only record the truth of history for the instruction and warning of

other generations.   If this truth were hidden, it would
be impossible to estimate aright the courage, foresight
and self-sacrificing spirit of Mr. Garrison and his associates.

Dr. Lyman Beecher was then at the head of the
Orthodox pulpit in Boston.   The great controversy
between Orthodoxy and Unitarianism was drawing
nigh to its culmination in the complete divorcement of
the two parties.   Dr. Channing, the leader on the Unitarian side, was a man of a gentle and humane spirit,
not liking controversy, while Dr. Beecher was a born
belligerent.   Mr. Garrison was conscientiously and
strictly Orthodox, and therefore naturally inclined to
seek support in the first instance from the Orthodox
pulpit and church.   When he was in Boston in 1828,
editing " The National Philanthropist," he became a
warm admirer of Dr. Beecher, partly on account of his
attitude on the Temperance question, but still more
because of his great powers as a preacher, and, naturally enough, he was the first minister to whom Mr.
Garrison appealed for support.   He was bitterly disappointed in finding him indifferent to the appeal.   " I
have too many irons in the fire already," said the Doctor.   " Then," said Mr. Garrison, solemnly, "you had
better let all your irons burn than neglect your duty
to the slave."   The Doctor, like almost all the clergymen of that day, was a colonizationist, believing that
freedom to the slaves with liberty to remain in the
United States would be a curse ; they must be sent to
Africa, whence their fathers had been stolen, and carry
to that country the Christianity of their masters.   To
him, therefore, Mr. Garrison's doctrine of immediate
emancipation upon American soil was repulsive, and he
told him so.   " Your zeal," he said, "is commendable ;
but you are misguided.   If you will give up your
fanatical notions and be guided by us (the clergy) we
will make you the Wilberforce of America."

Mr. Garrison had learned the doctrine of immediatism from Dr. Beecher himself. The very keynote of
the revivals of that day, in which the Doctor took so
prominent a part, was the duty of every sinner to
repent instantly and give his heart to Christ; but the
men who were most eloquent in urging this doctrine
in its application to the sin of unbelief were prompt to
deny it in its application to the sin of slavery. Sin in
general was something for which there could be no
apology or excuse, but the particular sin of treating
men as chattels and compelling them to work without
wages could only be put away, if at all, by a process
requiring whole generations for its consummation!
Such was the moral blindness of the time — a blindness not of the multitude alone, but of the professed
expounders of the will of God.

Mr. Garrison left Dr. Beecher with a disappointed
and saddened heart, for he had counted with confidence
upon his sympathy and support. He had sat under
his preaching with profit and delight, and he longed
to hear his eloquent voice pleading the cause of the
imbruted slave. Disappointed in this, to whom should
he next turn? He resolved to visit other clergymen
of the city and vicinity and seek their co-operation.
But, with hardly an exception, he found them unsym-
pathetic. Dr. Beecher, in speaking for himself, had
unconsciously spoken for the rest. Truth had indeed
fallen in the street, and Equity could not enter. He
resolved to go and see Jeremiah Evarts, Secretary of
the American Board of Commissioners for Foreign
Missions, who had been writing eloquently in behalf
of the Indians. Surely, he said to himself, I shall
find a helper in him. But no; Mr. Evarts, with all
his sympathy for the outraged Indians, would not
speak or write a word in behalf of the slave, or countenance any effort for his emancipation; and Mr. Garrison learned, to his unspeakable disgust, that not a

few of the Cherokees and Choctaws, for whom Mr.
Evarts was pleading so eloquently, were themselves
the owners of negro slaves!

It was in the midst of such darkness, discouragement and doubt that "The Liberator" was born — born
to fight slavery to the death, and to record its final
extinction. Started without so much as a single dollar of capital, or even one subscriber, it was sustained
for thirty-five years by such pluck and endurance, and
such faith in God as have been but rarely witnessed in
the history of mankind. In the character of its editor
it had a moral capital that no fire of persecution could
destroy or impair, and no flood of calumny overwhelm.
It fought for what is most of all fundamental in the
religion of Christ, for that without which it were indeed a mockery and a sham. God and Christ were
in the movement, and the gates of hell, though fortified and barricaded by traitor hands, could not prevail
against it. The hour had struck, and the man whom
God had commissioned to preach deliverance to the
captives and the opening of the prison to them that
were bound had come. It was in vain now that men
cried peace when there was no peace. The pulpit
might prostitute itself to the defence of slavery; statesmen might plead in its behalf the sacredness of the
Constitutional compacts and compromises; the press
might denounce as fanatical the plea for emancipation,
and mobs might howl upon the track of the Abolitionists. All in vain! for it was determined in the Divine
counsel that American slavery should be overthrown —
peaceably, if the nation were so minded, but otherwise
in blood! This was the dread alternative presented to
the American people. It was Mr. Garrison's hope that
the power of Christianity in the land was mighty enough
to accomplish the great work. The delusions of the
hour, he thought, would pass away, the pulpit would
awake to its duty, the churches — a mighty and invinci-

ble host—would come up to the help of the Lord against the great iniquity, and the statesmen of the land would show themselves men worthy of such a crisis. The slaveholders themselves, their first madness over, would listen to the voice of reason, and come speedily to see that their own safety and prosperity required that they should undo the heavy burdens and let the oppressed go free. With what earnestness of conviction and what eloquence of speech did he plead the promises of God to a nation that should put away its sin! "Loose the bands of wickedness, undo the heavy burdens, let the oppressed go free, break every yoke, hide not thyself from thine own flesh. Then shall thy light break forth as the morning, and thine health shall spring forth speedily; thy righteousness shall go before thee, the glory of the Lord shall be thy rereward, and thy darkness be as the noonday. And the Lord shall guide thee continually, and satisfy thy soul in drought, and make fat thy bones. Thou shalt be like a watered garden, and like a spring of water, whose waters fail not. They that shall be of thee shall build the old waste places. Thou shalt raise up the foundations of many generations; and thou shalt be called the repairer of the breach, the restorer of paths to dwell in. Thou shalt delight thyself in the Lord, and I will cause thee to ride upon the high places of the earth, and feed thee with the heritage of Jacob thy father; for the mouth of the Lord hath spoken it." Equally earnest and equally eloquent was he in depicting the calamities which, in the order of Divine Providence, would come upon the nation if it should persist in its sin: "Therefore, thus saith the Lord: Ye have not hearkened unto me, in proclaiming liberty, every one to his brother and every one to his neighbor; behold, I proclaim a liberty for you, saith the Lord, to the sword, to the pestilence, and to the famine."

That a nation, the great body of whose people be-

lieved in the plenary inspiration of the Bible, and that
its contents were designed for instruction in righteousness as well as for admonition and warning to the
whole human race till time should be no more, could
listen unmoved to passages like these from the Hebrew
prophets, so exactly descriptive of its condition and its
perils, would seem incredible if we did not remember
that the official and trusted expositors of the time taught
it to set them at naught, and filled its ears with apologies for slavery woven of texts from the same Book —
as Whittier says :

> " Torturing the pages of the hallowed Bible
> To sanction robbery, and crime and blood."

Stuart at Andover, Alexander at Princeton, Fisk at
Wilbraham, and others who in high places were training a new generation of ministers, were found, not
long afterwards, weaving ingenious arguments from
the Scriptures to prove that slaveholding was compatible with the Golden Rule, and that the plea for immediate emancipation was the wildest fanaticism. The
ready plea of the apologist for slavery was, that excitement upon the subject would inevitably quench the
influences of the Divine Spirit and put an end to the
revivals of religion, which were declared to be the
great instrumentality for the conversion of the world.
The voices of thousands who might otherwise have
borne a testimony against slavery were hushed to silence by this specious plea. A small remnant was
indeed "faithful among the faithless found," but they
fell under popular reproach, and in some instances
were subject to persecution among false brethren.

If we may accept for truth the declaration of the
Rev. Albert Barnes, "that there was no power out of
the church that would sustain slavery an hour if it
were not sustained in it," then it must be admitted
that the church was responsible for the failure to abol-

ish the system by moral power, and for all the blood spilled and treasure lost in the war of the Rebellion! There was no pretence *then* that Mr. Garrison was an infidel. That plea was invented years afterward, when the churches found it necessary to offer some plausible excuse for their delinquency; and it was no truer then than it would have been if offered at first. It was in the power of the churches, if they had had any heart for the work, to make the movement their own, to lead and guide it from its beginning to its consummation. This, indeed, was what Mr. Garrison desired and expected. He coveted not for himself the honors of leadership, but would have been content to serve the cause inconspicuously, if the men in power and influence had been persuaded to take it up. He was forced to the front when he would gladly have taken his place in the ranks.

III.

LYING open before me as I write is the first volume of "The Liberator," beginning and ending with the year 1831. It was small for that day, but how much more diminutive it looks in comparison with the weekly journals of the present time ! It is a folio of four pages. The page is fourteen inches in length by nine and three-tenths in width. The title at first was in bold-face black-letter, which gave place, at the end of four months, to an engraved head, with a "pictorial representation" of an auction, at which "slaves, horses and other cattle" are seen offered for sale, and of a whipping-post, at which a slave is receiving punishment. In the background is seen the Capitol of Virginia, with a flag, inscribed with the word "Liberty," floating over the dome. This picture of a scene familiar to every Southern eye was regarded as even worse than Mr. Garrison's "harsh language." At the South it was denounced as incendiary, while influential journals at the North declared that it was abominable thus to outrage the feelings of "our Southern brethren" and incite the slaves to insurrection ! Then, as now, the champions of "conciliation" thought it unpatriotic to drag into light the cruelties practised upon the negroes. For the sake of harmony, and to avert a dissolution of the Union, the disagreeable facts of slavery ought to be concealed. The Abolitionists were madmen and fools, and utterly devoid of "fraternal feeling" in making such a fuss about the Southern negroes, who were the most contented body of laborers in the world, and flogged only as they deserved to be for their innate laziness and insolence. But Mr. Garrison took little heed of these objurgations. The spirit of his chosen motto, "Our Country is the World, our Countrymen are all Mankind," pervaded and filled his heart, lifting him above the blind and selfish expediency of the time.

As I turn over the pages of this volume, what a flood of memories of that early day stirs my heart! It was indeed, as Lowell describes it, "the day of small things," when "one straightforward conscience" was "put in pawn to win a world." How vividly do I remember "that small chamber, dark, unfurnitured and mean," which after the first three weeks became the office of "The Liberator," and the only domicile of its brave editor and his associate. They had announced their determination to publish their paper as long as they could do so by living on bread and water; and so they made their bed on the office floor, and lived for a year or more on such food as they were able to procure at a neighboring bakery. More than once did I partake with them of their humble fare, Mr. Garrison doing the honors of the table with a grace worthy of a richer feast, and a cheerfulness that nothing could disturb. The office was in the third story of the building then known as Merchants' Hall. Everything about it had an aspect of slovenly decay, and Harrison Gray Otis well characterized it as "an obscure hole."

"Yet there the freedom of a race began."

The dingy walls; the small windows, bespattered with printer's ink; the press standing in one corner; the composing stands opposite; the long editorial and mailing table, covered with newspapers; the bed of

the editor and publisher on the floor; all these make
a picture never to be forgotten.   I was a frequent visitor from the first, but in the autumn I removed the
office of my own paper, "The Christian Soldier," into
an adjoining room, and for a year and a half thereafter
printed it on "The Liberator" press.   This brought me
into still closer relations with Mr. Garrison, making
me familiar with the daily current of his life, and fix-
ing and deepening my interest in the anti-slavery movement.   His courage, enthusiasm and devotion, so unlike
anything I had ever witnessed before, awakened my
admiration, and gave me a new conception of the majesty and power of a single human life.   I do not lightly
estimate the value of what the world calls an education, but I think Mr. Garrison did more and better for
me than any college or theological seminary could have
done.   The quickening, inspiring power of his conversation exceeded that of any other man I have ever
known.   His heart was all aflame with enthusiasm for
his cause, but never for a moment was his calm judgment overcome by heat.   A faith so absolute in the
sacredness and power of moral principles, a trust in
God so firm and immovable as his, I have never seen
exhibited by any other man.   Never for an instant did
he doubt the success of the movement to which, upon
his knees, with his Bible open before him, he had consecrated his life.   Whoever else might yield to discouragement, he never.   Though the Southern press
denounced him as a murderer and a cut-throat, and
every mail from that quarter brought him threats of
assassination if he did not desist from his work, he
never for one moment wavered in his purpose or indicated the slightest personal fear.   How often did I
hear him speak in tenderest pity of the deluded men
who stood ready to take his life at the first opportunity.   Not a word of vindictiveness or even of bitterness ever escaped his lips, and he would far sooner

have laid down his own life than taken that of an enemy.

That "obscure hole" was the scene of many a memorable talk. Among those who came to confer with the editor I remember Samuel J. May, who combined the courage of Paul with the lovingness of John, and who was ever afterward a conspicuous figure in the anti-slavery host; Ellis Gray Loring, then a rising young lawyer, with a clear head and a sound conscience, whose death in the prime of his powers left a vacancy that could not be filled; Samuel E. Sewall, of an honored Massachusetts family, a man fitted by his legal attainments and his judicial spirit for a high place on the bench, and who yet lives in a green old age to mourn the loss of the founder of "The Liberator"; David Lee Child, the bold editor and the faithful champion of the oppressed of every nation and clime; John G. Whittier, then almost unknown to fame, but whose flashing eye and intrepid mien foretold the songs of freedom with which he afterward thrilled and stirred the hearts of his countrymen; Joshua Coffin, the antiquarian, Whittier's old schoolmaster, and the subject of one of his characteristic lays; Arnold Buffum, the Quaker hatter, lately returned from England, where he had caught the spirit of Clarkson, Wilberforce, O'Connell and Buxton, and thus prepared himself to greet the rising Liberator of America; Moses Thacher, an Orthodox clergyman, one of the first of the profession to welcome the call for immediate emancipation; and Amos A. Phelps, then pastor of the Congregational church in Pine Street, whose labors in the cause as speaker and writer were for several years invaluable. Mr. Garrison was never too busy with his pen or his composing-stick to talk with those who cared enough for the cause to seek his presence. He was ever ready to answer inquiries for information, or to explain his principles, purposes and plans, and it was seldom that

any one who conversed with him for ten minutes failed
to be deeply and favorably impressed. At this time
he would have thought it impossible to address an audience for the space of one minute without first committing his remarks to writing; but as a talker he was
fluent, copious and strong, never hesitating for a word,
or failing to hit the nail squarely upon the head. It
was impossible to hear him and not be moved. Many
an opponent who thought to overcome him in argument
found himself, after a brief encounter, *hors de combat*,
and was obliged to retire with a broken lance. If an
antagonist had a conscience, Garrison was sure to enlist it on his side. In a few simple, well-chosen words
he cut his way through every web of sophistry, however cunningly woven, making slavery look the hideous thing that it is, and maintaining the humanity of
the negro with a cogency of reasoning that nothing
could resist.

The language of Mr. Garrison has been called bitter
by those whose sympathies for the slaveholders and
their apologists were superior to their sense of the sin
of slavery and their regard for the equal rights of the
negro. His bitterness, however, was only the inevitable bitterness of truth to men whose lives are stained
by flagrant sin. His descriptions of slavery and of the
sin of slaveholding were simply and scientifically accurate, as if he had said a spade is a spade, a brick is a
brick, a lie is a lie. Not a word was added from
malice or the love of severity, or with the purpose of
making men angry. He wounded only to heal. He
knew that the people of the United States could not be
roused to the work of abolishing slavery by smooth
phrases, in which the truth was rather concealed than
expressed. He knew that the consciences of slaveholders could be reached by no half-truths, and that
the torpid conscience of the North demanded not seda-
tives but a probe. In all this his judgment was as

cool and accurate as that of a mathematician in calculating the contents of the cube or the square. Some
of his timid friends thought the name of "The Liberator" sounded harsh and would inevitably create a
prejudice against the movement. One of these suggested that "The Safety-Lamp" would be a better
name, it sounded so gentle! But if he had been
capable of taking this advice he would have been
wholly unfitted for his work. "I will be," he said,
"as harsh as truth, and as uncompromising as justice.
. . . I am in earnest; I will not equivocate; I
will not excuse; I will not retreat a single inch; and
I WILL BE HEARD." . . "In attacking the system of
slavery, I clearly foresaw all that has happened to me.
I knew, at the commencement, that my motives would
be impeached, my warnings ridiculed, my person persecuted, my sanity doubted, my life jeopardized; but
the clank of the prisoner's chains broke upon my ear
— it entered deeply into my soul — I looked up to
Heaven for strength to sustain me in the perilous work
of emancipation, and my resolution was taken." The
Hebrew prophets and Jesus and his apostles were his
models; he would be like them even if he shared their
fate. Those who imagine that he used language
loosely, carelessly, recklessly, wholly mistake his character. He weighed his words as exactly and scrupu-
lously as the pharmaceutist weighs the constituents of
the physician's prescription, and those who read them
now that slavery is dead will find in them no other
bitterness than that which was necessarily involved in
their truth and justice. The spirit that dictated them
was kindred to that of Him who, while fearlessly
denouncing the leaders of the Jewish people for their
crimes, could yet exclaim: "O, Jerusalem, Jerusalem!
thou that killest the prophets and stonest them that
are sent unto thee! How oft would I have gathered
you as a hen gathereth her chickens under her wings,

but ye would not." The Rev. Henry Ward Beecher,
in his sermon on the death of Mr. Garrison, repeats
this charge of bitterness, but without citing a word of
proof.   IIc insists that, unlike Jesus and the prophets,
he was destitute of the spirit of love for those whom
he denounced.   It is very easy, at this distance from
the times in which the prophets and Jesus respectively
lived, to talk of their loving spirit as qualifying their
denunciations; but if Mr. Beecher had been the son of
one of that band of Pharisees whom Jesus indiscrimi-
nately denounced as a "generation of vipers" and
"hypocrites," who "devoured widows' houses, and
for a pretence made long prayers," and been called
upon after the crucifixion to deliver a discourse upon
his life and character, would he have been able to find
the soul of love in those denunciations?   I doubt it;
and yet it is there, as it is also in the epithets which
Garrison applied to slavery and to slaveholders.   Can
it for a moment be imagined that there was anything
in the character or conduct of the Scribes and Pharisees more fitted to excite the indignation of a noble
mind, and to call for and justify the use of strong epithets, than was seen in the example of the men who,
with the Declaration of Independence in one hand and
the Bible in the other, and the name of the blessed
Christ on their lips, held their fellow-beings in a state
of slavery which John Wesley, pronounced "the vilest
that ever saw the sun"?   Why, then, should men who
are able to find the fruits of love in the terrible denunciations that fell from the lips of Jesus, be so ready to
charge Mr. Garrison with bitterness?   Time has vindicated the Master, and it will yet vindicate IIis faithful disciple.

The men who are most prone to condemn as bitter
those who in this age of the world are called to wage
earnest war against iniquity in high places, are not so
blind as to the reasonableness of severe denunciations,

nor so unwilling to apologize for them, as is often supposed. I was forcibly struck, a short time since, with
a passage which I found in the Rev. Dr. W. T. G.
Shedd's address at the opening of the term in the
Union Theological Seminary. Dr. Shedd is a conservative of the conservatives, who stood carefully
aloof from Abolitionism, and it is worth while to note
the philosophical ground upon which such a man
apologizes for the use of "hard language." "The inflexible earnestness of the lover of truth," says the
learned Professor, "explains that phraseology, more
common in the century of the Reformation than now,
which is often cited in proof of the bitterness and
malignity of the theologian. Luther, and even the
mild Melanchthon, use words that are like drawn
swords, when speaking of the teachers of certain ten-
ets. Milton describes Salmasius in phraseology still
more vehement than that of the theologian. It is an
error to assume that in these instances, the energy of
the epithets is aimed at the persons. It is aimed at
their opinions. It is like the damnatory clause in the
Athanasian Creed; the real meaning of which is that
the denial of the deity of Jesus Christ, and of the
trinity of the Divine Being, is what an inspired apostle denominates a 'damnable heresy,' a fatal error.
That creed, in its damnatory clause, does not undertake to decide the state of the heart, and actually pronounce, in anticipation, the final judgment of God
respecting a particular individual; because the latitu-
dinarian person may be better than his creed, and the
orthodox person may be worse than his. But leaving
the person and the state of the heart to the judgment
of God, and having reference only to a tenet or a doctrine, both the creed and the theologian are authorized
to say that if the dogma of the deity of Christ is a
saving truth, then the dogma that He is only a creature is a fatal error. For this is only to say that if

the sum of two numbers is four, it cannot be six.
Respecting the unyielding earnestness of orthodoxy,
and the plain utterance which it sometimes necessi-
tates, the words of Lord Bacon are in point: 'Bitter
and earnest writing must not hastily be condemned ;
for men cannot contend coldly and without affection
about things which they hold dear and precious.   A
politic man may write from his brain, without touch.
and sense of his heart, as in a speculation that apper-
taineth not unto him ; but a feeling Christian will express in his words a character of zeal, and of love.' "
     It seems to come to this : that an Orthodox theolo-
gian, " when speaking of the teachers of certain ten-
ets," will be authorized, by his " inflexible earnestness "
as " a lover of truth," to " use words that are drawn
swords "; while the men who are called of God to fight
such a system of wickedness as American slavery was,
and whose souls are on fire with love of freedom, and
with sympathy for the oppressed and wronged, must
confine themselves to the use of soft phrases, on pain
of being denounced from Christian pulpits as bitter.
A mistaken theory as to the nature and offices of Christ
is worse than to sell him at auction in the persons of
those whom he calls his brethren.   " Damnatory
clauses " and " words that are like drawn swords " are
wholesome for men who have a twist in their theology,
but wholly inappropriate to the perpetrators of great
crimes and their defenders and apologists !
     The simple truth is, that this charge of bitterness has
been brought against every reformer who ever did
anything effectually for the redemption of the world
from any system of iniquity, and it never had less foundation in truth than in the case of Mr. Garrison.   Dr.
Channing has been accounted a mild man, but he
found justification for the " harsh language " of Milton
in the character of the times in which he wrote, and in
the nature of the evils with which he was forced to

contend; and in vindicating the great champion of English liberty he has made an unanswerable defence of the great advocate of negro emancipation:—

"Great evils were struggling for perpetuity, and could only be broken down by great power. Milton felt that interests of great moment were at stake; and who will blame him for binding himself to them with the whole energy of his great mind, and for defending them with fervor and vehemence? We must not mistake Christian benevolence, as if it had but one voice — that of soft entreaty. It can speak in awful and piercing tones. There is constantly going on in our world a conflict between good and evil. . . Men gifted with great power of thought and loftiness of sentiment are especially summoned to the conflict. . . They must speak with an indignant energy, and they ought not to be measured by the standard of ordinary minds in ordinary times. Men of natural softness and timidity, of a sincere but effeminate virtue, will be apt to look on these bolder, hardier spirits as violent, perturbed and uncharitable; and the charge will not be wholly groundless. But that deep feeling of evils which is necessary to effectual conflict with them, and which marks God's most powerful messengers to mankind, cannot breathe itself in soft and tender accents. The deeply moved soul will speak strongly, and ought to speak so as to move and shake nations."

Some of the modern talkers about reforming the world by love — by which they mean the reduction to moral flabbiness of every testimony against great systems of iniquity — would do well to study the life of John Milton.

That the slaveholders were seriously alarmed by the appearance of "The Liberator" was manifest by the efforts they made to prevent its circulation and frighten its intrepid editor from the field. The Vigilance Association of Columbia, S. C., composed, according to "The Charleston Mercury," of "gentlemen of the first respectability," on the 4th of October, 1831, "offered a reward of $1,500 for the apprehension and

prosecution to conviction of any white person who
might be detected in distributing or circulating 'The
Liberator,' or any other publications of a seditious
tendency." The authorities of Georgetown, D. C.,
enacted a law making it penal for any free person of
color to take from the post-office "the paper published
in Boston, called 'The Liberator.'" In Raleigh, N.
C., a grand jury found a true bill against the editor
and the publisher, evidently in the hope of finding a
way to bring them to that State for trial. A writer in
that grave and dignified old paper, "The National
Intelligencer," published in Washington, proposed
that Mr. Garrison should be indicted and tried in Virginia, and that, after conviction, a demand for his
surrender should be made upon the Governor of Massachusetts. Mr. Hayne of South Carolina, the champion of nullification, having received by mail a copy of
"The Liberator," wrote to the Hon. Harrison Gray
Otis, Mayor of Boston, asking to be informed who
sent it; and Mr. Otis, desiring to oblige his distinguished friend, sent a deputy to Mr. Garrison, hoping
to extract from him a confession that he was the guilty
man! Mr. Garrison, with the true Yankee instinct,
answered the interrogatory of Mr. Otis's agent by
propounding another, viz. : "By what authority does
the Hon. Robert Y. Hayne ask me such question?"
Thus were the great South Carolinian and his Northern
tool foiled in their attempt to make the anti-slavery
editor criminate himself and lay the foundation for a
requisition for his person upon the Governor of the
old Commonwealth. But it was left to the State of
Georgia to cap the climax of malignant folly in the
passage of a law offering $5,000 "to be paid by the
Governor to any person or persons arresting and
bringing to trial, under the laws of the State, and
prosecuting to conviction, the editor or publisher of
'The Liberator,' or any other person who shall utter,

publish or circulate said paper in Georgia." This was
nothing less than a bribe to any ruffian who might
choose on any dark night to go to the office of Mr.
Garrison and seize and convey him to a Southern vessel lying at the wharf not far distant. In response to
this threat, Mr. Garrison said: "Know this, ye patrons of kidnappers, that we despise your threats as
much as we deplore your infatuation; nay, more —
know that a hundred men stand ready to fill our place
as soon as it is made vacant by violence. 'The Liberator' shall yet live — live to warn you of your danger
and guilt — live to plead for the perishing slaves —
live to hail the day of universal emancipation. For
every hair of our head which you touch, there shall
spring up an asserter of the rights of your bondsmen,
and an upbraider of your crimes."

And how were these menaces and threats received
at the North? Not by any means with the indignation
they were fitted to excite in the breasts of freemen
jealous for the liberty of the press ; but generally with
cool indifference, if not with positive sympathy. The
Northern press made constant obeisance to "King Cotton," and dared do no more than to suggest, with
whispered humbleness, that perhaps it might be carrying things a little too far to kidnap the miserable
fanatic who was disturbing the peace of the South !
The newspapers that dared to speak in terms of honest
indignation of these attempts to destroy the freedom
of the press were those of smallest circulation, and
might be counted on one's fingers. The moral stupor
that rested upon the press and the people of the North
at that time seems utterly incredible now.

The Southampton (Va.) insurrection of slaves, led
by Nat Turner, occurred in the summer of 1831, when
"The Liberator" was only a few months old. Turner
was himself a slave, and he persuaded his deluded followers that he was a prophet sent by God to lead them

out of the house of bondage. There was never the
slightest reason to suppose that he had ever seen so
much as a single copy of "The Liberator," and if he had
he would have found in it nothing to encourage his
murderous project, but, on the contrary, much to dis-
suade him therefrom.   For Mr. Garrison from the
very start avowed his opposition to war and violence
under all circumstances.   In the very first number of
his paper he apostrophized the slaves in these memorable words :—

> "Not by the sword shall your deliverance be;
>   Not by the shedding of your masters' blood;
> Not by rebellion, or foul treachery,
>   Upspringing suddenly, like swelling flood:
>   Revenge and rapine ne'er did bring forth good.
> God's time is best! nor will it long delay:
>   E'en now your barren cause begins to bud,
> And glorious shall the fruit be! Watch and pray,
> For, lo! the kindling dawn, that ushers in the day!"

But, in spite of all such protestations, and notwithstanding the notorious fact that Mr. Garrison was a
non-resistant, the press at the North, as well as at the
South, insisted that he was responsible for the Nat
Turner insurrection, with all its cruelties and horrors.
Governor Floyd, in his message to the Virginia Legislature, said there was too much cause to suspect that
the plans of the insurrection had been "designed and
matured by unrestrained fanatics in some of the neighboring States."   That this was an allusion to Mr. Garrison and his associates was universally understood at
the time.   Northern newspapers found it hard to believe that a body of "contented laborers" like the Virginia slaves could revolt against the authority of their
kind masters unless they were invited to do so by mis-
chievous fanatics; and who but Garrison could be the
guilty cause of such madness?   There were moments
when it seemed as if the misguided public opinion of
the hour would demand the suppression of "The Lib-

erator," and it is not easy now to see what it was,
except the restraining interposition of Providence, that
prevented the people in their madness from doing all
that the slaveholders desired. Few newspapers of that
day exerted an influence so powerful as that of "The
National Intelligencer," in which the respectability,
learning, statesmanship and conservatism of the time
were incarnated. To the people of New England this
paper dared to appeal in these terms :—

" No one knows better than we do the sincerity with which
the intelligent population of New England abhor and repro-
bate the incendiary publications which are intended by their
authors to lead to precisely such results (as concerns the
whites) as the Southampton tragedy. But we appeal to the
people of New England, if not in behalf of the innocent
women and children of the whites, then in behalf of the
blacks, whose utter extermination will be the result of any
general commotion, whether they will continue to permit
their humanity to be under the reproach of approving or
even tolerating the atrocities among them which have already
caused the plains of the South to be manured with human
flesh and blood. To be more specific in our object, we now
appeal to the worthy Mayor of the City of Boston, whether
no law can be found to prevent the publication, in the city
over which he presides, of such diabolical papers [copies of
' The Liberator'] as we have seen a sample of here in the
hands of slaves, and of which there are many in circulation
to the south of us. We have no doubt whatever of the feelings of Mr. Otis on this subject, or those of his respectable
constituents. We know they would prompt him and them to
arrest the instigator of human butchery in his mad career.
We know the difficulty which surrounds the subject, because
the nuisance is not a nuisance, technically speaking, within
the limits of Massachusetts. But, surely, if the courts of
law have no power, public opinion has, to interfere, until the
intelligent Legislature of Massachusetts can provide a durable remedy for this most appalling grievance. The crime is
as great as that of poisoning a well. . . . We know
nothing of the man [Garrison] ; we desire not to have him
unlawfully dealt with ; we can even conceive of his motive

being good in his own opinion; but it is the motive of the man who cuts the throats of your wife and children."

Having thus deliberately accused Mr. Garrison of the most atrocious crimes, and sought to crush him by an inflamed public opinion under the forms of law, "The National Intelligencer" was true to itself and to the cause it served in refusing to publish his triumphant defence. It thus illustrated the spirit of American slavery, which could not endure the light of a free press, but was instinctively impelled to hide itself in perpetual darkness. In his reply, Mr Garrison said:

"I appeal to God, whom I fear and serve, and to its patrons, in proof that the real and only purpose of 'The Liberator' is to prevent rebellion, by the application of those preservative principles which breathe peace on earth, goodwill to men. I advance nothing more. I stand on no other foundation than this: 'Whatsoever ye would that others should do unto you, do ye even so unto them.' I urge the immediate abolition of slavery, not only because the slaves possess an inalienable right to liberty, but because the system, to borrow the words of Mr. Randolph, is 'a volcano in full operation'; and by its continuance we must expect a National explosion. . . . The present generation cannot appreciate the purity of my motives or the value of my exertions. I look to posterity for a good reputation. The unborn offspring of those who are now living wil reverse the condemnatory decision of my contemporaries. Without presuming to rank myself among them, I do not forget that those reformers who were formerly treated as the 'offscouring of the earth' are now lauded beyond measure; I do not forget that Christ and His apostles — harmless, undefiled and prudent as they were — were buffeted, calumniated and crucified; and therefore my soul is steady to its pursuit as the needle to the pole. If we would not see our land deluged in blood, we must instantly burst asunder the shackles of the slaves — treat them as rational and injured beings — give them lands to cultivate and the means of employment, and multiply schools for themselves and their children. We shall then have little to fear. The wildest beasts may be subdued and rendered gentle by kind treatment. Make the slaves free, and every inducement to revolt is taken away. . . . I see the design of the clamor raised against ' The Liberator.' It is to prevent public indignation from resting upon the system of slavery, and to concentrate it upon my own head. That system contains the materials of self-destruction."

"The National Intelligencer" spoke for the states-manship of that time; but how wild, incoherent, un-just and illogical were its utterances! Mr. Garrison was deemed a fanatic; but mark the wisdom and truth of his words, the reasonableness of his appeals, the justice of his denunciations and the calmness of his reliance upon the judgment of posterity! The extracts I have given above are of the body and spirit of the times. They reveal, as nothing else would, the delu-sion that rested upon the people at that day, and show those of this generation what courage, what faith in God, what love for humanity, and what a spirit of self-sacrifice it required to begin the fight with American slavery. If Garrison had faltered and retreated, what calamities might not have befallen the Nation! The fate of the Republic, according to our limited vision, depended upon the fidelity of a single man; for, if the Nation had gone on sinning against light for another generation, where would have been the hope of its res-cue from the ruthless clutch of the Slave Power? Already it had sunk into a stupor from which the most powerful and startling blasts of truth were barely suffi-cient to rouse it to life and some degree of moral sensi-bility. A little more drugging of conscience, and per-chance the call for reform would have been too late, and the Republic founded by Washington, Adams and Jefferson might have perished in the foul embrace of slavery!

Is there not in this a lesson for the present hour? On every side we hear the voices of men claiming to be statesmen, who brand as enmity to the South every earnest plea for the equal rights of the negro ; who ask us to stop our ears to the cry of men driven from the ballot-box and defrauded of their wages by violence, and to close our eyes to the frauds by which the South has been made "solid" in order to gain by political power the substance of what she failed to achieve by the sword. We are told on the one hand that it is perfectly patriotic and reasonable for the semi-civilized South to be a unit in her opposition to the vast majority of the intelligent people of the North ; and on the other that it is unpatriotic, unreasonable and cruel, a revival of all the worst passions and enmities of the war, for the latter to resist the efforts of the former to rule the Nation by an alliance with the men of the Northern slums! The sirens who are filling our ears with this song, disguised under smooth and seductive phrases, are the natural descendants of the men of a previous generation who were forever seeking to lull the North into indifference to the negro's wrongs, and always ready with some new compromise in the interest of the slaveholding class. If the enfranchised men of the South were white, the North would be all on fire with indignation over their wrongs, and ready to exert the last iota of constitutional power for their protection. Above all would they take care that the oppressors should not, by any political combination whatever, gain an ascendancy over the Republic. Let us have the principle and the courage to do for the negro what we should not hesitate to do for the white man. The voice of Garrison cries to us out of his freshly-made grave, bidding us not to waste the heritage won for us by his indomitable courage, and by the blood and bravery of our soldiers.

IV.

Mr. Garrison's Early Orthodoxy — No Odor of Heresy about him until long after the Churches and the Clergy had Rejected his Message — A Christian at the Last no less than at the First — Reluctance of Ministers to Pray in Anti-Slavery Meetings — Rev. Amos A. Phelps and his Book — The A. B. C. F. M. — The Methodist Church — Dr. Whedon's Denial — Testimony of Judge Jay — The Freewill Baptists.

So persistent have been the efforts made in certain quarters to excuse the hostility of the ministers and churches to the anti-slavery movement on the ground of Mr. Garrison's alleged infidelity, that it becomes im-. portant to set forth the truth on this subject with great clearness. In turning over the leaves of the first volume of "The Liberator," we find the evidences of Mr. Garrison's thorough-going Orthodoxy in great abundance. There was not about him the least odor of heresy of any kind, save in his belief in the perfect humanity of the negro, and in his denunciations of slavery as a sin. We find him pleading for the universal diffusion of the Bible as the chief instrumentality for promoting the cause. "Take away the Bible," he exclaims, "and our warfare with oppression, and infidelity, and intemperance, and impurity, and crime is at an end; our weapons are wrested away, our foundation is removed; we have no authority to speak, and no courage to act." That in later years he held the views of the Bible common among Quakers and Unitarians is not denied; but this was long after the American clergy and churches had repudiated the anti-slavery movement. Indeed, it was this repudiation on their part that led him to the investigations which resulted in the modification of his inherited views on

68   GARRISON AND HIS TIMES.

this and some other points. But to the very last the
Bible was to him "the Book of books," and he found
in its pages the truths on which his soul was fed, and
which were his chief reliance in the great struggle
with slavery. His writings and speeches from first to
last throb with quotations of the most striking appo-
siteness and power from that book. Above any minister of the Gospel whom I have ever known, he was
indeed "mighty in the Scriptures," and thousands have
confessed that before hearing him they were not half
aware of the quickening and inspiring power of the
volume around which so many of the most sacred
associations of the Christian world are clustered.

He was also the friend and champion of the revivals
of religion for which that period was distinguished;
looking to them with hope as likely to hasten the day
of emancipation. "Emancipation," he said, "must be
the work of Christianity and of the churches. They
must achieve the elevation of the blacks, and place
them on the equality of the Gospel. If the present
revivals be (as we trust they are) the fruit of the Holy
Spirit, we pray that they may embrace the nation, nor
cease till the bodies and souls of its population be
'redeemed, regenerated and disenthralled,' and every
man shall sit under his own vine and fig-tree, there
being none to molest or make him afraid. Take
courage, ye mourning slaves, for your redemption is
at hand." If, not long afterward, he found many of
the leaders in the revival movement closing churches
and pulpits against the advocates of emancipation, and
warning converts that if they would guard the flame of
their piety from extinction they must not allow themselves to become involved in the anti-slavery excitement, need we wonder that his faith in revivals, as
thus conducted, was somewhat shaken? And when,
not much later, the venerable Professor of Theology
at Andover was accustomed to say to his senior class,

"Young gentlemen, if you hope to be settled over intelligent, cultivated and prosperous parishes, you must be careful to keep aloof from the exciting questions of the day," is it any wonder that the champion of emancipation began to suspect there might be an important distinction between the Christianity of Christ and that of the American churches? Who was responsible for suggesting this thought to many earnest Christian minds is plain enough.

Another illustration of Mr. Garrison's evangelical Orthodoxy is found in his advice to the colored people of the country to set apart a day for fasting, humiliation and prayer on account of the wickedness of slavery, and the oppressions arising therefrom. "Who," he asked, "may estimate the importance of such a measure? We say to our dear colored brethren, 'Let us pray more, and fast more, and the Lord will do great and signal things for us.'" This is the sort of infidelity against which the American churches braced themselves when they turned their backs upon the anti-slavery movement.

Again, Mr. Garrison held and inculcated in "The Liberator" at first the most Orthodox views of the Sabbath. He would no sooner have gone to the post-office on that day to mail or receive a letter than he would have stolen the contents of a contribution-box. In "The Liberator" of April 16th, 1831, appeared from his pen the following sonnet: —

THE SABBATH DAY.

Faint prototype of Heaven, blest Sabbath day!
  Emblem of an eternal rest to come;
Emancipator from vile Mammon's sway,
  At whose approach a noisy world is dumb;
Unerring regulator, sacred pledge;
  Best friend and soother of the poor and weak;
A resting-place in our drear pilgrimage,
  Where soul and body may refreshment seek;
If thou wert blotted out, our moral sun,
  The huge eclipse would dress the world in gloom;

Confusion dire would seize on every one,
 And peace, love, order find a hasty tomb;
 Then would oppression reign, then lust rebel,
 Then violence abound, and earth resemble hell!

If this sonnet does not rank among the best of Mr.
Garrison's productions in verse, it is yet good enough
to show the hollowness of the pretence that the American clergy and churches rejected the anti-slavery movement because they were unwilling to follow the lead
of an infidel. Is it not time that men who would be
accounted honorable ceased to utter a calumny so
easily refuted?

It is certainly vain to attempt to blot from the page
of history the sad and disgraceful truth that the representatives of the popular Christianity of that day were
deaf to the groans and agonies of the slaves, insensible
of the humanity of the negro, indifferent to the sin
and shame of slavery, and disposed to take the slaveholder's part against every earnest effort for abolition.
True, there was "a glorious remnant," "faithful among
the faithless found," who espoused the cause with
ingenuous promptness, and did what they could to
rally the ministers and churches to their duty; but
they made themselves odious in the sects to which they
respectively belonged, so strong and overwhelming
was the tide of pro-slavery opinion and sympathy at
that day. There has been an attempt of late years to
make the fidelity of these exceptional men a shield and
covert for the churches that persecuted them; but the
justice of God will never permit such a travesty of the
truth of history. An attempt to show that the Jewish
nation did *not* reject and crucify Christ, because all his
disciples were Jews, and "the common people heard
him gladly," would not be a whit more preposterous.
As well deny that the United States was a slaveholding nation because thousands of its citizens were Abolitionists, as deny that the American churches were

"the bulwarks of American slavery" because a small remnant among them were found faithful. No clergyman of that day, however eminent, could have espoused the cause without risking the loss of his parish and his reputation at the same time. The swelling tide of ecclesiasticism had a power as irresistible as that of Niagara, and was sure to overwhelm and swallow up any clergyman who dared to resist it. I remember that the popular pastor of a Congregational church near Boston, a man who afterward achieved eminence as a writer as well as preacher, lost his pulpit because he delivered a lyceum lecture to the colored people of Boston, and because, in the face of many private remonstrances, he persisted in remembering the slaves in his public prayers. The leading members of the church were Boston merchants, and they informed the pastor that his leanings toward the anti-slavery cause were destroying his usefulness. He was constrained to avoid an open quarrel by resigning.

It was thus that the great body of the clergy were held captive in the interest of the Slave Power, many of them no doubt unwillingly and greatly to their own secret disgust. It was almost impossible sometimes to find in Boston a clergyman of any standing who would so much as consent to open an anti-slavery meeting with prayer. I remember that on more than one occasion I spent a whole day in a vain effort to persuade some one among a dozen white clergymen to perform this office, and had at last to accept the services of a " nigger " preacher from " nigger " hill ! That preacher was dear old Father Samuel Snowdon, one of the brightest, wittiest and best men, black as he was, that ever entered a pulpit. His genius was not below that of Father Taylor, who was also a preacher to seamen, and a Methodist; but of course " nigger " sailors could not worship with white ones on terms of equality in Boston, and so Father Snowdon found his sphere. His

prayers were as full of salt and as nautical in their
phraseology as those of his white brother.   The Abolitionists were proud of him, and his prayers were as remarkable for their oddity as for their fervor.   I remember that on the occasion above referred to he prayed
thus : " O Lord, bless the good British ship 'Buzzard,'
that rescued a cargo of slaves the other day on the
African coast.   Give her a fair wind, Lord, and drive
her right into port.   And, O God ! we pray that that
seven-headed, ten-horned monster, the Colonization
Society, may be smitten through and through with the
fiery darts of truth, and tormented as the whale is between the sword-fish and the thresher."

On one occasion, however, in 1833, we were to have
a meeting in the Representatives' Hall in the State
House.   How it happened that we got the use of the
hall I am not now sure ; but it had been granted to the
Colonization Society a short time before, and I believe
the simple-minded country members of the Legislature concluded that we ought to have it once, just to
make things even.   At any rate we were to have it,
and it was thought important that some white minister
of good standing should serve as chaplain on the occasion. It became my duty to procure such an one if possible.   I was then editor of a little paper, " The Christian
Soldier," which, being devoted to the resistance of the
then rising heresy of Universalism, was in favor among
the evangelical clergy of Boston, with many of whom
I was personally acquainted.   To one after another of
these I went with my plea, only to be met with a stern
refusal.   Not one of them could be persuaded so far
to countenance an Abolition meeting as to pray for it.
Last of all I went to my dear friend, the Rev. Amos
A. Phelps, pastor of the Pine Street Church, who had
but just begun his ministry in the city.   He had been
considering the slavery question, but had not fully
made up his mind what he ought to do.   I told him of

my ill-luck with the older and more conspicuous pastors, and besought him to come to the rescue. He at first declined, telling me he had just come to a struggling church and was afraid its prosperity might be endangered if he should comply with my request. At length, however, seeing how deeply I felt on the subject, he agreed to my proposal with fear and trembling. The censures bestowed upon him by his brethren, for thus giving countenance to the Abolition movement, led him to deeper reflection upon the subject, and he soon afterward took his stand openly as an Abolitionist. His subsequent services in the cause were invaluable. Up to that time the Abolitionists had been somewhat puzzled to find an exact definition of slavery, by which it could, under all circumstances, be distinguished from any any other human relation or institution. Mr. Phelps was distinguished as a logician, and when he entered upon the discussion of the subject he saw the need of a definition so clear as to exclude cavil, and after careful study and reflection he hit upon this: *Slavery is the holding of a human being as property.* In all subsequent discussions of the subject this definition, which was universally accepted, was of great value. It enabled us to sweep away at once a whole brood of sophistries that had sprung from the confounding of slavery with the relation of parent and child, of master and apprentice, of criminal and magistrate, etc., and to show that the system was in its very nature a sin against God and a crime against man. It was taken up by all the anti-slavery speakers, who found it would stand every test applied to it, and that it greatly simplified the argument against slavery, making it clear to the understanding of common men. Mr. Phelps was wont to say that he owed his conversion to the anti-slavery cause to me. If he was right, then I have not lived in vain nor been wholly useless to the cause in which so much of my life has been spent; for few men were

10

more successful than he in convincing the judgment
and swaying the convictions of men. As a lecturer
and editor during the period antecedent to the division
of 1839, he did the cause noble service. Of his course
after that date this is not the place to speak.

The American Board of Foreign Missions was then
rising into prominence and power, and drawing to itself the sympathy and almost idolatrous reverence of
the churches, especially in New England. It was natural to expect that the men who were contributing of
their wealth to redeem the heathen in the farthest ends
of the earth from their ignorance and debasement
would be among the first to respond to an appeal in
behalf of the heathenized and imbruted slaves at home.
But all such expectations proved vain. The managers
of the Board were deadly hostile to the anti-slavery
movement from the start. The piety of Boston was
subsidized in the interest of the cotton trade. The
champions of the Board appeared to think that if the
churches should become enlisted in the anti-slavery
cause, they would cease to feel a proper interest in foreign missions. And so, while the churches were constantly reminded of the ignorance and degradation of
the heathen abroad, every pains was taken to conceal
or excuse the enforced debasement of the heathen at
home. It was held to be a primary duty of the Amer-
can churches to send the Bible and the Gospel of Christ
to foreign nations sitting in darkness and the shadow
of death ; but at the same time it was held to be perfectly compatible with Christianity and the teaching of
the Holy Book to prevent men and women born and living in America from learning how to spell the name of
God, to compel them to work without wages under the
lash, and to sell them on the auction-block and put the
proceeds in the Lord's treasury ! Oh, what a night of
ignorance, delusion and sin was that from which the
anti-slavery movement delivered the American people !

While these sketches were passing through the columns of "The New York Tribune," the truthfulness of the statements made in the preceding pages concerning the attitude of the churches from 1830 to the close of 1833 was called in question by the Rev. Dr. Whedon, editor of "The Methodist Quarterly Review." Paying a tribute to my "profound honesty," he nevertheless is bold enough to pronounce my statements, "so far as Methodism is concerned, unhistorical and false." As the reader will observe, I had said nothing specifically of the Methodist church, but only alluded to the churches generally, as unfriendly to the anti-slavery movement. Why, then, this haste to put in a defence of Methodism, as if it had been particularly assailed? Whatever may have been the motive, my "profound honesty" will no doubt be accepted as a guaranty of my gratitude to any one who will detect any essential error in my statements. But, having duly considered Dr. Whedon's attempt to impeach my historical verity, I am constrained to re-affirm the statements of which he complained. It is true, as he says, that "Methodism," or a portion of the Methodist church, "responded early" to the voice of Garrison; but that response was not heard until 1835, as the files of the Methodist paper published in Boston at that period will show; and when it was at length heard, Dr. Whedon did all that he could to smother it, by heaping the grossest abuse upon Mr. Garrison, caricaturing his principles and misrepresenting his designs. The Doctor says, "it is certain that the delegates to our general conference of 1832 from the New England annual conference were, to a man, 'Garrisonian Abolitionists,' indorsing and affiliating with his societies." Now the only society representing Mr. Garrison's views at that period, so far as I can recollect, was the New England Anti-Slavery Society, which was organized in January, 1832, while the General Conference met

in May. I have before me now, a list of the delegates
to that conference from New England, and among them
I do not find one who, at that time, was known to me
as a "Garrisonian Abolitionist." I was the secretary of
the Anti-Slavery Society, and if these delegates were
to a man "affiliated" with it, it seems strange that I
should have been ignorant of the fact. The Rev. Dr.
Wilbur Fisk was one of the body of delegates who,
according to Dr. Whedon, "were *to a man* affiliated
with" Mr. Garrison. If *he* was an Abolitionist at that
period, then it will be safe to reckon John C. Calhoun
and George McDuffie in the same category. Other
histories besides mine will in that case demand correction at the hands of Dr. Whedon. The simple truth
is that the files of the Boston Methodist paper from
1831 to 1834, afford no more evidence of any excitement in the church on the subject of slavery than can
be found in any cemetery. The excitement that began in 1835, with the discussion opened in "Zion's
Herald" by Orange Scott, grew directly out of Mr.
Garrison's movement, after that long period of deadness and silence in the whole Northern church to which
I have referred in previous pages.

Dr. Whedon claims to have "coincided," as an anti-
slavery man, "with Benjamin Lundy;" but I venture
to say, that that sturdy old Quaker could have read
what Dr. Whedon wrote on the subject of slavery in
1835 with no other emotions than those of disgust
and indignation. The Doctor will find that Benjamin
Lundy's Quaker coat and hat will not avail him as a
rampart in his warfare against Mr. Garrison. There
was no such discrepancy in the views of those two reformers as he seems to suppose.

Again, Dr. Whedon says: "As to the earlier date
of my anti-slaveryism, I may say that I voted with the
germinal Liberty Party somewhere about 1834, for
Governor of Connecticut; with the same party for

James G. Birney," etc. According to this he was more concerned for the anti-slavery purity of his political party than for that of his church. He could not vote for a slaveholder or an apologist for slavery at the polls, but he could be a member and a minister of a church, thousands of whose members were permitted to buy and sell slaves as they bought and sold cattle in the market; and he gave his time and strength for years in opposing and hindering those who sought to free the church from this abomination. But I find it difficult to reconcile his claim to have been a voter "with the germinal Liberty Party somewhere about 1834," with the fact that in "Zion's Herald" of March 18, 1835, he endeavored to excite the public indignation against the Abolitionists on the special ground that they intended ultimately to make their movement a "political party agitation," and only "wanted strength" to do so at once. He even fortified himself in his assault by a quotation from Mr. Garrison, from which it would seem that the founder of the anti-slavery movement was himself the originator of the good Doctor's political party, in co-operating with which, even then, five years before its birth, he was finding relief for his intense hostility to slavery. In 1835 he arraigned Mr. Garrison as an unpatriotic and designing man, and held him up to public reprobation, for saying, " that the immediate emancipation of the slaves in the District of Columbia and the Territories is to be made a test at the polls ;" and yet, "somewhere about 1834," he was himself slily voting with "the germinal Liberty Party" for the same purpose!

The good Doctor having thus condescended to correct my "unhistorical and false " statements concerning Methodism, ventures to make, on his own account, this contribution to the history of the anti-slavery cause : " Every step he [Garrison] took and word he uttered maddened the slaveholders and solidified them into

hostile adamant." Dr. Whedon was more prudent.
He would have so organized the anti-slavery movement
as to please and conciliate the traffickers in human flesh.
He was wiser even than the Son of God, whose im-
prudences of speech "solidified" the Jewish nation, and
particularly the Scribes and Pharisees, "into hostile
adamant," bringing upon himself thereby a cruel death.
It is a pity that Dr. Whedon was not born early enough
to teach "the man Christ Jesus" a better way. But he
goes on : "Hence [*i. e.*, because he offended the slave-
holders], the great body of the best anti-slavery thinkers
stood apart from him ; and as these were generally
Christian, Mr. Garrison and many of his followers
grew rabid and hostile to evangelical Christianity. Infidels and semi-infidels gathered around him, opened
their batteries on the churches, and availed themselves
of the situation to discredit Christianity. Mr. Johnson's denunciation of the churches in his narrative is
written somewhat after that model."

Are these statements true? Let us see. From
1832 to 1839–40 the Abolitionists, under the lead of
Mr. Garrison, were a united body. The men referred
to as "the best anti-slavery thinkers" were in close
affinity with the movement. Moreover, the vast majority of the Abolitionists—including for a large portion
of the time Mr. Garrison himself — were evangelical
Christians. During this period there was no difference
of opinion between Mr. Garrison and the class whom
Dr. Whedon calls "the best anti-slavery thinkers," concerning the attitude of the American churches in respect to slavery. Those churches were denounced by
Mr. Garrison no whit more severely than they were by
eminent evangelical Christians, both clergymen and
laymen. If there were any infidels or semi-infidels
connected with the cause, they were to me unknown.
On the contrary, I believe the "Boston Investigator,"
the infidel organ of that day, was just as hostile to the

anti-slavery movement as the "Boston Recorder." If
there was any striking of hands with infidelity, it was
on the part not of the Abolitionists, but of their evangelical opponents. Indeed, during the whole history
of the movement, with the single exception of that
noble woman, Ernestine L. Rose, I do not remember
a single prominent speaker on our platform who could
truthfully have been called an infidel. Not that we
should have failed to welcome their aid, but that like
so many Christians of the period they were hostile or
indifferent. In all those years the lecturing agents of
the cause were for the most part evangelical men, many
of them ministers or theological students. It was during these very years that "the slaveholders were solidified into hostile adamant," not more by Mr. Garrison
than by Dr. Leavitt, James G. Birney, Amos A. Phelps,
and scores of other evangelical men, who stood
shoulder to shoulder with him.

The divisions of 1839–40, of which I shall give an account hereafter, did, indeed, take a large body of evangelical Abolitionists into the new organizations ; but
there were scores of others who remained with Mr.
Garrison, and there was never a moment when more
than one evangelical Christian was not found willing
to serve the cause upon the executive committee of the
American Anti-Slavery Society. After the division
there was no change whatever on the part of Mr. Garrison and his friends toward the churches, whether
evangelical or liberal ; no new "opening of batteries"
against them, and no assault upon their theological
beliefs. The charge that Mr. Garrison and his associates "availed themselves of the situation to discredit
Christianity" is wholly untrue. On the contrary, they
honored Christianity while faithfully denouncing pro-
slavery churches, and during most of the years when
the pro-slavery press was branding them as infidels,
they had the co-operation of that intensely or-

thodox body, the old-school Covenanters. The attempt to discredit what I have said in this work respecting the pro-slavery attitude of the churches, by the intimation that it is colored in the slightest degree by my theological views, is grossly unjust. I extenuate naught on the one hand, and on the other I set down naught in malice. My aim is to speak the exact truth without fear or favor. And in fact, I have said no more than I can prove by the most unimpeachable evangelical testimony. If Dr. Whedon attributes what I have said to hostility to evangelical religion, what will he say to this testimony of the Hon. William Jay, a distinguished member of the Protestant Episcopal church, and eminent during his life for piety and the love of Christian institutions? He was, moreover, I presume, one of "the best anti-slavery thinkers," to whom Dr. Whedon alludes as "standing apart" (after 1840) from Mr. Garrison. Writing in 1857,—twenty-three years after the period to which I referred, and when the churches had had ample time to correct any earlier mistakes,—Judge Jay says:—

"If we turn to the American church, a mournful scene meets our view. The church, whose office it is to distribute the bread of life, is scattering the apples of Sodom. . . . . . The northern church is, with rare exceptions, pursuing, in regard to slavery, a time-serving, man-pleasing policy, probably still more offensive to God than that of our pro-slavery politicians. The larger portion of our clergy, like the priest and Levite rebuked by our Lord, pass by on the other side, evincing neither sympathy for their wounded brother, nor indignation against his assailants ; while others pass over to the thieves, bless them in the name of the Lord, and aid in robbing their helpless victim. Of all our northern churches, the Methodist has offered the most striking and painful illustration of the corrupting influence of political and ecclesiastical union with slaveholders. The hypocrisy of this church is melancholy and astounding. Founded as an anti-slavery church, and recording in its standards the most express condemnation of slavery as sinful, it became the unscrupulous tool of the slaveholders."

Would it not be more manly in Dr. Whedon, and others like him, to plead to this indictment, drawn by the hand of Judge Jay, than to endeavor to break the force of similar statements, made by Mr. Garrison and his friends, by unscrupulous and false accusations of infidelity, and of a "rabid hatred of evangelical Christianity"?

It gives me great pleasure to mention one Christian denomination, somewhat numerous in parts of New England, as well as in other States, that deserves to be excepted from the censures I have been compelled to bestow upon the rest. I allude to the Freewill Baptists, who, from the beginning, refused to receive slaveholders into communion, and most of whom were prompt to espouse the doctrine of immediate emancipation. The "Morning Star," the organ of the denomination, did much to inform public sentiment on the subject of slavery, especially in New Hampshire, where it had a large circulation. The constituency of this church was mainly among the common people, where its influence was chiefly felt. Its leaders refused to follow the example of other churches in countenancing slavery, and for this reason they incurred much censure and some persecution. It is not too much to say that it was more through the influence of the "Morning Star" than from any other cause, that the power of the pro-slavery Democracy in New Hampshire was first broken, and John P. Hale elected to the senate of the United States. That the Freewill Baptists were in all respects consistent and as earnest as they should have been in their testimony against slavery, it would be too much to affirm; but, compared with the churches around them, they were as light in the midst of darkness. If all other Christian denominations had come up to their level, the chains of the slaves might have been broken by moral power.

11

·V.

Mr. GARRISON, even before starting "The Liberator," looked to the organization of anti-slavery societies, at the earliest possible day, as a necessary means of advancing the cause. He knew something of the work which the Abolitionists of England were doing by this means, and longed to see their example followed in America. The subject was constantly in his mind, and he did not fail to urge it upon the attention of others. The great benevolent societies, formed under the auspices of the different religious denominations as a means of extending Christianity, were then just getting under way, and beginning to awaken the enthusiasm of the churches. Bible, tract, missionary and temperance associations were common, and the revivals of the period had awakened the hope in multitudes of Christian bosoms that the millennium was coming on apace. Dr. Lyman Beecher, then at the head of the evangelical clergy of New England, if not of America, was full of this theme, and his eloquent words stirred the churches as the blast of a trumpet stirs the hearts of an embattled host. Mr. Garrison's heart responded warmly to these appeals, but he saw, as the leaders of the church did not, that these dreams of the millennium could never be realized until slavery

should be put out of the way. They, in their blindness, were afraid that any excitement on the subject of
slavery would quench the influences of the Holy Spirit,
stop revivals of religion, and paralyze the energies of
the churches ; while to his clearer vision it was manifest that slavery was the mightiest of all hindrances to
the growth of Christianity, and that the guilty com--
plicity of the pulpit and the church with the system
would inevitably counteract their efforts for the spread
of the gospel. He longed, therefore, to see anti-
slavery societies organized by the score, and the whole
country astir with anti-slavery excitement. But the
tide ran heavily against him, and it was not till near
the end of 1831 that any step toward organization was
taken. On the 13th of November fifteen persons
assembled in the office of Mr. Samuel E. Sewall, in
State Street, to consider the subject. Of course these
fifteen gentlemen were known to be warmly interested
in the cause, and it was agreed in advance that we
would form a society if the apostolic number of twelve
should be found ready for the movement.

Of this little company Mr. Garrison was, of course,
the central figure. He unfolded his purposes and
plans without reserve, telling us what the Abolitionists of Great Britain had done since, under the inspiration of Elizabeth Heyrick, they had put their movement on the ground of immediate, in distinction from
gradual, emancipation. He wanted societies formed
in America upon the same principle, and could not be
satisfied with any scheme of gradualism. The Rev.
Samuel J. May was one of the gentlemen present, and
in his "Recollections of the Anti-Slavery Conflict"
(p. 31) he states that only nine of the number were
believers in immediate emancipation. Upon this point
my recollection differs from his. I believe every man
present admitted the duty and safety of setting the
slaves free at once ; but six of the number doubted

the wisdom of incorporating that principle into the constitution of the society, believing that it would excite popular prejudice, and thus tend to defeat the object in view. They thought it would be better to leave the question of immediatism open for a time, until public opinion could be enlightened, and to admit to membership gradualists as well as immediatists. Nor did they doubt that "whosoever retains his fellow-man in bondage is guilty of a grievous wrong," but they doubted the wisdom of saying so in the constitution of the society, as they thought it would repel from membership many whose co-operation was desirable. But Mr. Garrison was firm in the conviction that the vitality of the movement depended upon a frank avowal of fundamental principles, however unpopular they might be ; and the vote upon the question showed that nine were in favor of organizing upon his plan, while six were opposed.

Another meeting was held at the same place on the 16th of December. Ten gentlemen were present, and, after considerable discussion, Messrs. David Lee Child, Samuel E. Sewall, William Lloyd Garrison, Ellis Gray Loring and Oliver Johnson were appointed a committee to draft a constitution for an Anti-Slavery Society, to be reported January 1, 1832. At the next meeting there was an additional attendance of Alonzo Lewis (known as the "Lynn Bard"), William J. Snelling (a man of some literary note), Dr. Abner Phelps, the Rev. Elijah Blanchard (editor of an anti-masonic religious paper) and Dr. Gamaliel Bradford. The body of the constitution reported by the committee was adopted, but the preamble was referred for revision to another committee, to be reported to an adjourned meeting to be held January 6, in the school-room under the African Baptist Church, in Belknap Street. Of that adjourned meeting my recollections are very vivid. A fierce north-east storm, combining snow, rain and hail in about equal proportions, was raging, and the streets were full of slush. They were dark too, for the city of Boston in those days was very economical of light on "Nigger Hill." It almost seemed as if nature was frowning upon the new effort to abolish slavery. But the spirits of the little company rose superior to all external circumstances. They knew that their cause was just, and that God and truth were on their side, and therefore nothing could discourage them. On that dismal night, and in the face of a public opinion fiercer far than the tempest of wind and hail that beat upon the windows of that "nigger school-house," were laid the foundations of an organized movement against American slavery that at last became too mighty to be resisted, and that drew into its wake the statesmanship as well as the piety and philanthropy of the country.

David Lee Child, editor of "The Massachusetts Journal," presided. The committee on the preamble to the constitution made its report. This preamble, as drawn by William J. Snelling, was in the following words : —

" We, the undersigned, hold that every person, of full age and sane mind, has a right to immediate freedom from personal bondage of whatsoever kind, unless imposed by the sentence of the law for the commission of some crime. We hold that man cannot, consistently with reason, religion and the eternal and immutable principles of justice, be the property of man. We hold that whoever retains his fellow-man in bondage is guilty of a grievous wrong. We hold that mere difference of complexion is no reason why any man should be deprived of any of his natural rights, or subjected to any political disability. While we advance these opinions as the principles on which we intend to act, we declare that we will not operate on the existing relations of society by other than peaceful and lawful means, and that we will give no countenance to violence or insurrection."

Behold in this the fanaticism, the incendiarism, and
the infidelity of the anti-slavery movement, which the
churches of America scorned and resisted, and against
which American statesmanship arrayed itself in fiercest
contempt and hostility! To the principles and spirit
of the above preamble the Abolitionists were faithful
from first to last. They assailed slavery in the name of
God, of Christ and the Bible, and not an infidel sentiment was ever uttered from their platform.

The preamble was the subject of earnest discussion
in the meeting. If I remember aright, no one denied
its truth, but further doubts were expressed as to the
expediency of putting the new society openly on the
basis of immediate emancipation. Among those who
took this view of the matter were David Lee Child,
Samuel E. Sewall and Ellis Gray Loring, than whom
there were no more earnest and devoted friends of the
cause. The majority, however, adopted the preamble, and then the Constitution was presented for signatures. Twelve persons (all white) signed it, as
follows :

William Lloyd Garrison, Oliver Johnson, Robert
B. Hall, Arnold Buffum, William J. Snelling, John
E. Fuller, Moses Thacher, Joshua Coffin, Stillman B.
Newcomb, Benjamin C. Bacon, Isaac Knapp, Henry
K. Stockton.

Of these twelve men I was the youngest, and I am
probably the only one now living. Messrs. Child,
Sewall and Loring refused their names at that time,
but they joined the society shortly afterward, and were
among its most useful and influential members. Of
the twelve original signers, I believe there were not
more than one or two who could have put a hundred
dollars into the treasury without bankrupting themselves! The society was called "The New England
Anti-Slavery Society." It was the first association
ever organized in this country upon the principle of

immediate abolition, and the parent of the numerous
other affiliated associations which in the next few years
created an anti-slavery agitation that shook the land
from end to end. The preamble, sound as it was in
principle, did not prove quite satisfactory, and its form
was changed at the end of the first year. The first
officers of the society were : Arnold Buffum (a Quaker), President ; First Vice-President, George C. Odi-
orne, a Boston merchant ; Second Vice-President,
Alonzo Lewis, the "Lynn Bard"; Corresponding
Secretary, William Lloyd Garrison ; Recording Secretary, Joshua Coffin, antiquarian (Whittier's schoolmaster) ; Treasurer, Michael H. Simpson ; Counsel-
lors, Moses Thacher, John E. Fuller, Oliver Johnson,
Robert B. Hall, Benjamin C. Bacon and Samuel E.
Sewall. These were respectable, but neither eminent
nor popular names, and I remember how their insignificance was often contrasted with the long list of
statesmen and divines that constituted the official
board of the Colonization Society. It was thought to
be excessively ludicrous that a small association of
"nobodies" should be talking of abolishing American
slavery, when the great body of the people believed
that the scheme was utterly impracticable. The Rev.
Joshua N. Danforth, agent of the Colonization Society,
often took occasion to sneer at "the men with more
blood than brains," who, under the lead of Arnold
Buffum, "the Quaker hatter," had undertaken a job
from which the great statesmen and divines of the
country shrank in utter dismay. In the then state of
public opinion such appeals to prejudice were exceedingly effective. But those who made them should have
remembered the words of Paul : "The foolishness of
God is wiser than men ; and the weakness of God is
stronger than men. . . . Not many wise men
after the flesh, not many mighty, not many noble are
called ; but God hath chosen the foolish things of the

world to confound the wise ; and God hath chosen the
weak things of the world to confound the things which
are mighty ; and base things of the world, and things
which are despised, hath God chosen, yea, and things
which are not, to bring to naught things that are ; that
no flesh should glory in his presence."

As the little company that formed the new society
were stepping out into the storm and darkness from
the African school-house, where their work was accomplished, Mr. Garrison impressively remarked : " We
have met to-night in this obscure school-house ; our
numbers are few and our influence limited ; but, mark
my prediction, Faneuil Hall shall ere long echo with
the principles we have set forth.   We shall shake the
Nation by their mighty power."   I well remember
those words as they fell from the lips of our great
leader, but I am indebted for their preservation to my
friend, the late Benjamin C. Bacon, among whose private memoranda they were found after his death, and
who doubtless wrote them down shortly after they
were uttered.   How well the prophecy they contain
has been fulfilled I need not say.

If our cause, like Christianity, started with the union
of twelve men, so also, our twelve, like that of Jesus,
had its one traitor.   The man to whom I allude was
then a theological student.   After entering the ministry he found the cross of abolitionism too heavy to
bear, as it interfered with his clerical ambitions, and
so he threw it off.   It was not long afterward that he
was compelled, by charges affecting his moral character, to leave the ministry.   He did not, however, like
Judas, go out and hang himself, but after some years
got elected to Congress as a " Know-Nothing."   I am
glad to say that while a member of that body he so far
returned to the faith of his earlier years as to vote
right upon the anti-slavery issues of the time.

The first thing which the new society did was to

make an appeal in a public address to the people of
New England. That appeal was written by the Rev.
Moses Thacher, one of the original "twelve," and the
editor of "The Boston Telegraph." In theology he
was of the school of Emmons, and wielded a powerful
pen. The address was alike strong in argument and
felicitous in style, and fitted in every way to stir the
heart of the reader. Mr. Thacher subsequently left
New England and became a minister of the Presbyterian Church, in whose service he died about two years
ago.

On the Fourth of July, 1831, the church of which
Dr. Beecher was the pastor held a morning meeting
for prayer, and the Doctor made an address, exhorting his hearers to support the Colonization Society,
and sneering at "the few foolish whites" who were opposing it, and advocating the immediate emancipation
of the slaves, "reckless of consequences." The good
Doctor thought it quite feasible to deport the whole
black population of the United States to Africa, but
ridiculed as impracticable the idea of emancipating the
slaves upon the soil. Mr. Garrison, who was a member of his congregation, answered him in "The Liberator," in part as follows :—

"After all, I think it will be easy to prove that the Doctor is not more sapient than immediate Abolitionists. I
never knew him to be wise enough in his pulpit to tell his
hearers that if they were habitually guilty of drunkenness,
of exercising cruelty, of stealing property, of committing
adultery, they must refrain from these crimes gradually, and
aim at an uncertain, indefinite, far-off reformation. Such a
doctrine might quiet the consciences and tickle the ears of
drunkards, tyrants, thieves and debauchees; but it would
hardly be tolerated, even from the lips of Lyman Beecher,
by the worshippers in Bowdoin Street meeting-house. Now,
slavery is a violation of every natural right; it is a system of robbery, adultery, cruelty and murder, and its perpetuity justly exposes the nation to the wrath of Heaven.

Yet he is foolish, in the Doctor's estimation, who tells the slaveholders to leave off their sins at once, and to be, to-day, honest and humane men.   For one, I cannot listen to any proposal for a gradual abolition of wickedness."

Mr. Garrison also reminded the Doctor that among "the foolish whites" who were "madly" calling for the immediate abolition of slavery might be reckoned a . very large majority of the wisest and best men in Great Britain, including Clarkson, Wilberforce, Brougham, Lushington, Stephen and O'Connell; and the most eminent clergymen of all denominations.   I refer to this only as illustrating the way in which the contest between the Abolitionists and the Church went on; for in reality Dr. Beecher spoke for the latter as really as Mr. Garrison did for the former.   Their encounter was but an epitome of the whole argument between the two parties; and which of them has most occasion to blush in view of the record it is needless to say.

After what I have said of the degeneracy of the Boston clergy in those days, it is pleasant to record the fact that Ralph Waldo Emerson, then pastor of a Unitarian church in that city, on Sunday evening, May 29, 1831, had the courage to open his pulpit for the delivery of an anti-slavery sermon by the Rev. Samuel J. May. What a powerful influence Mr. Emerson afterward exerted in moulding the public opinion that led to the abolition of slavery every intelligent American knows.

The new society began its work with a brave heart, in the full belief that success would ere long crown its exertions.   In social influence, as well as in pecuniary resources, it was indeed almost ludicrously weak; but in the strength of its principles, and in the firmness of its faith in God, it was not only mighty, but invincible.   They remembered (those infidels!) the truth afterward so vigorously expressed by Theodore Parker: "Truth is a part of the celestial machinery of God, and whoso puts that machinery in gear for mankind hath the Almighty to turn his wheel." But while on the one hand they were fully sensible that they had undertaken no holiday task, they were upon the other but feebly conscious of the power which slavery had acquired over the American Government and the American churches, and little aware of the amount of persecution and self-denial they would be called to endure. If they had known the worst, would their courage have been adequate to the work, or would they have shrunk back in utter despair? God only knows. Their weakness, whatever it may have been, was not unknown to Him, and it may have been His design to enlist them in the work, and then to develop their courage and devotion by such experiences as they were prepared to endure, until they should become capable at length of bearing all that would come upon them in their long and bitter struggle. In all great movements for the overthrow of giant evils this seems to be the way of Providence. If the leaders of the Protestant Reformation had foreseen all the suffering they would be called to endure, would their courage have been equal to their day? And if the fathers of our Republic had known from the start that they could establish their rights only by a long and bloody war with the mightiest nation on the globe, and by a complete severance of the political ties that bound them to the mother country, might they not have shrunk appalled from so mighty and so doubtful a task? In these, and in a hundred other similar instances, no doubt, men rushed with impetuous but honest impulse into a righteous contest, gaining the required courage and devotion as the fight went on, until at last they became invincible. In all such contests how many run well for a season, and then, unable to bear the cross, become stragglers and deserters! The anti-slavery movement, in this respect, was no exception to the general rule. Many a man who fought well so long as he felt sure that the victory would be speedily won, fell out of the ranks when he found that the battle would be fierce and long. It would be easy to give the names of some of these deserters, but I will not thus rescue them from deserved oblivion.

It seems ludicrous now, but I remember that the least enthusiastic of our number thought it would not take more than ten years at the utmost to abolish slavery! With the Declaration of Independence and the Bible, and God himself, on our side, how could the contest be any longer protracted? Our simplicity will seem all the more wonderful when it is remembered that we looked for emancipation through moral forces alone, and through the conversion of the slaveholders themselves to our doctrines. Our expectation, in spite of first untoward appearances, was, that the American Church and pulpit would be speedily enlisted on our side, that the free discussion of the subject would be at length tolerated in the South, and that the moral influences thus set in play would soon prevail over all opposition. How could the slaveholders long resist the evidence that slavery was not only wrong, but positively injurious to their best interests? With a free press pouring the light of truth into every dark place in the land, with the pulpit summoning the nation to repentance for its sin, with the churches overflowing with sympathy for the slave and bearing a faithful testimony against his wrongs, and with the voices of enlighted statesmen pleading for the right; how was it possible that the victory could be long delayed? Alas, alas! how little we then dreamed that slavery was to find in the pulpits and churches — then on fire with zeal for the conversion of the world to Christ — its chief bulwarks; that the authorized expounders of the Bible would "torture its hallowed pages" to show that slaveholding, instead of being sinful, was perfectly compatible with a Christian profession; that from Andover and Princeton and the other high places of the church would go forth voices to cheer and comfort the holders of slaves; that even the Golden Rule of the blessed Christ would be perverted by a New England Bishop to the service of slavery; that hundreds of pulpits would venture to mix the Bible's "bitter texts" against oppression "with relish suited to the sinner's taste"; that presbyteries, synods, associations, conventions and other ecclesiastical assemblies, and even the missionary bodies of the church, instead of pleading for the oppressed, would "daub with untempered mortar" in the service of the oppressor; that slaveholding preachers would find ready and approved access to Northern pulpits, while ministers advocating emancipation would be proscribed as fanatics; that the holders of slaves would be admitted without objection to Northern communion-tables, which the negro Christian could only approach as a pariah; and that the religious press, with few exceptions, would lend itself to the service of slavery. How blind we were to the fact that the Government, in every vein and artery, and even in its very heart, was poisoned by the insidious virus of slavery; that the Constitution itself was fatally infected; that our legislative, executive, judicial and diplomatic proceedings were largely under the sway of the slave power, ever watchful to advance its own interests; that the political parties were bound hand and foot to the ponderous wheels of the modern juggernaut; and that our statesmen, while eager to

> . . . Send, with lavish breath,
> Their sympathies across the wave,
> Where manhood, on the field of death,
> Struck for his freedom or a grave;

to plead warmly and eloquently

> For Greece, the Moslem fetter spurning,
> . . . .
> And Poland, gasping on her lance—

would yet stand dumb before American slavery and its
abominations, or open their mouths only to equivocate
and palter and stultify themselves !

The first thing that the new society did was to commission its Quaker president, Arnold Buffum, as a lecturing agent, with the understanding that he should
collect his own small salary, and as much more as possible. Mr. Buffum was then in the prime of life, a
man of excellent judgment, well versed in his subject,
and withal a pleasant and quite an effective speaker.
His Quaker dress and speech were accepted in some
quarters as an adequate excuse for his Abolitionism,
and so were an aid to him in his work. He had been
in England but a few years before, and made the
acquaintance of Clarkson, Wilberforce and others of
the anti-slavery leaders, from whose experience and
instruction he had gained some valuable lessons. In
some quarters he met with an encouraging reception,
and succeeded in gathering fair audiences, that gave
him respectful attention. Occasionally he found a
clergyman willing to open a church or vestry to him
without charge. In other places he was able to procure the use of a public hall at small expense. The opposition had not yet had time to organize itself, though
public prejudice was in many places very strong, and
the tone of the press far from friendly. In spite of many
adverse influences, Mr. Buffum's lectures were a good
beginning of the work that needed to be done. He
frequently encountered the agents of the Colonization
Society, never failing to give them battle as the chief
apologists of slavery, who denounced immediate emancipation as fanaticism, and declared that slaves should
be set free only upon condition of being exiled to Africa. The popularity of this Society arose from the fact
that it humored the popular prejudice against the negro as an inferior being, and did not claim for him the
rights accorded to white men. "Negro" then was al-

most universally spelled with two g's, and with this orthography it embodied a measure of contempt from which all manly and Christian sympathy and all reverence for human nature were eliminated. If the slaves had been so many wild beasts, people could not more coolly, or with less consciousness of cruelty in so doing, have denied to them the rights of men. Indeed, it was almost universally assumed that they *were* beasts in passion and revenge, and, if set free, would cut the throats of their emancipators! Slaves with white skins might be set free on the instant with perfect safety; but black slaves were so many wolves, held by the ears by their unfortunate masters, who could not let go without being devoured. The primary difference between the Abolitionists and their opponents lay in the fact that the former asserted, while the latter denied, the perfect humanity of the negro. It was this that made the anti-slavery movement dangerous in the eyes of the slaveholders — this that commended the Colonization Society to their favor and support. Mr. Buffum, true-hearted Quaker that he was, understood this perfectly, and therefore was able to strike effective blows. He was at once gentle and bold, cautious and faithful. He would not extenuate nor set down aught in malice.

"The gentle words which hung
Like a string of pearls from his cautious lip, .
On their silver thread, he was fain to clip,
Lest something more than the truth might slip,
For once, from a Quaker's tongue."

Such a man could not but exert a wholesome influence in the face of even such prejudices as he was compelled to encounter. He might have accomplished still more if the sect to which he belonged had given him its sympathy and support — nay, if it had not brought its strong social and ecclesiastical influences to bear against him. He became a mark for javelins stealthily hurled by false brethren. The Quaker sect, as such, was worshipping in the "house of Rimmon" like all the rest, its ears filled with cotton, its heart unresponsive to the cry of the slave. A few tender-hearted and noble members of the society were true to its principles and traditions, and these espoused the cause with zeal; but those who sat in high places and ruled the denomination discountenanced the movement, taking sides practically and effectively with the oppo-sition. Quaker meeting-houses, except in a few in-stances, were sternly closed against anti-slavery lec-turers, and members who attended anti-slavery meet-ings were often labored with as those who had strayed from the true path. The ground assumed by the lead-ers was that Quakers ought to keep by themselves and not mingle with "the world's people" in philanthropic work; that the Abolitionists were not truly inspired, but attempting to abolish slavery in their own strength, and that to pay men for lecturing against it was con-trary to the Quaker testimony against a "hireling min-istry." Talk like this was in many places the burden of Quaker preaching, and it was as effectual in its in-fluence upon the sect as open defences and apologies for slavery were in other denominations. But Mr. Buffum, though he became of no reputation among his brethren, and though he felt this opposition and de-traction very keenly, never faltered for a moment, but held on his way until, in subsequent years, the sect would gladly have blotted out all traces of its unfriendly course toward him. Others, too, were equally faith-ful. How invaluable and inspiring were the songs Whittier poured forth, heedless of the dominant in-fluences of the society, I need not say. He began early and continued even unto the end, and since the days of George Fox no man has done more than he to commend Quaker principles to the admiration of the world, or reflected higher honor upon the Quaker name. The name of Whittier indeed is a bright star in the Quaker firmament, to which every member of the society now points with a pride that rebukes the degeneracy of an earlier day. "Well, Perez, I hope thee's done running after the Abolitionists," said a high-seat Friend to one of his humbler brethren. "Verily, I have," said Perez; "I've caught up with and gone just a little ahead of them." There were a goodly number of men like Perez, in the society, after all.

At the time when the New England Anti-Slavery Society was formed, the movement in Great Britain against slavery in the West Indies was nigh its culmination. The whole kingdom was shaken by the eloquence of Wilberforce, Brougham, O'Connell, Thompson and others. The English press was full of the subject; but such was the power of slavery over the American press that the people here knew hardly more of the progress of the movement than they did of what was going on in the wilds of Africa. Some few rays of light did now and then steal into American minds from that source, but they were not sufficient to produce any wide illumination. American newspapers were afraid to print the truth lest it should help the Abolitionists, while the Abolitionists themselves, with their limited resources, were unable to give it any wide currency. Mr. Garrison was the recipient, now and then, of a batch of anti-slavery publications from England, by which his own heart was cheered, and which he used for the benefit of the cause in this country. Well do I remember with what emotions I first read in "The Liberator," where it appeared for the first time in America, the following passage from a speech by Lord Brougham:—

" Tell me not of rights — talk not of the property of the planter in his slaves. I deny the right— I acknowledge not the property. The principles, the feelings of our common nature rise in rebellion against it. Be the appeal made to the understanding or the heart, the sentence is the same that

13

rejects it. In vain you tell me of the laws that sanction such a claim! There is a law above all the enactments of human codes — the same throughout the world, the same in all times — such it was before the daring genius of Columbus pierced the night of ages, and opened to one world the sources of power, wealth and knowledge, to another all unutterable woes; such as it is at this day. It is the law written by the finger of God on the heart of man; and by that law, unchangeable and eternal, while men despise fraud, and loathe rapine, and abhor blood, they shall reject with indignation the wild and guilty fantasy that man can hold property in man."

While the hearts of British citizens and Christians were stirred by appeals like this from statesmen of renown, and by orators, ministers and philanthropists of every sort, the statesmen and the divines of America were weaving defences and apologies for slavery out of the Bible and the Constitution, thus leading the country toward the retribution that afterwards befel in the catastrophe of the Southern Rebellion.

VI.

Colorphobia Illustrated — Its Meanness and Cruelty — Doctors Gur-
ley and Bacon — A Contrast — The Nat Turner Insurrection —
Discussion in Virginia — Why it Failed to Accomplish Anything
— Power of Immediatism as a Principle.

WHEN it is remembered that the New England
Anti-Slavery Society sought not only to free the
slaves but to "improve the character and condition of
the free people of color," it may seem strange that
among those who took part in its formation there was
not a single individual of the latter class. But the
fact is easily explained. It was not from any lack of
interest on their part in the movement, for they saw
in it a bright star of promise for their race, and
thanked God for the sight. They had rallied, at least
the most intelligent among them, to the support of
"The Liberator," and were indulging in bright dreams
of speedy deliverance from civil and social proscription. Why then were they not conspicuous among
the formers of the new society? It was because they
instinctively knew that their presence and co-operation
would serve only to increase and intensify the prejudices which the society must encounter. Their very
anxiety for its success kept them aloof at first. They
were careful not to embarrass in its infancy a movement on which were staked their dearest hopes. An-
glo-Saxon prejudice against the negro is strong even
yet, but it is weak compared with what it was then.
No man with a black skin could enter a Christian
church without consenting to the degradation of the
"nigger pew." He could not ride in any public conveyance on terms of equality with others. A very

intelligent colored girl, the daughter of a devoted and
useful clergyman of Boston, was suddenly summoned
to the bedside of a dying relative in New Hampshire.
A seat was bespoken for her in the stage, then the only
means of public conveyance ; but the driver, on coming to the door and finding that she was a negro,
cracked his whip with an accompanying oath and
drove off without her. A colored man of Boston, in
trading with a white man, became the owner of a pew
in the central aisle of the Park Street Church, and,
thinking he might be profited by the ministrations of
an intelligent white minister, went to it one Sunday
morning with his family. They listened to the "stated
preaching of the Gospel" for once under the gaze of a
whole battery of frowning faces ; but they were not
permitted to enjoy the privilege a second time. The
trustees of the church found some technicality by
which to deprive the black man of his legal rights.
His appearance and that of his family in that fashionable house of worship was accounted by all Boston as
an outrage scarcely less flagrant than would have been
the use of the pew as a pigpen. A colored merchant
from Liberia, a man of intelligence as well as wealth,
and highly esteemed by Colonizationists, being on a
visit to Boston, took the opportunity of making the
acquaintance of the Abolitionists. As he wished to
hear Dr. Beecher preach, I invited him, as an act of
courtesy to a distinguished foreigner, to take a seat in
my pew. On my way out of church I encountered the
indignant frowns of a large number of the congregation ; but it was amusing to witness the change of countenance that fell upon the advocates of colonization as I
introduced to them "Mr. ——, of Liberia." They really
seemed to think his odor was not quite so offensive, after all, as they had suspected. The air of Liberia was
such a powerful disinfectant ! The slaveholders used to
think the atmosphere of their homes was perfectly de-

lectable when slaves in kitchen, dining-room, parlor and boudoir were as all-pervading as flies ; but there was no odor so offensive to them as that imparted to a "negro" when he was set free ; and Northern people in the days of slavery, while they required the free negro to occupy a separate apartment on steamboat and railcar, as being personally offensive to white olfactories, never thought of remonstrating when the slaveholders (in the hot summer weather, too !) claimed for their slaves all the privileges of first-class travellers. Strange that in a republican country freedom was so offensive, while slavery was so fragrant !

The meanness and cruelty of this hateful race prejudice, as it was often manifested in that day, was simply indescribable. A bright colored lad belonging to my class in Sunday school, in 1831, said to me, sadly, in reply to my efforts to awaken in him an ambition for self-improvement, "What's the use in my attempting to improve myself, when, do what I may, I can never be anything but a nigger?" I tried to cheer this boy, to kindle some hope in his breast, by reminding him that a few good men were struggling to deliver him and his unfortunate race from their terrible surroundings ; and I am glad to say that he became an honorable and useful man, and during the later years of his life he was a faithful servant of the United States in the Post Office Department. In that day no colored boy could be apprenticed to any trade in any shop where white men worked; still less could he find a place, except as a menial, in any store or office. I well remember what amazement was excited when Mr. Garrison and his partner first took a black boy as an apprentice in the office of "The Liberator." It was declared on every side that no "nigger" could learn the art of printing, and it was held to be evidence of arrant folly to try the experiment. If the negroes, under such circumstances, sometimes seemed

dull and even stupid, who can wonder? What race or
class of men is strong enough to keep its feet under
such a load of prejudice and contumely? The wonder
is that the negroes bore it so patiently and cheerfully,
keeping alive in their souls the hope of a better day to
come, when the hearts of Christians should be purged
from the foul spirit of caste. They could not have
done it if God had not made them gentle, patient and
forgiving above almost every other class of the human
family. The worst of it all was that the prejudice was
defended in pulpit and press as natural and therefore
justifiable. The scheme of African colonization rested
upon it as its corner-stone. If it had pleased God, in
a night to give the slaves a white skin, every man in
the United States would have arisen from his bed the
next morning a flaming Abolitionist. No need of any
colonies then, in Africa or elsewhere, and no danger that
the slaves, if set free, would cut the throats of their
masters. Every excuse and apology for slavery would
have been instantly swept away, and no premium for a
text of Scripture to support it would have been of any
avail, for no theological professor would have dared in
that case to torture the Bible, even for a reward.

Mr. Garrison won the grateful confidence of the free
colored people, not more by demanding the instant
emancipation of-the slaves than by his uncompromising assaults upon the spirit of caste. In short, his
recognition of the humanity of the negro was unqualified and complete, and he was firmly resolved to content himself with nothing less than the admission of
that, alike in principle and practice. He made open
war upon an old statute of Massachusetts inflicting a
fine of $50 upon any person who should join in mar-
riage any white person with any negro, Indian or
mulatto. He saw that this statute set a stigma upon
the negro, and therefore demanded its repeal. Perhaps of all his acts this was for a time the most unpop-

ular. The press poured upon it unmeasured ridicule and scorn, denouncing him as an "amalgamationist," and in the Legislature the petitions for repeal were at first treated with contempt. But every year they were repeated, until at last reason prevailed, and the obnoxious statute was repealed. Upon this question he would not equivocate, he would not excuse, he would not retreat a single inch, and his voice was finally heard and obeyed. It was this uncompromising spirit, this absolute devotion to principle, that distinguished him above other men, and made his influence so irresistible. How surely, even if slowly, does the world yield to the might of such a man! The tides obey the moon no more implicitly — the law of gravitation is not more certain in its operation.

"Men of a thousand shifts and wiles, look here!
    See one straightforward conscience put in pawn
  To win a world! See the obedient sphere
    By bravery's simple gravitation drawn!"

If there was among the colored people at first some distrust of the new movement, we need not wonder, since they had so often found themselves deceived by the spurious professions and promises of white men. The Colonization Society was even then exerting its influence, under spurious professions of friendliness toward them, to make their lot harder, and to compel them to take their choice between permanent degradation in their own country and exile to the inhospitable shores of barbarous Africa. "The African Repository," the organ of that society, declared : "The habits, the feelings, the prejudices of society — prejudices which neither refinement, nor argument, nor education, nor religion itself can subdue — mark the people of color, whether bond or free, as the subjects of a degradation inevitable and incurable. The African in this country belongs by birth to the very lowest station in society, and from that station he can never rise, be his talents,

his enterprise, his virtues what they may.   Here,
therefore, they must be forever debased; more than
this, they must be forever useless; more even than
this, they must be forever a nuisance, from which
it were a blessing for society to be rid." These words,
so insulting to the very spirit of Christianity, and so
full of baldest atheism, were written by a clergyman
educated in New England, the Rev. Ralph Randolph
Gurley, Secretary of the American Colonization Society; and what is still worse, they expressed the sentiments of a vast majority of Northern Christians. The
Rev. Dr. Leonard Bacon, of New Haven, then the
leading champion of Colonization in New England,
described the negro population of the country in "The
Christian Spectator" — a magazine of large influence —
as a class "which, even if it were not literally enslaved,
must forever remain in a state of degradation no better
than bondage.   Here a slave cannot be really emancipated. You cannot raise him from the abyss of his
degradation.   You may call him free, you may enact
a statute-book of laws to make him free, but you cannot bleach him into the enjoyment of freedom." It
was just as natural as breathing that the man who
thought there was no power in Christianity to overcome complexional and race prejudices, should be an
apologist for slavery ; and so we need not be surprised
to find Dr. Bacon saying: "The Bible contains no
explicit prohibition of slavery.   There is neither
chapter nor verse of Holy Writ which lends any countenance to the fulminating spirit of universal emancipation, of which some exhibitions may be seen in some
of the newspapers." What then did Isaiah mean when
he told the people of Israel to "break every yoke,"
and "let the oppressed go free"? And what did Jesus
mean when he said he had been anointed to "preach
deliverance to the captives, and to set at liberty them
that are bruised"? Were expressions like these in-

tended to suggest the duty of a distant and gradual breaking of the fetters of the enslaved, and to stigmatize as fanatical "fulminations" the demands for immediate emancipation?

Let no one suppose that I cite these utterances of Dr. Gurley and Dr. Bacon for any personal reason whatever. I might fill whole pages with similar extracts from the leading divines and statesmen of that day. Dr. Bacon, then a young man of ripe culture and highest promise, simply spoke the prevailing sentiment of the time — a sentiment which he afterward unlearned and repudiated. I am simply trying to make clear to my readers of the present generation the darkness, ignorance and moral degeneracy against which the early Abolitionists had to contend. There are those who, in the fancied interest of Christianity, would cover up these ugly blotches upon the escutcheon of the American church and clergy, and lead posterity to the conclusion that it was the so-called fanaticism and infidelity of the Abolitionists that repelled Christian sympathy and support. As God is just, all such attempts will be vain. . The ugly facts cannot be concealed, and they ought not to be if they could. Like the words written upon the wall of Belshazzar's palace, they should be emblazoned in history as a warning to men and nations in all coming time to obey the voice of God and respect the rights of human nature ; and, still further, as a warning that the true character of Christianity is to be sought, not in the churches bearing the name while they are false to the spirit of the Master, but in His own life and teachings, now and evermore. Let God and Christ be true, though all men are condemned as liars !

In contrast with the atheistic postulate cited above, that Christianity could do nothing for the negro in America, and that Providence had doomed him to inevitable degradation so long as he should foolishly

14

persist in sharing the advantages and blessings of our
glorious republic, let me quote a few sentences from
Mr. Garrison. Referring to the very passages above
quoted, and to others of a similar character, Mr. Garrison, writing in 1832, said : —

"Search the records of heathenism, and sentiments more
hostile to the spirit of the Gospel, or of a more black and
blasphemous complexion than these, cannot be found. I
believe that they are libels upon the character of my
countrymen, which time will wipe off. I call upon the spirits
of the just made perfect in heaven, upon all who have experienced the love of God in their souls here below, upon the
Christian converts in India and the islands of the sea, to
sustain me in the assertion that there is power enough in the
religion of Jesus Christ to melt down the most stubborn
prejudices, to overthrow the highest walls of partition, to
break the strongest caste, to improve and elevate the
most degraded, to unite in fellowship the most hostile, and
to equalize and bless all its recipients. Make me sure that
there is not, and I will give it up, now and forever.

"My countrymen! are you willing to be held up as tyrants and hypocrites forever? as less magnanimous and just
than the population of Europe? No — no! I cannot give
you up as incorrigibly wicked, nor my country as scaled over
to destruction. My confidence remains like the oak — like
the Alps — unshaken, storm-proof. I am not discouraged ; I
am not distrustful. I still place an unwavering reliance
upon the omnipotence of truth. I still believe that the demands of justice will be satisfied ; that the voice of bleeding
humanity will melt the most obdurate heart ; and that the
land will be redeemed and regenerated by an enlightened
and energetic public opinion. As long as there remains
among us a single copy of the Declaration of Independence,
or of the New Testament, I will not despair of the social
and political elevation of my black countrymen."

Let the reader compare these words of Garrison
with those of Doctors Gurley and Bacon, and judge
for himself whether the latter or the former accord
most perfectly with the spirit of Christianity.

I have already alluded to the Nat Turner insurrection of August, 1831; but I mention it again to call attention to the great debate to which it led in the Virginia Legislature, in the session of 1831-2. That debate was remarkable for the confessions it elicited as to the character and the cruel wrongs of slavery, and for the utter moral helplessness in dealing with it exhibited by the leading men of the State. Nothing that Garrison had said or could say of the evils of slavery exceeded what slaveholders themselves confessed in the course of this debate. Mr. Broadnax, forgetting that the people of Virginia had brought it upon themselves in defiance of God's law, described it as the "greatest curse that God in his wrath ever inflicted upon a people." Mr. Bolling said it was "the bane of our happiness, the most pernicious of all the evils with which the body politic can be afflicted." Mr. Chandler declared it to be "the greatest curse that has ever been inflicted upon the State." Mr. Moore said it was "the severest calamity that has ever befallen any portion of the human race," and that "its irresistible tendency was to undermine and destroy everything like virtue and morality in the community." Mr. Faulkner spoke of it as "that bitterest drop from the chalice of the destroying angel," and said the country was "groaning under the heaviest and blackest curse that ever afflicted freemen." Mr. Summers wished "to arrest the desolating scourge of our country, to save after ages from the accumulated ills of a then hopeless and remediless disease." Mr. Berry said it was "a cancer on the body politic, as certain, steady and fatal in its progress as any cancer on the physical system;" and Mr. McDowell, afterwards Governor of the State, said it was "not the fear of Nat Turner and his deluded, drunken handful of followers" that had so excited the people — "it was the suspicion eternally attached to the slave himself — a suspicion that a Nat Turner might be in every family, that the same bloody deed might be acted over at any time and in any place, that the materials for it were spread through the land, and were always ready for a like explosion."

It is impossible to doubt the sincerity of these men. They lived in the midst of slavery, most of them were slaveholders, and they all saw and felt how dangerous the system was, and how destructive of the very foundations of morality and prosperity. Why then did they not attack it boldly and insist upon its immediate abolition? It was because they were under the delusion, common in that day, and from which only a few Abolitionists had just been delivered, that, bad as slavery was, immediate emancipation would be worse; that the slaves, on being set free, would turn in vengeance upon the masters and give themselves up to riot and bloodshed. This delusion was long an absolute protection of slavery in communities where the slaves were numerous and where its strongest opponents dared not so much as hint its absolute sinfulness, or propose any other than an exceedingly gradual plan of emancipation. With what power these Virginians would have been clothed, if, seeing the terrible injustice of slavery and the dangers attending it, they had also seen with equal clearness that it would be perfectly safe to set every slave instantly free! But they were weak as water, while the champions of slavery, for the time-being, had all the advantages of a fortified position. If the former had been as willing to have "the way of God expounded more perfectly unto them" by Garrison and Elizabeth Heyrick as the Jew Apollos was to learn of Aquila and Priscilla, they might have demolished the fortifications of the slaveholders and beaten them on the open field; instead of which they were themselves utterly routed and silenced, and Virginia thenceforth bound hand and foot by the Slave Power, and given over to work the "iniquity" of slavery and

the domestic slave-trade " with greediness." The men
who had dared to assail slavery, and who afterward
aspired to public station, were compelled to eat their
own words, and thus descend to the same level with
those who openly declared, with Mr. Gholson, that
" the right of the slaveholder to his female slaves and
their increase, was the same as that to his brood mares
and their products."

To this vulgar complexion it came at last, and the
State of Washington and Jefferson was not ashamed
to owe her wealth chiefly to the profits derived from
the sale of slaves, deliberately raised for the market
like so many colts and calves ! If Garrison's plea for
immediate emancipation had been taken up and enforced by the Northern church and pulpit, the "mother
of Presidents" might have been saved from this degradation, and the freedom of the slaves assured without
the bloody arbitrament of a war that filled the land
with mourning and woe. Never in all history was
there another delusion so preposterous and absurd as
that which affirmed that it was dangerous to free the
slaves from their bonds. Not only was the delusion
contrary to common sense, and a libel upon human
nature and God, but its foolishness had been demon-
strated again and again by actual experiment, as it was
three years later by the results of emancipation in the
British West Indies. If Mr. Garrison, like his prede-
cessors in the cause, had been a gradualist, attributing
the sin of slavery (as the Rev. Dr. Leonard Bacon did)
to " those and those only who bore a part in originating
such a constitution of society," and assigning the duty
of emancipation to distant generations, he would have
been as powerless as those bewildered denouncers of
slavery in the Virginia Legislature, and his movement
would have come to naught. A good general is careful in selecting the ground upon which to fight the
enemy ; above all he avoids placing his army in a quag-

mire, where it can have no sound footing. The same
principle is as important in moral as in physical warfare, and Garrison was wiser than his generation in
that he saw that gradualism was a slough in which
many a well-meaning band of reformers had been swallowed up, and that it would be useless to assail slavery
on any other ground than that of its utter sinfulness
and the duty of every slaveholder instantly to emancipate his slaves. God's law of eternal justice and righteousness must be uplifted and honored, and men must
be made to understand the folly and wickedness of the
assumption that obedience to that law is not safe.
To attempt to abolish slavery while one's own mouth
was filled with apologies for it as a system for which
the generation then upon the stage was in no way responsible, and from which there was no way of present
escape, would be idle.

It was the doctrine of immediate emancipation that
imbued Garrison's arm with strength, and that made
all the difference between success and failure in the
movement he organized. As Wendell Phillips, standing over his coffin, said: "He seems to have understood—this boy without experience—he seems to have
understood by instinct that righteousness is the only
thing which will finally compel submission; that one,
with God, is always a majority. He seems to have
known at the very outset, taught of God, the herald
and champion, God-endowed and God-sent to arouse a
nation, that only by the most absolute assertion of the
uttermost truth, without qualification or. compromise,
can a nation be waked to conscience or strengthened
for duty."

It was the custom in that day to inveigh against immediatism as "impracticable." "You cannot," said our
opponents, "emancipate all the slaves at once; why,
then, do you propose so impossible a scheme?" Our
reply was, that slaveholding being a sin, instant eman-

cipation was the right of every slave and the duty of every master. The fact that the slaveholders were not ready at once to obey the demands of justice and the requirements of the Divine Law militated not against the soundness of the doctrine of immediatism or against its power as a PRACTICAL WORKING PRINCIPLE. The minister of the Gospel does not cease to proclaim the duty of immediate repentance for sin because he knows that his message will not be immediately heeded. It is his duty to contend for sound principles, whether his auditors "will hear or forbear." He dares not advise or encourage them to delay repentance for a single hour, though he knows that in all probability many of them will do so until their dying day.

' The fanaticism of the Abolitionists consisted in applying to the sin of slavery the general principle which they had learned from the American pulpit. There was no impracticability in the scheme of immediate emancipation save that which arose from the determination of the slaveholders to persist in their sin, and from the encouragement they received at the hands of men who made themselves partakers in their iniquity. Even at this day, after all the light shed upon the subject from the results of emancipation in the West Indies, and in the face of the recorded testimony of Clarkson and Wilberforce, Brougham and O'Connell, and other eminent philanthropists, there are men of eminence in the church who pronounce immediate emancipation "a fantastic abstraction," and seek to cast reproach upon American Abolitionists for advocating a doctrine so wild and impracticable. But the slaveholders, who had seen many a scheme of gradualism come to naught, knew right well that the voice of Garrison, pleading for the right of every slave to instant freedom, would, unless it could be silenced, prove the knell of their hateful system.

VII.

Battle with the Colonization Society — Garrison's "Thoughts" —
An Indictment with Ten Counts — Discussion — Mr. Garrison
gives the Colored People a Hearing — Attempt to Found a Negro
College in New Haven — The Town Thrown into an Uproar —
The Project Defeated — The Canterbury Disgrace — The Burleigh
Brothers — Why Windham County is Republican.

Mr. GARRISON, when he joined Lundy in Baltimore,
was a mild Colonizationist. Without investigating the
subject for himself, he took it for granted that a
scheme so earnestly supported by many of the best
people in the country was worthy of encouragement;
and in his Fourth of July address in Park Street
Church, Boston, in 1829, he commended it in a few
words which showed clearly enough that he did not
regard it as a remedy for slavery. The friends of Colonization indeed were dissatisfied with his address,
both for its uncompromising denunciations of slavery
and its lack of zeal in their favorite enterprise. Having consecrated his life to the work of emancipation,
he naturally sought the acquaintance and sympathy of
the free colored people, among whom he was glad to
find some men of intelligence, good judgment and high
moral worth. He was astonished to find that, without
exception, they regarded the Colonization Society with
feelings of strong aversion and abhorrence. They
held it to be a cunning device of Southern men to
avert some of the dangers that threatened the existence of slavery, and regarded as an affront to themselves the intimation that they were something less
than citizens of the United States, and must consent to
be deported to barbarous Africa in order to enjoy their

rights.   Mr. Garrison was at first inclined to remonstrate with them as the victims of a mistaken prejudice, but he soon found that they had studied the question, while he was ignorant of its bearings and consequences. They had read the reports of the Colonization Society and the speeches of its Southern as well as its Northern champions, and knew that the scheme rested upon the hateful spirit of caste as its chief corner-stone. Mr. Garrison, finding himself worsted in the argument by his colored friends, resolved to investigate the subject for himself.   He procured the annual reports of the American Colonization Society, together with files of its organ, "The African Repository," and copies of numerous pamphlets, official or friendly, and set himself to the task of examining them.   He found that his colored friends had not in any respect misrepresented or misunderstood the society — that the case was even worse than they had represented it.   In "The Genius of Universal Emancipation" he reviewed some of Henry Clay's Colonization speeches and writings, and it is creditable to the latter that this did not hinder him from entertaining, cordially and promptly, Mr. Whittier's proposition that he should pay the fine of his critic and release him from the Baltimore jail.

On returning to New England, after his imprisonment, he found that every little rill of honest sympathy for the negro, whether bond or free, had been made tributary to the Colonization scheme ; the agents of which at the North presented it as the only practicable remedy for slavery, while they denounced immediate emancipation as the wildest fanaticism.   The good people of the North, in their blind credulity, had given the Colonization Society a place in their sympathies side by side with the Bible, missionary and tract societies, and flattered themselves that in supporting it they were doing all that was practicable for the abolition of slavery.   It was easy to persuade them that

15

every attack upon this society and its scheme was aimed at the whole family of benevolent and charitable associations which had become entrenched in the affection and confidence of the churches as the agencies appointed of God for the conversion of the world. Behind this society as a rampart the apologists for slavery entrenched themselves, hurling the deadliest missiles at the heads of the Abolitionists. In these circumstances Mr. Garrison was inexorably compelled to justify his impeachment of the Colonization scheme, to tear the mask from its brow and show it up in its true colors, in the light of its own official documents. Having enlarged "The Liberator" at the beginning of the year 1832, and finding himself supported and cheered by an organized society, he addressed himself to this task with a courage that no opposition could subdue, and performed it with a thoroughness that made any further demonstration unnecessary. The result of his labors was seen in a bulky pamphlet, that came from the press in the spring, entitled " Thoughts on African Colonization ; or, an Impartial Exhibition of the Doctrines, Principles and Purposes of the American Colonization Society ; together with the Resolutions, Addresses and Remonstrances of the Free People of Color." As a compilation of facts and authorities it was unanswerable and overwhelming. It condemned the Colonization Society out of its own mouth, and by a weight of evidence that was irresistible. There was just enough of comment to elucidate the testimony from official sources and bring it within the comprehension of the simplest reader. His indictment contained ten averments, viz. : 1. The American Colonization Society is pledged not to oppose the system of slavery ; 2. It apologizes for slavery and slaveholders ; 3. It recognizes slaves as property ; 4. It increases the value of slaves ; 5. It is the enemy of immediate abolition ; 6. It is nourished by fear and selfishness; 7. It aims at the utter expulsion of the blacks; 8. It is the disparager of the free blacks; 9. It denies the possibility of elevating the blacks in this country; 10. It deceives and misleads the Nation. Each of these averments was supported by pages of citations from the annual reports of the society, from the pages of its official organ, "The African Repository," and from the speeches of its leading champions in all parts of the country. It was impossible to set this evidence aside, and equally so to resist the conclusions drawn therefrom. The work could not be, and therefore was not answered. There were nibblings, carpings and casuistical perversions, but nothing that deserved or even claimed the character of a reply. It did not indeed kill the Colonization Society, which was founded upon caste and drew the breath of life from the fetid atmosphere of slavery; but it smote it with a paralysis from which it never recovered, and sent it far to the rear of the benevolent associations to whose goodly fellowship it had unworthily aspired. Hundreds of ministers, who still hesitated to join the anti-slavery movement, thenceforth gave no further support to the Colonization scheme, feeling that they had been deceived as to its character and designs, and that the claim of some of its advocates that it was a practical remedy for slavery was either a delusion or an imposture. Only the blindest and most obstinate apologists for slavery thereafter lent it their support; but this was a numerous, wealthy and influential class, so that the treasurer's report still showed a large footing of receipts.

Just before the appearance of Mr. Garrison's "Thoughts," the American Colonization Society, taking alarm from his assaults in "The Liberator," and from the organization of the New England Anti-Slavery Society, sent to Massachusetts a Congregational clergyman, the Rev. Joshua N. Danforth, charged with

the duty of defending the Colonization scheme and resisting the progress of the abolition movement. The
Board of Managers of the Anti-Slavery Society
promptly challenged him to a public discussion with
its president, and took upon itself the responsibility
of providing a hall for the purpose. But Mr. Danforth was too discreet to expose himself to the fire of
our Quaker artillery. For four evenings the hall was
kept open, but only a squad of irresponsible advocates
of Colonization entered the lists. On one occasion,
however, he did venture to attend a lecture of Mr.
Buffum's, at Northampton, and, in response to the latter's courteous invitation, he made a speech sneering
at Mr. Garrison as one for whose head a reward had
been offered by a Southern Legislature, at Mr. Buffum
as "nothing but a hatter," and at the officers of the
Anti-Slavery Society generally as too insignificant for
notice. The good Quaker reminded the vain clergyman that this was not the first instance in which God
had chosen the weak things of the world to confound
the mighty ; that there was a story in an old-fashioned
book of twelve poor, illiterate fishermen taking the
lead in an enterprise upon which the Orthodox Scribes,
Pharisees and priests contemptuously frowned. He
reminded him also that if the Abolitionists were disposed to rest the merits of their cause upon the reputation of its champions, they might point with pride
to the names of Brougham, Clarkson, Wilberforce,
Buxton, Cropper, Allen, O'Connell, and a score of
others hardly less eminent. Mr. Danforth had sneered
at him (Mr. Buffum) as "a hatter," but he had read in
the old-fashioned book above referred to of one who
was despised and rejected of men, hissed at, spit upon
and called the son of a carpenter, but who yet was the
Son of God and the Saviour of the world. Paul was
a tent-maker, Franklin a printer, Roger Sherman a
shoemaker, and John Bunyan a tinker; but each of

these men had done a work in the world as important, perhaps, as that of any agent of the Colonization Society. But Mr. Danforth persisted in thinking it a very clever device on his part to contrast the names of the statesmen and divines who indorsed the Colonization Society with those of "the nobodies who led the movement for immediate abolition." However weak his arguments might be, this was sure to bring down the house, when there was no opportunity for reply!

The scheme of Colonization was urged, professedly, in the interest and for the benefit of the free colored people, but strangely enough, they were never consulted, nor were their opinions and feelings treated with the least respect. Indeed, the champions of the scheme no more thought of consulting their so-called beneficiaries than Mr. Bergh thinks of consulting the horses, dogs and cats which he is trying to protect from the cruelty of man. The utterance of an unfavorable opinion on their part was held to be an impertinence. What right had "niggers" to question the schemes of their benefactors, or to set up their opinions in opposition to those of the noble white men who proposed to send them from a civilized to a barbarous land? .

> "Theirs not to reason why,
> Theirs not to make reply,
> Theirs but to" go "and die!"

From the first organization of the society, in 1816, they cried out against the scheme as a piece of heartless injustice and cruelty ; but their protest was treated with contempt, and the society went on in its crusade against them, treating them as outcasts and pariahs, "a greater nuisance than the slaves themselves," and "scarcely reached in their debasement by the heavenly light." (*Vide* " The African Repository.") Is it any wonder that the people thus proscribed and trodden down took heart of grace from the appearance in the field of a champion who recognized their complete humanity and their right to a hearing upon the question whether or not they deserved to be expatriated from their native land? True, the Colonization Society proposed to send them away "with their own consent;" but what a mockery that was when this "consent" was to be extorted by denouncing them as nuisances, unfit to live in the land of their birth, and by visiting them with every form of proscription, political and social, that could be devised by the spirit of caste! Mr. Garrison for the first time gave these down-trodden people a hearing before the American people. He collected their protests from the different parts of the country—from New York, Philadelphia, Baltimore, Boston, Hartford, Providence, and from wherever else any considerable body of the class resided—and allowed them to speak in their own language; and verily, if his work had contained nothing else, this ought to have sufficed to settle the question.

Mr. Garrison, at every step in the controversy, was careful, as far as possible, not to impeach the motives of the good men who had been deluded by the spurious pretences of the Colonization Society, and not less so to make his appeal to the Christian sentiment of the country. In one place he says: " I address myself to high-minded and honorable men, whose heads and hearts are susceptible to sound logic. I appeal to those who have been redeemed from the bondage of sin by the precious blood of Christ, and with whom I hope to unite in a better world in ascribing glory and honor and praise to the Great Deliverer. If I can succeed in gaining their attention, I feel sure of convincing their understanding and securing their support." The work throughout is pervaded by a Christian spirit, and shows that its author was inspired by a faith in God such as has been rarely witnessed among men. Here is a prophetic passage that illustrates this: —

" It is the purpose of God, I am fully persuaded, to humble the pride of the American people by rendering the expulsion of our colored countrymen utterly impracticable, and the necessity for their admission to equal rights imperative. As neither mountains of prejudice, nor the massive shackles of law and of public opinion, have been able to keep them down to a level with the slaves, I confidently anticipate their exaltation among ourselves. Through the vista of time — a short distance only — I see them here, not in Africa, not bowed to the earth or derided and persecuted as at present, not with a downcast air or an irresolute step, but standing erect as men destined heavenward, unembarrassed, untrammelled, with none to molest or make them afraid."

If the man, who, in the thick darkness that enveloped this nation forty-seven years ago, was able to utter this prophecy, was not taught of God, from what other source did the heavenly light stream into his soul? And if the churches of America had received his message and followed that light, would they not now find their record stained by fewer blots, at sight of which they are constrained to blush?

The Abolitionists, from the very beginning, recognized the duty of devising some means for the education of colored youth. The schools, academies, universities and colleges of the land were, with hardly an exception, rigidly closed against pupils of African descent, and there was only too much reason to fear that many children of this class would grow up in ignorance, vice and crime, unless some sort of educational institutions were provided for their immediate benefit. Mr. Garrison's attention was called to this subject while he was in Baltimore, and it was a frequent topic of conversation between himself and some of the most intelligent colored citizens of that place. When he visited New Haven after his release from the Baltimore jail, the Rev. Simeon S. Jocelyn, whose death at the ripe age of eighty years occurred only a short time since, was the white pastor of a colored people's church

in that city.   Mr. Garrison naturally sought his acquaintance, and was happy to find in him a man after
his own heart, devoted to the welfare of the colored
people, and ready to co-operate in any feasible plan for
their improvement.   He had no faith in the Colonization scheme, and was ready to espouse the doctrine of
immediate emancipation the moment it was fairly presented to his mind.   So far as I know, he was the first
white man to conceive the idea of founding in this
country a college for negroes, and for what he did and
suffered in this cause, as well as for his anti-slavery
labors generally, he deserves honorable mention in these
sketches.   Mr. Arthur Tappan, to whom Mr. Garrison was indebted for his release from prison, was also
deeply interested in the proposed college, and offered
to be one of ten persons to contribute $1,000 each
toward the object.   To insure the success of the enterprise, it was deemed important that the colored people
themselves should co-operate therein ; and, as they were
to hold a National Convention in Philadelphia in June,
1831, Mr. Garrison, Mr. Jocelyn and Mr. Tappan
agreed to meet there for the purpose of laying the subject before them.   They were very cordially received,
and by invitation addressed the convention.   Mr.
Jocelyn, in his enthusiasm, had concluded that New
Haven was the best place for the college, and was full of
hope that the enterprise would command the cordial
and earnest support of the people of that city and of
the trustees and faculty of Yale.   He had even selected
a site for the college buildings — "the most beautiful
spot," says Mr. Garrison, "I have ever seen.   No
other part of New Haven compares with it."   They
proposed, in their wisdom, that the institution should
not be identified in any way with the new movement
for the abolition of slavery, but stand upon its own
merits and make its appeal to intelligent, upright and
humane men of every class, party and sect.   The idea

was that even those who were not prepared to promote a scheme for the immediate emancipation of the slaves would yet readily unite in an effort to improve the character and condition of colored people already free.

The convention embraced some men of more than ordinary intelligence and worth — men who in a white convention would have won distinction for ability, thoughtfulness and dignity. By these the proposal to found a college was enthusiastically received, and, after a day spent in debate, the project was unanimously approved, and the Rev. Samuel E. Cornish, a colored Presbyterian, of New York, was appointed an agent for the collection of funds. The matter was confided to a committee, consisting of the venerable James Forten, Joseph Cassey, Robert Douglass, Robert Purvis and Frederick A. Hinton, all of Philadelphia, and men of recognized mark and influence among the people of their class. The plan was for the colored people themselves to raise $10,000, and to collect an equal sum from white people. It was proposed to call the institution "A Collegiate School on the Manual Labor Plan," and the funds to be collected were to be deposited in the United States Bank, to the credit of Arthur Tappan. The committee obtained a rather cold endorsement of the plan by the venerable Bishop White, and his assistant, Bishop H. U. Onderdonk. It was also commended by the Rev. G. T. Bedell, afterward Bishop of Ohio, and by the Rev. Drs. Thomas McAuley and Ezra Stiles Ely, men of mark in the Presbyterian church.

Against a scheme so noble in its purpose, and so carefully and prudently devised, what could be said? Was it not rational to expect that Christians of every denomination, and the friends of education especially, would give it a cordial support? Who could have anticipated that the people of New England, proud as they were of their schools, academics and colleges,

would take offence at this effort to uplift an unfortunate and down-trodden class of American citizens?
Who could have deemed it possible that churches calling themselves Christian, and that were full of zeal to
establish schools in heathen nations, would treat with
contempt, indifference or hostility this effort to provide
the means of education for a large number of children
growing up in ignorance in their very midst? Yet it
was even so. If the proposal had been to establish an
institution for the propagation of leprosy, small-pox
or yellow fever, it could hardly have been scouted with
a fiercer indignation or resisted with a more vehement
energy. On every side was heard the exclamation,
"We don't want any negro colleges in America;
send them back to their own country." It was not
alone in places of low resort or among the ignorant
and degraded classes of society that this hateful spirit
of caste prevailed; it broke out like a leprosy in "good
society," and even in the Christian churches. The
Richmond "Religious Telegraph," edited by the Rev.
A. Converse, a recreant son of New England, and a
graduate of Dartmouth College, published, with editorial commendation, an argument to justify the keeping
of the slaves in ignorance, on the ground that it would
be "highly inexpedient, and, even dangerous to the
peace of the community, to teach them to read and
write"; while in regard to the free people of color,
the editor declared in so many words: "If they were
taught to read it might be an inducement to them to
remain in the country. We would offer them no such
inducement." When I add that the article in which these
views were urged was copied sympathetically, without
a word of comment or protest, in "The Boston Recorder," the expositor of New England orthodoxy, and
when it is remembered that this was the very spirit of
colonization, by which the Northern churches had become so extensively infected, no one at this day need

wonder at the hostility evoked by the proposal to found
a collegiate school for the instruction of negro children.
The only wonder is that Mr. Garrison and his associates, after the exhibitions they had witnessed of the
spirit of caste, were so simple as to imagine that their
plan was feasible. But they were very slow to be convinced that the Christianity of the North had become
so debased. They said, "It is only a mistake, a delusion,
that will quickly pass away, as the vapors of the night
are dispelled by the rising sun." It is the only point
in respect to which their prescience was seriously at
fault. But how could they readily suspect that the
churches under whose influence they had been trained,
and which they had been taught to revere as the representatives of Christ and his religion, had entered into
a moral eclipse so deep and dark? They would not
believe it, and they did not until they were compelled ;
and when at length the whole sad truth dawned upon
their unwilling minds, they surrendered their faith in
the churches while adhering more firmly than before
to their faith in Christianity and its Divine Founder.

In New Haven there was a high effervescence of hostility to the proposed college. A city meeting, duly
warned, was held (September 10, 1831), the Mayor,
the Hon. Denis Kimberly, in the chair. Distinguished
citizens, the Hon. Judge Daggett at their head, made
indignant speeches, and the meeting resolved, by a
vote of 700 to 4, "That the founding of colleges for
educating colored people is an unwarrantable and dangerous interference with the internal concerns of other
States, and ought to be discouraged"; that "the establishment in New Haven" of such a college "is incompatible with the prosperity if not the existence of the
present institutions of learning," and will be destructive
of the best interests of the city"; and that "the May-
or, Aldermen, Common Council and Freemen" will
"resist the establishment of the proposed college in this

place by every lawful means." Mr. Jocelyn, the white
pastor of the colored church, appears to have been the
only clergyman in the city who had the courage to protest against this frenzied exhibition of colorphobia.
The honored faculty of Yale assented by its silence to
this imputation put upon its character by the meeting.
Dr. Bacon, the popular pastor of the Centre Church,
a leading Colonizationist, and a powerful writer and
platform speaker, did not find his voice on this occasion, but, like his elders, bent before the storm. When
the whole tide of Colonization influence was running
with Niagara force against the proposed college, it
would have been an act of sublime heroism on his part
if he had lifted his voice in its defence, as, twenty
years later, he dared to protest against the repeal of
the Missouri Compromise. Of the public opinion that
could silence a man of such courage little need be said.

In the face of such opposition the plan of the proposed college seems to have been abandoned as impracticable. A year later Arnold Buffum, president of the
New England Anti-Slavery Society, made an effort to
establish a colored seminary, but the anti-slavery excitement increased so rapidly as to absorb the time and
means of the Abolitionists, and he was compelled to
abandon the scheme.

But another and still darker tale remains to be told.
In 1832, Prudence Crandall, a Quaker young woman
of high character, established in Canterbury, Windham County, Conn., a school for young ladies. Now
there was in that town a respectable colored farmer
named Harris, who had a daughter, a bright girl of
seventeen, who, having passed creditably through one
of the district schools, desired to qualify herself to be
a teacher of colored children. She was a girl of pleasing appearance and manners, a member of the Congregational church, and of a hue not darker than that of
some persons who pass for white. Miss Crandall, good

Quaker that she was, admitted this girl to her school. The pupils, some of whom had been associated with her in the district school, made no objection; but some of the parents were offended, and demanded the removal of the dark-skinned pupil. Miss Crandall made a strong appeal in behalf of the girl, and did her best to overcome the prejudices of the objectors, but in vain. After reflection she came to the conclusion, from a sense of duty, to open her school to other girls of a dark complexion. The announcement of her purpose threw the whole town into a ferment. A town-meeting was held in the Congregational Church, and so fierce was the excitement that the Rev. Samuel J. May and Mr. Arnold Buffum, the Quaker President of the New England Anti-Slavery Society, who had been deputed by Miss Crandall to speak for her, were denied a hearing. She had authorized these gentlemen to say that she would remove the school if her opponents would take her house off her hands on fair terms. Resolutions of the most denunciatory character were offered and supported by leading citizens and unanimously adopted. The leader in these proceedings was Andrew T. Judson, Esq., a lawyer of more than local reputation, a Democratic politician, much talked of as likely to be chosen Governor of the State. He was subsequently appointed Judge of the United States District Court. He avowed himself a Colonizationist, and said he was determined that no " nigger " school should be set up anywhere in Connecticut. The colored people were an inferior race; they could never rise from their menial condition in this country, and they ought not to be permitted to if they could. Africa was the place for them, and thither they should be sent.

But Miss Crandall, unmoved by these manifestations of hostility, received into her school fifteen or twenty colored girls from Philadelphia, New York, Providence and Boston. Then began a series of persecutions of the most inhuman character. The storekeepers of Canterbury refused to sell her anything, and she was compelled to send to the neighboring villages for household supplies. She and her pupils were insulted whenever they appeared in the streets. The doors and door-steps of her house were besmeared, and her well was filled with the most odious filth. Had it not been for the help afforded her by her father and another Quaker friend, who lived in the town, she would have found it impossible to obtain water or food. The pupils were excluded from the privileges of public worship by the officers of the Congregational church! An attempt was made to drive them away by the revival of an obsolete vagrant law, which provided that the selectmen of any town might warn any person, not an inhabitant of the State, to depart forthwith, and if the warning should be disregarded and the prescribed fine not be paid, then, after the lapse of ten days, the person might be whipped on the naked body not exceeding ten stripes! A warrant, under this law, was actually served upon one of the pupils from Providence, but when it was seen that she was not frightened, the proceeding was abandoned. Moreover, the persecutors were baffled by the Rev. Mr. May, of the neighboring town of Brooklyn, who gave the treasurer of Canterbury a bond in the sum of $10,000, signed by responsible gentlemen, to save the town from the vagrancy of any of the pupils. Then the persecutors procured the enactment of a law subjecting to fine and imprisonment any person who should set up anywhere in Connecticut a school for the instruction of colored pupils not residents of the State. When the news arrived in Canterbury of the passage of this infamous and unconstitutional law, the bells were rung, a cannon was fired, and the people gave themselves up to various demonstrations of joy. Miss Crandall was arraigned, bound over for trial, and thrust into jail, where she occupied a cell just vacated by a murderer. Such was the excitement that the local press dared not publish a line from Miss Crandall or any of her friends. In this emergency, Mr. Arthur Tappan, the noble New York merchant who had opened Garrison's prison door, furnished the Rev. Mr. May with funds to enable him to establish a newspaper, "The Unionist," and made himself responsible for whatever sum might be required to employ counsel for the defence for Miss Crandall. The story of the legal contest that ensued is too long to be told here. It was brought to an end by a technical error in the proceedings, so that no decision upon the merits was ever reached. The school, however, was finally broken up by violence. Miss Crandall's house was set on fire in the night, and it was saved from destruction only because the sill under which the combustibles were applied was so rotten that it would not burn quickly. A few nights after this — to wit, on the 9th of September, 1834 — the house was assaulted at midnight by a mob armed with heavy clubs and iron bars ; five window-sashes were demolished, and ninety panes of glass broken in pieces. For these outrages in this Christian town there was no redress, and the school was abandoned.

Two young men, brothers, who were afterwards widely and honorably known in connection with the anti-slavery cause, were first brought to public notice during the Canterbury conflict. I allude to Charles C. and William H. Burleigh. The former was the chosen editor of "The Unionist," the paper established by Mr. May for the defence of Miss Crandall. He had just fitted himself for the bar, and gave promise of eminence in his chosen profession. As an editor he did a good work, and so also did his brother as his assistant. Both of them afterwards entered the anti-slavery field as lecturers. Both were powerful and eloquent champions of the cause. William was

for some time editor of an anti-slavery paper in Pitts-
burgh. He was a poet of no mean reputation. In the
division of 1840, he joined the Liberty party; but
Charles continued his association with Mr. Garrison
to the close of the conflict. Few men did more than
the latter, by public speech, to form the public opinion which demanded the overthrow of slavery. He
was as remarkable for his clear-sightedness and devotion as for his eloquence.

If anybody wishes to know how it happens that
Windham County, by her large Republican majority,
has often saved the State of Connecticut from falling
into the hands of the Copperhead Democracy, he may
find the explanation in the facts above related, and in
the discussions that ensued. The Abolitionism of that
county was of the most thorough sort, receiving its im-
press and its impetus from men in full sympathy with
Mr. Garrison. In that county the Rev. Samuel J. May,
of blessed memory, did his earliest and best work, supported by the Bensons, the Burleighs, and others of a
no less sterling character. There was in the beginning a Garrisonian grip and vim in the anti-slavery sentiment of the county that was never lost, and that no
political arts could overcome. In other parts of the
State abolitionism was less intelligent and less thorough, and subject to unfortunate dilutions from men of
expediency, whose every word against slavery was sup-
plemented by two in opposition to "the extravagances
of Garrison." Milk and water is not the diet that
makes reform sinewy and powerful. If Connecticut
anti-slavery, like that of Massachusetts, had been fed
from the table of "The Liberator," that State, at no
time within the last twenty-five years, would have
been in danger of falling into the hands of the pro-
slavery Democracy. Every county in it would have
been as thoroughly abolitionized as Windham.

VIII.

Mr. Garrison goes to England — His Arrival Opportune — British Emancipation — Exposure of the Colonization Scheme — Protest of Wilberforce and Others — Death of Wilberforce — Mr. Garrison Speaks in Exeter Hall — Writes to the London "Patriot" — Taken for a Negro by Buxton — George Thompson — His Mission to America and its Results — He Returns to England — Preparing to Form a National Society — Mrs. Child's Appeal — Phelps's Lectures on Slavery — Western Reserve College — President Storrs and Professors Green and Wright — Death of President Storrs — Mob in New York.

SOON after the formation of the New England Anti-Slavery Society it became known to its managers that the American Colonization Society had sent an agent to England, who, under the false pretence that the Society favored or was calculated to promote the abolition of American slavery, was collecting considerable sums of money for its treasury from the too credulous Abolitionists of that country. To counteract the efforts of this agent, and to establish co-operative relations between British and American Abolitionists, Mr. Garrison, in the spring of 1833, was commissioned to visit England. It was not without difficulty that the funds to defray the expenses of this mission were obtained. The resources of the new society were hardly adequate to such an enterprise, but by persevering effort the object was achieved, and Mr. Garrison took his departure for the Old World with high hopes, followed by the prayers and sympathies of his devoted associates, and by the execrations of the pro-slavery party. He arrived in England at an opportune moment. The anti-slavery struggle in that country was approaching

17

its consummation. The leaders of the cause, from all parts of the United Kingdom, were holding a conference in London to prepare for their anticipated triumph in the passage of the Act of Emancipation. Mr. Garrison on presenting his credentials was received with open arms and invited to an honorary seat in a conference embracing such men as Clarkson, Wilberforce, Brougham, Macaulay, Buxton and O'Connell. He was then but twenty-eight years of age, but his modest bearing, combined with his grave earnestness and sound judgment, won the confidence of these eminent men, who were cheered by the hope that America, under the influence of so wise a leader, would be speedily redeemed from the curse of slavery. Every desired facility was offered him for fulfilling the objects of his mission. He put his work, "Thoughts on African Colonization," into the hands of eminent men, some of whom had been misled by the agent of the Colonization Society, and in public and private diligently explained the origin, purpose and spirit of the Colonization scheme, citing official documents in proof of his charges against it. The anti-slavery feeling of Great Britain was then at a white heat, and the Abolitionists were indignant in view of the attempt to dupe them into the support of a society controlled by slaveholders in the interest of slavery. The agent of the Colonization scheme found his position far from enviable; his occupation was soon gone', and not long afterward he returned to the United States. Mr. Garrison brought home with him a "Protest" against the Colonization scheme, signed by Wilberforce, Macaulay, Buxton, O'Connell, and others of scarcely less weight, in which they declared that its claims to anti-slavery support were "wholly groundless," and expressed their "deliberate judgment and conviction" that its professions were "delusive," its "real effects of the most dangerous nature." This protest, as well it might, had great weight with all sincere opponents of slavery in America, while it enraged the Colonizationists, who charged Mr. Garrison with deceiving the signers, though he had done no more than to call their attention to the utterances of the prominent advocates of the scheme. Thomas Clarkson, shortly before his death, addressed a letter to Mr. Garrison, in which he also repudiated the Colonization scheme in very earnest language.

Mr. Garrison's intercourse with the Abolitionists of Great Britain, and his studies of the work in which they were engaged, filled him with new hope and courage, and taught him some valuable lessons as to the ways and means of abolishing slavery at home. His faith in the potency of immediate emancipation as a working principle was confirmed by the experience of his British friends, and he saw more clearly than ever the danger and folly of compromises, and the delusive character of all partial and half-way measures. It was while he was in England that Wilberforce died, and it was his sad privilege to participate in the obsequies of that great and good man, and to follow his remains to Westminster Abbey. Whether the Act of West India Emancipation was passed before or after his return I am not sure ; but the measure was under discussion in Parliament while he was there, and he had the satisfaction of listening to the eloquence of some of its noblest champions in public meetings, if not in that body. The exhilarating effect of such scenes upon the mind of a young American, consecrated to the work of emancipation in his own country, may be more easily imagined than described.

Mr. Garrison had a hearing in Exeter Hall, where he made a powerful speech, denouncing American slavery in the severest terms, and sweeping away with an invincible logic the apologies offered in its behalf. He spoke of the inconsistency and guilt of his own

country in the strongest terms, giving great offence to
some Americans then in England. He also wrote a
letter, which was printed in the London "Patriot," in
which he handled the subject with the same plainness
of speech. "I know," he said, "that there is much
declamation about the sacredness of the compact which
was formed between the free and the slave States in
the adoption of the National Constitution. A sacred
compact, forsooth! I pronounce it the most bloody
and Heaven-daring arrangement ever made by men for
the continuance and protection of the most atrocious
villainy ever exhibited on earth. Yes, I recognize the
compact, but with feelings of shame and indignation;
and it will be held in everlasting infamy by the friends
of humanity and justice throughout the world. Who
or what were the framers of the American government,
that they should dare confirm and authorize such high-
handed villainy — such a flagrant robbery of the inalienable rights of man — such a glaring violation of
all the precepts and injunctions of the gospel — such a
savage war upon a sixth part of the whole population?
It was not valid then — it is not valid now. Still they
persist in maintaining it; and still do their successors,
the people of New England and of the twelve free
States, persist in maintaining it. A sacred compact!
a sacred compact! What then is wicked and ignominious?"

It is easy to say that this language is severe and even
bitter; but it is not possible to deny its truth. What
was it but a crime for a great nation, which had solemnly called upon the whole civilized world to bear
witness to its sincerity in declaring that all men were
created free and equal, to proceed to frame its government upon the condition that millions of human beings,
and their descendants after them, should be slaves as
long as it might please the masters to keep them in
bondage; to pledge its military power to keep them

from breaking their own chains, and to thrust back into the hell of bondage any slave who should presume to run away?

One incident of Mr. Garrison's first visit to England is worthy of mention here. Sir Thomas Fowell Buxton, before meeting him, desiring to do him honor, invited him to breakfast. Mr. Garrison presented himself at the appointed time at Mr. Buxton's house. When his name was announced, Mr. Buxton, instead of coming forward promptly to take him by the hand, scrutinized him from head to foot, and then inquired, somewhat dubiously, "Have I the pleasure of addressing Mr. Garrison, of Boston, in the United States?" "Yes," said Mr. Garrison, "I am he; and I am here in accordance with your invitation." Lifting up both hands, Mr. Buxton exclaimed: "Why, my dear sir, I thought you were a black man, and I have consequently invited this company of ladies and gentlemen to be present to welcome Mr. Garrison, the black advocate of emancipation from the United States of America." Mr. Buxton had seen some numbers of "The Liberator," and, supposing that no white American could plead for those in bondage as Mr. Garrison did, inferred that he was a black man. Mr. Garrison used to say, that of all the compliments ever paid to him, this was the one that pleased him most, because it was a testimonial of his unqualified recognition of the humanity of the negro.

Among the British Abolitionists with whom Mr. Garrison formed a close acquaintance was Mr. George Thompson, a man but little older than himself, and who had taken a conspicuous part in the struggle for West India emancipation. He was a man of surpassing force, eloquence and wit, who had vanquished the champions of slavery in England on many a field, and led the friends of emancipation to the victory that was just then crowning the grand struggle. He was for

years the only lecturing agent of the London Anti-
Slavery Society, and in this capacity performed an incredible amount of labor. He was in request in all
parts of the kingdom, and everywhere his lectures
were attended by crowds of the most intelligent people, who were enchanted by his eloquence and deeply
moved by his appeals. He was a religious man, a
Methodist, and in his youth had been the humble
assistant of the Rev. Richard Watson, the great Methodist theologian. The greatest men in the kingdom
— Brougham, Buxton, Wilberforce, O'Connell, and
scores of others that might be named — always listened to him with wonder and delight; and in the
House of Lords, at the time of the passage of the Act
of Emancipation, Lord Brougham said: "I rise to
take the crown of this most glorious victory from
every other head and place it upon George Thompson's. He has done more than any other man to
achieve it."

What wonder that Mr. Garrison, after listening to
the magic eloquence of this man, and hearing him commended by the greatest men in England for the purity
of his character and his unselfish devotion to the cause
of the oppressed, conceived the idea, now that the
freedom of the slaves in the West Indies had been secured, of inviting him to come to the United States
and devote his masterly powers to the work of emancipation here? How could he imagine that his fellow-
countrymen would greet such a man, — a Christian, a
friend and admirer of republican institutions, and a
philanthropist of world-wide sympathies — with malignant hisses as a "British emissary," with "pockets
full of British gold," and bent upon destroying the
Union? He knew, of course, that there were prejudices here against England and Englishmen; but how
could he, an American, loving his country, believe
that this prejudice would degenerate into utter violence

and brutality, and that such a man, inspired by a holy purpose and seeking only to aid us in breaking the fetters of our slaves, would be hunted by Americans as a wild beast is hunted, and compelled to flee from our shores to save his life? Thirty-four years afterward Mr. Garrison said: "I had nothing to offer him — no money — no reward of any kind, except that which ever comes from well-doing. I supposed he would meet with a good deal of opposition, but I did not invite him to martyrdom. I did not imagine he would be subjected to such diabolical treatment as was afterward shown to him. I only felt sure that if he could but obtain a fair hearing it would ere long be all over with slavery. I was confident that no audience would be able to withstand the power of his eloquence and the force of his arguments." But it was the knowledge of his great power that maddened the champions and apologists of slavery; and from the time that he landed in New York, in the fall of 1834, until his departure a year later, he was denounced in the press, and not infrequently in the pulpit, as an enemy of the country, an emissary of the British Government, sent hither to destroy our institutions. The Abolitionists, of course, received him with open arms, and found in him all and more than had been promised. Invitations poured in upon him from every quarter, and he was heard in Boston, Portland, Providence, Concord, N. H., and in many other places in Massachusetts, Connecticut, New York, Pennsylvania and Ohio. In some instances he was even admitted to pulpits on Sunday. In every place where he spoke there are to this day undying traditions of his matchless eloquence and power. In many instances, men who went to scoff, or perhaps meditating violence against him, were completely subdued and won to the cause. But all this only made the supporters of slavery the more angry, until at length his appearance in almost any place became the signal for a mob. An announcement, unauthorized and false, that he would address the Female Anti-Slavery Society of Boston, October 21, 1835, threw that city into a fearful state of excitement. He had been secreted by his friends some time before, and had no intention of being present at the meeting in question. On the morning of the day, October 21, the streets of the city were placarded with the announcement that "that infamous foreign scoundrel, Thompson," would speak in the afternoon at No. 46 Washington Street, and "the friends of the Union" were reminded that there would be "a fair opportunity to snake him out." It was announced that "a purse of one hundred dollars" would "reward the individual" who should "first lay violent hands on Thompson, so that he may be brought to the tar-kettle before dark." This was the incitement to that famous Boston mob of "gentlemen of property and standing," of which an account will be given in another place. A month later Mr. Thompson embarked privately in a small English brig bound from Boston to St. Johns, from which port he sailed for England.

I have told the story of Mr. Thompson's first visit to this country a little out of the chronological order, because it seemed naturally to connect itself with the account of Mr. Garrison's first visit to England, and having gone thus far, I may as well complete here what I have to say of this distinguished champion of the anti-slavery cause. After his return to England he took an active part in the movement for the abolition of the wretched apprenticeship system in the West Indies, and was engaged with Cobden and Bright in the great Corn law agitation which revolutionized the commercial policy of Great Britain. He was also enlisted in the defence of the people of India against the tyrannous practices of the East India Company, and in pursuit of that object passed several years in the

East, returning home in broken health. He was elected
to Parliament from the Tower Hamlets of London,
but does not seem to have found the situation altogether
congenial to his tastes and habits. In 1850, during
the Fugitive Slave law excitement, he came to this
country again, and remained, I think, nearly a year.
Fifteen years had not sufficed wholly to remove the
prejudices awakened by his first visit, but his life
was no longer in danger. He was received with high
honors in many places, and cheered by the mighty
change wrought in public sentiment since the time
when he was constrained to flee in secret from our
shores. He was still a powerful speaker, and was
heard in many places with delight. When the slaveholders' rebellion broke out in 1861, he devoted himself to the championship of the Northern cause among
his countrymen. It was by his labors and those of a
few kindred spirits that the laboring people as well as
the middle class of the English population were kept
informed of the nature and progress of our war, and a
public opinion developed there that deterred the British
Government from openly espousing the rebel cause.
His labors in this direction were highly appreciated by
President Lincoln and Secretary Stanton, and when,
before the end of the war, he came again to the United
States, the hall of the House of Representatives was
opened for his reception, and thronged by such an
assembly of people from the loyal States as is rarely
seen within those walls. The Vice-President of the
the United States was in the chair, and President Lincoln, with most of the members of his cabinet, was
present. On this occasion, though in feeble health and
suffering from some of the infirmities of age, he spoke
with not a little of his old fire, calling forth the universal
applause of his great audience. The President invited
him to the Executive Mansion, and showed him every
mark of respect. In many of the cities and towns of

the country he was welcomed and honored with equal
heartiness and enthusiasm. By invitation of the Secretary of War, he and Mr. Garrison accompanied
Major Anderson and his party, on board of the "Arago,"
in April, 1865, to see the star-spangled banner once
more unfurled on the walls of Sumter. He marched
in the procession, more than a mile long, extemporized
by the Freedmen, which escorted the visitors from the
North through the principal streets of Charleston; singing the while, —

"John Brown's body lies mouldering in the grave,
   But his soul is marching on " —

and giving cheer after cheer for Abraham Lincoln and
others of their Northern friends. Thus did America,
"redeemed, regenerated and disenthralled" from the
execrable system of slavery, atone in part for the insults
and persecutions inflicted at an early day by so many
of her deluded citizens upon this noble champion of
universal liberty.

Mr. Thompson was a genuine lover of republican
institutions, and had the courage to avow that love
under the shadow of the British throne, and in the
presence of the British aristocracy. America never
found in any foreign land a truer or more disinterested
friend. The motives of Lafayette and Steuben and
Kosciusko, in coming over the Atlantic to help us in
our Revolutionary struggle, were not purer than those
of Mr. Thompson in coming hither to take part in the
movement for the overthrow of the system of slavery,
and his name deserves to be handed down to posterity
on both sides of the Atlantic, among those of the
noblest benefactors of mankind. The attachment
between him and Mr. Garrison was as warm as that
between David and Jonathan. Their souls were knit
together by common purposes, hopes and aspirations,
and they were not far divided in their death, Mr.

Thompson's departure occurring only a few months before that of his devoted friend.

Before Mr. Garrison's departure for England, and during his absence, there was much serious talk among Abolitionists about organizing a National Anti-Slavery Society. The need of such an association was seriously felt, and the only question was whether the time for its organization had come. Already a considerable number of local auxiliaries to the New England Anti-Slavery Society had been formed, and the cause was gaining a strong foothold in many places. The circulation of "The Liberator" was extending, and its power was felt in many quarters. A considerable number of clergymen of different denominations had espoused the cause and opened their pulpits to anti-slavery lectures, while others were anxiously considering the subject. There was, moreover, a most auspicious beginning of an anti-slavery literature. Mrs. Lydia Maria Child, "than whom," said "The North American Review" of the period, "few female writers, if any, have done more or better things for our literature, in its lighter or graver departments," published in the summer of 1833 a most valuable book, creditable alike to her literary skill and her womanly courage. She was the most popular female writer in the country — popular at the South as well as at the North; and she not only made a sacrifice of her popularity, but exposed herself to an overwhelming tide of obloquy and abuse by lending her powerful pen to the cause of the slave. Nothing could have been more pertinent or timely, and, I may add, more convincing, than her "Appeal in Favor of that Class of Americans called Africans." It showed up the slave-system in the light of the laws framed for its regulation; cited multitudes of authentic facts showing that the system was of necessity barbarous and cruel; proved by the laws of human nature and the testimony of experience the perfect safety of immedi-

ate emancipation; vindicated the humanity of the
negro, and exposed the character and designs of the
Colonization Society. The book was received with
joy by the Abolitionists, with rage by their opponents. "Uncle Tom's Cabin" came long after this,
and only when the way had been prepared for
it by toils and sacrifices of which the people of this
generation know very little. The "Appeal," though
sneered at and denounced in high quarters, was widely
read, and converts were multiplied by its influence.
And having introduced the name of this excellent woman, I will add that from that early day to the end of
the conflict her pen was always at the service of the
cause. Her anti-slavery writings, too various to be
enumerated here, were of the highest value, and "The
National Anti-Slavery Standard," under her editorship,
exerted a wide and powerful influence. It was her
privilege to witness the final triumph of the cause she
served so faithfully; and now, in a green old age, her
mental powers are unimpaired, her pen still employed
in the service of mankind.

Another book of equal power and value with Mrs.
Child's "Appeal" was published before the end of the
year (1833). I allude to "Lectures on Slavery and
its Remedy," by the Rev. Amos A. Phelps, pastor of
the Pine Street Congregational Church, Boston. The
author, a young man of fine ability and promise, a
graduate of Yale (both College and Theological Seminary), was full of zeal in the cause. While his book
was passing through the press, it occurred to him that
it would be a good thing to publish with it a declaration of anti-slavery sentiment, signed by a number of
clergymen of different denominations. He accordingly
drew up such a declaration and sent it out for signatures among his clerical brethren. One hundred and
twenty-four names were returned from Maine, New
Hampshire, Vermont, Massachusetts, Rhode Island,

Connecticut, New York, New Jersey, and Ohio, and
their appearance in the book encouraged the Abolitionists to hope that the churches would soon espouse the
cause in a body. The substance of the declaration
was: "1. That colonization is not an adequate remedy for slavery, and must therefore be abandoned for
something that is; and 2. That the scheme of immediate emancipation is such a remedy, and is therefore
to be adopted and urged." In looking over the list
of signers I find a few eminent names, among them
those of the late George Shepard, of Bangor; David
Thurston, of Winthrop; Professor William Smyth, of
Bowdoin College; Jacob Ide, of Medway, Mass. (still
living at well-nigh a hundred years of age); D. C.
Lansing, of Utica; Beriah Green, of the Oneida Institute; Joshua Leavitt, editor of "The New York
Evangelist"; Asa Mahan, of Cincinnati (afterward
President of Oberlin); Professor John Morgan, of
Lane Theological Seminary; Charles B. Storrs, President of the Western Reserve College, and the sainted
Samuel J. May. I may also include the name of the
late Rev. Dr. Joel Parker, who afterwards settled in
New Orleans and made shipwreck of his anti-slavery
faith. These and some others were men of considerable influence at that day, but the signers, for the most
part, were undistinguished. "Not many wise men
after the flesh, not many mighty, not many noble," had
accepted the new gospel of freedom. The cause had
a charm for ingenuous, uncalculating young men, while
the timid, the ambitious and the self-seeking naturally
stood aloof. Pastors of wealthy churches in the cities
and larger towns, men who aspired to leadership in
their respective denominations, as a general rule,
resisted the movement with all the weapons at their
command.

Another event that greatly encouraged the Abolitionists was the favor shown to their cause by the pres-

ident and several of the professors of the Western
Reserve College at Hudson, Ohio. " The Liberator"
and Garrison's " Thoughts on Colonization " had found
their way to this institution, where they exerted an
instant and powerful influence. The president and at
least two of the professors espoused the cause with
their whole hearts, and not only discussed the subject
themselves, but invited discussion on the part of the
students. The president was the Rev. Charles B.
Storrs, a gifted younger brother of the late Richard S.
Storrs, D.D., of Braintree, Mass. No other man of
his age in the United States was in higher repute as an
eloquent preacher and a man of fearless devotion to
every principle of truth and righteousness than he.
"The fear of man that bringeth a snare" had no place
in his noble nature. He loved liberty — liberty for all
men — with his whole heart, and could see no reason
why a black man more than a white one should be
reduced to slavery. He felt himself bound as a Christian to testify against every form of despotism, and to
"remember them that were in bonds as bound with
them." Convinced of the iniquity and danger of American slavery, he wrote and preached against it with an
earnestness and eloquence that stirred the hearts of all
who listened. Professor Beriah Green, a man of kindred spirit and a no less powerful preacher, was another
convert to the cause ; and so also was Professor Elizur
Wright, a layman, who wielded a pen as keen as a
Damascus blade. These men, by their discussion of
the slavery question, produced a profound excitement,
not only in the college, but all over Northern Ohio.
The trustees were alarmed, thinking if the excitement
continued the college would be ruined. A controversy
ensued, which resulted in the resignation of these three
men — a blow to the college from which it did not recover for years. President Storrs soon afterward fell a

victim to consumption, dying at the house of his brother
in Braintree. His last effort to guide a pen was in the
attempt to append his name to the declaration of sentiment printed with the lectures of Mr. Phelps. His
paper was ruled for him, and all things prepared. He
took the pen, traced all the letters of his first name,
but found that one of them was transposed, laid down
the pen calmly and said : "I can write no more — I've
blundered here. Brother, will you write my name
and give the date and place where I am? Those principles are eternal truths, and cannot be shaken. I
wish to give them my testimony." One of the first of
Whittier's anti-slavery poems — perhaps, with the exception of his Lines to Garrison, the very first — is his
tribute to this noble man, from which I select these
stanzas : —

> "Thou hast fallen in thine armor,
>   Thou martyr of the Lord!
> With thy last breath crying 'Onward!'
>   And thy hand upon thy sword.
> The haughty heart derideth,
>   And the sinful lip reviles,
> But the blessing of the perishing
>   Around thy pillow smiles.
>
> Oppression's hand may scatter
>   Its nettles on thy tomb,
> And even Christian bosoms
>   Deny thy memory room ;
> For lying lips shall torture
>   Thy mercy into crime,
> And the slanderer shall flourish
>   As the bay-tree, for a time.
>
> But, where the south wind lingers
>   On Carolina's pines,
> Or, falls the careless sunbeam
>   Down Georgia's golden mines;
> Where now beneath his burden
>   The toiling slave is driven ;
> Where now a tyrant's mockery
>   Is offered unto Heaven —

Where Mammon hath its altars,
    Wet o'er with human blood,
And pride and lust debases
    The workmanship of God —
There shall thy praise be spoken,
    Redeemed from Falsehood's ban,
When the fetters shall be broken,
    And the slave shall be a man!

In the evil days before us,
    And the trials yet to come,
In the shadow of the prison
    Or the cruel martyrdom,
We will think of thee, O brother!
    And thy sainted name shall be
In the blessing of the captive,
    In the anthem of the free."

Beriah Green was called to the presidency of the
Oneida Institute, where, as teacher and preacher for
many years, he exerted a great influence, being widely
known and beloved. He was equally eloquent with
voice and pen. Professor Wright was called to serve
the American Anti-Slavery Society, shortly afterwards
formed, as Corresponding Secretary — an office that he
filled with consummate ability for four or five years.
The annual reports from his pen were masterly presen-
tations of the society's principles and objects. He edited the society's publications, "The Emancipator,"
"Human Rights," "Anti-Slavery Record," and "Quarterly Anti-Slavery Magazine," making them all powerful agents for promoting the cause. At a later date he
was editor of "The Massachusetts Abolitionist," and
later still of a Boston daily paper, "The Chronotype."

Mr. Garrison's account of what he had seen and
heard in England greatly encouraged the friends of the
cause, and he was himself no less cheered when he
found, on his return, that a call had been issued for a
convention to meet in Philadelphia on the 4th, 5th and
6th of the ensuing December, to form a National Anti-
Slavery Society. He entered into the project with all
his heart. The public mind was in an exceedingly fev-

crish condition. The enemies of the anti-slavery cause, seeing that it was rapidly gaining ground, and stung to madness by what they called the "impertinent interference" of Wilberforce and other English Abolitionists with the "domestic institutions" of the United States, began to show symptoms of a purpose to resort to violence in order to suppress the agitation. The formation of an Anti-Slavery Society in New York, which took place on the day of Garrison's landing in the city on his return from England, was made the occasion of a mob. The Abolitionists defeated their opponents by a ruse. Foreseeing that their meeting, if held at the place where it was first appointed, would be broken up, they went to the old Chatham Street Chapel, where they organized their society, and then retired through a rear door as the mob entered at the front. The disturbers encountered but one man, the noble old Quaker, Isaac T. Hopper, who, when his fellow Abolitionists retired, concluded to stay and see what the mob would do. He was found sitting in imperturbable quiet, in a meditative mood, on one of the benches, not in the least disturbed by the entrance of the mob, whom he badgered and shamed by his unfailing wit. The mob was instigated by the press, notably by James Watson Webb's "Courier and Enquirer" and Colonel Stone's "Commercial Advertiser." Not that these papers, in so many words, recommended a resort to violence, but that their inflammatory denunciations and misrepresentations of the Abolitionists were precisely adapted, if not even intended, to produce that result.

This mob occurred after the call for the National Convention was issued. If it had occurred sooner, possibly the Convention might have been delayed, and possibly it might not. The Abolitionists, though courageous, were not reckless. They did not desire to provoke violence; far from it. But they felt that their

cause was just — that God was on their side ; and they
were sure that, whatever of reproach, persecution or
violence they might be called to endure, the cause
would eventually triumph.   They were resolved to act
a worthy part, as men and Christians who loved their
country, and who meant, by the help of God, to deliver it from the crime and curse of human bondage.
And so they held their Convention.

IX.

Formation of the American Anti-Slavery Society — Character and Spirit of the Convention — The Declaration of Sentiments Drafted by Garrison — Close of the Convention — The Society Begins its Work — Headquarters in New York — The First Anniversary — The Bible Society Tested and Found Wanting — Hostility of the Press — Attitude of the Churches — Apologies for Slavery — Mobs — Judge Jay — W. I. Emancipation.

THE National Convention which met in Philadelphia Dec. 4, 1833, to form the American Anti-Slavery Society, was a very remarkable body of men, and its proceedings were of the highest interest and importance from their bearing upon the progress of the cause and the welfare of the nation. It was composed of sixty-two delegates from eleven different States. Without a single exception, I believe, they were Christian men, most of them members, and a dozen or so ministers of evangelical or Orthodox churches. Only two or three of the small denomination of Unitarians were present, but one of these, the late Samuel J. May, was a host in himself. Both branches of the Society of Friends, Orthodox and Hicksite, were represented. I was not myself a member of the Convention. Before it was called I left Boston for a visit to Ohio, under circumstances which made my attendance impossible. This to me has been a subject of life-long regret, for no public gathering during the whole anti-slavery struggle was more memorable than this. It was composed of men, most of whom had never seen each other before, but who were drawn together by convictions and purposes as high as any that ever animated the human soul. They were of one heart and

one mind, their bond of union being the common love
of freedom which the founders of the Republic declared to be inalienable, and which is of the very soul
and substance of Christianity; a common hatred of a
system which made merchandise of humanity, and a
common purpose to do what they might, by the help
of God, to deliver their country from such a crime
and curse.   They knew that they were undertaking no
holiday task.   They saw the black cloud that was
gathering around them, and heard the mutterings of
the storm that was so soon to burst upon their devoted
heads.   Philadelphia, then a Southern city in its sympathies, met them with angry frowns.   The press
teemed with misrepresentations and menaces that fell
upon the Southern hot-bloods gathered in the medical
schools, and upon other mobocratic elements of the
population, as sparks upon tinder.   The very air of
the city was sulphurous, ready at any moment to burst
into a devouring flame.   They were officially warned
to hold no evening meetings; the Mayor could only
assure them protection in the daytime !   This in the
city of "Brotherly Love," whence issued, but fifty-
seven years before, the Declaration of American Independence !   In such circumstances we need not wonder that some of the delegates, at a preliminary conference, resolved, if possible, to persuade some
distinguished and well-known citizen of the city, whose
name might be a shield, to act as president of the Convention.   Thomas Wister and Robert Vaux, two eminent philanthropists, Quakers both, were successively
waited upon, and earnestly entreated to accept the position, but they both declined.   Robert Vaux was the
one last applied to, but, though he was a professed
Abolitionist, he could not be persuaded to face the
gathering storm.   When the committee retired from
his house they were conscious that they had at least
gone quite as far in their search for a distinguished

presiding officer as their self-respect would allow; and
Beriah Green said, in a sarcastic tone, "If there is not
timber amongst ourselves big enough to make a president of let us get along without one, or go home and
stay there till we have grown up to be men."

The delegates, on their way to the Adelphi. Building, where the Convention was held, says Samuel J.
May, "were repeatedly assailed with most insulting
words." As they passed through the door, guarded
by a body of policemen, and took their seats in the
hall, we need not wonder if they were awed by a
sense of the greatness of their task and of their need
of Divine help. If I may believe the testimony of
some who were present, the disciples of Jesus, when
they were assembled together after the crucifixion, to
consider what they should do for the propagation of
the Christian faith, were no more solemn, tender or
prayerful in their mood, than were the members of
this Convention in view of the work before them. In
such an hour men forget all the petty differences of
sect and party, and remember only their humanity and
the sacredness of their work. "Never," says Samuel
J. May, "have I seen men so ready, so anxious to rid
themselves of whatsoever was narrow, selfish or merely
denominational. If ever there was a praying assembly, I believe that was one." After a fervent prayer,
in which all the members seemed to unite, the Convention was organized by the appointment of the Rev.
Beriah Green, of Whitesboro, N. Y., as President,
and Wm. Green, Jr., and John G. Whittier as Secretaries. After a free and somewhat informal interchange
of thought, it was unanimously agreed that the time
had come for the organization of a National Society,
and committees were appointed to draft a Constitution
and nominate officers. The reports of these committees occupied the Convention during the afternoon.
The object of the new Society, as set forth in the

Constitution, was "the entire abolition of slavery
in the United States." While admitting that each
State had exclusive right to legislate in regard to its
abolition, it avowed its aim to be to convince the people of the slave States by arguments addressed to their
understandings and consciences, that slaveholding was
a heinous sin against God, and that duty and safety
required its immediate abandonment, without expatri-
ation. It maintained the duty of Congress to abolish
slavery in the District of Columbia, and the trade in
slaves between the several States, and urged the duty
of elevating the character and condition of the free
people of color. It pledged the Society, moreover,
to discountenance the use of force to secure the freedom of the slaves. From this it will be seen that the
members of the Convention were fully aware of all
the limitations of the United States Constitution, and
that it called upon the National Government to exercise only such powers in relation to slavery as, by the
common consent of statesmen of all parties, up to
that time, it possessed. It is important to observe
this, since the Abolitionists were charged by their opponents with an unintelligent and reckless zeal that
overleaped all the barriers of the Constitution, and
would free the slaves by means which that instrument
forbade. The discussions in Congress and in the newspapers, so far as our opponents were concerned, went
on for years upon this false assumption. The slaveholders and their apologists knew that they could
resist us successfully only by appeals to popular ignorance and prejudice, and by exciting a wild clamor, in
the midst of which the reasonableness of our purposes
and plans should be overlooked.

But the Constitution of the Society, as an exposition
of its principles, purposes and plans, was thought to
be insufficient. It was instinctively felt that there was
need of a document of a more imposing character,

which should be to the anti-slavery movement what the
Declaration of Independence was to the fathers in the
Revolutionary struggle. The duty of preparing such
a document was assigned to a committee of ten, composed of Messrs. Atlee, Wright, Garrison, Jocelyn,
Thurston, Sterling, William Green, Jr., Whittier,
Goodell and May. This committee, after a consultation of several hours, in which the nature and design
of the proposed paper were carefully considered, appointed a sub-committee of three to draft the same.
This sub-committee was composed of Messrs. Garrison, Whittier and May, and after consultation it was
determined that Mr. Garrison should write the document. He sat down to the task at ten o'clock in the
evening, and when, at 8 o'clock the next morning,
Messrs. Whittier and May, according to previous
agreement, went to meet him, they found him, with
shutters closed and lamps burning, just writing the
last paragraph of his admirable draft. The sub-committee, after careful examination and a few slight alter-
ations, laid it before the committee of ten, which, after
three hours of careful consideration, reported it to the
Convention. It was read to that body by Edwin P.
Atlee, chairman of the committee. "Never in my
life," says Mr. May, "have I seen a deeper impression
made by words than was made by that admirable document upon all who were there present. After the
voice of the reader had ceased there was silence for
several minutes. Our hearts were in perfect unison.
There was but one thought with us all. Either of the
members could have told what the whole Convention
felt. We felt that the word had just been uttered
which would be mighty, through God, to the pulling
down of the strongholds of slavery." The Convention
then proceeded to consider the paper. It was taken
up, paragraph by paragraph, sentence by sentence, and
after five hours of discussion, unanimously adopted.

Then it was engrossed upon parchment by the late
Abraham L. Cox, M. D., of New York, and on the
last day of the Convention, signed by all the delegates,
sixty-two in number.

Of this "Declaration of Sentiments," the Magna
Charta of the anti-slavery movement, what shall I say?
As a specimen of vigorous and pure English it certainly
will not suffer by comparison with its model, the
Declaration of Independence. The great struggle
which it heralded, and whose principles and purposes
it so clearly defined, is now over, and most of those
whose names were appended to it have entered upon
the life beyond; but no man possessed of ordinary
human sympathies can read it even now without being
deeply moved. It is full of power. Its sentences
throb with moral and intellectual vitality. It stirs the
heart like the blast of a trumpet. No one who reads
it and considers its high purpose and import will think
John G. Whittier extravagant when he said: "It will
live as long as our national history. I love, perhaps
too well, the praise and good-will of my fellow-men;
but I set a higher value on my name as appended to
that Declaration than on the title-page of any book.
Looking over a life marked with many errors and shortcomings, I rejoice that I have been able to maintain the
pledge of that signature, and that in the long interven-
ing years

'My voice, though not the loudest, has been heard
Wherever Freedom raised her cry of pain.'"

The Declaration is too long, of course, to be copied
here, but I must bring before the reader a few of its
terse and thrilling sentences: —

" With entire confidence in the overruling justice of God,
we plant ourselves upon the Declaration of our Independence
and the truths of Divine Revelation as upon the Everlasting
Rock.

"We shall organize anti-slavery societies, if possible, in every city, town and village in our land.

"We shall send forth agents to lift up the voice of remonstrance, of warning, of entreaty and rebuke.

"We shall circulate unsparingly and extensively anti-slavery tracts and periodicals.

"We shall enlist the pulpit and the press in the cause of the suffering and the dumb.

"We shall aim at the purification of the churches from all participation in the guilt of slavery.

"We shall spare no exertions nor means to bring the whole nation to speedy repentance.

"Our trust for victory is solely in God. *We* may be personally defeated, but our principles never. Truth, justice, reason, humanity, must and will gloriously triumph. Already a host is coming up to the help of the Lord against the mighty, and the prospect before us is full of encouragement.

"Submitting this declaration to the candid examination of the people of this country, and of the friends of liberty throughout the world, we hereby affix our signatures to it, pledging ourselves that, under the guidance and by the help of Almighty God, we will do all that in us lies, consistently with this declaration of principles, to overthrow the most execrable system of slavery that has ever been witnessed upon earth, to deliver our land from its deadliest curse, to wipe out the foulest stain that rests upon our National escutcheon, and to secure to the colored population of the United States all the rights and privileges which belong to them as men and as Americans, come what may to our persons, our interests, or our reputation; whether we live to witness the triumph of liberty, justice and humanity, or perish untimely as martyrs in this great, benevolent and holy cause."

Such was the purpose, such the spirit of Garrison and of the whole anti-slavery movement; such it was in the beginning, such it was in every hour of its progress, and to the very end. Here is the fanaticism, the "coarse vituperation" (*vide* Dr. Whedon), and the "infidelity" from which the American churches turned away in affected digust; and yet there are those in the

20

churches, even at this day, who would, were it possible, hide from future generations the shame of their delinquency, their recreancy to humanity and to Christ, and meanly throw the responsibility therefor upon those whose only fault was that they showed them the right way and besought them with many prayers and tears to enter into it. There never was an hour when the ministers and churches of this land, if they had had any heart for the work, or any earnest purpose or desire to overthrow slavery, might not have assumed complete control of the anti-slavery movement, and when the persecuted and maligned Abolitionists would not have received them with shouts of gladness, and, to make room for them, consigned themselves, if necessary, to utter obscurity. It was not that they did not choose to follow Mr. Garrison — that of itself was a small matter — but it was that with the whole question within their grasp, with power to appoint such leaders as they pleased, they did nothing — nay, that they virtually took sides with the slaveholders, and tried to screen them from rebuke, weaving apologies for them out of perverted texts of Scripture, and encouraging them to persevere in their sin.

The Convention, after a session of three days, having completed the work for which it convened, adjourned *sine die*, in a very serious yet hopeful frame of mind, its members returning to their respective homes to do what they might for the furtherance of the cause. The President, the Rev. Beriah Green, made a parting address of singular eloquence and power, that melted the whole body into tears. His closing words were these : —

" But now we must retire from these balmy influences and breathe another atmosphere. The chill hoar frost will be upon us. The storm and tempest will rise, and the waves of persecution will dash against our souls. Let us be prepared for the worst. Let us fasten ourselves to the throne of God as with hooks of steel. If we cling not to Him, our names to that document [the Declaration] will be as dust. Let us court no applause; indulge in no spirit of vain boasting. Let us be assured that our only hope in grappling with the bony monster is in an Arm that is stronger than ours. Let us fix our gaze on God, and walk in the light of His countenance. If our cause is just—and we know it is—His omnipotence is pledged to its triumph. Let this cause be entwined around the very fibres of our hearts. Let our hearts grow to it, so that nothing but death can sunder the bond."

Instantly upon closing his address, the President lifted up his voice in a prayer so tender, so solemn, so fervent, so heartfelt, that all present were deeply touched and awed; and then, under the influence of this baptism from on high, the members bade each other farewell, and went out to fight a great battle for God and humanity.

The new Society began its operations promptly and vigorously, making New York its headquarters. Its office was on the corner of Nassau and Spruce streets, on the very spot now occupied by the Tribune Building. Among its officers were a few men of considerable distinction. Arthur Tappan, the President, stood high as a merchant, and was widely known as a liberal supporter of the religious and benevolent societies of the day. His brother Lewis, a man of very remarkable executive force and fertile in plans for promoting the cause, was a member of the Executive Committee. Professor Elizur Wright, Jr., from the Western Reserve College, was the Domestic Corresponding Secretary; William Lloyd Garrison, Secretary of Foreign Correspondence. The Committee, as a whole, was a well chosen and very efficient body of men — every one of them, if I mistake not, an Orthodox Christian. One of its first measures was the adoption as its own of "The Emancipator," a weekly paper which had ex-

isted for several months, under the editorship of Rev.
C. W. Denison. William Goodell, a powerful writer
and thoroughly familiar with the slavery question, was
appointed editor. Arthur Tappan subscribed $3,000
— a large sum for that day to be given to any benevolent cause; John Rankin, $1,200, William Green,
Jr., $1,000, and other friends lesser sums, to promote
the cause. Tracts were printed and sent flying through
the land. Among these tracts, if I remember aright,
were the Rev. Dr. Samuel Hopkins's "Dialogue on Slavery," and Dr. Jonathan Edwards's famous anti-slavery
sermon. Lecturing agents were also sent out. The
Society began its work so vigorously and with such a
determined purpose, that while its friends were much
encouraged, its enemies became more and more angry.
Accessions to the cause of both ministers and laymen
were numerous, so much so that for a time the hope was
indulged that the leaders of the different religious
denominations at the North would soon give up their
opposition, that the whole body of the churches would
wheel into line and the pulpit lift up a united voice in
opposition to slavery. This was what we all longed for;
for this we incessantly toiled and prayed, for we were
then fully aware of the truth, afterward proclaimed by
Albert Barnes, that "there was no power outside of the
church that would sustain slavery an hour if it were
not sustained in it." We saw, therefore, that the terrible responsibility for the existence of slavery rested
upon the churches; and we appealed to them, in the
name of God and of Christ, and by arguments drawn
from the Bible, to abandon their position of open con-
nivance, or of a not less guilty silence, in respect to
the sin which made Jefferson tremble for his country
when he remembered that God is just. But our plead-
ings, for the most part, so far as the leaders in the
churches were concerned, fell upon dull ears and consciences hardened by long complicity with sin. One

powerful ally of our cause at this time was "The New
York Evangelist," then edited by the Rev. Joshua
Leavitt. It had a considerable circulation, and exerted
a wide influence among the "New School" Presbyterians, who were active in the revivals that occurred in
connection with the labors of the Rev. Charles G. Fin-
ney. It advocated the cause with zeal and earnestness, and many clergymen and laymen were led by it
to declare themselves Abolitionists. When Mr. Leavitt withdrew from "The Evangelist" to become editor
of "The Emancipator," the anti-slavery tone of the
former became quite feeble, in compliance, no doubt,
with the well-understood desire of the larger number
of its readers. It was never afterward an Abolition
paper, but, with certain anti-slavery tendencies, a
supporter of the New School Presbyterian Church,
which James G. Birney said was one of the "bulwarks
of slavery."

The Society held its first anniversary May 6, 1834,
taking the place in "Anniversary Week" which it ever
afterward held among the religious and philanthropic
associations of the country. At this meeting it took
one step which caused much excitement. The American Bible Society had been engaged in supplying every
family in the United States with a Bible, and had announced to the British Society the completion of this
work. But it had taken no more account of the scores
of thousands of families of slaves than of "the cattle
upon a thousand hills," or of the wild beasts that
roamed the forests. The Anti-Slavery Society passed a
resolution calling public attention to this omission, and
offering, if the Bible Society would appropriate $20,-
000 for this purpose, to put into its treasury one-
quarter of that sum. A committee, of which Mr.
Lewis Tappan was the chairman, was made the bearer
of this proposition to the board of managers of the
Bible Society. Mr. Tappan having presented it, asked

permission to say a few words in explanation; but he
was denied a hearing, and no mention of the matter
whatever appeared in the official report of the society's
proceedings. Considering that the slaveholders and
their allies always insisted that the Bible sanctioned
slavery, their unwillingness that the slaves should read
it for themselves appears not a little strange.

The agitation had now gained such headway that the
pro-slavery party became desperate. The press of
the country, with some noble exceptions, teemed with
misrepresentations and denunciations of Abolitionists,
which sounded strangely enough when compared with
the complaints made of them in the same quarter on
account of their alleged severity. I regret to say that
the religious was not less abusive than the secular
press. Here and there a religious paper treated the
subject with something like reasonable fairness, but
as a general rule the organs of the different sects were
bitterly hostile. The Methodist paper of New England, "Zion's Herald," which was not under ecclesiastical control, was friendly; but "The Christian Advocate" of New York, the official organ of the Methodist
church, was filled with gross abuse of the Abolitionists. As there appears to be a disposition in some
quarters to deny or conceal these ugly facts, and to
make the Abolitionists themselves responsible, through
their alleged imprudence and recklessness, for the opposition they met with, let me fortify my own testimony by citing that of the Rev. William Goodell, who
was a Calvinist of the Calvinists to the day of his
death. "The religious presses," he says, "of the principal sects at the North, particularly of the Congrega-
tionalist sect, in the hands of the conservative party,
were the first to traduce, to misrepresent, to vilify
and to oppose the Abolitionists, representing them as
anarchists, Jacobins, vilifiers of great and good men,
incendiaries, plotters of insurrection and disunion, and

enemies of the public peace." And now behold! When the shameful complicity of the churches of that day with slavery, their bitter opposition to the anti-slavery movement, and their persecution of such of their own members as were Abolitionists, are exposed, the attempt is made to build a wall for their protection out of the toils and sacrifices of the men whom they opposed and denounced. In other words, the fidelity of a proscribed and persecuted Christian minority is imputed as a merit to the whole church, while the attempt is made to conceal from the present and future generations the shameful action of the ruling majority. Does any Christian imagine that God can look with any other feelings than those of abhorrence and indignation upon such efforts to pervert the truth of history? In the interest of Christianity itself, and as a warning to the ages to come, let the truth be proclaimed without fear or favor. Perish all the arts of evasion and concealment by which ambitious ecclesiastics would defend their craft at the expense of truth and justice, and hide the blot, not on Christianity, but on the escutcheon of a recreant church! Judgment in this case, as of old, must begin at the house of God — with those, in other words, whose religious professions gave them power to mislead the community and pervert the right way of the Lord.

But I may be asked, did the leaders of the churches, the men of influence and might, openly advocate slavery as a good thing? Oh, no indeed! If they had done that we should speedily have overmastered them. Their hostility was disguised under a great variety of specious pleas and pretences. They were "just as much opposed to slavery as the Abolitionists, but,—" and then would follow one or more of such allegations as these : Immediate emancipation would be dangerous ; the slaves would cut their masters' throats if set free ; they are not prepared for freedom ; they are

contented and happy, and wouldn't take their freedom
if it were offered to them ; they ought not to be set free
in this country, but to be taken back to Africa, where
they belong ; would you like to marry your daughter
to a "nigger"? the Bible sanctions slavery ; the curse
of Ham doomed his posterity to bondage forever, and
the Scriptures must be fulfilled ; the chosen people of
God held slaves by Divine permission ; Jesus did not
condemn slavery, and Paul expressly sustained the
system by sending the slave Onesimus back to his master ; the agitation of the subject will divide the churches
and divert their attention from religious work ; the
Abolitionists are too indiscriminate in their denunciations ; of course, slavery in the hands of bad men is
wrong, but there are thousands of good slaveholders,
who treat their slaves kindly ; the slaves are property,
and it would be cruel to deprive the masters, without
compensation, of that for which they paid their money ;
the Constitution guarantees slavery, and without such
guarantees the Union never could have been formed ;
the discussion of the subject is dangerous to the peace
of the country, and tends to a dissolution of the Union.
In this list of excuses, which might be greatly extended, there is not the slightest touch of caricature, as
every Abolitionist of that day now living will testify.
I have heard them myself, *ad nauseam*, from the lips
of clergymen and laymen, and read them a hundred
times in the newspapers. Slavery, it was insisted, was
not in itself a sin ; and, curiously enough, the innocent slaveholders were always those who were most
enlightened, who were members of the Christian
Church, and whose example, therefore, did more than all
else to sustain the system. Men who would have
blushed to affirm that pious men might be gamblers or
pickpockets, were not ashamed to plead that slavery was
sanctified by the goodness and piety of the masters.
The profane man, who swore at his slaves and treated

them cruelly, was a great sinner of course; but the religious man, who called them in to family prayers and instructed them in their duties to God and to one another, was no sinner. Slavery, when mixed up with oaths and curses and cruelty, was indeed dreadful; but when well seasoned with prayers, exhortations and hosannas, it was very tolerable! Ecclesiastical bodies, feeling the necessity of seeming at least to oppose slavery, passed cunningly-worded resolves, in which "holding slaves for gain" was condemned, it being quietly assumed, if not asserted, that religious slaveholders held their slaves from other and higher motives. Learned expositors of Scripture — men to whom the churches looked with confidence as safe guides — wrote ingenious articles in magazines and reviews, in which they put forth all their dialectical skill and metaphysical subtlety to prove that holding property in man was not necessarily sinful, and that the demand for immediate emancipation was pure fanaticism. These expositors found an echo in the religious press, and preachers, instead of rebuking iniquity in high places, volunteered, in many instances, to

"Hang another flower
Of earthly sort about the sacred truth,
And mix the bitter text
With relish suited to the sinner's taste."

Thus the slaveholders who felt the force of the warnings and rebukes of the Abolitionists, were comforted in their sin, and encouraged to resist the demand for emancipation. Under such influences is it any wonder that the South "hardened her neck as in the day of provocation," and went on from one step of madness to another, until at last, in the hope of perpetuating her diabolical system, she plunged into a bloody rebellion? And when slavery was thus defended in church and pulpit and in all the high places of the land, what wonder if the lower stratum of society

21

caught the infection and became infuriated in its hostility to the Abolitionists? Is it strange that a meeting of the Abolitionists of New York, assembled on the Fourth of July to listen to a famous orator from Philadelphia, was broken up by a mob, and that for several successive days and nights the city was in the possession of the rioters, who assaulted private dwellings and places of public worship? I am not sure whether it was in this or a subsequent riot that the Laight Street Presbyterian Church, of which the Rev. Dr. Samuel Hanson Cox was the pastor, was violently assailed and much damaged. Dr. Cox had lately been in England, and having caught the anti-slavery fire from the clergy of that country, he came home full of zeal, and evidently impressed with the belief that he could speedily enlist the churches of this country in a crusade against slavery. He preached on the subject in his own pulpit with much warmth, and in one of his sermons, on the subject of prejudice against color, he happened to remark that Jesus, born as he was in an Oriental clime, was probably a man of a swarthy complexion, who, if living in this country, might not be received into good society. This observation was reported with exaggerations in the newspapers, and commented upon in such a way as to inflame the passions of the vulgar. While the mob was engaged in smashing the windows of the church, a gentleman who had been drawn to the spot by motives of curiosity, asked one of the rioters what was the reason for the attack. "Why," said the rioter, in reply, "Dr. Cox says our Saviour is a nigger, and —— me if I don't think his church ought to be torn down." It was in these days that the house of Mr. Lewis Tappan, was sacked and its furniture destroyed. There were riots also in Philadelphia about the same time, in which the houses of many colored people were assailed, and several lives were sacrificed. The public mind throughout the country was in an inflamed condition, and the press, by misrepresentations and appeals to popular ignorance and prejudice, was constantly fanning the excitement.

But in the midst of this darkness there was a sudden gleam of light, which filled the hearts of the Abolitionists with fresh hope. The Hon. William Jay, noble son of a noble sire, espoused the cause, and put forth a work in its defence which will live as a monument of his intellectual power as well as of his philanthrophy and courage. It was entitled "An Inquiry into the Character and Tendencies of the American Colonization and the American Anti-Slavery Societies." It was full of light and truth, and admirably adapted to convince any candid person who would read it of the righteousness and wisdom of the anti-slavery movement. It appeared at a most opportune moment, and exerted a powerful influence in many quarters. But the author's noble name and his judicial eminence did not save him from the fierce denunciations of the pro-slavery press. He was roundly abused on all sides, and not long afterward lost his place on the bench in consequence of his abolitionism. He was appointed a member of the Executive Committee of the American Anti-Slavery Society, and filled the place for many years with great fidelity. His trained mind, his ripe judgment and wide legal knowledge were a great acquisition to the cause. He was a devoted Christian and a man of large influence in the Protestant Episcopal Church. How faithful he was in rebuking that Church for its complicity with slavery, all the friends of the cause gratefully remember. His pen was always at the service of the oppressed, and his collected anti-slavery writings are a monument of his industry and devotion, and an illustration of the nobleness and the grandeur of the cause which the American churches rejected and contemned.

This year (1834) was also signalized by the peaceful emancipation of 800,000 slaves in the British West India Islands. The event took place on the 1st of August, and the Abolitionists awaited the result with intense interest, but not a shadow of doubt. They knew that obedience to God in the breaking of the chains of so many slaves would be perfectly safe; and so it proved, for not a drop of blood was shed; the negroes received their freedom with grateful joy as a boon from Heaven, and all the predictions of the pro-slavery party were falsified. Naturally enough, American Abolitionists were mightily encouraged by this intelligence to persevere in their labors.

X.

MR. ARTHUR TAPPAN, not long after he procured
Mr. Garrison's release from the Baltimore jail, gave
ten thousand dollars to the Lane Theological Seminary, at Cincinnati, upon the condition that Dr. Lyman Beecher should become its President. The
churches of the North and East were then just beginning to perceive that the day was not far distant when
the centre of moral and political influence in this
country would be in the vast and then comparatively
unsettled region drained by the Mississippi; and
hence there was much zeal and not a little organized
effort to anticipate the oncoming tide of population
that was so soon to fill that immense territory, and to
provide, in advance, educational institutions suited to
its needs. The founding of Lane Seminary, at the
gateway of the great West, was a part of this plan,
and Dr. Beecher, being generally recognized as the
leader of New England Revivalism, and the strongest
representative of the advanced school of Orthodoxy at
that day, Mr. Tappan thought that he of all others was
the man best fitted to train a body of ministers for the
new field. The Doctor, after considerable delay, and
to the great grief of his Boston church, accepted the

appointment. Such was his fame, that a large class of students, of unusual maturity of judgment and ripeness of Christian experience, was at once attracted to the Seminary. In the literary and theological departments together, they numbered about one hundred and ten. Eleven of these were from different slave States; seven were sons of slaveholders; one was himself a slaveholder, and one had purchased his freedom from | cruel bondage by the payment of a large sum of money, which he had earned by extra labor. Besides these there were ten others who had resided for longer or shorter periods in the slave States, and made careful observation of the character and workings of slavery. The youngest of these students was nineteen years of age; most of those in the theological department were more than twenty-six, and several were over thirty. Most if not all of them had been converted in the revivals of that period, and were filled with the revival spirit, in which Dr. Beecher so much delighted. A more earnest and devoted band of students was probably never gathered in any theological seminary. The Doctor had great pride as well as confidence in them.

Soon after the Seminary was opened the students formed a Colonization Society, and were encouraged by the faculty to manifest such an interest in the slavery question as was compatible with a scheme for sending the negroes to Africa. So much, it was thought, might be permitted without endangering the union of the States or the peace of the churches, and with safety to the Seminary itself. In the winter of 1833–34, after the publication of Garrison's "Thoughts on Colonization," and the organization of the American Anti-Slavery Society, with Arthur Tappan at its head, the students began to think about slavery and their duties to "the heathen at home." They proposed to hold meetings for the discussion of the subject, and so informed their teachers. Most of the faculty advised them to let the subject alone ; but Dr. Beecher said to the committee that waited upon him "Go ahead, boys — that's right; I'll go in and discuss with you." The students, thus encouraged by the President, were confirmed in the conviction that, as men intending to be ministers of the Gospel, in a slaveholding country, it was their duty to study the subject of slavery patiently and thoroughly; and, as there were among them representatives of the slave as well as of the free States, they thought a frank, open and friendly discussion would be both interesting and profitable.

The discussion began in February, 1834. An earlier day was at first proposed, but the disputants on the pro-slavery side asked for more time to prepare themselves for the argument. "You Abolitionists," they said, "have studied the subject ; the rest of us haven't; you must give us more time." This request was cheerfully granted. When the time for opening the discussion came, it was agreed to consider two questions, viz. :

1st. Whether the people of the slaveholding States ought to abolish slavery at once, and without prescribing, as a condition, that the emancipated should be sent to Liberia, or elsewhere, out of the country?

2d. Whether the doctrines, tendencies, measures, spirit of the Colonization Society were such as to render it worthy of the patronage of Christian people?

Dr. Beecher, instead of appearing at the first meeting, according to his declared purpose, sent a note to Mr. Weld, saying that, upon the whole, he thought it was not best for him to be present, but that his daughter Catherine would attend as his representative. The students afterwards learned that the Doctor changed his purpose by advice of the trustees. His daughter attended the first meeting, which was wholly occupied by the speaker to whom had been assigned the duty of opening the debate. The next day she sent a letter replying to the speaker's argument, and asking that it might be read to the students. This request was complied with at the next meeting, the speaker who was thus reviewed answering Miss Beecher, point by point, as he read her communication. One member of the faculty, Prof. John Morgan, honored himself by attending the discussion throughout. He was ever afterwards an outspoken Abolitionist. For the last forty-five years he has been a distinguished member of the theological faculty of Oberlin.

The questions were taken up in their order, and each of them discussed, during nine evenings. I have often conversed with some of the men who took part in the debate, and they agree in assuring me that from first to last it was conducted in a candid, prayerful and Christian spirit. There was great earnestness, but no unworthy heat, and no impeachment of the motives of the disputants on either side. The whole discussion was marked by a strong desire to discover and follow the truth, and by a depth of fraternal feeling that was most remarkable. The leader in the discussion was Theodore D. Weld, a young man from Connecticut, famous as a public speaker even before he entered the seminary; a man of great originality and force of character, and highly esteemed for his piety and self-consecration. He had travelled in the South, keeping his eyes and ears open, and gathering information in relation to slavery, which enabled him to debate the subject intelligently as well as eloquently. The result of the discussion, when it is remembered that the disputants embraced men from the slave as well as the free States, seems very remarkable. Upon the first question debated every student voted in the affirmative. "The North gave up, the

South kept not back," both being united in proclaiming immediate emancipation to be the right of the
slave and the duty of the master. When the vote
upon the second question was taken, one faint voice
only was heard in the affirmative ; and that was
the voice of a man who said in the beginning that he
"defied the Abolitionists to wring out of him a vote
against the Colonization Society." If he was convinced, it was against his will, and so his opinion was
not changed.

The students immediately organized an anti-slavery
society, while the Colonization Society, previously
formed, perished because the blood was all drawn from
its veins. The anti-slavery work wrought in the minds
and hearts of the students was so deep and thorough
that it could only be ascribed to the influences of the
Divine Spirit. They were not only brought into
closer affinity with each other, but a missionary spirit
was kindled in their hearts, impelling them, like their
Master, "to seek and to save the lost." Their attention was naturally drawn to the three thousand colored
people of Cincinnati, most of whom had been slaves.
They formed a committee, each member of which
pledged himself to give one evening a week to teaching the colored people, and to furnish a substitute in
case of emergency. Thus two evening schools, with
pupils from fifteen to sixty years of age, were in progress each evening, except Sunday. Augustus Wattles, one of the students, taking Mr. Weld with him,
went to Dr. Beecher and opened his heart in substance
as follows : " When I came here three months ago," he
said, "from the State of New York, I had been for a
year the President of a Colonization Society ; I had discussed and lectured in its favor; I did unremittingly
what I now see was a great wrong. I must do what I
can to undo that wrong. Here in Cincinnati are three
thousand colored people, most of them in great igno-

. 22

rance. Last night I could not sleep. My present
duty is plain, which is to take a dismission from the
seminary, throw myself among these three thousand
outcasts, establish schools, and work in all practicable
ways for their elevation." Dr. Beecher, as well as
Mr. Wattles, was moved to tears. The Doctor gave
him his dismission, adding, "Go, my son, and may
God be with you."

Mr. Wattles at once established, in one of the colored churches, a school, which he taught gratuitously.
A colored man, once a Kentucky slave, gave him his
board; another lodged him. His advent among these
people was to them as life from the dead. In a few
months, in co-operation with a committee of Abolitionists in the seminary, he had established four more
schools, taught by four noble young women, who came
from Connecticut and New York, and one (a sister of
Prof. Elizur Wright, Jr.) from the Western Reserve.
All these came in the spirit of missionaries and martyrs, identifying themselves with the colored people,
living sometimes in their families, at other times board-
ing themselves, and at all times and in all ways doing
with their might what their hands and hearts found to
do for the three thousand victims of pro-slavery prejudice and scorn, among whom they had cast their lot.
"I know," says the friend from whom I have obtained
these facts, "of no nobler consecration than that of
these four young women, and of Augustus Wattles, in
their tireless labors of love in the lanes and alleys of
Cincinnati, in their unselfish ministry to the poorest
of the suffering poor. One of the students, who was
acquainted with Arthur Tappan, wrote to him the details of Wattles's work at the outset, and of the offer
of the four young women to teach, without price, the
schools that he was establishing. Mr. Tappan immediately authorized the student to draw upon him at
sight for the travelling expenses of the young women

from their homes to Cincinnati; for books, maps and fixtures for their schools and for that of Mr. Wattles, and *carte blanche* for whatever in his judgment might be necessary for their personal comfort, and to secure the most substantial practical results of their labors of love."

Cincinnati, though on the northern bank of the Ohio, was saturated with the spirit of slavery. Its trade was derived largely from the South, and many of the inhabitants were from that region. It was scarcely less fatal to a man's reputation to be known as an Abolitionist there than it would have been in Richmond or New Orleans. The laws of Ohio in respect to negroes, having been dictated by emigrants from the South, were infamous in their proscriptive force. Against these cruel laws the churches lifted up no voice of protest, while religious men of every denomination aided in enacting and enforcing them. The average Cincinnatian was as ready to catch and return a fugitive slave as he was to return to his owner a stray horse or dog. The press of the city was hardly less servile to the slaveholders than that of Charleston or Mobile. No wonder, therefore, that the discussion in Lane Seminary, and the results to which it led, caused intense excitement in that slavery-ridden city. "Mr. Wattles and the lady teachers," says the friend to whom I am indebted for many of the facts in this narrative, "were daily hissed and cursed, loaded with vulgar and brutal epithets, oaths and threats; filth and offal were often thrown at them as they came and went; and the ladies especially were assailed by grossest obscenity, · called by the vilest names, and subjected to every indignity of speech which bitterness and diabolism could frame. So also the students, known to be conspicuous as Abolitionists, were constantly in receipt of letters filled with threats, to be executed unless they discontinued lectures and teachings among the colored people. These letters often enclosed pictures of hearts thrust full and through with daggers; throats cut, heads cut off, bloody tongues hanging from bleeding mouths, etc. One of the students had a special place of deposit for these Satanic curiosities, and kept piling them in till, from sheer nausea, his gorge so rose that he emptied the contents of the reeking tophet into their own place."

Two of the students, James A. Thome of Kentucky, and Henry B. Stanton of Connecticut, went by invitation to the first anniversary of the American Anti-Slavery Society in New York, in 1834, and electrified the country by their eloquent testimonies against slavery. Then there burst immediately upon Lane Seminary and its brave students a storm of indignation, before which the managers of the institution quailed. These young men might have gone to a meeting of the Bible Society or of the A. B. C. F. M., to make a plea in behalf of the heathen abroad, and no one would have accused them of any impropriety — nay, they would have been universally applauded for doing a work appropriate for young men studying for the ministry; but that they should presume to expose the wrongs of American slaves, or speak a word for over "two millions of human beings in this Christian Republic," who, according to the testimony of the Presbyterian Synod of Georgia and South Carolina, uttered but a few months before, were "in the condition of heathen, and in some respects in a worse condition," and such as "justly to bear a comparison with heathen in any part of the world," was regarded as an impertinence deserving the severest rebuke. Mr. Thome, by the revelations he made of slaveholding practices in Kentucky, of which he had been an eye-witness, made himself an exile from his native State, and the religious press of the country treated him as one who had received no more than he deserved!

In every part of the free States there were Christian men, and godly women not a few, who prayed to God night and day that Lyman Beecher might be imbued with strength and courage to stand up nobly in the face of the storm that raged around him, and maintain the right of his pupils, as candidates for the Christian ministry, to investigate and discuss the subject of slavery, and to bear their testimony against it as a sin, and a mighty hindrance to the spread of the Gospel. They remembered the brave words he had spoken against the then fashionable sin of intemperance; they called to mind his earlier denunciations of duelling as a crime; they thought of his zeal to carry the Gospel to the dark places of the world; and they were unwilling to believe that in this terrible crisis he would yield to the demands of the Slave Power, and seek to put a padlock upon the lips of the noble young men in whom he had taken so much pride, and upon whose future he had built such exalted hopes. They knew that, by force of all that was noblest and grandest in his nature, he belonged to freedom's side, and they could not bear to think that he would commit such an outrage upon himself as to go with the pro-slavery party in such a crisis. He had been my pastor in my fresh young manhood, and my affection for him was deep and strong. He had married me with his blessing to the wife of my youth, and had shown me many attentions, such as a young man prizes very highly when received from one so eminent; and to the last moment I kept alive in my heart the hope that he would, in spite of previous waverings, make a final stand for freedom of speech, in the seminary as well as elsewhere, for the purification of the church, and for the overthrow of the foulest system of oppression with which the groaning earth was cursed. But I was doomed to a bitter disappointment. The fancied temporary interests of the semi-

nary and of the Presbyterian Church were in one
scale, the eternal principles of liberty and the rights
of the trampled and outraged slaves in the other;
and the latter, by the touch of his hand, were made
to kick the beam! In the absence of the faculty,
during vacation, the trustees had made a rule requiring the students to disband their anti-slavery society,
and, to give an appearance of consistency, the Colonization Society as well, though since the anti-slavery
discussion it had been dead beyond the power of
resurrection. Other restrictions were also put upon
the students, for the purpose of effectually preventing
the agitation of the slavery question in the future.

One of the trustees was the Rev. Asa Mahan, afterwards for twenty years the President of Oberlin
College. Of course he opposed the passage of the
gag-law, which, as originally introduced to the board,
forbade the students to discuss the question of slavery
at all, even in private,—the words being "at the table
and elsewhere." Dr. Mahan—so I learn from high
authority—moved that these words be stricken out.
The motion was at first stoutly opposed, but upon the
suggestion being made that such a cast-iron rule, laid
upon the students of a Theological Seminary, would
savor more of the dark ages, the Inquisition, and the
Star-chamber, than of the enlightenment of the nineteenth century, it was voted to omit the words—on
the score of policy!

Dr. Beecher and his associates in the faculty, on
returning to their duties in the fall, had to decide
whether they would or would not consent to enforce
these disgraceful laws, set up in the interest of the
Slave Power. Their conclusion to obey the behest
of the trustees, though a cruel disappointment to the
students and to the struggling friends of freedom
throughout the country, was hailed with exultation by
the pro-slavery press. It was a sad day for the slaves

and their friends, and a sad day also for Lane Seminary; for the anti-slavery students, though plied with all the arts of persuasion of which Dr. Beecher was master, calmly refused to bend their necks to the yoke. Nearly all of the theological students, seventy or eighty in number, took their dismission from the institution, leaving it in a bare and crippled condition for years. Before doing so, however, they issued, under their own names, an eloquent and impressive appeal to the Christian public, prepared by a committee consisting of Theodore D. Weld, James A. Thome, George Whipple, Henry B. Stanton, and Sereno W. Streeter. In the main, no doubt, it was the production of Mr. Weld, who, in point of native ability, it is not too much to say, was the peer of Dr. Beecher himself. After a long period of invaluable service in the anti-slavery field as lecturer and writer, he has for many years devoted his great powers, enriched by ripest culture and experience, to the instruction of the young. Mr. Thome, after serving fifteen years as a professor at Oberlin, became pastor of a church in Cleveland. He is now dead. Mr. Whipple was a professor at Oberlin for twenty years, then for a long period Secretary of the American Missionary Association, and finally, at the time of his decease, President-elect of Howard University at Washington. Mr. Streeter was for some years Professor of Mental and Moral Philosophy in an Ohio College, and has since been a pastor. Mr. Stanton, served the anti-slavery cause until 1840, after which he entered the legal profession.

The answer of the faculty to the appeal of the students, though dialectically and rhetorically skilful, was weak and sophistical in argument. Some parts of it read strangely enough in the light of the present day. The faculty admitted that the students had not been drawn away from their studies, or led into any neglect of duty by the discussion which had given so much offence. "We never witnessed," they said, "more power of mind or capacity of acquisition, or of felicitous communication in popular eloquence, in the same number of individuals; and we add that the attainments of the past year, as developed by daily intercourse and by the closing examination, were honorable to them and satisfactory to us. We always have believed, and still do believe, that they have acted under the influence of piety and conscience." Why, then, were they gagged? Oh, because discussions on slavery had "a bearing upon a divided and excited community;" because the subject was one of "great national difficulty and high political interest;" and because the discussion, though under the control of "piety and conscience," and pursued without any interruption of the course of study, had yet been "conducted in a manner to offend needlessly public sentiment, and to commit the seminary and its influences contrary" to the advice of the faculty. And so the faculty deliberately committed it and its influences to the pro-slavery side! Moreover, some of the students had been very "imprudent." One of them, who had gone from Walnut Hills to the city to deliver an evening lecture to the colored people, being "too much indisposed to return to the seminary, accepted ('give ear, O Earth!') the hospitality of a respectable colored family to pass the night with them." Another, a teacher of a colored school ("hung be the heavens in black!"), actually "boarded in a colored family." How could it be expected that the people of Cincinnati would be able to reconcile their delicate feelings to outrages like these? And what would the American churches, which were sending their missionaries to war against caste in India, say to such imprudent disregard of caste at home? Worse than all (O horror of horrors!), "several female colored persons," wishing, doubtless, to see some of the students in regard to their missionary work, "visited the seminary in a carriage," and were courteously received by the young missionaries! The faculty, in this awful state of things, called the students together, not to commend and encourage them for behaving worthily of their Christian profession, but to persuade them, in deference to the vulgar pro-slavery spirit of the times, "to abstain from the apparent intention of carrying the doctrine of intercourse with the colored people into practical effect," and pressing "a collateral benevolent enterprise in a manner subversive of the confidence of the entire Christian community." "The entire Christian community!" Let these words be remembered, for they show by plain implication what the Abolitionists in their godlike work had to contend with, and what was the real attitude of the church and the ministry at that time. We are asked to believe that the men who had not the courage to rebuke the meanest and most inhuman exhibition of caste that the world has ever seen were chosen of God to bear upon their shoulders the Ark of the Covenant in the presence of a scoffing world, and to keep the fire on God's altar from going out!

I verily believe that, if Lyman Beecher had been true to Christ and to liberty in that trying hour, the whole course of American history in regard to slavery would have been changed, and that the slaves might have been emancipated without the shedding of blood. The churches at that hour were halting between the good and the evil side, and it only needed the example of one strong man like Dr. Beecher to rally them to their legitimate place as the foremost champions of justice and liberty. He sacrificed a great opportunity, as Webster did in 1850, and linked his name forever with those of the trimmers and compromisers of that day. He inflicted a wound upon his own reputation from which he never recovered. He lost the

23

confidence of the friends of freedom; while the
champions and apologists of slavery respected him
far less than they would if he had shown himself
worthy of his New England blood. As Lowell
sings : —

" Man is more than [institutions]; better rot beneath the sod,
Than be true to Church and State, while we are doubly false to
    God."

Some of the exiled students completed their education in the freer air of Oberlin, while a few did noble
service in the anti-slavery cause as lecturing agents.
Conspicuous among the latter were Theodore D. Weld,
Henry B. Stanton and Marius R. Robinson, who, by
their logic and eloquence, did much to enlighten the
people and create the public sentiment which finally
led to the overthrow of slavery. Mr. Weld's Bible
argument against slavery, his " Slavery as It Is, or, the
Testimony of a Thousand Witnesses," and other publications of a similar character, which were scattered
broadcast by the American Anti-Slavery Society, exerted a great influence. Mr. Stanton was for a time
one of the Secretaries of the National Society, devoting himself to the work of organizing the system of
petitioning Congress for such anti-slavery action as that
body could constitutionally take, and in the collection
of funds for the Society's treasury.

Of Mr. Robinson there is a tale to be told, which
coming generations ought to hear. A more gentle,
sweet-spirited and self-consecrated man I have never
known. He was exceedingly modest, never seeking
conspicuity, but willing to work in any place, however
obscure, to which duty called him. For a time, after
leaving the Seminary, he devoted himself to the welfare of the colored people of Cincinnati, and, for aught
that I know, was one of those who were so "imprudent " as sometimes to take a meal with a colored fam-

ily. It would have been just like him to do so, simple-hearted man that he was. Then he was for a time in the office of Mr. Birney's "Philanthropist," and, when the mob came to destroy the types, it was his tact and courage that saved the ". forms " from being broken up, so that the paper of the week was printed in an adjoining town and delivered to its subscribers on time. At a later day he entered the lecturing field in Ohio, where he did noble service, enduring all manner of hardness like a good soldier of freedom. He was a capital speaker, with much that we call magnetic force for lack of a better term, and he was sure to make a deep impression wherever he could get a hearing. It was during the " reign of terror," and he was often harried by mobs and other exhibitions of pro-slavery malevolence. At Granville, Licking County, he was detained some time by severe illness. One day a constable obtruded himself into his sick-room, and served upon him a paper, a copy of which I herewith present as a specimen of the pro-slavery literature of that day : —

"LICKING Co., GRANVILLE TOWNSHIP, ss.
" *To H. C. Mead, Constable of said Township*, GREETING.

" *Whereas*, we, the undersigned, overseers of the poor of Granville Township, have received information that there has lately come into said Township a certain poor man, named Robinson, who is not a legal resident thereof, and will be likely to become a township charge ; you are, therefore, hereby commanded forthwith to warn the said Robinson, with his family, to depart out of said Township. And of this warrant make service and return. Given under our hands this first day of March, 1839.

CHARLES GILMAN, } Overseers of
S. BANCROFT,   } the Poor."

It was nearly two years before this that he went to Berlin, Mahoning County, to deliver several lectures. On Friday evening, June 2, 1837, he spoke for the first time, and notice was given that on the following

Sunday he would deliver a lecture to vindicate the Bible
from the charge of supporting slavery. This was more
than the public sentiment of Berlin could bear, and so,
on Saturday evening, he was seized by a band of ruffians
— two of them, I am told, members of the Presbyterian Church — dragged out of the house of the friend
with whom he lodged, carried several miles away, and,
besides many other insults, subjected to the cruel
indignity of a coat of tar and feathers. In this condition he was carried some miles further, and, in the
darkness of a chilly Sunday morning, having been
denuded of much of his clothing, left in an open field, in
a strange place, where he knew no one to whom to look
for aid. After daylight he made his way to the near-
est house, but the family was frightened at his appearance, and would render him no aid. At another house
he was fortunate enough to find friends, who, in the
spirit of the good Samaritan, had compassion on him
and supplied his needs. The bodily injuries received
on that dreadful night affected his health ever afterwards, and even aggravated the pain of his dying
hours. But they brought no bitterness to his heart,
which was full of tenderness toward those who had
wronged him. He gave himself with fresh zeal to the
work of reform, and few men have ever done more
than he did to make purer and sweeter the moral
atmosphere of the region in which he lived. In 1851
he became editor of "The Anti-Slavery Bugle," at
Salem, Ohio, and conducted it till the time of its discontinuance, after the abolition of slavery was substantially assured. His editorial services were of great
value, and won for him the admiration and the confidence of those who profited thereby. He died in
Salem less than a year ago, respected and beloved by
the whole community.

It seems incredible now that the pulpit of that day
was generally silent in the presence of outrages like

those inflicted upon Mr. Robinson, and that leading newspapers spoke of them rather to condemn the victims than the authors. But such is the fact. Those who imagine that the conflict with the Slave Power began with the organization of the anti-slavery political parties need to be reminded that no such parties could have had an existence but for the grand moral struggle that preceded them, and that was sustained for years by men and women who endured, bravely and unflinchingly, the reproach and scorn of hostile communities, and whose property and lives were often in peril.

XI.

Progress of the Cause — Madness of the Opposition — Southern
Threats and Northern Menaces — Firmness of Arthur Tappan —
Northern Colleges — Mutilation of Books — Beginning of a
"Reign of Terror" — Movement of Conservatives in Boston
— James G. Birney — Anti-Slavery Publications Sent to the
South — Post-Office in Charleston Broken Open by a Mob —
Pro-Slavery Demonstration in Boston — Mob of "Gentlemen
of Property and Standing" — Garrison Dragged Through the
Streets and Thrust into Jail — Dr. Channing's Tribute to the
Abolitionists.

FROM the time of the organization of the American
Anti-Slavery Society in 1833, to the end of the following year, the anti-slavery agitation grew more and
more intense, until at last it arrested the attention of
the whole country. "The Liberator" in Boston, and
"The Emancipator" in New York, had each enlarged
its circulation. "The New York Evangelist," under the
editorship of the Rev. Joshua Leavitt, was doing the
cause good service in the places most under the influence of the revivals of that period, while a small number of other papers in different parts of the country
were friendly to the movement. The American Society was sending out its agents and scattering its tracts
and other publications broadcast through the land.
Anti-slavery societies were springing up on every side,
ministers here and there ventured to preach against
slavery, and there were movements in some of the
ecclesiastical bodies that seemed to presage a favorable
change in the attitude of the churches. There were
signs of an effort on the part of the Methodists of New
England to break the silence so long imposed by the ·

leaders of that church. Hitherto all efforts to crush
the new movement had not only proved unsuccessful,
but actually aided in fanning the excitement. The
South was full of rage and fury, and the apologists of
slavery at the North were growing more and more
reckless and unscrupulous. The air was full of misrepresentations of the principles and designs of the
Abolitionists, who were pelted by the pro-slavery press
everywhere with the most odious epithets, such as "fanatics," " disorganizers," " amalgamationists," " traitors," "jacobins," " incendiaries," " cut-throats," " infidels " — the latter term being directed especially
against those who were so bold as to deny that the
Bible sanctioned slavery. This tide of abuse, issuing
from political and religious journals of wide influence,
had a powerful effect upon the lower stratum of society in the cities and large towns, and indeed in smaller
places as well. Anti-slavery meetings were often interrupted, and in some instances broken up by mobs ;
and instead of condemning these outrages, popular newspapers apologized for them, throwing the
blame not upon those who organized and took part
in them, but upon the Abolitionists, who, it was
alleged, persisted in discussing a subject with which
they had no right to intermeddle. The enemies of
the cause appeared to be under the delusion that it
could be crushed out by persecution and violence ;
that the men who had undertaken the work of abolishing slavery were so wanting in courage that they would
fly from the field to save their property and their persons from harm. These men had somehow contrived
to read the lessons of history backwards, imagining
that the way to stop a conflagration was to pour oil
upon the flames !

Such was the state of things at the beginning
of the year 1835, which has often been described as
pre-eminently the "mob year" in the history of the

cause. True, the pro-slavery mobs neither began nor
ended with that year, but they were more numerous
then than at any previous or subsequent time. The
social, ecclesiastical and commercial pressure brought
to bear upon leading Abolitionists during that year
was tremendous. Arthur Tappan, especially, was beset by leading merchants and moneyed men, presidents
of banks and insurance companies, and by influential
members of the churches, who besought him, by his
regard for his public and private reputation, as well as
for his business interests, to resign the office of President of the American Anti-Slavery Society and withdraw himself from the agitation. "You ask me," he
said in reply, "to betray my principles, to be false to
God and humanity: I WILL BE HANGED FIRST!" The
Rev. Samuel J. May, while sitting upon the platform
at the anniversary of the American Anti-Slavery Society in 1835, was called to the door by a partner in
one of the most prominent mercantile houses in New
York, who said to him, "Mr. May, we are not such
fools as not to know that slavery is a great evil, a
great wrong. But it was consented to by the founders
of our Republic. It was provided for in the Constitution of our Union. A great portion of the property
of the Southerners is invested under its sanction; and
the business of the North as well as the South has become adjusted to it. There are millions upon millions
of dollars due from Southerners to the merchants and
mechanics of New York alone, the payment of which
would be jeopardized by any rupture between the
North and the South. We cannot afford, sir, to let
you and your associates succeed in your endeavor to
overthrow slavery. It is not a matter of principle
with us; it is a matter of business necessity. We
cannot afford to let you succeed; and I have called
you out to let you know, and to let your fellow-laborers know, that we do not mean to allow you to suc-

ceed. We mean, sir," said he with increased emphasis, —"we mean, sir, to put you Abolitionists down —
by fair means if we can, by foul means if we must."*
Beyond all doubt, this merchant expressed the feelings
and the purposes of his class. The virus of slavery
at that day poured in a strong tide through every ave-
nue of commerce between the North and the South.
Northern men, many of them prominent in the church
and liberal contributors to benevolent societies, took
security for debts owed them at the South, in the
shape of mortgages upon "slaves and souls of men,"
and, in case of foreclosure, sold the human chattels and put the proceeds in their pockets, with as
little fear of censure as they would have experienced
in selling so many sheep or swine. In many instances
such men occupied the most eligible pews in churches,
and frowned upon ministers if they even dared to pray
in public for the slaves. In Northern colleges, the
whole power of faculties and trustees was exerted to
prevent agitation among the students. In some of
these colleges were bodies of Southern young men,
who stood ready to display the "manners of the plantation" upon such of their fellow-students as dared to
whisper a word against the divinity of slavery. Pub-
lishers at the North, in reprinting English books,
erased from their pages the passages likely to give
offence to the traffickers in human flesh. Even the
American Tract Society and the Methodist Book Concern engaged in this work of mutilation, and hardly
had the grace to be ashamed of it when they were exposed. At the very time when slavery was thus ob-
truding itself into every Northern interest and relation,
demanding of us the meanest of all services in its behalf, we were told that it was none of our business,

* Mr. May's "Recollections," p. 127.

and that the discussion of the subject was nothing less than treason against the government.

The spirit of the South at this time is indicated in the following paragraph from "The Richmond Whig," one of the most respectable and influential journals of that section:—

"Let the hell-hounds at the North beware. Let them not feel too much security in their homes, or imagine that they who throw firebrands, although from, as they think, so safe a distance, will be permitted to escape with impunity. There are thousands now animated with a spirit to brave every danger to bring these felons to justice on the soil of the Southern States, whose women and children they have dared to endanger by their hell-concocted plots. We have *feared* that Southern exasperation would seize some of the prime conspirators in their very beds, and drag them to meet the punishment due their offences. We fear it no longer. We hope it may be so, and our applause as one man shall follow the successful enterprise."

The Columbia (S. C.) "Telescope" uttered itself thus:—

"Let us declare, through the public journals of our country, that the question of slavery is not and shall not be open to discussion—that the very moment any private individual attempts to lecture us upon its evils and immorality, in the same moment his tongue shall be cut out and cast upon the dunghill."

It was not alone the *politicians* of the South who were meditating schemes of vengeance; the clergy were filled with the same evil spirit.

"Let your emissaries," said the Rev. Thomas S. Witherspoon of Alabama, in a letter to the editor of the "Emancipator," "dare to cross the Potomac, and I cannot promise you that your fate will be less than Haman's. Then beware how you goad an insulted but magnanimous people to deeds of desperation."

"Let them" [the Abolitionists], said the Rev. Wm. S. Plummer, D. D., of Richmond, "understand that they will be caught if they come among us, and they will take good care to keep out of our way. If the Abolitionists will set the country in a blaze, it is but fair that they should receive the first warning of the fire."

"At the approaching stated meeting of the Presbytery," said the Rev. Robert N. Anderson, D. D., writing to the sessions of the Presbyterian churches of Hanover (Va.) Presbytery, "I design to offer a preamble and string of resolutions on the subject of the treasonable and abominably wicked interference of the Northern and Eastern fanatics with our political and civil rights, our property, and our domestic concerns. If there be any stray goat of a minister among you, tainted with the blood-hound principles of abolitionism, let him be ferreted out, silenced, excommunicated, and left to the public to dispose of in other respects."

"If you wish to educate the slaves," said the Rev. J. C. Postell (Methodist) of South Carolina, writing to Rev. La Roy Sunderland of New York, "I will tell you how to raise the money without editing 'Zion's Watchman.' You and old Arthur Tappan come out to the South this winter, and they will raise a hundred thousand dollars for you. New Orleans itself will be pledged for it."

During this same year twenty thousand dollars reward was offered in New Orleans for the seizure of Arthur Tappan, and ten thousand dollars in some other place for that of Rev. Amos A. Phelps. Several other Northern Abolitionists were honored in a similar way, and the fires of persecution burned fiercely. In March, 1835, the Noyes Academy in Canaan, N. H., was opened for the reception of pupils without distinction of color. The whole State was thereby thrown into a fierce commotion. "The New Hamp-

shire Patriot" at Concord, and many other papers,
teemed from week to week with the most vulgar attacks upon the school and its managers, until, on the
10th of August, a great body of the inhabitants of
Canaan and the neighboring towns assembled together,
and, with a team of one hundred yoke of oxen,
dragged the school building from its foundations and
left it on the highway, a useless ruin. The leader of
this mob was a member of the Congregational church
in Canaan. The outrage was regarded with cool indifference, if not with approbation, by the great body of
citizens in all that region.

At Worcester, Mass., on the same day, the Rev.
Orange Scott, a Methodist clergyman of high standing,
while delivering an anti-slavery lecture, was assailed
by a son of ex-Governor Lincoln, who, with the assist-
ance of an Irishman, tore up his notes and offered him
personal violence. Not far from the same time, the
Rev. George Storrs, another Methodist clergyman, of
the highest character, while delivering a lecture in
Northfield, N. H., was arrested on the charge of being
"a common rioter and brawler," and sentenced by a
magistrate to three months imprisonment in the house
of correction. The case was appealed to a higher
tribunal, and the sentence was not executed. The
man who instigated this proceeding was afterwards a
Democratic member of Congress.

The incidents above related were but the beginning
of the reign of terror, of which I shall have more to
say hereafter. I wish now to notice briefly an effort
made in Boston at the beginning of the year (1835)
to organize a conservative anti-slavery society, — one
that should not displease the slaveholders, nor make
any uncomfortable excitement at the North. The
most obstinate and virulent of the clerical opponents
of abolition were at the head of this scheme; and the
purpose frankly avowed by some of them was to "put

down Garrison and his friends." A call for a convention was, by a curious oversight, issued at first in terms so broad as fairly to include the Abolitionists, and leave open the question of forming a new society. The blunder was discovered before the convention assembled, and a new call issued, but not in time to prevent the attendance of some leading Abolitionists, who were prepared to discuss the question with their opponents, and to show them that if they were really opposed to slavery and prepared to adopt efficient measures for its overthrow, there was no need whatever of a new organization. If the call had not been changed, the promoters of the scheme would have been sure to be outvoted by clergymen and laymen of their own denominations. The new society was wanted, not as a means of opposing slavery, but only as a feint to deceive the unwary and the unsuspecting, and make an appearance of doing something, while actually doing nothing to any purpose. The name of the society was "The American Union for the Relief and Improvement of the Colored Race;" and the constitution was so worded, as while it was seemingly opposed to slaveholding, it did really permit the cunning apologists of slavery to become members and to control its action. "The *system* of slavery" was pronounced "wrong," while nothing was said against individual slaveholding. A motion to substitute the word "sinful" for the word "wrong" was most strenuously objected to, on the ground that the object was to "conciliate and unite," and that the word wrong would not be so offensive to gentlemen of the South, and would better accord with the views and feelings of *wise* men at the North." One of the clergymen present said: "Many of the men on whom we are to operate are not professors of religion, and the word wrong does not sound to them as the word sin does; it is less offensive." Brave

reformers these, who were more concerned not to
give offence to the slaveholders and their friends than
they were on account of the wrongs done to the
slaves! The new society, being rooted in nothing but
hatred of the Abolitionists and a desire to put down
the anti-slavery agitation, soon went to its own place.
Its supporters, finding that they could do nothing by
its means to accomplish their real purpose, and that
the public saw through their thin disguise, abandoned
it to its fate. Founded upon no principle of genuine
hostility to slavery, it died an ignominious death,
while most of its members became even more than
ever embittered against the Abolitionists.

In the midst of the persecutions of this period the
Abolitionists were cheered by the intelligence that a
distinguished slaveholder, Mr. James G. Birney, had
espoused their cause, and given freedom to his slaves.
He was a native of Kentucky, but for some years had
been a distinguished member of the bar at Huntsville,
Ala. He had for several years been the agent of the
Colonization Society in the Southwestern States. As
early as 1832 he met Theodore D. Weld at the house
of Rev. Dr. Allen of Huntsville, and in conversing
with him was led into a closer examination of the moral
character of slavery. The final result was a conviction
in his mind of the sinfulness of slaveholding, and of
his own duty to emancipate his slaves. He thereupon
summoned them all into his presence, acknowledged
the wrong that he had done them in holding them in
bondage, and announced that he had executed deeds of
emancipation for each and all of them, and that henceforth they would be free. He offered to retain them
all in his service and to pay them wages, if they
should desire to remain with him. The negroes,
instead of proceeding at once, as according to the
current pro-slavery theory they ought to have done,
to cut Mr. Birney's throat and burn his house over his

head, gratefully took up the "shovel and the hoe," and
went to work for him with right good-will. Naturally
enough, Mr. Birney was received with open arms by
the Abolitionists. Wherever he was announced to
speak crowds flocked to hear him. As Mr. May
says : "He was mild yet firm, cautious yet not afraid
to speak the whole truth, candid but not compromis-
ing, careful not to exaggerate in aught, and equally
careful not to concede or extenuate." But the Northern sympathizers with slavery, though they could
not charge him with any violence or fanaticism, and
though they could not deny that he was a calm,
dignified and cultured gentleman and Christian, liked
him not a whit better than they did Mr. Garrison.
The tide of detraction against the anti-slavery cause
was not diminished or softened in the least by his
appearance among us. Indeed, he was the object of
peculiar hatred, because, having lived in the South
from his birth, he was able to throw a flood of light
upon the workings of the slave system, and thus to
show the folly and absurdity of all the defences made
of it by its apologists and supporters.

The American Anti-Slavery Society, soon after its
formation, adopted the practice of sending its most important publications — those especially which explained
its principles and designs — to leading citizens at the
South. This would seem to have been required on the
score of principle as well as courtesy. Seeking the
abolition of slavery, not by external force, but by appeals to the reason and judgment as well as the conscience of the masters, the Abolitionists desired nothing so much as to have their movements thoroughly
understood at the South. They would gladly have
sent thither living agents, to meet the holders of slaves,
and, if possible, persuade them, not only for their own
peace of mind, but as a means of advancing their pecuniary interests, to give freedom to their bondmen.

In the beginning, indeed, it was their hope that the
Southern people would shortly become reasonable
enough to permit, if not to invite, the presence of such
agents. Meanwhile, the least that they could do was
to send their publications to men whose names were
found in public documents or obtained from private
sources. This they did openly, availing themselves
of the postal service of the United States. Not one
of their documents was ever addressed by them to a
slave. To him, indeed, they had nothing to say, save
to entreat him never to attempt to redress his wrongs
by violence, but to wait patiently for his chains to be
broken by

> "The mild arms of Truth and Love,
> Made mighty through the living God."

In the summer of 1835, large quantities of anti-slavery publications were sent through the mails to citizens
of the South, from the anti-slavery office in New York.
A tremendous excitement in that part of the country
was the consequence. If, indeed, the Society had furnished every slave with a bowie-knife, and advised him
to cut his master's throat therewith at the earliest possible moment, the rage of the South could hardly have
been greater than it was. The documents were pronounced incendiary, and though they were addressed
exclusively to white men, and generally to the foremost slaveholders, it was coolly assumed, at the North
as well as at the South, that they were intended to
excite an insurrection and deluge the South in blood!
Fresh torrents of misrepresentation and abuse were
thereupon heaped upon the heads of the Abolitionists,
whose voices of explanation and protest were drowned
in a worse than Niagara roar of calumny. In Charleston, on the 29th of July, the post-office was broken
open by a mob, and the anti-slavery publications that
had accumulated therein, and which the postmaster
had obligingly left in a pile for the convenience of the

rioters, were taken out and burned in the presence of an exultant crowd. Shortly afterwards a public meeting was held to denounce the "incendiaries" of the North, and to complete the work of the mob by ferreting out and punishing any Abolitionist, or friend of Abolitionists, who might happen to be in the city. "This meeting," said the "Charleston Courier" in its report, "the clergy of all denominations attended in a body, lending their sanction to the proceedings, and adding by their presence to the impressive character of the scene." John G. Whittier was moved to embalm this impressive scene for the benefit of coming generations, in a poem entitled "Clerical Oppressors," a few stanzas of which are here copied : —

"Just God! and these are they
    Who minister at Thine altar, God of Right!
Men who their hands, with prayer and blessing, lay
    On Israel's Ark of light!

What! preach and kidnap men?
    Give thanks, and rob Thy own afflicted poor?
Talk of Thy glorious liberty, and then
    Bolt hard the captive's door?

Pilate and Herod friends!
    Chief priests and rulers, as of old, combine!
Just God and holy! is that church, which lends
    Strength to the Spoiler, Thine?

How long, O Lord, how long
    Shall such a priesthood barter truth away,
And, in Thy name, for robbery and wrong
    At Thy own altars pray?

Woe to the priesthood! woe
    To all whose hire is with the price of blood!
Perverting, darkening, changing, as they go,
    The searching truths of God!

Their glory and their might
    Shall perish; and their very names shall be
Vile before all the people, in the light
    Of a world's liberty!"

25

The postmaster at Charleston took the responsibility
of refusing to deliver anti-slavery publications until
he should receive instructions from Washington. The
postmaster-general, Amos Kendall, a man of New
England birth, told his subordinate that he had " no
legal authority to exclude newspapers from the mail,
nor to prohibit their carriage or delivery on account of
their character or tendency, real or supposed." Having made this admission, he proceeded to say : " We
owe an obligation to the laws, but a higher one to the
communities in which we live ; and, if the former be
permitted to destroy the latter, it is patriotism to disregard them.   Entertaining these views, I cannot sanction, and will not condemn the step you have taken."
The scoffers at a Higher Law easily discovered a lower
one when it was necessary for the accomplishment of
their evil designs. Postmasters generally at the South
followed the example set them at Charleston, and this
action on their part was widely commended at the
North.

Shortly after the occurrences above related there
were movements for holding great public meetings in
the chief cities at the North.   And what does the
reader suppose was their object? Was it to protest
against the outrages at Charleston and elsewhere, and
to vindicate the liberty of the press and the sanctity of
the mails? On the contrary, it was to apologize, openly
or covertly, for those outrages, and to intensify the
public hostility against the Abolitionists on account of
their lawful and peaceful efforts to abolish slavery.   In
other words, it was to "PUT THE ABOLITIONISTS
DOWN," and thus protect the South from all danger of
interference with her system of slavery.   New York,
Philadelphia, Boston, and some of the smaller cities
gave utterance to the prevailing madness.   The Abolitionists asked for Faneuil Hall, wherein to explain
their objects and defend themselves against the assaults

of their enemies. Their request was rudely denied; but on the 15th of August the doors of the "Old Cradle" were opened to their enemies and made to echo with their misrepresentations and calumnies. The mayor took the chair, and the blood of Boston, already at fever heat, was still more inflamed by intemperate harangues from the lips of Harrison Gray Otis, Richard Fletcher and Peleg Sprague. Daniel Webster, for some unexplained reason, was reserved for later immolation upon the bloody altar of slavery. The resolutions adopted were full of the most preposterous assumptions in the interest of slavery, and of the grossest libels upon the Abolitionists. It was not long after this that Mr. Garrison was hung in effigy at his own door, and there seemed only too much reason to fear that his life might fall a prey to the madness of the time. In the midst of all these proceedings, which menaced the overthrow of the freedom of speech and of the press, the destruction of the sanctity of the mails, and the perpetual rule of the Slave Power, the Pulpit of New England was either apologetic or dumb; or, if here and there some minister, braver than his brethren, ventured to remonstrate, his single voice seemed only to emphasize the surrounding silence.

The Faneuil Hall meeting, by intensifying the public hostility to the Abolitionists, led naturally to the Boston mob of "gentlemen of property and standing," on the 21st of October, 1835. As I have stated in a previous chapter, the avowed design of the mob was to do violence to Mr. George Thompson, the eloquent anti-slavery lecturer from England. The annual meeting of the Boston Female Anti-Slavery Society was advertised to be held on that day in the Anti-Slavery Hall, 46 Washington Street. A larger hall had been engaged for the purpose of holding the meeting at an earlier date, but the owners, fearing a mob, declined to open its doors; and, after a week's postponement,

196   GARRISON AND HIS TIMES.

the meeting was notified to be held as above. A false
report that Mr. Thompson would deliver an address on
the occasion added to the public excitement. The
morning papers referred to the meeting in terms well
calculated to excite a mob. One of them — "The
Commercial Gazette" I think it was — said it was "in
vain to hold meetings in Faneuil Hall; in vain that
speeches are made and resolutions adopted, assuring
our brethren of the South that we cherish rational and
correct notions on the subject of slavery, if Thompson
and Garrison, and their vile associates in this city, are
permitted to hold their meetings in the broad face of
day, and to continue their denunciations of the planters of the South. They must be put down if we
would preserve our consistency. The evil is one of
the greatest magnitude; and the opinion prevails very
generally that if there is no law that will reach it, it
must be reached in some other way." This and other
similar articles had their natural results in the gathering of an immense mob — of "*gentlemen* of property
and standing," one of the papers called it — that filled
all the streets in the vicinity of the meeting. The
anti-slavery women, as they passed into the hall
through this crowd of chivalrous friends of the South,
were assailed in a rude and indecent fashion. They
entered quietly, and went calmly about their business.
The president, Miss Mary S. Parker, read a portion
of Scripture, and then lifted up a firm but gentle voice
in fervent prayer to God for his blessing upon the
slave's cause, for the forgiveness of its deluded enemies and persecutors, and for succor and protection to
its friends in the hour of peril. She offered thanks
that "though there were many to molest, there were
none that could make afraid." "It was," says Mr.
Garrison, who was present by invitation to address the
meeting, "an awful, sublime and soul-thrilling scene —
enough, one would suppose, to melt adamantine hearts,

and make even fiends of darkness stagger and retreat. Indeed, the clear, untremulous voice of that Christian heroine in prayer occasionally awed the ruffians into silence, and was heard distinctly even in the midst of their hisses, yells and curses; for they could not long silently endure the agony of conviction, and their conduct became furious." The Anti-Slavery Office was separated from the hall by a board partition, and to this Mr. Garrison retired, by advice of the President, in company with Mr. C. C. Burleigh, who locked the door to preserve the contents of the Depository from being destroyed. The mayor, who had shown his sympathy with the object which the genteel ruffians had in view by presiding with alacrity at the Faneuil Hall meeting, instead of taking the necessary means to disperse the mob and protect the Society, entered the meeting to *command* the ladies to retire. Seeing that no efforts of theirs could induce him to do his sworn duty, they adjourned to the house of one of their number, encountering again, as they passed into the street, the jeers and curses of the ruffian crowd. The mob having bravely demolished the anti-slavery sign, which the mayor had ordered to be given up to them, and appropriated the Testaments and prayer-books that had been thrown out of the windows, next turned their attention to Mr. Garrison, whose place of retreat was easily discovered. "We must have Garrison! Out with him! Lynch him!" they cried. By advice of the mayor he attempted to escape at the rear of the building. He got safely from a back window on to a shed, making, however, a narrow escape from falling headlong to the ground. He reached a carpenter's shop, where a friend tried to conceal him, but in vain. The rioters, uttering a yell, furiously dragged him to a window, with the intention of throwing him from that height to the ground. But one of them relented and said, "Don't kill him outright." So they drew

him back, and coiled a rope around his body, probably
intending to drag him through the streets therewith.
He descended to the street by a ladder raised for the
purpose. He fortunately extricated himself from the
rope, but was seized by two or three of the leading
rioters, powerful and athletic men, by whom he was
dragged along bareheaded, a friendly voice in the crowd
shouting, "He shan't be hurt! he is an American!"
This seemed to excite sympathy in some breasts, and
they reiterated the same cry.   Blows, however, were
aimed at his head by such as were of a cruel spirit,
and at last they succeeded in tearing nearly all the
clothes from his body.   Thus was he dragged from
Wilson's Lane into State Street, in the rear of the
City Hall, over ground that was stained with the blood
of the first martyrs in the cause of Liberty and Independence, in the memorable massacre of 1770; and
upon which, only a few years before, had been unfurled,
with joyous acclamations, the beautiful banner presented by the young men of Boston to the gallant
Poles.   At the south door of the City Hall the mayor
attempted to protect him; but as he was unassisted by
any show of authority or force, he was quickly thrust
aside.   There was a tremendous rush to prevent
him from being taken into the hall. For a time
the conflict was desperate; but at length a rescue was
effected by a posse that came to the help of the mayor,
and he was taken up to the mayor's room.   Here he
was furnished with needful clothing, the mayor and his
advisers declaring that the only way to preserve his
life was to commit him to jail as a disturber of the
peace!   Accordingly a hack was got ready at the door,
and, supported by Sheriff Parkman and Ebenezer
Bailey, Esq. (the mayor leading the way), he was
put into the vehicle without much difficulty; the
crowd not recognizing him at first in his new
garb.

THE BOSTON MOB OF OCTOBER 21, 1835.

"But now," says Mr. Garrison, "a scene occurred that baffles description. As the ocean, lashed into fury by the spirit of of the storm, seeks to whelm the adventurous bark beneath the mountain waves, so did the mob, enraged by a series of disappointments, rush like a whirlwind upon the frail vehicle in which I sat, and endeavor to drag me out of it. Escape seemed a physical impossibility. They clung to the wheels, dashed open the doors, seized hold of the horses, and tried to upset the carriage. They were, however, vigorously repulsed by the police—a constable sprung in by my side—the doors were closed—and the driver, lustily using his whip upon the bodies of his horses and the heads of the rioters, happily made an opening through the crowd, and drove at a tremendous speed for Leverett Street. But many of the rioters followed even with superior swiftness, and repeatedly attempted to arrest the progress of the horses. To reach the jail by a direct course was found impracticable; and after going by a circuitous direction, and encountering many hair-breadth escapes, we drove up to the new and last refuge of liberty and life, when another desperate attempt was made by the mob to seize me, but in vain. In a few moments I was locked up in a cell, safe from my persecutors, accompanied by two delightful associates—a good conscience and a cheerful mind. In the course of the evening several of my friends came to my grated window, to sympathize and confer with me, with whom I held a strengthening conversation until the hour of retirement, when I threw myself upon my prison-bed, and slept tranquilly."

In the morning the prisoner inscribed upon the walls of his cell, with a pencil, the following lines:—

"William Lloyd Garrison was put into this cell on Wednesday afternoon, Oct. 21, 1835, to save him from the violence of a 'respectable' and influential mob, who sought to destroy him for preaching the abominable and dangerous doctrine that ' all men are created equal,' and that all oppression is odious in the sight of God. 'Hail Columbia!' Cheers for the Autocrat of Russia, and the Sultan of Turkey!

" Reader, let this inscription remain till the last slave in this despotic land be loosed from his fetters.

> "When peace within the bosom reigns,
>   And conscience gives the approving voice,
> Though bound the human form in chains,
>   Yet can the soul aloud rejoice.
>
> "'Tis true my footsteps are confined—
>   I cannot range beyond this cell;
> But what can circumscribe my mind ?
>   To chain the winds attempt as well !
>
> "Confine me as a prisoner — but bind me not as a slave.
> Punish me as a criminal — but hold me not as a chattel.
> Torture me as a man — but drive me not like a beast.
> Doubt my sanity — but acknowledge my immortality."

"In the course of the forenoon," says Mr. Garrison, "after passing through the mockery of an examination, for form's sake, before Judge Whitman, I was released from prison; but at the earnest solicitation of the city authorities, in order to tranquillize the public mind, I deemed it proper to leave the city for a few days, accompanied by my wife, whose situation was such as to awaken the strongest solicitude for her life."

Those who imagine, as too many ill-informed persons do, that the anti-slavery movement began with the organization of the Liberty, the Freesoil, or the Republican party, are the victims of a great mistake. They little know by what toils and sacrifices a highway for those parties was cast up by men and women who trod the field with bleeding feet, and stood firmly for the right in the presence of such fiery trials as beset only the paths that martyrs are called to tread. If the Abolitionists at this earlier period had given way

before the minions of the slave power, the Liberty
party could not have been born for a century, if indeed the republic could in that case have been saved
from destruction. Dr. Channing, though critical of
some of their modes of action, gave them unqualified
praise for their brave defence of the freedom of speech.
"To them," he said, "has been committed the most
important bulwark of liberty, and they have acquitted
themselves of the trust like men and Christians. Of
such men I do not hesitate to say, that they have rendered to freedom a more essential service than any
body of men among us. The defenders of freedom
are not those who claim and exercise rights which no
one assails, or who win shouts of applause by well-
turned compliments to liberty in the days of her triumph. They are those who stand up for rights which
mobs, conspiracies, or single tyrants put in jeopardy ;
who contend for liberty in that particular form which
is threatened at the moment by the many or the few.
To the Abolitionists this honor belongs. From my
heart I thank them. I am myself their debtor. I
am not sure that I should this moment (Nov. 4, 1836,)
write in safety, had they shrunk from the conflict, had
they shut their lips, imposed silence on their presses,
and hid themselves before their ferocious assailants. I
thank the Abolitionists that in this evil day they were
true to the rights which the multitude were ready to
betray. Their purpose to suffer, to die, rather than
surrender their dearest liberties, taught the lawless
that they had a foe to contend with whom it was not
safe to press."* This tribute, be it remembered, was
written almost twenty years before the organization of
the Republican party, and before the Liberty party was
conceived. I would not detract in the least from the
praise due to the noble men who fought the Slave

* Channing's Works in six volumes — Vol. II., pp. 159, 160.

26

Power by means of a political party, on the floor of
Congress and elsewhere, without flinching, hampered
as they were by the compromises of a blood-stained
Constitution; but I would have them remember that
the cause met its Thermopylæ before any anti-slavery
political party was born, and that whatever was done
through the ballot-box was accomplished by the aid of
moral forces previously accumulated, and that alone
made such a political party possible.

XII.

Effects of the Boston Mob — Francis Jackson's Bravery — Harriet
Martineau — Mrs. Chapman and her Work — Mobs in Montpelier,
Vt., and Utica, N. Y. — Gerrit Smith — Alvan Stewart — Burning
of Pennsylvania Hall — Attempts to Put the Abolitionists Down
by Law — Demands of the South — Gov. Everett — Prosecution
of Dr. Crandall — Flogging of Amos Dresser — Requisition from
the Governor of Alabama — Harsh Language.

THE "gentlemen of property and standing" in
Boston were not long in discovering that the weapons
which they had formed for the suppression of the
anti-slavery agitation did not prosper. One of the
first effects of the riot was seen in the bravery of
Francis Jackson, who, while Mr. Garrison was in jail
and the rioters were yet patrolling the city and exult-
ing that they had "put the Abolitionists down," sent
a letter to the President of the Female Anti-Slavery
Society, offering his dwelling for its use whenever it
should desire to hold another meeting. This brave
act thrilled the hearts of the Abolitionists and awed
their enemies. How brightly "shines a good deed in
a naughty world!" The invitation was accepted, and
on the 19th of November a memorable meeting was
held in Mr. Jackson's house. It was a solemn occasion, for those present were not sure that the house
would not be sacked or burned. Harriet Martineau
was then in Boston. She had travelled extensively in
the country, at the South as well as at the North.
Conservative Unitarians and others had done their utmost to prejudice her against American Abolitionists;
but she deemed it her duty, in view of the persecu-

tions to which they were subjected, to attend this
meeting, and see for herself whether the aspersions
cast upon them were just. Being invited to address
the meeting, she responded promptly. "I had supposed," she said, "that my. presence here would be
understood as showing my sympathy with you. But
as I am requested to speak, I will say what I have said
through the whole South, in every family where I have
been, that I consider slavery inconsistent with the law
of God, and incompatible with the course of his providence. I should certainly say no less at the North
than at the South concerning this utter abomination,
and now I declare that in your principles I fully
agree." This brave, yet modest little speech brought
upon Miss Martineau a tide of denunciation only less
violent than that which had beat for months on the
head of her noble countryman, George Thompson.
Up to that moment her society had been courted by
the *élite* of Boston, especially by the Unitarians, with
whom she was religiously associated. But now she
was slighted as one who had committed an unpardon-
able offence. Her brave words were imbued with
power, and while they greatly cheered and encouraged
the Abolitionists, they filled the pro-slavery party with
rage. Her experience at this time prepared her to
write that admirable little work, "The Martyr Age of
America," which did so much to bind the hearts of
Abolitionists in England to the struggling friends of.
the cause in the United States. From that day to the
end of our conflict her powerful pen was always
at the service of the cause; and I doubt if any
other person ever did so much as she to give the people of Great Britain a clear understanding of the
nature of our struggle, of the mighty obstacles it
encountered, and of the ways in which they could
help us.

Ten righteous men, it is said, would have availed to

savo the ancient city of Sodom. Boston was spared
for one ; but that one was in himself a host, and able to
put ten thousand enemies of freedom to flight. Ever
afterwards, to the day of his death, which occurred
during the war of Rebellion, Mr. Jackson was foremost in the anti-slavery conflict. He served for many
years as President of the Massachusetts Anti-Slavery
Society, presiding at its meetings with a dignity that
commanded the public respect; his house was ever
open to the faithful workers in the cause, and to shelter the fugitive slave ; and he gave generously of his
substance for the support of lecturers and the printing
and distribution of anti-slavery periodicals and tracts.
Modest and unobtrusive in manner, he was firm as a
rock in his adherence to the cause, quick to discern, and
prompt to repel danger, and brave enough to endure
without flinching and without complaint the reproaches
heaped upon his head by the minions of slavery. His
name in Boston, where he was conspicuous for integrity in public affairs as well as in private life, was a
tower of strength.

Another name, that of a woman, was brought into
wide conspicuity amidst the events above related.
Maria Weston Chapman, the wife of Mr. Henry
G. Chapman, a Boston merchant, and for many
years the treasurer of the Massachusetts Anti-Slavery
Society, was the pride and charm of the most cultured social circle in Boston. She had enjoyed some
of the best opportunities of culture which Europe
offered to an ambitious American girl, and encountered
the temptations to a worldly and fashionable life to
which so many others yielded. Possessing in an
eminent degree the graces of person, the intellectual
acquirements and the wit that are so fascinating in
womanhood, she yet consecrated herself and her great
gifts to the service of a righteous but most unpopular
cause. She was a member of the Boston Female

Anti-Slavery Society before the mob, and a close
observer of the events of that trying period; and not
long afterwards she gave to the world a most remarkable *brochure*, entitled "RIGHT AND WRONG IN BOS-
TON," in which the conspirators against Liberty were
depicted in their true character and held up to the
scorn of mankind for all coming time. She was the
cotemporary historian of Boston's mob of "*gentlemen*
of property and standing," and the leading actors
therein cowered under the well-deserved strokes of
her lash. Her pamphlet is of great historic value. It
will forever bring a blush of shame to the cheeks of
some whose misfortune it will be to trace their line of
ancestry through that stormy period. But such are
the revenges of Time.

From this period to the close of the conflict Mrs.
Chapman occupied a position of great usefulness and
power. Her counsel in emergencies was invaluable.
She was quick to detect and expose any sign of
treachery to the cause, and any attempt to lower the
standard to meet the requirements of intriguing and
selfish men. Her executive power was remarkable.
She could keep more irons in the fire, without burning
one of them, than any person I ever knew. For many
successive years she was an inspiring force in the
cause, laying out plans of labor on the widest fields,
and superintending their execution with unsleeping
vigilance. Her pen, keen as a Damascus blade, was
like a lance in rest, ready on the instant for any
required service. During many years a very large
proportion of the funds used in carrying on the cause
were raised by means of an annual fair in Boston. Of
this fair Mrs. Chapman and her three sisters (Miss
Anne Warren, Miss Caroline, and Miss Deborah
Weston) were the chief managers. The most beautiful articles for the fair were contributed by the faithful
friends of the cause in Great Britain and France, with

whom Mrs. Chapman was in constant correspondence, and who are entitled to the eternal gratitude of the American people for the help they gave us in our struggle to abolish slavery. I might mention the names of some of these foreign helpers, but I fear that in doing so I might seem to be invidious in omitting others equally worthy of recognition. In connection with the fair, and as a special means of advancing the cause, Mrs. Chapman published a beautiful little annual, " THE LIBERTY BELL," which she edited with rare skill and taste. The volumes, a dozen or more in number, are worthy of preservation as memorials of the cause and specimens of the literature it produced. In them will be found contributions from a large number of the most prominent anti-slavery writers of the time, both men and women.

In a *jeu d'esprit*, by James Russell Lowell, published many years ago, and embracing a description of prominent persons attending one of the annual fairs in Boston, I find these lines : —

> "There was Maria Chapman, too,
> With her swift eyes of clear steel blue,
> The coiled-up mainspring of the Fair,
> Originating everywhere
> The expansive force, without a sound,
> That whirls a hundred wheels around;
> Herself meanwhile as calm and still
> As the bare crown of Prospect Hill;
> A noble woman, brave and apt,
> Cumæa's sybil not more rapt,
> Who might, with those fair tresses shorn,
> The Maid of Orleans' casque have worn;
> Herself the Joan of our Arc,
> For every shaft a shining mark."

The 21st of October, 1835, is memorable, not alone for the Boston riot, but for two other similar attempts to put the Abolitionists down by violence. One of these took place at Montpelier, the capital of Vermont, and in the very church where, a little more than three years before, I had delivered my first anti-slavery lecture. Samuel J. May, who, on account of his gentleness of speech, was called our Apostle John, was the speaker of the occasion. No sooner did he begin his address than a mob, led by some of the foremost citizens of the place, commanded him to be silent, and the meeting was broken up. For the state of public sentiment which made this and other similar riots possible in that State, no other newspaper was so much responsible as the "Vermont Chronicle," which, from the very beginning of the anti-slavery movement, had persistently misrepresented its principles and designs, and done what it could to make its champions odious. It was the organ of the Congregationalists, the most numerous and influential sect in the State, and hence its power for mischief was very great. It was for this reason that Vermont was so long tolerant of the designs of the Slave Power. Nothing could be more offensive to a pure conscience than the hair-splitting, Bible-perverting metaphysics by means of which the brothers Tracy prevented the churches of Vermont from taking their true position as the uncompromising opponents of the slave system. The moral atmosphere of the State is even now not quite disinfected of the taint derived from that source.

But there was a far more formidable riot on the same day, in Utica, N. Y., where a convention to form a State Anti-Slavery Society was to meet. A worse than Ephesian uproar ensued. Leading citizens declared that the convention must be broken up ; Utica must not be disgraced by an assembly of "fanatics and incendiaries." The court-house having been engaged for the convention, a public meeting of the pro-slavery party was held in advance, and arrangements were made to pre-occupy the building before the hour at which the Abolitionists were to assemble, and by any means to prevent them from effecting their object.

The whole city was in an uproar, and the disturbance was led by eminent citizens. The convention, composed of from six to eight hundred delegates,
was driven from the court-house to the Second Presbyterian Church, where it barely succeeded in organizing the proposed society before it was broken up.
The chief of the mob was the Hon. Samuel Beardsley,
then a representative of the district in Congress, who
declared that "the disgrace of having an Abolition
Convention held in the city would be a deeper one
than that of twenty mobs," and "that it would be better to have Utica razed to its foundations, or to have
it destroyed like Sodom and Gomorrah, than to have
the Convention meet here."

Up to this time, Gerrit Smith, though an earnest
opponent of slavery, had adhered to the Colonization
Society and kept aloof from the anti-slavery cause.
He came to the Utica Convention to be a spectator of
its proceedings, and to inform himself more fully of
the designs and purposes of the Abolitionists. He
was so disgusted, shocked and alarmed by the action
of the pro-slavery party, and so impressed by the
earnestness, devotion and patience of the members of
the Convention, that he felt the hour had come for him
to take his stand openly with the friends of immediate
emancipation. He invited all the members of the
Convention to repair to Peterboro, his place of residence, thirty miles distant, and finish their proceedings. A large proportion of the members accepted
the invitation, and on the next day they assembled in
the Presbyterian church of Peterboro, where Mr.
Smith made an address of surpassing eloquence and
power, in which he avowed his purpose from that time
forth to act with the Abolitionists. The accession to
our ranks of a man of such high social and moral distinction filled us with encouragement and hope, and
helped us to bear patiently the persecution that still

27

remained for us. Ever afterwards his name was a
tower of strength for the cause. His pen, his voice,
his purse were always at its service. His house was
a refuge for the fugitive slave and for the toil-worn
lecturer, and of his great wealth he contributed generously to the promotion of every form of anti-slavery
effort.

It did not require a mob to make an Abolitionist of
that eminent advocate, Alvan Stewart. With his clear
head, his warm love of liberty, and his keen sense of
the wrong of turning a man into a chattel, he could be
nothing else. But while the mob was not needful to
his conversion, it did rouse him to put forth his great
energies in behalf of the cause. His commanding eloquence as a speaker, his quick perception of the ludicrous, his power of sarcasm and ridicule, combined
with his high moral tone, his indignation at every
form of injustice, and his imperturbable good-nature,
made him a powerful champion of our struggling
enterprise. He died in the very maturity of his
powers, revered and lamented by all who could appreciate his sterling worth. He was more especially
interested in the political aspects of the slavery question, and if he had lived he would no doubt have taken
a high place in that group of great men whose services
in the cause of freedom form so large a part of the
history of the last twenty-five years. It will be a misfortune if a personage so unique, and whose life exhibited such varied powers, should fail to find a biog-
rapher.

On the 17th of May, 1838, Pennsylvania Hall, a
commodious structure erected by the friends of freedom in Philadelphia, at a cost of $40,000, and conse-
crated to the free discussion of all subjects interesting
to American citizens, was burned by a mob three days
only after its dedication. During those three days
the hall was used for meetings to promote education

and temperance, and to awaken sympathy for the Indians and the slaves. The pro-slavery party was greatly excited by the fact that at last there was a hall in the city which would be open to Abolitionists in common with others, and a mobocratic spirit was roused. The anti-slavery meetings had been addressed by Charles C. Burleigh, Arnold Buffum, Alvan Stewart, William Lloyd Garrison, Angelina Grimké Weld, Maria Weston Chapman and Abby Kelley. The building was surrounded and menaced by a mob. The city authorities took no efficient steps to prevent a riot. The mayor informed the proprietors that if they would hold no meeting on the evening of the 17th, but place the building in his hands, he would disperse the mob. But the rioters did not prove as tractable as he expected. In spite of his feeble and inadequate efforts to protect the building, it was burned to the ground under his very eyes. The conflagration was no doubt regarded with pleasure by a very large proportion of the inhabitants of the city, including not a few men of wealth and high social standing. In short, the public sentiment of the city afforded no protection against such outrages. The burning of the hall was followed during the next two days by brutal attacks upon the colored people, their churches, institutions and private dwellings. The "Shelter for Colored Orphans" was set on fire, and colored people were attacked while passing quietly in the streets. During all of these outrages the conduct of the mayor was most disgraceful.

The mobs of which I have given an account may be taken as samples of a great number of similar disturbances which occurred about the same time in different parts of the country, and which I have not room even to mention. The whole land was hot with pro-slavery wrath, ready at any moment to break out in riotous demonstrations. There was, in fact, an

epidemic of mobs, which, if not directly instigated by
men of respectable standing in society, were at least
winked at by such men as well as by the press.   The
announcement, almost anywhere, of an anti-slavery
lecture was pretty sure to evoke a disturbance.   This
state of things, in some portions of the country,
continued to a greater or less extent from 1834 to
1838, and did not wholly cease even then.

But not by mobs alone was the attempt made to
suppress the anti-slavery agitation.   From the very
beginning there were mutterings of a design on the
part of the slaveholders and their Northern allies to
effect this object by law — by common law, where the
courts were sufficiently compliant, and elsewhere by
statutory enactments.   The demands for such laws
on the part of the Southern press were alike frequent
and insolent; and they were sometimes echoed at
the North.   As early as March, .1832, Judge Peter
Thatcher of the Boston Municipal Court, in a charge
to the Grand Jury, pronounced it "an undoubted misdemeanor, and indictable as such at common law," to
publish in one State with the intent to send it to another, a paper designed to excite slaves to murder their
masters; it being always taken for granted that such
was the object of the anti-slavery papers.   "If any
publications," said the Judge, "which have a direct
tendency to excite the slave population of other States
to rise upon their masters, and to involve their families and property in a common destruction, are here
published and circulated freely, may not the citizens
of those States well imagine that such publications
are authorized by our laws?   If such publications
were justified and encouraged here, it would tend to
alienate from each other the minds of those whose
best political happiness and safety consist in preserving in its full strength the bond of the Union."   The
argument of the Judge was drawn out at length, and

not only published promptly in the Boston newspapers, but in the "American Jurist," a periodical of
high repute in the legal profession. It was itself as
infamous a libel upon a body of peaceable, orderly
citizens as was ever published; and, in the then state
of the public feeling toward Abolitionists, was a thou-
sand-fold more likely than "The Liberator" to incite
men to commit murder.

It was not far from the same time that "The Boston
Courier" (Joseph T. Buckingham, editor), which had
been distinguished above other journals in that city
for its zeal for freedom of the press, came out une-
quivocally in favor of enacting statute laws for the
suppression of "The Liberator." "The people of
New England," said the editor, "would stop this
publication with as much zeal as the citizens of
Charleston."

Another Massachusetts man, the Hon. William
Sullivan, wrote a pamphlet in 1835, in which the
same doctrine was put forth. "It is to be hoped and
expected," he said, "that Massachusetts will enact
laws declaring the printing, publishing and circulating
of papers and pamphlets on slavery, and also the
holding of meetings to discuss slavery and abolition,
to be public indictable offences, and provide for the
punishment thereof in such manner as will more
effectually prevent such offences."

Symptoms like these of a readiness on the part of the
North to put the Abolitionists down by law naturally
encouraged the South to demand legislation for that
purpose. Gov. McDuffie, in his message to the Legislature of South Carolina, after declaring slavery to
be "the corner-stone of the Republican edifice," and
that the laboring population of any community,
"bleached or unbleached," is a "dangerous element in
the body politic," and after predicting that the laboring people of the North would be virtually reduced

to slavery within twenty-five years, declared that "the
laws of every community should punish such interference," as that of the Abolitionists with slavery,
" with death without benefit of clergy." The Legislature, responding to the Governor's recommendation,
promptly resolved, "That the Legislature of South
Carolina, having every confidence in the justice and
friendship of the non-slaveholding States, announces
her confident expectation, and she earnestly requests,
that the government of these States will promptly
and effectually suppress all those associations within
their respective limits purporting to be abolition societies." The Legislatures of North Carolina, Alabama and Virginia adopted resolutions of the same
character. These demands were sent in due form to
the governors of the non-slaveholding States. In
what spirit were they received? I have not been able
to find a single instance in which they awakened the
least degree of surprise or indignation, or called forth
such a rebuke as they deserved. My impression is
that most of the Northern governors contented themselves with a formal and perfunctory transmission of
them, without comment, to their respective Legislatures. Not so, however, the governor (W. L. Marcy)
of New York, who took occasion to say that, " without
the power to pass such laws " as the South demanded
" the States would not possess all the necessary means
for preserving their external relations of peace among
themselves." Whatever measure of individual popularity Governor Marcy may have gained at the South by
this slavish utterance, he did not succeed in persuad-
ing the Legislature of the Empire State to enact the
proposed laws. The people in those days were less
servile than their political leaders. In the Legislature
of Rhode Island, even before the Southern demands
were received, a bill in conformity to those demands
was actually presented by a committee to which the

subject had been referred. It was defeated by the strenuous efforts of Mr. George Curtis (father of George William Curtis) and Mr. Thomas W. Dorr.

Edward Everett was at that time Governor of Massachusetts. In 1826 he had revealed his servility by declaring on the floor of Congress that "there was no cause in which he would sooner buckle a knapsack to his back and put a musket on his shoulder than that of putting down a servile insurrection at the South." "The great relation of servitude," he added, "in some form or other, with greater or less departure from the theoretic equality of men, is inseparable from our nature. Domestic slavery is not, in my judgment, to be set down as an immoral and irreligious relation. It is a condition of life as well as any other to be justified by morality, religion and international law." Mr. Everett having been trained for the pulpit, these utterances surprised and shocked some people who had not quite unlearned the teaching of an earlier day in respect to slavery. Mr. C. C. Cambreling, a member of Congress from New York, and a native of South Carolina, sharply rebuked the recreant New Englander on the spot. If he (Mr. Everett) had learned such sentiments in the University of Gottingen, he should, said Mr. Cambreling, instead of returning to his native land, have journeyed eastward, "followed the course of the dark-rolling Danube, crossed the Euxine, laid his head upon the footstool of the Sultan, and besought him to place his feet upon the neck of the recreant citizen of a recreant republic." We need not wonder that a man of such antecedents, occupying the post of Governor of Massachusetts, insulted the people of that Commonwealth in his response to the demands of his Southern masters. "Whatever by direct and necessary operation," said this smooth-faced champion of slavery, "is calculated to excite an insurrection among the slaves,

has been held, by highly respectable legal authority,
an offence against the people of the Commonwealth,
which may be prosecuted as a misdemeanor at common
law." "The patriotism of all classes," he added,
" must be invoked to abstain from a discussion which,
by exasperating the master can have no other effect
than to render more oppressive the condition of the
slave ; and which, if not abandoned, there is great
reason to fear, will prove the rock on which the Union
will split." In other words, the South would consent
to remain in the Union only upon the condition that
Northern freemen should wear a padlock upon their
lips !

This portion of the Governor's message, together
with the insolent resolves of the Southern Legislatures,
was referred to a joint committee of the two Houses,
of which Senator George Lunt of Newburyport, a
doughface of the first water, was chairman ; and there
was only too much reason to fear that in the then state
of public sentiment, Massachusetts might be disgraced
by some sort of compliance with the Southern demands. Neither press nor pulpit had the least appreciation of the crisis, and it depended alone upon the
Abolitionists to make such resistance as they could to
this effort to destroy the sacred right of free discussion. Mr. Garrison and his friends promptly bestirred
themselves, and the scheme was defeated. The conduct of the chairman of the committee toward Dr.
Follen, William Goodell, and others, who appeared
before them to explain and defend the Abolitionists,
was so arbitary and insolent as to excite general indignation.

Mr. Lunt, in behalf of the committee, made a report,
in which he spoke of the demands of the South as " of
the most solemn and affecting character ; as appeals to
our justice as men, to our sympathies as brethren, to our
patriotism as citizens ; to the memory of the common

trials and perils of our ancestors and theirs ; to all the
better emotions of our nature ; to our respect for the
Constitution ; to our regard for the laws ; to our hope
for the security of all those blessings which the Union
and the Union only can preserve to us." The conduct
of the Abolitionists was pronounced "not only wrong
in policy, but erroneous in morals," and such as to
justify the censures that the Southern Legislatures had
bestowed upon them. And yet Mr. Lunt did not
venture to propose a compliance with the Southern
demand for penal enactments ; his courage was only
equal to the presentation of resolutions expressing
"entire disapprobation of the doctrines avowed and
the general measures pursued by such as agitate the
general question of slavery." But even this vicious
little mouse, which the Committee had brought forth
with so much and such painful labor, was laid on the
table, whence it fell into that bottomless limbo reserved
for things evil. The country members, though not
Abolitionists, had too much common-sense to follow
the advice of the Committee.

No person known to be an Abolitionist could travel
in those days at the South except at the peril of his
life. If any one was suspected, in view of circumstances ever so slight, to be an enemy of slavery, he
was sure to meet with some indignity. Meanwhile
Southerners could travel at the North, bring their
slaves with them, go where they listed, and denounce
Abolitionists as incendiaries and cut-throats at every
step, and no one thought of imposing any restriction
upon their liberty ! It was an offence against public
opinion to oppose slavery, but none whatever to apologize for it or defend it outright. Dr. Reuben Crandall (a brother of Prudence Crandall, the founder of
the Canterbury school for colored girls), a gentleman
of the highest character, went to Washington to teach
botany. On the 11th of August, 1835, he was arrested

28

and thrown into jail, on the charge of circulating incendiary publications, with a view to excite an insurrection of slaves. The evidence against him was, that some of his botanical specimens were wrapped in old copies of anti-slavery papers, which had probably been bought in the market as waste paper, and that he had lent an anti-slavery pamphlet to a white citizen. The passages read in court from these publications were no more inflammatory than many that may be found in the writings of Jefferson and Patrick Henry. The prosecuting attorney, however, made a desperate effort to secure his conviction, though without success. But his close confinement for a long time in a damp dungeon brought upon him a lingering consumption, which terminated his life in 1838.

Amos Dresser, a young theological student (a native of Berkshire County, Mass.), went to Nashville, Tenn., in the summer of 1835, to sell the "Cottage Bible." His crime was that he was a member of an anti-slavery society, and that he had some anti-slavery tracts in his trunk. For this he was flogged in the public square of the city, under the direction of a Vigilance Committee, composed of the most distinguished citizens, some of them prominent members of churches. He received twenty lashes on the bare back from a cowskin. On the previous Sunday he had received the bread and wine of the communion from the hands of one of the members of that Vigilance Committee! Another member of the Committee was a prominent Methodist, whose house was the resort of the preachers and bishops of his denomination.

In the latter part of 1835, Governor Gayle, of Alabama, demanded of the Governor of New York that Ransom G. Williams, publishing agent of the American Anti-Slavery Society, should be delivered up for trial under the laws of Alabama (a State in which he had never set his foot), on an indictment found

against him for publishing in "The Emancipator," of
New York, these two sentences :—

"God commands, and all nature cries out, that men
should not be held as property. The system of making
men property has plunged 2,250,000 of our fellow-countrymen into the deepest physical and moral degradation, and
they are every moment sinking deeper."

The land was ringing with the charge that the
Abolitionists were incendiaries, and engaged in
stirring up an insurrection of slaves; but the Grand
Jury of Tuscaloosa, with something less than a cart-
load of anti-slavery publications before it, cited the
above sentences as the worst, the most incendiary
that they could find. Read them again, and see how
false and hollow was the pretence that the Abolitionists brought themselves into difficulty by a reckless
use of harsh language! It was the *doctrine* of the
Abolitionists — the doctrine that slavery was a sin
against God and an outrage upon humanity, and that
immediate emancipation was therefore a duty — and
not the language in which that doctrine was presented,
that filled the South with madness. Dr. Channing
and others thought they could express their hostility
to slavery in terms so gentle and a spirit so calm, that
the South would welcome their soft rebukes; but they
found their mistake, and that the slaveholders, in
their wrath, made no discrimination in their favor.
Dr. Channing, though he criticised the Abolitionists
sharply, was just as intensely hated at the South as
Garrison himself, and the recipient of the same odious
epithets that were hurled at him.

XIII.

Persecution of James G. Birney — Press Destroyed — The Martyrdom of Lovejoy — Meeting in Faneuil Hall — Dr. Channing —
Wendell Phillips — Edmund Quincy.

I HAVE already alluded to Mr. James G. Birney's
conversion to the anti-slavery cause, to his emancipation of his slaves, and to his consecration of himself to
the work of freedom. The Abolitionists built large
hopes upon the accession of such a man to their ranks.
They argued therefrom the feasibility of their efforts to
convince slaveholders of the sinfulness of slavery and
persuade them to break the chains of their slaves; and
they felt sure that his example and eloquence would
have great weight at the North. They soon discovered, however, the truth of the prophet's words:
" Truth faileth, and he that departeth from evil
maketh himself a prey." The South broke out upon
Mr. Birney in a storm of wrath. His gentleness,
candor, and freedom from exaggeration counted for
nothing. Allied by birth and marriage to a large
circle of slaveholders, his name was at once cast out
by them as evil, and he could find no rest for the sole
of his foot in the State where he was born. The
Supreme Court of Alabama made haste to expunge
his name from the roll of attorneys entitled to practice
at the bar; and in the University of the State, of
which he had been a trustee, several literary societies,
which had elected him an honorary member, passed
resolutions of expulsion. In the face of all these
angry ebullitions he was not dismayed. He resolved
to establish a paper at Danville, Ky., and make open

war upon the slave system. On the 12th of July, 1835, the slaveholders of that place and its neighbor-hood held a public meeting and openly declared that the establishment of the proposed paper should be prevented, by violence if necessary. Mr. Birney thereupon determined to go to Cincinnati ; but he soon found that he could not safely set up his press there. He went to New Richmond, twenty miles above Cin-cinnati, on the Ohio, where Quaker influences were dominant, and from that place appeared the first num-bers of "The Philanthropist."

The new paper was well received, and Mr. Birney ere long ventured to remove it to Cincinnati. It had been published there only about three months, when at midnight, on the 12th of July, 1836, the office was visited by a mob which did much damage to the press and types. Handbills appeared on the streets, offering rewards for the arrest of Mr. Birney and his delivery in Kentucky as a fugitive from justice. On the 21st of July a public meeting was held, to see if the people of Cincinnati "will permit the publication or distribu-tion of abolition papers in this city." The postmaster of the city, a clergyman, presided. A committee of thirteen men of wealth and high social position, eight of them communicants in Christian churches, was ap-pointed to wait upon Mr. Birney and his associates and warn them that if the obnoxious paper were not dis-continued, the meeting would not be responsible for the consequences. At the head of this committee was Jacob Burnet, an ex-Senator of the United States, and ex-Judge of the Supreme Court of Ohio. The com-mittee met Mr. Birney and the Executive Committee of the Ohio Anti-Slavery Society, in a spirit of inso-lence worthy of the object it had in view. It would listen to no fair proposal on the part of the Abolition-ists. Judge Burnet declared that if the paper were not promptly suppressed, "a mob unusual in numbers, determined in purpose and desolating in its ravages," would be the consequence. Five thousand persons, he predicted, would engage in such a mob, and two-thirds of the property-holders of the city would join it. Mr. Birney and his friends felt that they could not yield to the demands of the committee without betraying a sacred trust and inflicting upon themselves an indelible disgrace. They must remain firm, at whatever hazard to their persons or their property. The threatened mob followed promptly. On the evening of August 1st, the rioters assembled, organized, and resolved to destroy the press and types of "The Philanthropist," and to warn the editor to leave the city within twenty-four hours. Under cover of darkness the office was pillaged, the types were thrown into the street, and the press was broken in pieces and thrown into the river. Mr. Birney, not long after these events, was appointed Secretary of the American Anti-Slavery Society, and "The Philanthropist" passed under the control of Dr. Gamaliel Bailey. Twice after this, however, its types and press were demolished; but ultimately the right of free speech was respected in Cincinnati. Mr. Birney served as Secretary of the National Society till the division of 1840, when he was nominated by the Liberty party as a candidate for President of the United States.

The tragic story of Elijah P. Lovejoy must next be told. He was a native of Maine and a graduate of Waterville College, in the class of 1826. He settled in St. Louis as a teacher, and for a time edited a political paper. In 1832 he resolved to enter the ministry, and after passing some time in the Theological Seminary at Princeton, was licensed to preach by the Presbytery of Philadelphia. Returning to St. Louis, he became the editor of a religious paper called "The Observer." He was not an Abolitionist in the full sense of the word, but was a friend of free discus-

sion, and some of his remarks on the subject of slavery
gave great offence to the people of St. Louis. He was
called to account for this exercise of his freedom in a
slaveholding community, but did not prove tractable.
In response to those who sought to curb him into
silence he reminded them that the blood in his veins
was kindred to that which flowed at Lexington and
Bunker Hill, and declared that his own should flow
like water before he would surrender the right of free
discussion. In the spring of 1836, a negro who had
killed an officer to avoid arrest, was taken out of jail
by a mob, chained to a tree and burned to death. An
attempt being made to punish the murderers, the judge
(appropriately named Lawless), in his charge to the
Grand Jury, laid down the doctrine that when a mob is
hurried by some "mysterious, metaphysical and almost
electric frenzy" to commit a deed of violence and
blood, the participators therein are absolved from guilt
and are not proper subjects of punishment. If the
jury should find that such was the fact in that case,
then, he said, "act not at all in the matter; the case
transcends your jurisdiction; it is beyond the reach of
human law." Mr. Lovejoy commented upon this infamous charge, and upon the crime it was intended to
screen from punishment, in the spirit of a freeman;
and for this his office was destroyed by a mob. He
determined to remove his paper to Alton, but his
press, on being landed there, was at once broken into
fragments. The citizens reimbursed him for his loss.
The pro-slavery party in Alton soon found occasion of
offence, and in the month of August, 1837, the office and
press were destroyed by a mob. Another press was
purchased, but before it could be set up it also was
broken in pieces and the fragments thrown into the
Mississippi.

In the midst of these events a convention to form a
State Anti-Slavery Society, which had been called to

meet at Upper Alton, was broken up by a pro-slavery
assemblage. Two days later, however, the convention
met in a private house and organized the contemplated
society. Among the resolutions adopted was one
declaring that "the cause of human rights, the liberty
of speech and of the press, imperatively demand that
the press of 'The Alton Observer' be re-established at
Alton with its present editor," and pledging the Society, with the aid of Alton friends and "by the help of
Almighty God," to take measures for its re-establishment. Among those who took an active part in this
convention, was the Rev. Dr. Edward Beecher, President of Illinois College, who drew up the preamble to
the Constitution of the Society, and also a bold and
comprehensive declaration of sentiments. The town
was in a fearful state of excitement. A colonization
meeting was held Oct. 31st, in which speeches, calculated if not designed to inflame the mobocratic spirit,
were made. Prominent among the speakers was the
Rev. Dr. Joel Parker, who, having in 1833 declared
himself in favor of immediate emancipation, afterwards
went to New Orleans to adapt the Gospel to the tastes
and desires of the traffickers in human flesh. A fit
person was he to appear on the scene at Alton, in this
fearful crisis, to lend a stimulus to the mob that was so
soon to imbrue its hands in the blood of Lovejoy.

At a public meeting, held Nov. 3d, to consider
whether the publication of "The Observer" should be
any longer permitted, Mr. Lovejoy made an eloquent
and powerful speech. "I am impelled," he said, "to
the course I have taken because I fear God. As I
shall answer to my God in the great day, I dare not
abandon my sentiments, or cease in all proper ways to
propagate them. I am fully aware of all the sacrifice
I make in here pledging myself to continue the contest to the last. I am commanded to forsake father
and mother, wife and children, for Jesus' sake; and

as His professed disciple, I stand pledged to do it. The time for fulfilling this pledge in my case, it seems to me, has come. Sir, I dare not flee away from Alton. Should I attempt it, I should feel that the angel of the Lord, with drawn sword, was pursuing me wherever I went. It is because I fear God that I am not afraid of all those who oppose me in this city. No, sir, the contest has come here, and here it must be finished. Before God and you all, I here pledge myself to continue it, if need be, till death; and if I fall, my grave shall be made in Alton."

This speech made a powerful impression, and for a moment it seemed possible if not probable that the mob might be foiled. Dr. Edward Beecher says he was never before so overcome with the powers of intellect and eloquence. "Many a hard face," he says, "did I see wet with tears as Mr. Lovejoy struck the chords of feeling to which God made the soul to respond. Even his bitter enemies wept. It reminded me of Paul before Festus, and of Luther at Worms." At the critical moment, when it was hoped that the liberty of speech would be vindicated, a Methodist preacher named John Hogan arose, and, in a violent, vindictive harangue, rekindled the mobocratic spirit and prepared the way for the tragedy that followed.

Mr. Lovejoy's new press arrived on the morning of Nov. 7th, and the news of its arrival was proclaimed to the mob by the blowing of horns. The mayor superintended its transfer to the warehouse and aided in storing it away. Great excitement prevailed during the day, but at nine o'clock in the evening, there being no sign of an assault, most of the defenders of the press retired, leaving a dozen persons or so, who were willing, if necessary, to risk their lives in defending the freedom of speech. An hour or two later, the mob, thirty or forty in number, issued from the grog-shops, prepared to do the work to which they had been

29

incited by the speeches of the Rev. Dr. Joel Parker and the Rev. John Hogan. The defenders of the press were armed, and resolved to do what they thought to be their duty. Mr. Lovejoy himself was among them. The mob threw stones at the building, broke windows and fired several shots. Then the cry went up, "Burn them out!" Ladders were obtained and preparations made to set the building on fire. The mayor came, with a justice of the peace, and they were sent into the building to propose the surrender of the press, on condition that its defenders should not be injured. The mayor told the owner of the warehouse that it was not in his power to protect the building. He reported to the rioters that their terms were rejected, whereupon they set up the cry, "Fire the building, and shoot every d——d Abolitionist as he leaves." The mob mounted the building and fired the roof. Five of the defenders rushed out of the warehouse, fired upon the mob and returned. Mr. Lovejoy and two others then stepped out, and were fired upon by rioters concealed behind a pile of lumber. Mr. Lovejoy received five balls, three of them in his breast. He lived long enough to return to the counting-room, where, after exclaiming, "I am shot! I am shot!" he almost instantly expired. After his death his friends offered to surrender, but the offer was refused. As they left the burning building they were fired upon, but no one was killed. The mob then rushed in, broke the press in pieces and threw them into the river. The next day the body of the martyr was buried by his friends, the infuriated mobocrats regarding the scene with manifest exultation. Alton, from that very day, went under a cloud, from which she did not emerge for years. Her prosperity was smitten with a moral blight. Her very name became repulsive. Emigrants of intelligence and character could not be attracted to a place whose citizens allowed a man to be ruthlessly murdered for daring to speak against slavery. The grave of the martyr, which was made upon a bluff overlooking the Mississippi, was unmarked for many years, but an appropriate monument now indicates the spot. For centuries to come, that monument, I venture to say, will attract more visitors than any other object that Alton will have to show. To the friends of liberty it will be a shrine, reminding them how much they owe to one noble man, who preferred to die rather than surrender the dearest right of an American citizen.

The Alton tragedy set everybody to discussing the slavery question. As a general rule, the newspapers condemned the mob, and criticised Mr. Lovejoy at the same time for his alleged imprudence. Here and there a pulpit spoke out bravely in condemnation of the outrage; but a larger number offered apologies for it, and made it an occasion for denouncing the Abolitionists. Dr. Channing was deeply moved, and at once proposed to hold a public meeting in Faneuil Hall of those who wished to condemn the outrage as it deserved. The first application for the hall was denied, on the ground that the resolutions and votes of the proposed meeting might be considered in other places "as the public voice of the city." This decision was certainly significant as to what was understood to be the real public sentiment of Boston in respect to the tragedy. Dr. Channing appealed from the decision of the Board of Aldermen to the people themselves, in a letter of such power that it admitted of no reasonable answer from the other side. A second application for the hall proved successful; and the proposed meeting was held on the 8th of December, 1837, — in the daytime, lest, if it should be held in the evening, Boston might once more try her hand at a mob. A large audience assembled. Hon. Jonathan Phillips, an eminent citizen, and a particular friend of

Dr. Channing, presided.   Dr. Channing made a calm
but most impressive address; after which, a series
of resolutions — written by him — temperately yet
strongly condemning the Alton outrage, and expressing a deep sense of the value and importance of the
unrestricted freedom of the press, was read by B. F.
Hallett.   George S. Hillard followed in an earnest
and able speech in support of the resolutions.   When
he had concluded, uprose (in the gallery) James T.
Austin, Attorney-General of the State and a member
of Dr. Channing's congregation, who, in a brazen
way, imposed himself upon the meeting to deliver a
most abusive and insulting speech.   He compared the
emancipation of slaves to turning loose the wild beasts
of a menagerie, and declared that Lovejoy had " died
as the fool dieth."   The Alton mob against the freedom
of the press was justified by a comparison therewith
of the destruction of the tea in Boston Harbor in
Revolutionary days.   The speech was as offensive in
manner as in matter.   The speaker probably hoped
that his utterances would create confusion and defeat
the object of the meeting.   If such was his expectation, he was doomed to a bitter disappointment.
When he took his seat, a young man — then unknown
to fame, but destined soon to achieve a reputation as
a public speaker second to that of no other in the land
or in the civilized world — stepped upon the rostrum.
It was Wendell Phillips, his brow still wet with the
dews of youth, the best blood of Boston in his veins,
the best culture of Harvard in his head, and his
tongue set aflame by the righteous indignation that
filled his breast.   Mr. Phillips, a few months before
this, had openly identified himself with the Abolitionists.   The trumpet-tones of Garrison had fallen upon
his ear and touched his ingenuous heart.   He had
spoken several times in small anti-slavery meetings,
charming all who heard him by his eloquence, grace,

and devotion ; but this was his first appearance before a large assembly. I had heard him once before myself, as a few others in that great meeting probably had, and my expectations were high ; but he transcended them all, and took the audience by storm. Never before, I venture to say, did the walls of the "Old Cradle of Liberty" echo to a finer strain of eloquence, or to more exalted and ennobling sentiments than those which then fell from the lips of the young orator of freedom. It was a speech to which not even the completest literal report could do justice ; for such a report could not bring the scene — the occasion and the manner of the speaker — vividly before the reader. It was before the days of phonography, and the reporter seems to me to have caught only a pale reflection of what fell from the speaker's lips ; but here is a portion of the exordium, as reported by B. F. Hallett, one of the best of the profession at that day : —

"Mr. Chairman, when I heard the gentleman (Mr. Austin) lay down principles which placed the rioters, incendiaries, and murderers of Alton, side by side with Otis and Hancock, with Quincy and Adams, I thought those pictured lips [pointing to the portraits in the hall] would have broken into voice to rebuke the recreant American, the slanderer of the dead. Sir, the gentleman said that he should sink into insignificance if he dared not gainsay the principles of the resolutions before this meeting. Sir, for the sentiments he has uttered on soil consecrated by the prayers of Puritans and the blood of patriots, the earth should have yawned and swallowed him up."

From this time till the close of the conflict Mr. Phillips, above all other men, was the orator of the anti-slavery cause. The announcement that he would speak, whether in city or country, was sure to attract a crowd ; and this not once or twice merely, but constantly, year after year. As a young member of the

bar, a brilliant career was open before him.   He had
but to keep steadily on in the traditional path, and he
might hope to win any honors that the old Commonwealth had to bestow.   But when he heard the cry of
suffering humanity, the voice of worldly ambition was
hushed; and he gave all his great powers to the work
of "delivering the needy, the poor also, and him that
had no helper."   Exalted natural endowments, the
ripest culture America could give, and social advantages of the highest order, all were made tributary to
an unpopular but righteous cause.   His example, in
this act of early self-consecration, and in the firmness
of his adherence to the principles embraced in his
early manhood, may be safely commended to the
young men of coming generations.   Perhaps no man,
save Mr. Garrison himself, did more than he to create
the public sentiment which opened the way to the
emancipation of the slaves; and never, surely, was
eloquence of the highest order consecrated to a nobler
cause.   Many of his friends will recall with pleasure
these humorously descriptive lines of James Russell
Lowell, written many years ago : —

> "There, with one hand behind his back,
> Stands Phillips, buttoned in a sack, —
> Our Attic orator, our Chatham;
> Old fogies, when he lightens at 'em,
> Shrivel like leaves; to him 'tis granted
> Always to say the word that's wanted,
> So that he seems but speaking clearer
> The tip-top thought of every hearer;
> Each flash his brooding heart lets fall
> Fires what's combustible in all,
> And sends the applauses bursting in
> Like an exploded magazine.
> His eloquence no frothy show,
> The gutter's street-polluted flow;
> No Mississippi's yellow flood,
> Whose shoalness can't be seen for mud;
> So simply clear, serenely deep,
> So silent, strong, its graceful sweep,
> None measures its unrippling force,
> Who has not striven to stem its course."

Another young man of Boston, and one bearing a name most honorably associated with American history from the earliest period, was led by the Alton tragedy to identify himself with the despised cause of abolition. I allude to Edmund Quincy, youngest son of Josiah Quincy, Sr., formerly a member of Congress from Boston, afterwards for several years mayor of the city, and later still president of Harvard University. Mr. Quincy was a graduate of Harvard, a young man of great intellectual ability, ripe culture, fine literary tastes, and unswerving rectitude of character. In a letter asking that his name might be enrolled as a member of the Massachusetts Anti-Slavery Society, he said : "I have deferred too long enrolling my name on the list of that noble army, which for seven years past has maintained the right, and gallantly defended the cause of our common humanity, undismayed by danger and undeterred by obloquy ; but I hope that in whatever fields yet remain to be fought you will find me in the thickest of the fray, at the side of our veteran chiefs, whether the warfare be directed against the open hostility of professed foes, or the more dangerous attacks of hollow friends." And well did he fulfil the promise conveyed in these words, though in doing so he incurred a measure of social obloquy which few others in our ranks were called to endure. Not once did he shirk any service for the cause which it was in his power to render. At the meeting called by the Massachusetts Anti-Slavery Society to commemorate the death of Lovejoy, he made his first anti-slavery speech, and a noble one it was, revealing a firm grasp of principles and a moral insight clear as the noonday sun. As a speaker, though impressive and forcible, he was not the equal of Phillips ; but as a writer upon the questions of the day, he was highly gifted. His name and presence as a presiding officer lent dignity to many of our meetings, and his contributions to

"The Liberator" and "National Anti-Slavery Standard," from the time that he entered our ranks to the
end of the conflict, were as important and valuable as
they were numerous.   It often fell to his lot to contribute editorial articles to "The Liberator," in the absence of the editor, and he was for twenty years or
more an editorial writer and correspondent of "The
Standard," which was established by the American
Anti-Slavery Society in New York in 1840, to replace
the "conveyed" "Emancipator," and which was continued, like "The Liberator," to the end of the conflict.   During a considerable part of this time he was
associated with James Russell Lowell, another man
who deserves honorable mention for consecrating his
fresh young manhood and his fine literary abilities to
the cause of the slave.   Some of his noblest poems
made their first appearance in "The Standard."   Mr.
Quincy's leaders, in their adaptation to the needs of
the hour, and in respect of their literary quality, were
equal to the very best to be found in any other journal ; while his letters from Boston — in "The Standard," under the signature of "D. Y.," and in "The
New York Tribune" under that of "Byles,"—for their
felicitous treatment of passing events as connected
with the anti-slavery cause, and for both playful and
caustic wit, were of the highest interest.   In the days
of Webster's apostacy and Boston's degradation as a
hunting-ground for fugitive slaves, Mr. Quincy was
our "Junius," and a great deal besides.   It would be
impossible to exaggerate the value to our cause of a
writer of such varied gifts.   I am certain that no
series of editorial essays, written for any other journal during the Rebellion, and dealing with its ever-
changing phases, would so well bear examination now
as those written by Mr. Quincy for "The Standard."
They were remarkable for soundness of judgment in
regard to past events, and equally so for that pre-

science which is a characteristic of the highest wisdom. Mr. Quincy lived to see the fruits of his self-sacrificing labors in the broken chains of the slaves, and in their transformation from chattels to citizens. It was my privilege to be intimately associated with him in the conduct of "The Standard" for many years, and were it needful, I could recall many illustrations of the nobility of his character and of his unreserved devotion to the cause. He was exceedingly modest, sometimes even shy, never seeking conspicuity or courting applause; but when the camp was beleaguered by foes, or in danger of betrayal by traitors within, his sagacity and courage were equal to the occasion. He hated meanness and treachery, whatever guise they assumed, and could set a hypocrite in the pillory with a skill that left him no chance of escape.

20

XIV.

Attitude of the Churches — Anti-Slavery Agitation among the
Methodists — Persecution of Abolitionists — The Wesleyan Secession — The Division of 1844 — The Methodist Church a Type
of Others — The Baptists — Orthodox Authorities — Old School
Covenanters — The Free Presbyterians — The Quakers.

IN not a few instances, in the preceding pages, I
have spoken of the hostility of the great religious denominations of the country to the anti-slavery movement, but there is need of a more distinct presentation
of this branch of my subject. I am the more convinced of this because, while some of my sketches
were passing through "The Tribune," complaints were
made in some quarters that my statements respecting
ministers and churches were unhistorical and false. I
shall, therefore, devote this chapter to the subject.
And I begin with the Methodist church, not only because it is one of the largest and most influential of
American sects; but because I have been charged by a
distinguished minister of that church with misrepresenting it.

The Methodist Episcopal church, in its earlier years,
set itself strongly against slavery, apparently with a
fixed determination not to be defiled by it; but long
before the anti-slavery movement began, its good resolutions had been forgotten, and it had surrendered
to the enemy. Its degeneracy began early. During
the Revolutionary period, the influence of Wesley on
the rising church was withdrawn, and "the infernal
spirit of slavery," as Bishop Asbury called it, gained
ascendancy over the "dear Zion;" the rules against

slavery were relaxed; the foul flood began to per-
colate the dikes erected by Wesley, and they were
at length practically swept away by its force. The
church, so far as respects its laity, became a slaveholding church, nursing at its bosom a system of oppression which Wesley truly stigmatized as " the vilest
that ever saw the sun." Whatever rules of discipline
unfavorable to the system still remained upon its
records, in the presence of this damning fact were as
worthless as the Ten Commandments would be if inscribed on the walls of a gambling den. They could
only serve to make the guilt of the church the more
conspicuous. And yet there are those at the present
day who point to these tattered remnants of laws contemned and violated, as proofs that the church, with
thousands of slaveholders in her bosom, holding scores
of thousands of slaves, buying and selling them at
pleasure, keeping them in ignorance and degradation,
and working them without wages under the lash, was
yet an anti-slavery church, with, in the language of
the Rev. Dr. Whedon, " a historic anti-slaveryism of
her own, of which she is not a little proud." It seems
to me that the pride which is built upon such a foundation must be of the sort that " goeth before destruction,"
indicating a " haughty spirit " that betokens " a fall."
Shame and confusion of face, and tears of contrition
would better befit a church in such circumstances.
The prodigal son did not seek to make his early but
broken resolutions of virtue a cover and excuse for
" wasting his substance in riotous living," nor talk with
" pride " of his " historic " merit. God's moral law,
let it be remembered, is the same for churches as for
individuals.

Slavery having once gained a foothold in the church,
its power was augmented with every passing year.
The period following the war of the Revolution was
marked by a laxity of morals on every hand, which

affected the Methodist church in common with others.
The country, weary with excitement, longed for repose, and was little inclined to enter into any moral
struggle. There was, moreover, a common feeling,
that the spirit of liberty, which had triumphed over
the tyranny of England and made the nation an independent republic, had gained such momentum, that,
without any special efforts on the part of the people,
it would of itself sweep slavery and other forms of
oppression entirely away. Then came the era of the
Constitution, with its sinful compromises, to work a
still further demoralization. The invention of the
cotton-gin, by augmenting the profits of slave labor,
deadened the conscience of the whole country to the
iniquity of slavery, and the testimonies against it at the
North grew feebler and feebler until they dwindled at
length, after the Missouri spasm in 1820, into almost
utter silence. The voice of Lundy was indeed heard
"crying in the wilderness," but heard by few outside of
the Quaker sect. But Garrison's trumpet-call, instinct with a living principle and an indomitable purpose, awoke the sleeping land. The Methodists in
New England were among the first to show signs of
sensibility and interest. They were but slightly affected by the conservatism that pervaded other sects in
that part of the country. They were a simple-minded
people, with deep religious convictions, and therefore
peculiarly susceptible to moral truths. Methodist
preachers began early to read " The Liberator," which
set them thinking not only about slavery, but about
the guilty connection of their own church therewith.
Wesley's denunciations of slavery were brought freshly
to mind, and a desire to do something for the purification of the church that he had founded sprang up among
both ministers and laymen. Methodist preachers here
and there sought Mr. Garrison's acquaintance, and began to testify against slavery in their own pulpits, and

to open them to the agents of the anti-slavery societies.

At the beginning of 1835, the columns of " Zion's
Herald " were opened to the discussion of the subject,
pro and *con*. The Rev. Orange Scott led off on the
anti-slavery side in a series of able articles, which
made a very powerful impression within and even beyond New England. He opposed the Colonization
scheme, denounced slavery as a sin, and vindicated the
doctrine and the duty of immediate emancipation. His
abolitionism, in short, was avowedly Garrisonian.
There was no disingenuous effort then to make it appear that the impulse to the discussion had been derived from Methodist traditions alone, and that nothing
was due to Mr. Garrison on that score. That folly
was reserved to be put forth by a Methodist divine in
1879, fourteen years after emancipation ! He pre-
sumes too far upon human forgetfulness and the uncer-
tainties of history in making such a claim. So far as
human foresight can discover, if Garrison had not
spoken, the Methodist church might have slept to this
day, as it had been sleeping for years, over the sin and
crime of slavery, sinking deeper and deeper into the
slough from which she was finally delivered, not by
her own inherent virtue or by the operation of her
discipline, but by the bloody desolations of a retribu-
tive war.

From this point the agitation of the slavery question
in the Methodist church went on, with various alterna-
tions, until the day of emancipation. It spread from
New England to the Middle States and to the West,
and stirred the South to impotent madness.

It does not lie within the scope of my work to trace
the history at length. Any one who wishes to do so
will find it set forth in " The History of American
Slavery and Methodism," by the Rev. Lucius C. Matlack, a new edition of which, I understand, will

shortly appear. The agitation was marked on the one
side by a brave and earnest advocacy of anti-slavery
principles, and on the other by a spirit of proscription
which has few parallels in modern ecclesiastical history. The central authority of the church was dominated by the Slave Power, and though it piled no
faggots and kindled no literal fires for its victims, it
was yet able to make the air around them hot with the
flames of persecution. Ecclesiastical chains and
thumbscrews were in requisition on every hand. Anti-
slavery ministers, who dared to preach or write against
slavery and in favor of immediate emancipation, were
marked for such forms of proscription as are still possible in the light of the nineteenth century. The
power which the Methodist discipline confers upon
bishops, and upon the presiding elders appointed by
them, and the moral and ecclesiastical weight of the
great General Conference, were employed to crush the
leaders of the anti-slavery agitation. Specious and
professedly affectionate appeals were first tried, and
when these failed, ecclesiastical stones hurtled in the
air. The Bible was appealed to for proof that slaveholding was an innocent practice, and the friends of
immediate emancipation were pelted with opprobrious
epithets. A New England bishop declared that "the
right to hold a slave is founded on this rule : 'Therefore, all things whatsoever ye would that men should
do unto you, do ye even so unto them.'" Dr. Wilbur
Fisk, the great leader of New England Methodism,
declared that "the general rule of Christianity not only
permits, but in supposable circumstances enjoins, a
continuance of the master's authority." "I have never
yet," said Bishop Soule, "advised the liberation of a
slave, and I think I never shall." "There is," said
the editor of "The Christian Advocate and Journal,"
"no express prohibition to Christians to hold slaves."
The Southern Conferences were allowed to pronounce

opinions favorable to slavery, and to fulminate their
hostility to the Abolitionists, in such language as their
vindictive temper might suggest; but when Northern
Conferences essayed to utter a testimony against
slavery and in favor of emancipation, the presiding
bishops refused to put the question to vote, claiming
it as their prerogative to decide what subjects, outside
of the prescribed disciplinary routine, should be acted
upon. The minions of the Slave Power on the floor of
Congress were no more arbitrary or insolent than these
bishops and their tools.

But it was all in vain. The agitation went on in
spite of the most desperate efforts to extinguish it;
indeed, as might have been expected, these efforts only
added to its intensity. The great body of the preachers in New England soon became Abolitionists, as did
those, if I mistake not, of some other Conferences.
Their leaders, Sunderland, Scott, Horton, Storrs, Lee,
Matlack and others, were powerful men, and they
fought a brave battle; but they could never carry the
main fortress of the enemy, commanded as it was by
the central powers of the church. Mr. Sunderland
established an anti-slavery paper, "Zion's Watchman,"
in New York, and conducted it for years, with great
ability, bringing upon himself a load of persecution,
social and ecclesiastical, that he found hard to bear.
" The result of this extensive series of proscriptions,"
says Mr. Matlack in his History, p. 296, "was soon
felt and manifested. It generated a loss of confidence
in the integrity of the prime ministers, who, in many
cases, were the prime movers of these measures. This
was associated with a decrease of attachment to the
church itself, while many desired to give a powerful
testimony against slavery that should be felt throughout the land. These things combined prepared the
way for the withdrawal from the Methodist Episcopal
Church, on the alleged ground that it was hopelessly

wedded to slavery, and could only be waked up to see
its true position by such decided action."

The Wesleyan Methodist Church, composed of six
thousand members, most of them seceders from the M.
E. Church, and seventy-five or eighty pastors, was
organized at Utica, N. Y., May 31, 1843. Its discipline condemned slavery as a sin. This movement
alarmed the old church. The new organization was
gaining rapidly in numbers, when the General Conference of the old church assembled in New York in May,
1844. The pro-slavery party, sobered by the secession
of so large a body of members, and apprehensive of
still further losses, began to think that discretion was
the better part of valor, and that it was best for
the old church to take some sort of action that would
have a tendency to stem the tide of anti-slavery secession. An occasion was furnished in the circumstance
that J. O. Andrew, one of the Southern Bishops, had
become a slaveholder by marriage. No instance of
this sort having occurred before, it was resolved by
the members to make a virtue of passing some form of
censure upon the bishop. It was hoped at first that
the Southern members, after all that their Northern
brethren had done to protect the system of slavery
from the assaults of the Abolitionists, would themselves
quietly consent to this action, which was necessary
to save the Northern wing of the church from further
disintegration.

But Southern Methodists were in no mood to submit
to this arrangement, merely for the purpose of enabling
their Northern brethren to say, " See ! we are opposed to
slavery ; have we not unfrocked a slaveholding bishop ?"
The Southern brethren, having for years received from
their Northern associates the comforting assurance that
slaveholding was no sin, but a practice sanctioned by
the Bible and not forbidden by the discipline, could
not understand why a censure should be passed upon

Bishop Andrew for doing only what the whole body of the Southern laity and many of the preachers had been permitted to do without objection for half a century. If "the right to hold a slave" was "founded upon the Golden Rule," as Bishop Hedding said it was, why should a bishop of the church be denounced for exercising that right? Had the lay members and preachers a monopoly of the rights conferred by the Golden Rule? If Bishop Andrew were pronounced a sinner for being a slaveholder, would not a stigma be fastened by implication upon every other slaveholder at the South? This was the logic of the case to the Southern members, and they felt that to yield what the Northern brethren demanded, on grounds of expediency, merely to help them out of a difficulty, would be nothing less than a surrender of the very citadel of slavery. They firmly refused to do as they were requested, and threatened to secede if their favorite bishop were censured. Having ruled the church so long, they were not inclined to give up the reins of authority now.

Here was a dread alternative for the Northern brethren. If they should let the slaveholding bishop pass without censure, the Wesleyans would devour their heritage; if they dared to censure him, they would drive out almost the whole body of Southern Methodists, to retain whom they had stooped in the past to every form of self-stultifying humiliation. In view of what they had said of slavery in previous years, they could not pretend to act upon any ground of principle, but only upon one of expediency, in censuring the bishop. The Baltimore Conference, either hoping that the more Southern conferences would not carry out their threats, or holding that a secession on that side would be the least of two evils, concluded to join the North in censuring the bishop, and so the measure was carried. The Southern conferences thereupon seceded. And now the church North proceeded to

exalt itself as an anti-slavery body, though slavery
still existed, exactly as before, in no less than eight of
its conferences, and though she had exerted all her
powers of persuasion to induce the whole church
South, with her thousands of lay slaveholders and her
hundreds of slaveholding preachers, to remain in full
fellowship with her. It strikes me that the refusal to
sanction in a single bishop what had for half a century
been freely allowed to tens of thousands of laymen
and multitudes of preachers, was a very narrow foundation on which to set up a claim for an anti-slavery
reputation ; but that was what the Methodist Episcopal
Church did after the Southerners withdrew. She did
not even trouble herself to make a single effort to free
the twenty thousand or more slaves still held within
her pale, nor call to account the slaveholding preachers
whose names still remained upon her rolls. And
to-day there are Methodists blind enough to claim that
the refusal to endorse a slaveholding bishop was an
adequate atonement for conniving with slavery for
scores of years, for all the apologies and defences
of the system woven from Scripture texts by bishops
and theological professors, for the desperate attempt
pursued for years to put down the anti-slavery agitation, and for the dreadful persecutions visited upon
Sunderland, Scott, and other faithful friends of the
slave !

Does any one ask why I have told this story of the
complicity of a great church with slavery? I answer :
Because I would pay a tribute of respect and admiration to the brave champions who fought the battles of
the slave against such tremendous odds, bearing reproach with meekness and patience ; because the anti-
slavery agitation in the Methodist Church was part of
the great movement that originated with Garrison ;
and finally, because the interests of truth require the
exposure, for the warning of men in all time to come,

of every such betrayal of the interests of humanity
and of the cause of Christ. I do not for a moment
imagine that Hedding and Fisk, and Olin and Bangs,
and their associates, had any love for slavery in itself
considered. What they desired was to build up a
great and united church. For this they were willing
to close their ears and steel their hearts to the cry of
suffering humanity, and to torture the Bible in the
interest of the slave-masters. Grant even that they
were pro-church rather than pro-slavery in their
hearts; this does not in the least diminish the heinous-
ness of their sin. For that sin the present generation
of Methodists is no otherwise responsible than as it
apologizes therefor and seeks to cover it up. The
only honorable course involves a frank acknowledgment of the sin of the fathers. The Divine declaration, "He that covereth his sins shall not prosper; but
whoso confesseth and forsaketh them shall have mercy,"
is as true of churches as it is of individuals. An apology might be framed for the politicians and parties
that "bent the knee to the dark spirit of slavery," on
the same ground upon which it is sought to excuse the
clergy and the churches for the same offence. Northern Whigs and Democrats did not love slavery for its
own sake; they only wished to preserve and augment
the strength of their parties. If they had seen a way
of doing this while fighting slavery, they might have
adopted it eagerly. But this view of the matter aggra-
vates rather than diminishes their inhumanity and
guilt. What worse indeed *could* we say of any man,
than that his love for his party overmasters his love
for humanity, and that his desire for the external prosperity of his church exceeds his solicitude for its
purity and his regard for the law of God?

I have said nothing specifically thus far of the Baptist denomination. If space permitted, however, I
could "a tale unfold" of the complicity of that branch

of the church with slavery, of heroic but unsuccessful
struggles to redeem it from blood-guiltiness, and of
opprobrium and persecution endured by noble men in
the prosecution of that work, in most respects parallel
with that which I have told concerning the Methodists.
Northern and Southern Baptist churches were in close
affiliation with each other; in the latter, slavery existed in its most odious form, and the whole power of
the denomination, from first to last, was exerted to
screen slaveholders and slaveholding churches from
censure. Some of the men who fought for freedom
and purity in this denomination with little success,
were Rev. Cyrus P. Grosvenor, Rev. Duncan Dunbar
and Rev. Elon Galusha. The Rev. Richard Furman,
of South Carolina, was the first president of the Tri-
ennial Convention in which Northern and Southern
Baptists met in fraternal union. After Mr. Furman's
death his estate was sold at auction, and was advertised in these terms: "A plantation or tract of land
on and in Wateree Swamp; .... a library of a
miscellaneous character, *chiefly theological;* 27 NE-
GROES, some of them very prime; 2 mules, 1 horse,
and an old wagon." Dr. Wayland, President of
Brown University, was the Coryphæus of the Baptist
denomination, and while, in his "Moral Philosophy,"
he pronounced slavery wrong, he could never be persuaded that the Baptist churches at the North ought to
do anything to abolish it, or that it was wrong for
them to be in religious fellowship with those who sold
human beings (perhaps Baptist Christians) at auction,
along with mules, horses and old wagons. In 1838,
when the consciences of Northern Christians were
beginning to be tender on this subject, he published a
book, "The Limitations of Human Responsibility," in
which, after wading through a great array of prelimi-
naries and drawing a great many fine distinctions on a
variety of subjects, he came to the one point which he

seems to have had in view at the start; viz., that the people of the North were in such relations with the South, constitutionally and otherwise, that they ought not to agitate the subject of slavery, and that it would be an act of bad faith for Congress to abolish slavery in the District of Columbia!

Making due allowance for differences of ecclesiastical organization, the Methodist and Baptist churches, in their relations to slavery, may be taken as types of all the other great denominations of the country. The Episcopalian, Presbyterian, Congregational, Unitarian and Universalist churches, with some differences as to method, location, etc., were essentially alike in spirit, in their firm resistance to the anti-slavery movement, and in their refusal or neglect to adopt any efficient measures for the overthrow of slavery. They were alike in exerting their ingenuity to evade the subject entirely; and when this was found to be impossible, they all alike made their action as feeble and meaningless as lay in their power. When public opinion compelled them, as it sometimes did, to take some sort of action that would *seem* to be anti-slavery, it was usually put in such a shape as to amount to little or nothing — in short, mere buncombe. Denunciations of the *system* of slavery, with mental reservations for individual slaveholding, were often put forth to deceive the unwary and as a sop for uneasy consciences. And when passably satisfactory resolutions were adopted, as they sometimes were, by local ecclesiastical bodies, they became worthless for lack of corresponding action. What would be thought of a great church that contented itself with adopting an occasional resolution of sympathy for the heathen, recognizing their need of the gospel, but which established no missions, sent forth no missionaries, and never took up a contribution for any missionary treasury? Would such a church have credit for sincerity? I trow not. And

now I ask what one of all the great churches in this
Christian country ever formed a purpose to overthrow
or assist in overthrowing slavery, and then proceeded
either to adopt measures of its own for that purpose,
or to assist in carrying out measures proposed by
others to that end?   In the days when African colonization was accepted at the North as a remedy for slavery, the churches (or many of them) used to take up
contributions in aid of the scheme ; but how often did
the anti-slavery movement, in any of its forms, have
the benefit of such aid?   Admit, for the sake of the
argument, that the churches had good reason for standing aloof from Garrison, was that a justifiable excuse
for doing nothing?   If others were seeking the abolition of slavery by unwise methods, or even making
their opposition to the system a cover for their hostility
to the churches, was it not all the more the duty of
the churches to array their whole moral power in support of some wise movement against that gigantic
national crime?   If the churches had any plan of their
own for the abolition of slavery, what was it?   If they
ever struck hands with each other to break the shackles
of the slaves, when was it?   That with one consent
they received slaveholders to their communion and
admitted them to their pulpits, contending the while
that holding slaves was perfectly compatible with Christianity, I know full well.   But in what way did they,
as organized bodies, bring the power of Christianity
to bear *against* slavery and its supporters?   Brave men
there were in all these folds, who struggled to bring
their several denominations to a sense of their responsibility, and lead them to take earnest anti-slavery
action.   These men were maligned and persecuted,
while the churches closed their ears to such entreaties,
and rushed on in their pro-slavery course.   And now
behold ! an effort is made, with some professedly anti-
slavery men assenting, to shield the churches behind

these very men, and to blot out a chapter of history
as disgraceful as any that can be found in ecclesiastical
annals.   The effort will be abortive — the ugly facts
will be proclaimed, for the instruction and warning of
men in all coming time.

There are men, who, when the truth on this subject is spoken, stand ready to say it is all a slander of
those who hate Christianity, at least in the " evangelical" meaning of the term.   It is important to unmask
these men, and show that not Garrisonian Abolitionists
alone, but men of the strictest orthodoxy have made
precisely the same allegations against the churches, on
account of their pro-slavery attitude and course, as
were made by Mr. Garrison.   For this purpose I cite
the following testimony : —

JAMES G. BIRNEY, *Presbyterian.*

The American churches are the bulwarks of American
slavery.

REV. MR. McLANE, *Mississippi.*
[In Presbyterian General Assembly at Buffalo.]

We have men in our churches who buy slaves, and work
them, because they can make more money by it than any
other way.   And the more of such men we have the better.
All who can, own slaves ; and those who cannot want to.

MR. STEWART, *Ruling Elder, of Illinois.*
[In General Assembly of 1835.]

Ministers of the gospel and doctors of divinity may engage in this unholy traffic [separating brothers and sisters,
husbands and wives, parents and children], and yet sustain
their high and holy calling.   Elders, ministers, and doctors
of divinity are with both hands engaged in the practice.

ALBERT BARNES, *Presbyterian.*

Let the time come when, in all the mighty denominations
of Christians, it can be announced that slavery has ceased
with them forever ; and let the voice from each denomination
be lifted up in kind, but firm and solemn testimony against

the system — with no "mealy" words; with no attempt at
apology; with no wish to blink it; with no effort to throw
the sacred shield of religion over so great an evil — and the
work is done. There is no public sentiment in this land —
there could be none created, that would resist the power of
such testimony. There is no power out of the church that
could sustain slavery an hour if it were not sustained in it.

These words of Mr. Barnes, mild as they are, justify, and more than justify, every accusation brought
against the American churches by Mr. Garrison, or
any one else in the anti-slavery ranks. Having the
power to strike the chains from the slaves at any time,
they not only refused to exercise that power, but did
what they could to hinder those who were working
with that end in view. They did not even emancipate
the slaves within their own pale, but continued to hold
them as long as they could, and until their shackles
were broken by war.

RALPH WARDLAW, *Scotland.*

So long as a church holds that slavery is authorized by
the scriptures, it is an anti-Christian church, and not a church
of Christ.

HON. WILLIAM JAY, *Episcopalian.*

The shocking insensibility of our churches, religious societies, and religious men to the iniquities of slavery, of course
involves them in gross inconsistencies, degrades the character of the gospel of Christ, and gives a mighty impulse to infidelity. . . From men like Paine and most of his followers the church has little to fear. But a new class of converts
to infidelity is springing up, men whose fearless and disinterested fidelity to truth, mercy and justice extort unwitting respect. These men reject the gospel, not because it rebukes
their vices, but because they are taught by certain of its
clergy, and the conduct of a multitude of its professors, that
it sanctions the most horrible cruelty and oppression, allowing
the rich and powerful forcibly to reduce the poor and helpless
to the condition of working animals, articles of commerce,

and to keep their posterity in ignorance and degradation to the end of time.

It is certainly no exaggerated statement, that not one sermon in a thousand delivered at the North contains the slightest allusion to the duties of Christians towards the colored population; while at the South multitudes of the clergy are as deeply involved in the iniquity of slavery as their hearers. It is no libel on the great body of our Northern clergy to say that, in regard to the wrongs of the colored people, instead of performing. the part of the good Samaritan, their highest merit consists in following the example of the priest and Levite in passing by on the other side without inflicting new injuries on their wounded brother.

What does the church? She declares from her lowest to her highest judicatories that slavery shall not be interfered with; that the system is legal — nay, even Scriptural — and that they who declare it an outrage against Republicanism and the Bible, are fanatics and incendiaries.

LEWIS TAPPAN— 1855.

The Abolitionists have not only to contend with the slave power, with a pro-slavery government, with ecclesiastical bodies and national societies in complicity with slavery, but with a large body of ministers, editors and church-members, in the free States, who style themselves anti-slavery people, and yet afford aid and countenance to the iniquitous system by their apologies, mystifications, glosses and misstatements.

ARTHUR TAPPAN — 1857.

We appear to be making no progress in enlisting the churches in favor of anti-slavery missions, or in bringing them to our views respecting fellowshipping slaveholders and slaveholding churches. What can we expect from the almost universal church in this country, that, even in the free States, grinds the face of the colored people with the denial of every, or nearly every, political and religious, civil and social privilege? Even here, in Orthodox Connecticut, they are driven to associate in separate churches, separate schools, and to lie in separate burying-grounds, and are ignored in all their civil rights as citizens, except that of paying taxes.

22

I could fill a hundred pages with citations not less emphatic than these, from scores of earnest evangelical men, against whom there was never a suspicion of heresy. I have taken these simply because they were close at hand. When anybody can exculpate the American clergy and churches from the above charges, he will have nothing further to do to sweep away as lies the accusations of Mr. Garrison and his associates. Until then let men cease their attempts to evade the issue by charging Abolitionists with enmity to evangelical religion.

I have already given the Freewill Baptists credit for their refusal to admit slaveholding churches to their communion. The Old School Covenanters also deserve mention for their firm and consistent opposition to slavery. Some of them heartily co-operated with the Garrisonians. The Rev. J. R. W. Sloane, then of New York, now of Allegheny, Penn., never hesitated to stand on our platform even when charges of infidelity were flying thickest about our heads. Moreover, it should not be forgotten that "The Free Presbyterian Church" was organized somewhere about 1850, by seceders from the two larger Presbyterian bodies, on account of their pro-slavery attitude. One of the leaders in this movement was the Rev. John Rankin of Ohio, who bore a faithful testimony against slavery even before the days of Mr. Garrison; another was the Rev. Arthur B. Bradford, of Enon Valley, Penn., one of the most faithful friends of freedom.

It has often been said that the Abolitionists did not recognize the anti-slavery work done by ministers and private Christians. This is a great mistake. Such men were always honored, and received on our platform with an eager welcome. We were too grateful for their help to neglect them. If men from the churches came in a half-hearted spirit, their mouths filled with apologies for their pro-slavery brethren, and with only hard words for the Abolitionists, and seeking to lower the standard in deference to the feelings and wishes of the apologists for slavery, they were stoutly resisted, of course. But no earnest Christian worker was ever repelled.

It is often said that Garrisonian Abolitionists singled out evangelical ministers and churches for censure, letting the liberals escape. There is not a shadow of truth in this accusation. I doubt if evangelical ministers and churches were ever once spoken of as a class distinct from others. Certainly there never was any occasion for such discrimination, for the liberal churches were as recreant as the evangelical, and our resolutions included them all alike. We did not even make the Quakers an exception, for they, in their associated capacity, were scarcely less delinquent than the rest. The ministers, elders and overseers were opposed to the anti-slavery agitation, and private members were often proscribed and sometimes disowned for their abolitionism. Many Quaker preachers were in the constant practice of alluding in their ministrations to the anti-slavery movement as organized "in the will of man," and therefore unworthy of the support of Friends; and the members of the body were exhorted to "keep in the quiet," to "mind their own business," and not mix themselves with the agitators of the day. One of the bitterest and most vehement pro-slavery preachers I ever heard was an eminent minister of the Society of Friends in New York. It was the monthly meeting dominated by this man that disowned the venerable Quaker, Isaac T. Hopper, the sweet-hearted Charles Marriott, and James S. Gibbons, the faithful friend of the slave, for nothing but their activity in the anti-slavery cause. Quaker meeting-houses were generally closed against anti-slavery lecturers.

Rev. Samuel J. May, in his "Recollections of the

Anti-Slavery Conflict," tells us that when, in 1835, at
the suggestion of some Friends, he went to Newport at
the time of the New England Yearly Meeting, in the
hope of finding some opportunity of presenting the
claims of the cause to the Quakers who were expected
to assemble there, he found that the leaders of the body
had hired every hall in the city to prevent him from
gaining a hearing; and they even attempted, though
unsuccessfully, to exclude him from one of the board-
ing-houses frequented by members of the sect.   During
the two years that I was the Secretary and General
Agent of the Rhode Island Anti-Slavery Society, there
was no influence working against the cause more insidious or potent than that of the Quakers.

When the facts illustrating the pro-slavery attitude
of the churches are presented as above, we are often
referred to the uprising of the clergy of New England
to resist the repeal of the Missouri Compromise, and to
what they did afterwards in support of the Republican
party, especially during the war.   Yes, thank God!
they *did* rally in that crisis, and I am not sure that
without their aid the country could have been saved.
For what they did at that time and afterwards let them
have the full measure of credit that is their due.   But
I insist that their activity then neither disproves what
I have said of their attitude during the twenty preceding years, nor furnishes any excuse for the course they
pursued during that period.   But for their indifference
to the wrongs of the slave, their apologies for slaveholding, or their guilty silence on the subject, the
Slave Power would probably not even have thought of
repealing the Missouri Compromise.   After the slaveholders had received for years from Northern professors of theology the comforting assurance that slaveholding was not a sin, and that the Abolitionists were
fanatics, meddling with what did not concern them,   .

and when they had observed that the great body of Christian men at the North apparently cared nothing for slavery in any way, what more natural than that they should conclude that the compact of 1820 could be annulled without more than a ripple of excitement? If the churches had been alive to the slavery question from 1830 to 1850, that compact would never have been annulled.

XV.

Activity of Women — Example of England and Virginia — Mrs
Mott in the Convention of 1833 — Female Societies — Sarah and
Angelina Grimké — Their Visit to New York — Their Labors in
Massachusetts — The "Brookfield Bull" — Whittier's Poem —
"Southside" Adams and Governor Wise.

ONE special sign of the rapid progress of the cause
from 1835 to 1838 was seen in the increasing activity
of women in its behalf. The reports current among
us of the mighty work which had been done by the
women of England, especially in the way of petitioning Parliament for the immediate emancipation of the
slaves of the West Indies, had awakened a deep interest and created no little enthusiasm. American
women were learning to imitate the example of their
sisters in Great Britain. Nor were they without an
example of a similar kind among the women of their own
country—even in Virginia! Many reproaches have
been heaped upon the anti-slavery women of the North
for forsaking their "appropriate sphere," but the credit
for originality in taking that dreadful step, so much
deplored by sentimental apologists of slavery, belongs
to the women of the Ancient Dominion. Honor to
whom honor is due. After the Southampton insurrection of 1831, at least two petitions from women
were presented in the Virginia House of Delegates.
One of these was from Augusta County, and signed
by three hundred and forty-three of the sex; the
other was "the memorial of the female citizens of
Fluvanna." Of the purport of the first of these petitions I have no knowledge, save that it was referred

to by Benjamin Watkins Leigh as being of an anti-slavery character. The second was a most eloquent appeal to the House of Delegates to devise a method for the abolition of slavery, the evils of which were most feelingly depicted by the petitioners. If the Legislature of Virginia had given heed to this appeal, and entered upon the work of abolition in friendly co-operation with the Abolitionists of the North, in what a different channel might have run the tides of American history!

In the Convention which formed the American Anti-Slavery Society a small number of women were in constant attendance, not as members, but as specta-tors. The names of three only of these have been preserved: Lucretia Mott, Esther Moore, and Lydia White—all Quakers, the first a minister of her sect in high standing. So broad and free was the spirit of the Convention, and so glad were its members of any manifestation of interest in the cause, that the pres-ence of these women was not felt to be an impropriety; and when Lucretia Mott arose to speak, as she did more than once, not one of the clerical members cried shame, or even remembered to throw at her a text from St. Paul. At first, when she seemed to be hesi-tating lest she should be deemed an intruder by some, the orthodox President, Rev. Beriah Green, was prompt to encourage her. "Go on, madam," he said, "we shall all be glad to hear you," and out of the Convention came other voices also, saying heartily, "Go on," "Go on." Thus welcomed, she did go on, and Mr. May says that "she made a more impressive and effective speech than any other that was made in the Convention, excepting only our President's closing address." She spoke repeatedly after this, and so pertinently that some of her suggestions upon topics before the Convention were adopted. Esther Moore and Lydia White also took part in the discussions.

When humanity is uppermost in the hearts of men, and a noble cause inspires their enthusiasm, how quickly prejudice melts away! If the propriety of woman's speaking in public had been introduced in that body as an abstract question, how many of the members would have been quick to cite the authority of Paul against the practice. But when the women themselves were actually present, and seeking an opportunity to speak for the enslaved, no one even thought of objecting. Near the close of the Convention a resolution was introduced and adopted in these words :—

" That the thanks of the Convention be presented to our female friends for the deep interest they have manifested in the cause of anti-slavery during the long and fatiguing session of this Convention."

And this is the way that " the woman question " was first introduced into the anti-slavery cause. "Ah," says some one, " but those women were not enrolled as members of the Convention; they only spoke, in an exceptional way, by sufferance." Very true ; but how is the principle involved in any way affected by the question of membership? Was not Paul's injunction to " keep silence " as binding upon spectators as upon members? I am quite sure that if Paul himself had been a member of the Convention — as he would have been very likely to be if he had been living in that generation—and had once looked into the face of Lucretia Mott, he would have been among the first to cry out, " Go on, madam, we shall all be glad to hear you." He would have been quick to perceive that his rule of " silence," however proper and necessary at the time and for the people among whom it was promulgated, would be an absurdity if applied to the women of America, and especially to such women as honored that Convention by their presence. St. Paul was no fool, whatever folly may be attributed to him by those who would like to use his words as a cudgel to beat back the friends of progress in their onward march. It is not too much to say that Lucretia Mott, who, as I write, still lives in revered old age, to make sweeter and purer, by her gracious presence, the moral atmosphere of the world, must be reckoned among those who have done the most to break the fetters of the American slaves. She was an Abolitionist in the days when, even in her own sect, the name was one of reproach, and when the rulers in the church would have been glad to silence her voice or cast her out of the synagogue. No more shining example of all the virtues that exalt womanhood, and make it a power for the redemption of the human race from ignorance and sin, can be found in the history of the world. The bigotry that would silence a voice so potent for good as hers, or presume to limit her "sphere" by any ancient rule or law, belongs rather to the middle ages than to the nineteenth century. It is not that she is or has been eloquent above many others, but that the simplest words spoken by her are endued with a power which CHARACTER alone can give to any human utterance.

The reader has already seen with what courage the Boston Female Anti-Slavery Society faced the mob of "gentlemen of property and standing" in 1835. Similar societies were formed in other cities and towns, and in May, 1837, a convention of anti-slavery women from the different States was held in New York. It was an object of scorn and ridicule on the part of the press, both secular and religious, but its members were too deeply in earnest in their work to care for that. When they thought of the degradation and helplessness of the slave women of the South, their hearts told them it was their duty to do what they could for their deliverance from so terrible a fate. They took counsel together as to the ways and means by which they might hope to succeed in arousing the women of the North to a sense of their responsibility for the crimes and woes of slavery. A stream of vulgar abuse was poured upon their heads, and their proceedings were shamefully perverted and travestied in the newspapers. I venture to say that during the ensuing three months more pulpits made that convention a subject for stinging reproach than were moved to utter a testimony against slavery itself. But what a change! The ground which the anti-slavery women won in face of such a' storm of missiles, and which they trod with bleeding feet, is now occupied by the women of the popular churches, who ride over it, four-in-hand, with the applause of the world ringing in their ears. No meetings now are more popular than those of women associated in missionary societies and in other agencies for benevolent work. They are not even aware of the toils and sacrifices by which the highway on which they travel with so much ease and pleasure was cast up for their use, and many of them will, no doubt, be ready to cast stones at those who shall presume to take any new step forward. But this is no ground for discouragement; it has been so from the beginning, and will be so doubtless to the end. Let the words of Lowell cheer us: —

> "Get but the Truth once uttered, and 'tis like
> A star new-born, that drops into its place,
> And which, once circling in its placid round,
> Not all the tumults of the earth can shake."

It was in the darkest hour of the movement, when many were fainting by the way, that two noble women from South Carolina came among us with words of hope and cheer. Sarah and Angelina Grimké, daughters of Judge John F. Grimké, and sisters of the late Thomas S. Grimké, of Charleston, who took so prominent a part in resisting the tide of Nullification in that State in 1831–32, left South Carolina because they

could no longer endure existence in an atmosphere
polluted by slavery, and because they desired to do
something to arouse the white women of the country
to a sense of their responsibility for the wrongs and
woes of their sisters in bondage. They had resided
in Philadelphia several years before " The Liberator "
first appeared. They had been brought up in the
Episcopal Church; but they found that church so
wedded to slavery, that they withdrew from it and
joined themselves to the Orthodox Quakers, among
whom Sarah, the elder of the two, became an approved
minister. In 1836 Angelina published a heart-moving
"Appeal to the Women of the South," on the subject
of slavery. The appearance of this pamphlet suggested to Mr. Wright, the Secretary of the American
Anti-Slavery Society, that the author and her sister
might do a great deal of good if they would consent
to come to New York, and address companies of women
in private houses, disclosing to them what they had
witnessed of the degrading influences of slavery in
their native State. They entered upon this work at
Mr. Wright's invitation, though at their own expense.
So much interest did they awaken that no parlor or
drawing-room could hold the crowds of women who
pressed to hear them. The Rev. Dr. Dunbar, the
Scotch pastor of the Baptist church in McDougal
Street, opened his lecture-room to them; and when
this in turn became too small, they spoke several times
in the church of the Rev. Henry G. Ludlow. Their
appearance was most impressive, and the revelations
they made of the wrongs and immoralities of slavery
produced a powerful effect. Angelina, in the words of
Lucy Stone, "had rare gifts. The eloquence which
is born of earnestness in a noble purpose gave her
anointed lips." She was then in her womanly prime,
handsome in person and graceful in manner, with a
musical and ringing voice, as penetrating as it was

pleasant.   In her simple Quaker garb, her intelligent
face lighted up with animation, as she stood before an
audience, she presented a most lovely picture of
womanhood.   She was entirely self-possessed, without a suggestion of masculine assurance, and mistress
of her facts and of all the questions to which they
were related.

As might have been expected, the appearance at the
North of these women, self-exiled from the land of
slavery, and devoting themselves to the work of creating sympathy for their sisters in bonds, caused no
little excitement.   The slaveholders were angry and
abusive, and so also were their Northern apologists.
But the Abolitionists regarded them with affection and
reverence for their works' sake, and indulged the
brightest hopes from the influence they were fitted to
exert.   When the Seventy agents of the American
Anti-Slavery Society gathered in New York for instruction, these women consented to meet with them and to
give them the benefit of their knowledge and experience
of the workings of slavery.   They also attended the
Women's Anti-Slavery Convention referred to above,
and took an active part in the proceedings.   Early in
1837 the Massachusetts Anti-Slavery Society invited
them to come and labor among the women of that
State.   Thither they went at the close of the New
York anniversaries, and spent nearly or quite a year.
They went from place to place, as the way opened before
them, speaking sometimes in private parlors, sometimes in vestries or halls, and occasionally in a church.
It mattered not whether the place were large or small,
it was sure to be overcrowded.   Women, as they returned from the meetings, gave glowing accounts of
what they had heard, and often expressed the wish that
their fathers, husbands and brothers might enjoy an
opportunity of listening to what affected them so
deeply.   The interest and curiosity awakened by

their labors increased so much that many men desired
to hear them. It was known that the ladies themselves had no objection to the presence of men in
their meetings. Quakers that they were, they had no
horror of addressing promiscuous assemblies. At
length the Rev. Amos A. Phelps, General Agent of
the Massachusetts Anti-Slavery Society, being in Lynn
at the time when they were speaking to a crowd of
women in the great Methodist church on the Common,
overcome by curiosity, forgot the injunction of Paul,
stepped inside the door with a friend and stayed till the
addresses were over. After this no effort was made
to exclude men from the meetings, and they flocked to
them in crowds. The efforts of Mr. Phelps to induce
a restoration of the rule, which he had been the first to
break, were ludicrous enough; but his Orthodox
brethren had been quick to add this to the list of his
sins in becoming an Abolitionist, and to charge the
anti-slavery movement with a tendency if not a design
to put woman out of her sphere and to disturb the
sacred foundations of social life. This added not a little to the burdens which Mr. Phelps had been required
to bear in becoming an Abolitionist, and which I am
glad to say he had borne firmly and bravely. He was
fitted by ability and culture for a high place in his denomination, and here was a fresh obstacle laid in his
path by his own hand. The women at that day, as in
the present, were the strongest allies of the clergy, and
in many things their main reliance. The ladies from
South Carolina were making a very deep impression
upon their sex wherever they went, and pro-slavery
ministers felt that some strong measures must be taken
to counteract their influence. I believe they were
more afraid of those two women than they would have
been of a dozen lecturers of the other sex.

When the General Association of Congregational
Ministers met that summer in West Brookfield, the

managers laid their heads together and came to the conclusion to make the usual Pastoral Letter the vehicle of an assault upon the obnoxious ladies as enticing women from their appropriate sphere and loosening the foundations of the family. The preparation of the document, whether by special appointment or the regular working of the ecclesiastical red-tape I know not, was assigned to the Rev. Dr. Nehemiah Adams, who afterwards, by his subserviency to the Slave Power, earned for himself the *sobriquet* of "Southside." He was the man just fitted to produce that combination of shallow sophistry with pious sentimentalism, in a letter to the churches, which the occasion required. The document opened the subject by referring to "perplexed and agitating subjects" (meaning the one subject of slavery), "which are now common amongst us," and then mildly suggested that they "should not be forced upon any church as matters for debate at the hazard of alienation and division." As the pro-slavery party was certain to create "alienation and division" in any church where slavery was discussed, this could only mean that the subject should not be introduced at all in any church. "We are compelled to mourn," said this Protestant encyclical, "over the loss of that deference to the pastoral office which no minister would arrogate, but which is at once a mark of Christian urbanity, and a uniform attendant of the full influence of religion upon the individual character." The churches were reminded of "the importance of maintaining that respect and deference to the pastoral office which is enjoined in the Scriptures, and which is essential to the best influence of the ministry on you and your children." "One way," said these "overseers," "in which this respect has been in some cases violated; is in encouraging lecturers or preachers on certain topics of reform (meaning slavery) to present their subjects within the parochial limits of settled pastors without their consent. Your minister is ordained of God to be your teacher, and is commissioned of God to feed the flock over which the Holy Ghost hath made him overseer. If there are certain topics upon which he does not preach with the frequency or in the manner that would please you, it is a violation of sacred and important rights to encourage a stranger to present them. Deference and subordination are essential to the happiness of society, and peculiarly so in the relation of a people to their pastor."

This is High Church Congregationalism in all its naked deformity. It is gravely assumed that every clergyman settled over a parish holds a commission from God, and is empowered by the Holy Ghost to determine what subjects shall be discussed, and what lecturers shall be permitted to open their mouths within the parochial limits; and the members of the churches are reminded that they cannot disregard this Divine arrangement without a "violation of the most sacred and important rights," nor without endangering the loss of their piety. "Obey them that have the rule over you, and *submit yourselves,*" said these parish popes, who, indifferent themselves to the wrongs of the slaves, would, if possible, have stopped the mouth of any other person whose humanity impelled him to remember those in bonds as bound with them.

In the next place, these lords over God's heritage call the attention of the churches to "the dangers which at present seem to threaten the female character with widespread and permanent injury." From what source did these dangers arise? Were these men, "commissioned of God" to rule the parishes of Massachusetts, alarmed by the fact that a vast body of women at the South were degraded to the level of chattelhood, bought and sold, like calves and pigs, at the pleasure of their owners; with no right or power to protect their own virtue, kept in the lowest ignorance and

degradation, and often compelled to toil in the field
under the lash of a brutal overseer? Were these men
awake at last to "the dangers that threatened the
female character" while these infamous crimes were
tolerated? Oh, no! Their tender sensibilities were
aroused by the appalling fact that two educated and
refined Christian women had come to Massachusetts
to expose these crimes, and to entreat their sisters to
do what they could to prevent them! In this terrible
phenomenon they saw ground for serious apprehension
lest the natural delicacy of womanhood should be impaired! Of course they were in favor of all proper
forms of activity on the part of woman. In "unobtrusive and private" ways she might exert a "softening
influence on man's opinions." She might teach in the
Sunday school, and "lead religious inquirers" to her
pro-slavery "pastor for instruction." But she must
not transcend the "modesty of her sex." "We cannot
but regret," the parish popes go on to say, "the mistaken conduct of those who encourage females to bear
an obtrusive and ostentatious part in measures of reform, and countenance any of the sex who so far forget themselves as to itinerate in the character of public
lecturers and teachers." "Itinerate!" how shocking!
If they would only settle over a parish, it would not
be so bad. "We especially deplore," said these nicely
scrupulous guardians of female purity, "the intimate
acquaintance and promiscuous conversation of females
with regard to things 'which ought not to be named,'
by which that delicacy which is the charm of domestic
life, and which constitutes the true influence of woman
in society, is consumed, and the way opened, as we
apprehend, for degeneracy and ruin." The unblushing
licentiousness of the slave system gave them not the
least concern; but that the iniquity should be exposed
to the women of Massachusetts, in such language as
refined Christian ladies know how to use, was more than

the tender sensibilities of these ministers, who claimed
to be commissioned of God and to speak in the name
of the Holy Ghost, could bear!

Strange as it now seems, scores of churches or
vestries that might otherwise have been opened to the
sisters Grimké were now rigidly closed. In some
instances men, and women too, who had acted with
the Abolitionists, bowed their necks under the yoke
imposed upon them by their pro-slavery pastors, and
thenceforth closed their ears to the cry of suffering
humanity. It was a compensation for this melancholy
blindness and subserviency to hear the ringing voice
of Whittier in lines worthy of the occasion:—

> "So this is all — the utmost reach
>   Of priestly power the mind to fetter!
> When laymen think, when women preach,
>   A 'war of words' — a 'Pastoral Letter!'
> Now, shame upon ye, parish Popes!
>   Was it thus with those, your predecessors,
> Who sealed with racks, and fire, and ropes
>   Their loving-kindness to transgressors?
>
> "A 'Pastoral Letter,' grave and dull!
>   Alas! in hoof and horns and features,
> How different is your Brookfield bull
>   From him who thunders from St. Peter's!
> Your pastoral rights and powers from harm,
>   Think ye, can words alone preserve them?
> Your wiser fathers taught the arm
>   And sword of temporal power to serve them.
>
>   .   .   .   .
>
> "Your fathers dealt not as ye deal
>   With 'non-professing' frantic teachers;
> They bored the tongue with red-hot steel,
>   And flayed the backs of 'female preachers.'
> Old Newbury, had her fields a tongue,
>   And Salem's streets could tell their story
> Of fainting woman dragged along,
>   Gashed by the whip, accursed and gory!
>
> "And will ye ask me why this taunt
>   Of memories sacred from the scorner?
> And why, with reckless hand, I plant
>   A nettle on the graves ye honor?

34

Not to reproach New England's dead
This record from the past I summon,
Of manhood to the scaffold led,
And suffering and heroic woman.

"No, for yourselves alone I turn
The pages of intolerance over,
That, in their spirit, dark and stern,
Ye haply may your own discover!
For, if ye claim the 'pastoral right'
To silence Freedom's voice of warning,
And from your precincts shut the light
Of Freedom's day around ye dawning;

"If, when an earthquake voice of power,
And signs in earth and heaven, are showing
That forth in its appointed hour
The Spirit of the Lord is going;
And, with that Spirit, Freedom's light
On kindred, tongue, and people breaking,
Whose slumbering millions, at the sight,
In glory and in strength are waking;

"When for the sighing of the poor,
And for the needy, God hath risen,
And chains are breaking, and a door
Is opening for the souls in prison;
If then ye would, with puny hands,
Arrest the very work of Heaven,
And bind anew the evil bands
Which God's right arm of power hath riven;

"What marvel that, in many a mind,
Those darker deeds of bigot madness
Are closely with your own combined,
Yet 'less in anger than in sadness'?
What marvel, if the people learn
To claim the right of free opinion?
What marvel, if at times they spurn
The ancient yoke of your dominion?
            .   .   .   .

"But ye, who scorn the thrilling tale
Of Carolina's high-souled daughters,
Which echoes here the mournful wail
Of sorrow from Edisto's waters,
Close while ye may the public ear,
With malice vex, with slander wound them;
The pure and good shall throng to hear,
And tried and manly hearts surround them.

"O, ever may the Power which led
Their way to such a fiery trial,
And strengthened womanhood to tread
The wine-press of such self-denial,
Be round them in an evil land,
With wisdom and with strength from heaven,
With Miriam's voice and Judith's hand,
And Deborah's song, for triumph given!

"And what are ye who strive with God
Against the ark of his salvation,
Moved by the breath of prayer abroad,
With blessings for a dying nation?
What, but the stubble and the hay
To perish, even as flax consuming,
With all that bars his glorious way,
Before the brightness of his coming?"

Whether the attempt of the leading Congregational clergy of Massachusetts, under a direct and most audacious assumption of power from God, to exclude from their parishes the light of heaven upon the guilt and danger of American slavery, was a less revolting crime against Liberty than the efforts of statesmen and politicians to put down the anti-slavery agitation by statutory enactments, or than the alliance of "gentlemen of property and standing" with the mobocratic elements of the country to effect the same object, let the reader judge for himself. And let it be remembered that, of the men who committed that crime, not one ever lost, on that account, his standing in his denomination. "Southside" Adams, the author of the "Pastoral Letter," though he served the cause of slavery with a willing mind until it was overthrown by war, was honored in his death as a saint "without spot or wrinkle," and that, too, by men of strong anti-slavery professions! The Rev. Dr. Nathan Lord, also, President of Dartmouth College, while enjoying the uninterrupted fellowship of his denomination, was permitted for twenty years or more to teach the young men under his care (New England boys, some of them candidates for the Christian ministry!) that "slavery

is an institution of God according to natural religion,"
and "a positive institution of revealed religion." If
he had swerved but a hair's-breadth from any doctrine
of the Orthodox scheme of theology, the churches
would speedily have found a way of ejecting him from
his chair; but as he only covered a great national crime
with the mantle of Christianity, he was left undisturbed
for a score of years as a teacher of practical atheism in
a New England college. The men who extended the
right hand of Christian fellowship to Doctors Adams
and Lord while they lived (taking no note of their pro-
slavery attitude and utterances as of any account), and
canonized them in death, made the air of New England
hot for years with denunciations of Garrison and
other faithful friends of the slave, as infidels! These
facts are wormwood and gall, but there is no bitterness
in my statement of them — only a feeble effort to set
them in their true light, that generations to come may
know amidst what darkness and against what odds the
Abolitionists of the United States fought their battle.

There is an incident in the career of "Southside"
Adams, which, as I shall not have occasion to refer to
him again, may as well be told here. It is certainly
too good to be lost. In 1854 he conceived the idea
that "the Northern antagonism to slavery" might be
"diverted into a mutual effort with the South to plan
for the good of the African race;" and thus "effectually supersede the present bitter abolition feeling and
measures." The pro-slavery divines, though intensely
opposed to immediate emancipation, often prated in a
vague way of their anxiety to do something "for the
good of the African race." The slaves, for all them,
might perish in their chains, but "the African race"
commanded their sympathy. Dr. Adams in meditating upon his scheme, was so fascinated that he resolved
to attempt its execution. He was sure that the dear
slaveholders, who had been so much abused by the

Abolitionists, would respond to his wishes most heartily; and so he sent to a number of them in different States a series of mild interrogatories, which he begged them to answer. Among the Southern men thus addressed, and whose aid Dr. Adams fondly hoped to secure in furtherance of his most benevolent scheme, was the Hon. Henry A. Wise, of Virginia. Mr. Wise replied in a letter which first met the eye of the Doctor in a public journal. It contained this passage, from which the spirit of the whole may be safely inferred :—

"What business have you to interest yourself about it [slavery]? Why take a thought about benefiting the race of my slave, more than about benefiting the race of my ox or my ass, or anything else that is mine?"

This was certainly a poser. What answer the Doctor made, if any, I know not; but if Mr. Wise had watched the course of the great body of the Northern clergy on the slavery question, he might with good reason have inferred that they cared as little for the slave as they did for the ox, or the ass, or any other of of the slaveholder's chattels. The Richmond "Enquirer" gave the Doctor this bit of instruction :—

"Mr. Adams's hope of handling slavery with silk gloves, and of bringing slaveholders to tolerate the mildest possible opposition to slavery, is a fallacy. Mr. Wise is as fierce on Mr. Adams as he is on Mr. Garrison; and that man must be a veritable verigreen who dreams of pleasing slaveholders, either in church or state, by any method but that of letting slavery alone."

And yet, after this snub, Dr. Adams went on with his "Southside View," and probably remained "a veritable verigreen" to the day of his death.

But "Carolina's high-souled daughters" found work enough to do in Massachusetts, in spite of the "Brook-

field Bull." There were churches and even ministers
in the State who did not acknowledge the Divine
jurisdiction of the " parish popes," and were not unwilling that women, possessing the proper qualifications, should plead the cause of the slave. The
proscribed women were heard in more than fifty cities
and towns, and did not once fail to make a powerful
moral impression. Angelina spoke several times in
the " Odeon," in Boston, to large and deeply interested
crowds, and in the spring she addressed a Committee
of the Massachusetts Legislature in the Representatives' Hall, having among her hearers many of the
most eminent citizens of the State, ladies as well as
gentlemen. Her public labors in the cause, and those
of her sister as well, ended with her marriage to
Theodore D. Weld in May, 1838. The elder sister
died some years since. Mrs. Weld's earthly life
closed only a few days before these pages were written. Her memory will be fondly cherished by all who
have any knowledge of her character or of the work
she did for the slave.

XVI.

The Woman Question — The New England Convention Admits Women — Mr. Garrison's "Heresies" — The Clerical Appeal — A Confession — Attempts to Narrow the Platform — Sectarian Assumptions — Whittier's Testimony — Catholicity of the Movement — The Peace Discussion and its Fruits — Attempt to Revolutionize the Massachusetts Society — A New Paper — "New Organization" — Mrs. Chapman's History, "Right and Wrong in Massachusetts."

THE events recorded in the preceding chapter set the Abolitionists of Massachusetts to thinking upon two subjects — the rights of women and the assumptions of divine authority on the part of the clergy — the first of these particularly. It was soon discovered that the constitutions of the anti-slavery societies admitted to membership "any person" who accepted their principles and contributed to their funds; and as, from the beginning, women had done much of the work of the societies, in circulating petitions, collecting funds, etc., their right to full membership, to vote and speak, if they wished, was generally regarded as unquestionable. Many excellent women, perceiving this, were more than willing to avail themselves of their constitutional rights. So strong did this sentiment become, that the New England Convention of 1838 adopted this resolution :—

" *Resolved*, That all persons present, or who may be present at subsequent meetings, whether men or women, who agree with us in sentiment on the subject of slavery, be invited to become members, and participate in the proceedings of the Convention."

It was adopted without a single negative vote. A very large number, if not a majority, of those who voted for it were persons holding evangelical senti- ments, who desired in this way to express their con- tempt for the "Brookfield Bull." Eight orthodox clergymen, however, immediately removed their names from the roll of the Convention, and eight others remained to protest against the introduction of a topic which they said was foreign to the platform. The majority, however, insisted that they had taken no action, and should take none, upon any question of woman's rights, except so far as to recognize her right of membership in the anti-slavery societies. They had simply acknowledged her to be a "person," within the meaning of that term as used in the anti-slavery con- stitutions, and resolved to treat her accordingly. The question, they insisted, had not been arbitrarily foisted upon the Convention; but had come up of itself, in the natural course of events, and it was a duty to decide it promptly and justly. When noble women wished to join our ranks, we could not beat them back in deference to conventional usages or sectarian preju- dices, which, in their nature, were evanescent. We simply left them free to act with greater or less public- ity, according to their own individual convictions. It was not for us to define their sphere; to do so would be a usurpation. We assumed that they were compe- tent to take care of themselves, and needed not that we should put them under any restrictions.

The local anti-slavery societies in Massachusetts quickly followed the example of the New England Convention, as the State society also did at its next meeting; and thus our movement there was put upon the broad ground of equal rights, without regard to sex. There was no desire or intention on the part of those who took this step to embarrass or annoy their stricter brethren; still less was there a purpose to drive them out of the ranks. We felt sure that, after the first excitement was over, they would be reconciled to so reasonable and inevitable a change, which we did not doubt would vindicate itself by the happiest results. But there is nothing more obstinate than prejudice, and, when fortified by a dash of temper, it does not readily yield to argument. The press was clamorous in its denunciation of the new "fanaticism," and the pro-slavery clergy attacked us on all hands as having openly repudiated the authority of the Scriptures, and cast contempt upon the Apostle Paul. They urged all this vehemently, in the hope of creating a division in our ranks, which they thought might prove fatal to our movement. Orthodox Abolitionists, and ministers especially, were harried worse than before, and charged by their brethren with lending aid to a movement tending directly to unsettle the foundations of social life, and disturb the faith of the young in the infallibility of the Bible. Great use was made of the fact that Mr. Garrison was no longer so orthodox as he had been. His views of the Sabbath, though in substantial accord with those of Luther and Calvin and many others of the orthodox school, were denounced as dangerous, while it was more than suspected that his views upon some other subjects were not such as would pass muster at Andover. True, they could not allege that he had ever introduced his peculiar religious opinions, whatever they might be, in anti-slavery meetings; but he did sometimes introduce them, incidentally, in "The Liberator," which, being his own property and the organ of no society, he did not confine exclusively to the discussion of slavery. Then there was his doctrine.of non-resistance, which was said to be turning the heads of many people, and unfitting them for political opposition to slavery. Then, again, an appeal was made to orthodox prejudices on the ground that some of the persons most prominent in the anti-slavery

35

ranks were Unitarians, while others had departed still
farther from "sound views." Members of orthodox
flocks were constantly warned of the danger of asso-
ciating with such men, and entreated to withdraw
themselves before making shipwreck of the faith.   In
some instances hints were thrown out that if Garrison
could only be put out of the way, the clergy would
take the lead in organizing a new anti-slavery movement, effectually guarded against the intrusion of men
of unsound opinions.

   No one who understands the force of religious prejudices and fears will wonder that some excellent people
in our ranks were much perplexed by all this clamor,
insomuch that they began to waver in their allegiance
to the cause as then organized.   Far be it from me to
impeach their motives.   It is no disgrace to a man to
love his church or to seek its peace and security when
he believes it to have been Divinely founded.   These
men were simply bewildered.   They did not comprehend the breadth of the anti-slavery platform, nor do
justice to the spirit and purposes of their more liberal
associates.   For the slave's sake they desired to secure
the co-operation of the great body of the church and
ministry in the anti-slavery cause, and to accomplish
so important an object it was right for them to take
any reasonable and honorable step.   But they had no
right to take up a false accusation against their associates and to turn their backs upon them, in order to
conciliate the favor of men who for years had rejected
and contemned the cause of the slave.

   In the summer of 1837, "The Liberator," in the
absence of its editor, was under my charge.   During
that time there came to Boston a Presbyterian clergyman from the South, who was reported to be a slaveholder and who was afterwards proved to be such, and
to have uttered, in the General Assembly of the Presbyterian Church, the most atrocious sentiments respect-

ing slavery. "The Liberator," after proper inquiries as to the facts in the case, alluded in appropriate terms to his admission as a preacher to Massachusetts pulpits, as illustrating the complicity of Northern churches with slavery. About the same time there were reports that Dr. Blagden, pastor of the "Old South" Church in Boston, who was known to be an ardent sympathizer with the South, was a slaveholder. "The Liberator" alluded to this fact also, and called for information. Forthwith appeared in a Boston paper an "Appeal of Clerical Abolitionists on Anti-Slavery Measures," signed by five Orthodox clergymen, two of them residing in Boston and three in the vicinity. The authors of the "Appeal," taking occasion from what had appeared in "The Liberator" respecting the two ministers above referred to, accused leading Abolitionists of "hasty, unsparing and almost ferocious denunciation of a certain gentleman, because he had resided in the South," without first ascertaining whether he was a slaveholder or not. They also accused "The Liberator" of making "hasty insinuations" respecting Dr. Blagden, of making various unreasonable demands of the clergy generally, and of denouncing Christian men because they were not prepared to endorse all our measures. With a single exception, the signers of this manifesto had not been in any way prominent as Abolitionists ; but as their accusations were an echo of what pro-slavery men had been saying for a long time, it made considerable stir. Curiously enough, its reputed author and first signer was a man whose habit of severity in discussing slavery was as notorious as it was offensive to the taste of his associates. That such a man was found posturing as an apostle of gentleness could only be accounted for on the supposition that he had volunteered or been selected to speak for others rather than for himself. The document was no doubt put forth in the expectation that it would prove a moral bombshell

of the largest dimensions, and bring upon Mr. Garrison
and the other persons marked for censure a weight of
condemnation that would force them to fall to the rear,
while the conservatives would march to the front with
colors flying, music from a full band and a general
fusillade of applause.   But its accusations were found
upon examination to rest upon so slight a basis of fact,
that the document fell flat from the press.   Mr. Garrison and the Rev. Amos A. Phelps, then the General
Agent of the Massachusetts Anti-Slavery Society, replied to it, not so much because in itself it needed an
answer, as because it offered an excellent opportunity
to show the unreasonableness of charges long and persistently brought against the Abolitionists from many
quarters.   The signers of the "Appeal" won no following, but fell into immediate obscurity.   Some
years afterwards, the author, in a letter to Mr. Garrison, confessed that he had done wrong.   "I feel," he
said, "bound in duty to say to you, that to gain the
good-will of man was the only object I had in view in
everything that I did relative to the 'Clerical Appeal.'
As I now look back upon it, in the light in which it has
of late been spread before my own mind (as I doubt
not by the Spirit of God), I can clearly see that in all
that matter I had no regard for the glory of God or
the good of man."   This is certainly an honorable
confession, and I am sure it won for the writer the
sympathy and respect of those who had been the subjects of his accusations.   Men so rarely honor themselves in this way, that the confession is worthy of permanent record as an example for others to follow.

It is not my purpose to revive the controversies of
that day in any spirit of partisanship, or to give needless pain to any one who took part in them.   My only
desire is, in the exercise of such impartiality as is possible to one who fought earnestly for principles which
he deemed equally sound and important, to make clear

to my readers the ground upon which Mr. Garrison and his friends actually stood and the difficulties with which they had to contend. Probably the fault was not wholly on one side. It would be strange indeed, if, in fighting such a battle for the freedom of the anti-slavery platform against foes within as well as foes without the camp, there were not some words spoken that call for the exercise of a generous charity. Without impeaching the motives of others, I may at least claim that Mr. Garrison and those who rallied around him as their leader, were moved by a sincere conviction that they were repelling a most mistaken and dangerous assault upon the integrity of the anti-slavery movement — an insidious effort to narrow its platform in conformity to the wishes of men, who, however sincerely they loved the cause, yet loved their sects far more.

It was one of the noblest, as it was one of the most conspicuous characteristics of the anti-slavery movement that it invited the co-operation of every friend of immediate emancipation, without distinction of sect, party, caste, or sex. A majority of its founders were no doubt Orthodox men, but they no more designed to make their orthodoxy a test of membership, or to repel any friend of the slave on account of his opinions upon other subjects, than they thought of rehabilitating the Inquisition. If it had been proposed in the National Convention of 1833 to set up any test in order to repel the approaches of men of the Liberal faith, or even to keep out unbelievers and infidels, I am sure the proposal would have been rejected, indignantly and vehemently, by the whole body. And if no one, in entering the society, was to be interrogated as to the orthodoxy or heterodoxy of his religious faith, then surely no one, after becoming a member, could be either excluded, proscribed, or arraigned on that account. What if Mr. Garrison had changed his

religious opinions, or even avowed himself an infidel?
In doing so he would have committed no offence for
which he could be arraigned on the anti-slavery platform, and so long as he was true to the slave, and
refrained from intruding his opinions on other subjects
upon his fellow-laborers when engaged in anti-slavery
work, there could be no ground of complaint against
him.

Now I am prepared to affirm that in no single instance did Mr. Garrison ever violate the catholicity of
the platform. When he was Orthodox, he never obtruded his orthodoxy upon his Liberal associates; and
he was, if possible, still more careful to observe the same
law of propriety and good faith after his religious opinions changed. He only claimed for himself the liberty
which he cheerfully accorded to others. If a Presbyterian joined the society, he was not supposed to put himself under any restriction as to propagating Presbyterian
opinions anywhere outside of anti-slavery meetings.
If he were a preacher, he was not expected to abandon
his pulpit; if he were an editor, he might in his own
columns mix Abolitionism and Presbyterianism in such
proportions as suited his own judgment. Why, then,
should it have been deemed an offence in Mr. Garrison,
if, in his own paper, for which no anti-slavery society
was responsible, he chose to discuss the question of
non-resistance, the rights of woman, the proper observance of Sunday, or any question of theology in
which he happened to feel an interest? As a matter
of fact, there was comparatively little in regard to
such topics in "The Liberator"—perhaps two columns
or so weekly to twenty devoted to the anti-slavery
cause. But Mr. Garrison would never consent to be
gagged in his own paper. When an Orthodox editor,
without prejudice to his anti-slavery standing, could
print twenty columns of orthodoxy to two of Abolitionism, Mr. Garrison was not able to see what ground

of objection there was to *his* printing his Abolitionism
along with his religious views, in inverse proportions.
Nor could he understand why a man of liberal opinions,
standing on the anti-slavery platform, should be required to wear a strait-jacket, or hold himself under
ban, while an Orthodox man was at perfect liberty to
saturate his speech or his prayer through and through
with his religious opinions. John G. Whittier, in
some remarks suggested by the "Clerical Appeal," put
this point very clearly. "How often," he says, "has
the Unitarian Abolitionist heard from the lips of anti-
slavery lecturers the doctrine of the Trinity advanced,
as if no one ever called it in question? How often has
the Quaker listened to the declaration, from the same
source, that without the Bible the slaves must *necessarily* die unvisited of God, and candidates for the
prison-house of eternal despair? How often have the
Unitarian and the Restorationist been told that the
slave and his master are both going down to that everlasting perdition, a belief in which they consider un-
scriptural and absurd? Have *they* no right to complain? Who edits the 'Anti-Slavery Magazine,'
'Record,' and 'Human Rights'? A Presbyterian,
Trinitarian and Sabbatarian, who believes that a saving
knowledge of God can only be derived from the Holy
Scriptures. Who edits 'The Emancipator'? Joshua
Leavitt, a Presbyterian clergyman, who, in spite of
himself, occasionally 'sifts in' some of his peculiar
views and doctrines. Yet these papers are the official,
accredited organs of a Society made up of all denominations. . . . Each one who differs from the Cal-
vinistic creed has as good and substantial reasons for
offering his appeal or protest as the five gentlemen
who have taken offence at 'The Liberator.'" Orthodox men, as lecturers or speakers, were never expected to put themselves under any particular restraint.
They were not asked to divest themselves of their

Orthodox harness and talk like Unitarians. No offence
was taken if they employed an Orthodox phraseology
in describing the sin of slavery and its consequences,
or if they sometimes appealed to motives the force of
which could be felt only by those of the Orthodox faith.
If an Orthodox man opened a meeting with prayer, no
Liberal objected if, according to habit, he closed with
an ascription to the Trinity. But some of the Orthodox brethren, while themselves exercising this unrestricted liberty, were often exceedingly critical of the
speech of men of Liberal opinions, taking offence if
there was anything in what they said that did not
accord with the Orthodox theology.

Against this sectarian spirit, which seemed at times
bent upon either subordinating the anti-slavery movement to the evangelical churches, or breaking it up
altogether, Mr. Garrison contended with might and
main, deeming it contrary to the genius as well as to
the fundamental principles of the organization, and
seeing very clearly that its effects upon the cause could
only be disastrous. If Episcopalians, Presbyterians,
Baptists, Methodists, Unitarians, Universalists, unbelievers, Whigs and Democrats, could combine
together to build railroads, dig canals, erect manufac-
tories, and promote all sorts of schemes for money-
making, without so much as thinking of their religious
and political differences, why should not members of the
same sects and parties join in a common movement for
the overthrow of the execrable system of slavery?
Why, with such a gigantic crime against humanity
confronting them, and demanding their utmost efforts
for its suppression, should they haggle with one another for precedence, or thrust their sectarian notions
forward as conditions of united action?

Mr. Garrison's appeals for the catholicity of the
platform rang out clearly from every issue of "The
Liberator," and, throbbing as they did with the spirit

of humanity, they drew to his side a large majority of the anti-slavery host, who were inspired by the purpose to be true to the principle so clearly enunciated. A majority even of the Orthodox friends of the slave rallied around him, indignantly repelling the accusations of his enemies, and maintaining his right, in common with others, to hold such opinions and discuss such subjects, outside of the anti-slavery meetings, as he pleased.

When the news of the Alton tragedy reached Boston, Mr. Garrison expressed his sorrow in view of the fact that Mr. Lovejoy had died with arms in his hands. "We cannot in conscience," he said, "delay the expression of our regret that our martyred coadjutor and his unfaltering friends in Alton should have allowed any provocation, or personal danger, or hope of victory, or distrust of the protection of Heaven, to drive them to take up arms in self-defence. Far be it from us to reproach our suffering brethren, or weaken the impression of sympathy which has been made on their behalf in the minds of the people. God forbid. Yet, in the name of Jesus of Nazareth, who suffered himself to be unresistingly nailed to the cross, we solemnly protest against any of his professed followers resorting to carnal weapons, under any pretext, or in any extremity whatever."

Many who were not themselves Non-resistants felt deep regret on account of Mr. Lovejoy's course, being seriously apprehensive that it would tend to lower the tone of the movement and lead ultimately to a bloody conflict. In the face of all the attempts to put the Abolitionists down by force, it had been of great advantage to them to refer to the principles of peace incorporated in their "Magna Charta;" but now it was feared that the contest would assume another and a less noble shape. Mr. Lewis Tappan was anxious to have the subject discussed. "I was much gratified,"

he said, in a letter to Mr. Garrison, "with your remarks respecting the mode in which our brother
Lovejoy met death.   Is it not now a very suitable time
to discuss, in 'The Liberator,' the Peace question fully?
It can be done without offending any of your readers ;
and I believe Abolitionists generally, on both sides of
the question, and those who think they are at present
on neither side, would rejoice to see the arguments,
for and against, on the Peace question."

And yet, for following this excellent advice, Mr.
Garrison was arraigned by some of his associates upon
the charge of intruding "a foreign topic" into his
paper; and when, in 1838, the discussion bore fruit
in the organization of "The New England Non-Resistance Society," a storm burst upon his head as surprising as it was fierce.   It was insisted by many that he
was no longer entitled to a place on the anti-slavery
platform, or that, at least, he should take a back seat.
Non-resistance was held to be a disqualification for the
complete discharge of the duties of an Abolitionist.
James G. Birney so far forgot himself as to say of those
who felt it a duty to "love their enemies," that "it
would seem that the duty of withdrawing from the
Anti-Slavery Society was altogether plain.   Justice to
those with whom they are associated, and to the slave,
requires it."   Strange language this to be applied,
among others, to the founder of the anti-slavery movement!

A plan was set on foot by certain men to rally a
party at the annual meeting of the Massachusetts
Society, in 1839, vote down Mr. Garrison's Annual
Report, turn him and his friends out of office, and put
the society under other management.   Such, at least,
was the report that came to Mr. Garrison and others,
and to which they gave credit.   It is only fair to say,
however, that some of those who were implicated by
the report denied its truth.   A great excitement fol-

lowed, "The Liberator" sounded an alarm, and the meeting was very largely attended. Whatever may have been the truth in respect to the alleged design, by a secret movement, to revolutionize the society, a party hostile to Mr. Garrison and "The Liberator" was found to be present. His non-resistance views were made a ground of attack, and it was urged that a new anti-slavery paper was needed in Massachusetts, which should confine itself strictly to the question of slavery. The discussion occupied the whole of the first day, and the meeting did not reach a vote until nearly midnight. The result of the vote was over-whelming in Mr. Garrison's favor. The defeated party, however, a short time afterwards, established a new paper, — "The Massachusetts Abolitionist," — of which Mr. Elizur Wright became the editor. A little later, the Rev. Amos A. Phelps resigned his place as one of the board of managers of the Massachusetts Society, alleging, as his reason for that step, that "the society is no longer an anti-slavery society simply, but, in its principles and modes of action, a woman's rights, non-government anti-slavery society." This change of front on the part of Mr. Phelps, who had been so prompt to condemn the "Clerical Appeal," was a great disappointment to many, — to no one more than to myself, for I had placed the highest confidence in his clear-sightedness as well as his integrity. I lamented his course quite as much for his own sake as for that of the cause, for I felt sure that he was preparing for his own lips a cup of bitter disappointment.

Thus a nucleus for an anti-Garrison abolition move-ment in Massachusetts was established. Mr. Phelps and some other Orthodox Abolitionists seemed to have got it into their heads that there was a great body of evangelical men ready to espouse the cause the mo-ment they should see an anti-slavery organization which they could join without — to use one of the.

phrases of the time — "swallowing Garrison." Of
course, therefore, there must be a new society; and,
accordingly, the "Massachusetts *Abolition* Society"
was organized in Boston, in May, 1839. After the
organization had been completed, the Rev. George
Trask, one of its members, came into the New England Anti-Slavery Convention and made a speech, in
which he said: "Sir, we want the men of influence in
our ranks. It is in vain that you attempt to carry
on any cause in this country without them. We want
the Honorables, the D. D.s, the Rabbis of the land.
Now, our new organization will get them. They will
come to us, and we shall give them offices. Sir, they
won't come unless we give them offices." Mr. Trask
had not, on his own account, a particle of hostility to
Mr. Garrison; but he was full of the notion that "the
men of influence," whom the editor of "The Liberator"
repelled, would join a society of which he was not the
leader. How mistaken he and his associates were was
soon made apparent. The new society did not, I
verily believe, draw to itself so much as one of the
men whose co-operation was thought to be so desirable
and important. Their real hostility to Garrison, as
the result showed, was inspired far less by any objection they felt to his religious opinions than by their
bitter opposition to his uncompromising Abolitionism.
The new society had but a short and feeble existence;
and "The Massachusetts Abolitionist," which was to
supersede "The Liberator," and bring the grumbling
sectarians over to the cause in troops, under a new
leadership, lasted but a few years, when it took the
less obnoxious name of "Free American," and soon
afterwards went out of sight. "The Liberator" and
the Massachusetts Anti-Slavery Society, on the contrary, continued in the field till liberty was proclaimed
"throughout the land, to all the inhabitants thereof."
Such is the story, in brief, of "New Organization"

in Massachusetts. Those who wish to see that history
in all its lights and shades are referred to Mrs. Maria
W. Chapman's admirable *brochure*, "Right and Wrong
in Massachusetts," and to the papers of the day, especially "The Liberator" and "The Massachusetts
Abolitionist." A considerable number of excellent,
well-intentioned people were no doubt engaged in
the movement, but it had its root in a most unreasonable distrust of Mr. Garrison, and in an utter miscon-
ception of the grounds upon which the clergy and the
churches opposed him. So far as the latter were concerned, it was a case of false pretences, pure and
simple, as their behavior afterwards abundantly de-
monstrated.

XVII.

The American Society in 1839 Admits Women — Strong Protest
Against the Measure — Scheme for Rescinding the Action in
1840 — Struggle of the Two Parties — Transfer of "The Emancipator" — A Steamboat Excursion — The Admission of Women
Confirmed — A Woman on the Business Committee — A New
National Society — Its History — Its Decease — American Missionary Association — The Old Society — "National Anti-Slavery
Standard" and its Editors — Garrison's Tribute to Arthur Tappan — John A. Collins — N. P. Rogers — Abby Kelley.

IN 1839 the American Anti-Slavery Society, after a
long and somewhat unpleasant discussion, decided to
interpret the word "person" in its constitution as
including women as well as men. The vote stood —
yeas, 180; nays, 140. The nays, it will be observed,
were much more numerous in New York than they
had been in Boston, showing that the influence of
"Carolina's high-souled daughters" had been more
potent in Massachusetts than elsewhere — perhaps
because there an attempt had been made to silence
them by an ecclesiastical bull. The act, it was understood, was not favorably regarded by the Executive Committee; but in an address to the public they
said: "The vote of the Society, being grounded on the
phraseology of its constitution, cannot be justly regarded as committing the Society in favor of any con-
troverted principle respecting the rights of women to
participate in public affairs." This was exactly what
the friends of the measure had said in the discussion;
while the opponents had sought to defeat it upon the
assumption that its passage would commit the Society

to the doctrines of woman's rights, in all their length and breadth. Dr. Leavitt, in "The Emancipator," not only endorsed what the Executive Committee had said, but went further in the remark that "a contrary decision, unsupported by the constitution, would have been taking sides on a question respecting which the Society is bound to entire neutrality." In view of these expressions of opinion at headquarters, those who voted in the majority hoped that there would be no further controversy on the subject, and that the minority, while doubtful of the wisdom of the course that had been taken, would cheerfully acquiesce in the decision.

As the year went on, however, it became more and more manifest that the Executive Committee of the Parent Society sympathized with the new organization rather than with its old and faithful auxiliary in Massachusetts. There was a strong suspicion among the friends of the latter that the committee in New York was hardly acting in good faith toward the society from which it had received its appointment, and that it was actually playing into the hands of the new organization, in the hope of being able, at the next meeting, to reverse the action upon the woman question, and put the whole movement into a hostile attitude toward its founder. I do not affirm that this suspicion was just; I only say it was entertained upon grounds that were thought to be tenable. The friends of the old organization, therefore, were in an anxious frame of mind during that whole year. As the time of the anniversary of 1840 drew near, information was received in Boston that confirmed them in their belief that a plan was on foot to capture the National Society in the interest of the new organization. We were assured that private circulars had been issued for the purpose of securing a large attendance of those who were supposed to be friendly to such a scheme, and that measures had been taken to enlist the support of large

numbers of Abolitionists in New York and its immediate vicinity.   Again let me say I do not affirm that
these reports were true ; I only affirm that they were
honestly believed to be so.   Then, just three weeks
before the annual meeting, came the sudden announcement that " The Emancipator," the weekly organ of the
society, had been transferred — professedly for lack of
funds to maintain it longer, and for that reason only —
to the New York City Anti-Slavery Society, upon the
condition that it should be continued under the editorship of the Rev. Joshua Leavitt.   As the paper was
the property of the society, and had been published at
its expense for years, this was regarded as an act of
bad faith, designed to keep the paper out of the hands
of its rightful owners, in case the scheme for revolu-
tionizing the society should miscarry.   Hot words
were used to characterize the act, and the friends of
the old organization never saw any reason for withdrawing them.   It was felt that if the Executive Committee were really unable to publish the paper for three
weeks, until the society could have an opportunity to
decide for itself what disposition to make of it, the
only honorable course to take was to suspend it for
that brief period.   I do not now impeach the motives
of the committee ; I only say, upon compulsion, as one
bound to speak the truth, that they *were* impeached at
the time, and that the committee defended themselves
warmly.   Those who wish to enter into the full merits
of the question are referred to the anti-slavery papers
of that day.   I will state, however, first, that those
concerned in the transaction stoutly denied, during the
controversy which it provoked, that their motive for
making the transfer was either partly or wholly to keep
it out of the hands of Mr. Garrison and his friends.
At any rate, they put forth another reason as the only
one existing.   Secondly, Mr. Lewis Tappan, who had
participated in the transaction, writing seven years

afterwards to Miss Maria Waring, an English lady, used these exact words : " The paper was transferred, *not* alone on account of the pecuniary difficulties of the society, but *because the Executive Committee did not wish to continue it themselves, or leave it in the hands of their successors of different principles.*" If this avowal had been frankly made at the time, there would have been no difference of opinion among impartial men as to the character of the transaction.

Under the circumstances above described, the friends of the old organization in Massachusetts felt compelled to take some efficient measures to defeat what *they* thought an unworthy plot to change the whole character of the anti-slavery movement and place it upon a sectarian basis. What they did was to charter a steamer, to take from Providence to New York as large a number of delegates as might choose to attend. They put the fare at a low rate, and sent out a rallying-cry through " The Liberator " to all who desired to keep the good ship Anti-Slavery on her right course.

The call was promptly responded to. Over four hundred delegates, many of them women, went to New York in the steamer " Rhode Island," prepared to do what they could to preserve the integrity of the anti-slavery movement. A happier crowd I never saw, and surely a more respectable body of people never went on board a ship. They were all animated by what they regarded as a high and noble purpose. They were of one heart and one mind, of " one accord in one place." Songs and speeches filled up the evening hours until the time for sleep, when such as were fortunate enough to obtain berths retired for the night. Those less fortunate appropriated to themselves such portions of the steamer's floors, in cabin or on deck, as they found available. There are some people, with memories better than mine, who could tell some very

17

amusing stories of that passage through the Sound, and of the entertainment provided, or *not* provided, for them upon their arrival in New York. Truth to say, the fun of the occasion was mixed with some serious annoyances, of which I shall not pretend to give an account. Mr. John A. Collins, the General Agent of the Massachusetts Anti-Slavery Society, had done what he could — and his qualifications as a quartermaster and commissary were of no mean order — to provide for the wants of those modern crusaders; but the quarters engaged for their accommodation were altogether inadequate, and scarcely less "dark, unfurnitured, and mean" than the "obscure hole" in which Harrison Gray Otis found the editor of "The Liberator" some six or seven years before. There were no tents, and if there had been, it would not have been quite safe to set them up in the City Hall Park, or anywhere else under the jurisdiction of the New York police of that day. But all annoyances were borne with a good-natured patience that would have done credit even to veterans, and the whole company were ready for roll-call at the appointed place and time.

The anniversary of the Society was held in the forenoon in the Presbyterian church on the corner of Madison and Catherine streets, and everything passed off pleasantly enough. The only circumstance that I remember very distinctly is, that Henry Highland Garnett, then a young man fresh from the Oneida Institute, where he had enjoyed the instruction of Beriah Green, made on this occasion his maiden speech. It was only half-believed among white people at that day that a negro could make a speech worth listening to; but Mr. Garnett's effort banished any lingering skepticism upon this point from the minds of those who heard it. The meeting for business was held in the same place in the afternoon. The house was crowded by an audience that waited eagerly for the conflict that all knew was to come. Arthur Tappan, the President, foreseeing a division, was absent, and the chair was taken by one of the Vice-Presidents, Francis Jackson of Massachusetts. The Chair, having been instructed to nominate a Business Committee, named for one of its members a well-known Quaker young lady, Abby Kelley, of Lynn, Mass., who had just entered the field as a lecturer, and to whom no objection could be made except on the ground of sex. Considering the fact that full half the members of the Society were women, whose rights as such had been duly acknowledged the year before, this action on the part of the Chair was eminently proper. The nomination, however, being objected to, an exciting debate followed, in which the: whole "woman question," as connected with the anti-slavery cause, was pretty thoroughly discussed. It was the largest business meeting the Society had ever held. The party opposed to women's membership had rallied in great strength, confirming the suspicion that extraordinary efforts had been made to secure a rever-: sal of the action of the previous year. Finally the: Society was brought to a vote, with this result :—In favor of Miss Kelley's appointment, 557 ; against it, 451. The only mistake, if there were any, was that. Mr. Jackson did not give her a companion of her own sex on the committee. Whether this was an oversight, or because he did not happen to remember the name of another woman who would be willing to serve, I do not know. Some of the most distin-. guished women of the Society had gone to England as delegates to the London Anti-Slavery Conference. If they had been present, perhaps Miss Kelley would not have been the only woman appointed. It is to be observed that much of the ridicule excited by the appointment turned upon the fact that one woman was sent alone into the company of six or eight men. This was a circumstance easily turned to

account by the vulgar, and they fed upon it with a
relish, making it a basis for the vilest insinuations.
If I should cite what some newspapers of high repute
said about this at the time, I should disgust no less
than astonish my readers. It is impossible that a
woman should not feel such insults most keenly; but
Miss Kelley bore them bravely for the sake of her sisters
in bonds, and thus, with bleeding feet, broke a path
through a thorny jungle for those who should come
after her.

Then went up all over the land the cry that the
American Anti-Slavery Society had become a woman's
rights association, and would henceforth, besides its
other fanaticisms, seek to overturn the family relation
and destroy the faith of men in the Bible. It had,
so it was alleged, openly defied the authority of
Paul, and thus shown itself infidel in spirit and purpose. Those who had opposed the admission of
women declared that Mr. Garrison and his friends had
"packed the meeting;" but the Rev. Joshua Leavitt
said, "I don't think there's any room for *us* to talk
about that." Mr. Lewis Tappan, soon after the resolution admitting women to membership was passed,
invited those who had voted against it to meet in the
lecture room under the church, for the purpose of
organizing a new society. The great body of ministers present accepted the invitation, as did many
others, and the "American *and Foreign* Anti-Slavery
Society" was speedily organized, with a constitution
carefully guarded against the intrusion of women,
though their activity in conventional ways, in behalf
of the cause, was commended. The new society took
with it all the members of the old Executive Committee, with the single exception of James S. Gibbons,
a highly respected member of the Society of Friends,
who had borne a faithful testimony against the transfer of "The Emancipator," and been true in every way
to the old society's platform. It was curious to ob-

serve that while the pro-slavery press poured measureless denunciation and ridicule upon the old society, it
complimented the new one upon its great respectability, and praised its founders for their good sense in
cutting loose from Garrison and his fanatical associates. It seemed to us that, considering their source,
the compliments were harder to bear than the abuse —
that our side, after all, was the one really complimented.

It is not to be denied that the new society presented
a formidable front, embracing in its ranks as it did
Abolitionists of high standing and great popularity.
It is not for me to cast any imputations upon the men
who thus separated themselves from the old society.
Doubtless the great body of them believed that they
had taken the course best calculated to advance the
cause. Many of them were no doubt sincerely alarmed
by Mr. Garrison's alleged heresies, believing that it
was actually his design to wage war upon the most
sacred institutions of society. The charges against
him were equally baseless and cruel, but for all that they
may have been sincerely accredited. It was no doubt
the belief of our accusers that they would speedily
draw to their more conservative and "prudent"
society the support of a large body of the evangelical
ministers and laymen who had stood aloof because, as
they said, "they could not swallow Garrison." In this
respect, however, they were doomed to a bitter disappointment. The men whom they hoped to conciliate
and win, however strong their aversion to Garrison,
yet loved the anti-slavery cause no more than they
loved him. They still stood aloof, grumbling and
carping over everything that either society did. Of
which of the two societies they were most afraid it
was easy to see, by the direction they gave to their
abuse. Some people, perhaps, may be inclined to
doubt the accuracy of these statements. Let me then

cite the testimony of Lewis Tappan, the founder and
leader of the new society. In his life of his brother
Arthur, (p. 329) he says : —

"It was said that the abolition body was largely composed of irreverent men, some of them of infidel sentiments ;
that their publications were couched in harsh language, that
the lecturers were intemperate in their speeches; that the
measures of the society set public opinion at defiance.
These allegations were notoriously untrue, as it regarded a
major part of the advocates of the anti-slavery reform, and
with reference to the rest of them were much exaggerated.
And it is worthy of remark that when the division took
place and a portion of the Abolitionists drew off and formed
a separate society, endeavoring to adopt such language and
such measures as Christians could not reasonably object to,
those who had been loudest in their opposition and most
offended with what they termed the unchristian spirit of the
Abolitionists, kept aloof as well from the American and
Foreign Anti-Slavery Society as they did from the American Society, of which Mr. Garrison was the head."

In another place he says : —

"At this time (1851), and previously, most of the ministers kept away from the anti-slavery platform, especially in
the large cities.   He by whom actions are weighed witnessed
throughout the anti-slavery contest the enormous mistakes
and even guilt of ministers of the Gospel, elders and dea-
cons of churches, officers of ecclesiastical bodies, editors of
religious newspapers and leading laymen in the churches
and on committees of benevolent and religious societies, putting themselves in the scales with slaveholders to weigh
down the poor slaves and their advocates."

Mr. Tappan, let it not be forgotten, was the man
who led in the secession, dividing the anti-slavery host
for the purpose of securing the co-operation of men,
who, as it was afterwards proved, had not a drop of
anti-slavery blood in their obdurate hearts, being "like

the deaf adder that stoppeth her ear; which will not hearken to the voice of the charmer, charming never so wisely." So much for concession and compromise as a means of reform — for "enticing words of man's wisdom" as a means of turning the hearts of apologists for sin, whose teeth needed rather to be broken by the "fire and hammer of Divine truth." (See Psalm lviii: 6.) The new society failed to gain the support of this class of men because, although it had turned its back upon Garrison, it still denounced slavery as a sin and urged immediate emancipation as a duty. It was Mr. Garrison's anti-slavery principles after all, and not his "hard language," that repelled these men; hence they would no more follow Mr. Tappan's lead than his. And this shows what a mistake it was to divide the anti-slavery body in response to the heartless clamor of such men, merely because women were admitted to membership! The good the new society did — and I do not deny that it did much — was but a poor compensation for the evils produced by the division. The seceders were never so strong afterwards as they were at the instant of their departure; they sent no agents into the field, and contributed little to increase the agitation of the slavery question. They held an anniversary, usually not half as well attended as that of the old society; they issued some excellent pamphlets from the pen of Judge Jay; and they are said to have founded "The National Era" in Washington. None of these things do I disparage; I only say that if the seceders had stood firmly by the old organization, and the united body had continued to "move upon the enemy's works" with steady and unflinching step, far more might have been accomplished than was possible to be done by a divided host. The reasons for the division, I think, were not such as should have had influence with men who loved the anti-slavery cause more than they did

their sects. The new Society, after a feeble existence
of thirteen years, expired for want of moral vitality.
Many of its members transferred their interest to the
American Missionary Association — a body of great
moral value as a protest against the pro-slavery course
of the American Board, and which has done and is
still doing a noble work among the emancipated
slaves. Others became absorbed in political measures, and lost their appreciation of purely moral instrumentalities. During the seven years immediately
preceding the war, when, if ever, there was the utmost
need of the highest moral influences in the warfare
with slavery, the seceders from the old society were
not in the field in any organized capacity. They had
fallen from their elevation as preachers of righteousness to the level of political action, directed merely
against the further extension of slavery.

The secession, it must be confessed, left the old
society in a very crippled condition. It was strong
only in its principles and in the unswerving loyalty and
faith of its members. It had no depository, no newspaper, no funds. The secession had carried away
nearly all the Abolitionists of New York and vicinity,
so that it was hard to find there a sufficient number of
persons qualified to constitute an Executive Committee.
But the Garrisonians were determined not to yield
their foothold in New York. They re-organized the
Executive Committee with such men as James S. Gibbons ("faithful among the faithless found"), the
venerable Isaac T. Hopper, William P. Powell, and
others. In the course of a few weeks the abstracted
"Emancipator" was replaced by a large, handsome
journal, the "National Anti-Slavery Standard," started
without a subscriber, and without so much as a dollar
in the treasury. It was the story of "The Liberator"
over again, save that the new paper was without a
permanent editor, and was compelled for a time, like

a Yankee schoolma'am, to "board round." It was
conducted during the summer by James S. Gibbons,
James C. Jackson, and William M. Chace—on just
what plan of co-operation I do not remember. I only
know that it was a very able and interesting sheet,
and that it mightily pleased those on whose patronage
it depended for support. Its prompt appearance, after
what Mr. Garrison not inaptly described as "the
scuttling of the old ship," greatly cheered the friends
of the old society. An office was opened in Nassau
Street above Beekman, and the venerable Quaker,
Isaac T. Hopper, put in the place of office agent.
The original design was to procure the services as
permanent editor of Nathaniel P. Rogers, so soon as
he should return from the London Anti-Slavery Conference, whither he had gone in company with Mr.
Garrison at the close of the annual meeting. He had
been for two years editor of the "Herald of Freedom,"
at Concord, N. H., and by his peculiar genius had
made it very popular. He could not, however, be
persuaded to leave New Hampshire, and the paper
with which he had become so pleasantly identified, for
a residence in New York; but in the autumn it was
arranged that he should write for the paper every
week, and that I should take the place of local editor.
This arrangement continued until May, 1841, when
Mrs. L. Maria Child was persuaded to take the editorship. She occupied the position for two years, giving
the paper a high character and securing for it a large
circulation. She was succeeded by her husband,
David Lee Child, who filled the place until the spring
of 1844, when Sydney Howard Gay became local editor
and agent, with Edmund Quincy and James Russell
Lowell as contributing editors. Mr. Gay proved to
be the right man for the place, and with the help of
his associates made the paper a great power. He

38

remained at this post till 1858, doing excellent work,
and commending himself to the confidence and affection
of his fellow-Abolitionists by his ability as a writer and
his unswerving devotion to the cause. From 1853 till
1858 I was associated with him, and when he retired
to accept a position on "The Tribune," the local editorship devolved wholly upon me. I filled the place
until 1865, when, agreeing with Mr. Garrison that
slavery being abolished, there was no longer any need
of anti-slavery societies or anti-slavery papers, I resigned. Mr. Quincy retired at the same time and for
the same reason. Mr. Lowell had dissolved his relation with the paper many years before. It now
passed, together with the American Anti-Slavery
Society, under the management of Wendell Phillips
and his friends, and Mr. Aaron M. Powell, shortly
afterwards, became the editor. It was discontinued
some years afterwards, at the same time that the
society was dissolved. Thus, while "The Emancipator," a few years after its transfer, was reckoned
among "things lost upon earth," the "National Anti-
Slavery Standard," which, under the most discouraging
circumstances, was established in its place as the
organ of the original American Anti-Slavery Society,
lived, together with that society, to record the death
of American slavery and the enfranchisement of its
victims. "New Organization" was certainly not a
success. Making a formidable show in the beginning,
it dwindled year by year, and died long before the
abolition of slavery; while "old organization," fear-
fully crippled as it was by the secession, lost neither
heart nor hope; but, standing upon the original
foundation, working on the old plan, and seeking the
co-operation of all the friends of immediate emancipation, without regard to sect, party or sex, remained in
the field to the very end, fighting the enemy with constantly increasing energy and power, and at last

mingling its shouts of victory with those of four millions of ransomed slaves.

I have now told the story of the great division in the anti-slavery movement. I have told it frankly, as I understand it, and with such candor as is possible to one who was an earnest actor in the controversy, but who has no enmities to gratify, and no reproaches to visit upon anybody. I have dwelt upon the main features of the case, entering only into such details as were necessary to a clear understanding of the main event. I would gladly have avoided the subject, but it was impossible. I have always believed that many of those who took part in the secession regretted it afterwards, seeing the mistaken impressions upon which they acted, in respect to Mr. Garrison on the one hand, and on the other in regard to those whose support of the cause they so much desired to secure. Mr. Garrison was deeply pained by the division, partly because he was himself, unjustly as he thought, made the occasion thereof, but more because it alienated from him, for a time, not a few men to whom he was fondly attached, and in whom he had long had the highest confidence. He was especially pained that a cloud should fall between him and Arthur Tappan, to whom he was indebted for his release from the Baltimore jail, and whose character he greatly admired. He never believed that the division was inspired or much promoted by him. When Mr. Tappan died, in 1866, Mr. Garrison, casting behind him all unpleasant memories, addressed a letter to one of his family, in which he spoke of "his Christian graces and virtues" as "making his character illustrious," and of his "proving his love for God by his love for man, without regard to country, race or clime;" and then he added: "At all times 'ready to be offered' in the service of God, and the cause of suffering humanity, he was serene in the midst of fiery trials and imminent

perils, being crucified to that 'fear of man that bringeth a snare,' and having 'his life hid with Christ in
God.' Now that the nation has decreed universal
emancipation, I doubt not that he is cognizant of the
glorious event, and, with the liberated millions rendering praise and thanksgiving to God."

Three persons, alluded to in this chapter, are entitled to further notice on account of important services rendered by them to the cause of the slave.
Mr. John A. Collins came to us from Andover Theological Seminary at the time of the division in Massachusetts, taking the place of General Agent, left
vacant by the retirement of the Rev. Amos A. Phelps.
His executive power was remarkable. He did much
to infuse courage into our broken ranks, to overcome
opposition, to collect funds, and devise and execute
large plans of anti-slavery labor. He travelled much
at home, and once went to England on a mission in
behalf of the cause. A man of tremendous energy,
nothing could stagnate in his presence. He could set
a score of agents in the field, and plan and execute a
campaign on the largest scale. At one time a series
of one hundred conventions, extending over several
States, East and West, was held by an organized
corps of lecturers under his superintendence. He
came to us in a critical hour and his services were
exceedingly valuable.

How shall I bring before the reader that rare man,
Nathaniel P. Rogers, who was often compared to
Charles Lamb, and who had a hold upon the affection
of his fellow-Abolitionists such as few others were priv-
ileged to acquire? He espoused the cause at an early
day, and articles from his pen, appearing from time to
time in the anti-slavery papers, won attention by their
raciness and striking originality of style as well as
thought. He was at this time a member of the bar in
Grafton County, N. H., but cared more for literature

than for his briefs. The "Herald of Freedom" was established in Concord by the New Hampshire Anti-Slavery Society in 1835. Its first editor was Joseph Horace Kimball, who, in 1837, was sent, in company with James A. Thome, to observe and report the results of emancipation in the British West Indies. Not long after his return from this expedition he died of consumption, when Mr. Rogers, by the spontaneous suffrages of the Abolitionists of New Hampshire, was selected to fill his place. He made the paper as brilliant as it was able. His style was remarkable for terseness, for vivid flights of imagination, for odd and striking turns of thought, and for a wit all his own. The paper attained high popularity under his management, while personally he became a great favorite with all who had the privilege of his acquaintance. He was a man of exquisite taste and refinement, warm-hearted and hospitable, and therefore a most delightful host as well as guest. In the early days of the cause he was strictly Orthodox in opinion and feeling, but grew liberal, as many others did, as he observed how the clergy and the churches hardened their hearts against the cry of the slave. He attained at length to the honor of excommunication by a church that thought it worse to be an Abolitionist with a deficient creed than to be a slaveholder. During the later years of his life he carried his ideas of individual freedom so far that he could not tolerate a presiding officer in an anti-slavery meeting. This brought him into conflict with the New Hampshire Anti-Slavery Society, which had founded the "Herald of Freedom," and made him its editor. The publisher claimed that the title to the paper had in some way lapsed, and that it was no longer the property of the Society. The Society, however, or its Executive Committee, still claimed it. Mr. Garrison, Mr. Quincy and others were summoned from Boston, as umpires in the dispute. They decided

that the title remained with the Society.   It was the
universal wish, however, that Mr. Rogers should continue to edit it.   His health was seriously impaired at
the time, and such was his extreme nervous sensibility
that he took offence at the decision, and refused to
acquiesce in it.   A most unfortunate controversy was
the result, and he became alienated from Mr. Garrison,
without cause or reasonable provocation, as the latter
thought and many others believed.   In this state of
mind he died in 1846.   His estrangement from his old
friends, and especially from Mr. Garrison, was a
subject of general lamentation.   It never could have
happened, I am sure, but for a morbid sensitiveness
that was the result of ill-health.   This, I know, was
the opinion of many of his best friends, though not of
all of them.   Mr. Garrison loved him tenderly, and
was never for an instant conscious that he had done
him wrong.   Mr. Rogers remarked, at the time of the
secession from the old Society, that "the quarrels of
Abolitionists were better than other people's peace";
but I am afraid this philosophy did not console him in
this last extremity.   But I am sure that he and Garrison
and Quincy are friends now. . Surviving Abolitionists
everywhere will gladly forget any faults of his last
days — the fruit, no doubt, of nervous prostration —
and remember only his noble nature, his rare endowments, his ripe culture and his consecration to the
cause of the slave.   It is greatly to be regretted that
the Rev. John Pierpont, in his Introduction to "A
Collection from the Newspaper Writings" of Mr.
Rogers, allowed himself to make statements of a partisan and most preposterous character respecting the
controversy between Mr. Rogers and his old friends,
for which he was afterwards constrained to apologize,
and which he promised to correct in another edition —
which, however, was never published.   Aside from
this most mistaken partisanship, the book is a worthy
monument of Mr. Rogers's character and genius.

Abby Kelley (now Mrs. Stephen S. Foster) was the first woman, after the Grimké sisters, to enter the field as an anti-slavery lecturer. No one who ever knew her doubted that she felt herself called of God to the work, and she entered upon it in a spirit of self-consecration that inspired the deepest respect of all observers. She did not begin in any careless or random way, but studied her subject thoroughly. She no doubt expected to become a target for the pro-slavery press, but I am sure she did not anticipate the weight of odium that fell upon her on account of the brave step she felt it her duty to take. There are newspapers that ought to be blushing to-day, and editors who should be clothed in sackcloth and ashes, for their shameful abuse of this noble woman. Her exalted worth did not exempt her from insinuations of the vilest sort. She was denounced and ridiculed by the pulpit as well as the press, and her meetings were sometimes assailed by mobs. She bore all this load of reproach with unmurmuring patience, keeping quietly on in her work, until at last she conquered her true place in the public esteem. She was a very popular and successful lecturer, and labored much not only in New England, but in New York, Pennsylvania and the West. In Ohio, and particularly on the Western Reserve, she did a noble work. She may be said with truth to have founded "The Anti-Slavery Bugle," and I doubt if the Western Anti-Slavery Society, which, as an auxiliary of the National Society, did such noble work, especially in Eastern Ohio, would ever have been organized but for her. James Russell Lowell describes her in these lines : —

> " A Judith there, turned Quakeress,
> Sits Abby, in her modest dress.
> .   .   .   .
> No nobler gift of heart or brain,
> No life more white from spot or stain,
> Was e'er on Freedom's altar laid
> Than hers — the simple Quaker maid."

It was Mrs. Foster's misfortune to be often confounded by the press (sometimes mischievously) with
Abigail Folsom, an innocent monomaniac on the subject of free speech, who used to torment the anti-slavery
meetings with grotesque interruptions, and who was
not unfrequently removed by gentle force. The mobocratic fringe that so often hung around the doors at
anti-slavery gatherings always cheered this woman
vociferously whenever she arose to speak. She accepted such cheers as "the voice of the people," and
sometimes annoyed us excessively by her insane talk,
which, however, was frequently spiced with the keenest
wit. Once I assisted in carrying her gently out of the
Marlboro' Chapel. She made it a point of conscience
not to resist. She was placed in a chair, and as Wendell Phillips, William A. White and myself were
carrying her down the aisle, through a crowd, she
exclaimed, "I'm better off than my Master was; He
had but one ass to ride — I have three to carry me."
Mrs. Folsom was perfectly rational on every subject
except that of free speech. She was a woman of rare
benevolence, and Theodore Parker and others often
made her their almoner.

XVIII.

Formation of the Liberty Party — Complicated with "New Organization " — Mr. Garrison's Opposition, and the Reasons thereof —
Samuel E. Sewall and John G. Whittier — Parties Limited by
the Constitution — In Danger of Degenerating — Slavery Abolished by Southern Madness rather than by Northern Principle —
Moral Agitation of Paramount Importance — Testimony of
Frederick Douglass.

WHILE the divisions of which I have given an
account in previous chapters had their origin mainly in
sectarian fears and jealousies, and in the delusion that
large numbers of Orthodox ministers and laymen stood
ready to espouse the cause if they could only do so without endorsing or following the lead of Mr. Garrison,
they were yet complicated, to a large extent, with the
organization of the Liberty political party. It is probably true that the first man to suggest such a party,
and to take steps toward its formation, was the late
Hon. Myron Holley, of Rochester, N. Y., who was, I
suspect, as profoundly indifferent as any man could
well have been to the complaints of Orthodox Abolitionists in respect to Mr. Garrison. Many of the
New Organizationists, however, seized upon that movement, and used it as a makeweight to effect their ends.
The organization of the Liberty party, if it had stood
simply upon its own merits, might and probably would
have left the anti-slavery societies intact, to pursue the
work for which they were formed. It might have
weakened, but could hardly have destroyed them.
Mr. Garrison and others would have opposed the
measure strenuously, but not in such a way as to give

its friends any provocation for withdrawing themselves
from the work of moral agitation. For Mr. Garrison,
though himself a Non-resistant, and therefore pre-
cluded from taking any part in the management of
political parties, still looked to political action as an
important means of advancing the anti-slavery cause.
The anti-slavery movement, first in the order of time,
was before all others in his regard. It could not wait
for the people to be converted to his principles of
peace, but must go on in the use of those instrumentalities whose rightfulness the people did not question.
Outside of anti-slavery meetings he would do what he
could for the spread of his Peace principles; but on
the anti-slavery platform he had neither the right nor
the wish to introduce that subject. No Abolitionist
rejoiced more heartily than himself in observing the
growth of anti-slavery sentiment in the political parties, and in witnessing the agitation of the subject in
Congress and the State Legislatures. He knew that all
this was the natural, as it certainly was the anticipated
result of the moral agitation created by anti-slavery
societies, newspapers, tracts, lectures, conventions,
etc.; and therefore he desired to multiply these agencies a hundred-fold, in order to induce the nation, at
the earliest possible day, to do all that could be done
by political action for the overthrow of slavery. No
man appreciated more highly than he did the noble
service in the cause of freedom rendered by the earliest
agitators of the question in Congress — such men as
John Quincy Adams, William Slade, Seth M. Gates
and Joshua R. Giddings. He saw in their action the
fruit of his own labors, and a sure augury of the success of the movement which he had planted. The
kind concern manifested by a certain class of persons
as to his consistency in all this he duly appreciated,
but thought himself fully capable of taking care of his
own reputation in this respect. He was no Roman

Catholic, any more than he was a politician, and could not in conscience have become a member of the Catholic Church; but if that ancient and powerful denomination had lent itself to the work of abolishing American slavery, he would have rejoiced with joy unspeakable. No reproaches of the Pope would have fallen from his lips on the anti-slavery platform. He was indeed a member of *no* religious sect, nor would he have joined any one of all the churches around him ; but not the less on this account would he have been glad to see any one of them take a position of active hostility to slavery. It was indeed his constant effort and desire to induce them all to do this. His relation to the political parties was exactly similar to his relation to the churches, and he felt no more scruple in urging the one than the other to take an anti-slavery course.

Mr. Garrison's opposition to the formation of the Liberty party was often attributed to his non-resistance sentiments. But this was a great mistake. Thousands of the most earnest Abolitionists in the land, who had no sympathy with his non-resistance views, were as warmly opposed to it as he was. Such an organization was indeed in direct contravention to numerous avowals, official as well as private, of the Abolitionists. " We have opened," said the American Anti-Slavery Society in its third annual report, " and shall open, no road to political preferment. The strength of our cause must be in the humble, fervent prayer of the righteous man, which availeth much, and the blessing of that God who had chosen the weak things of the world to confound the mighty." A year later it said, " It is to be expected that some political wolves will put on the clothing of abolitionism, and seek to elevate themselves and manage the anti-slavery organ-ization, to secure their own purposes. But they ought to be met on the threshold, and stripped of their dis-

guise. The best safeguard against their entrance is for
the Abolitionists, while they firmly refuse to vote for
a man who will not support abolition measures, to
avoid setting up candidates of their own." Later still
the society said, "Abolitionists have resolved from the
first to act upon slavery politically, not by organizing
a new political party, but by making it the interest of
the parties already existing to act upon abolition principles." "Abolitionists," said the "Quarterly Anti-
Slavery Magazine" for January, 1837, "have but one
work — it is not to put anybody into office or out of it,
but to set right those who make officers." "The exhibition of truth in Christian faithfulness," said the Hon.
Wm. Jay, "appears to me to be the great instrument
by which we are to operate. Should political anti-
slavery ever be substituted for religious anti-slavery,
the consequences. would probably be disastrous."

Mr. Garrison thought, in the first place, that it was
wholly unnecessary for Abolitionists to organize a
political party, since one or both the existing parties
would be compelled to espouse the cause so soon as
public opinion should call for anti-slavery action.
Their true course, he thought, was to persevere in the
work of moral agitation, enlightening the people as to
the character of slavery and their duties concerning it,
quickening their consciences, and seeking to form a
public sentiment that would impel the National and
State Governments to exercise all their constitutional
powers in opposition to slavery. The results then
already accomplished were a demonstration of the
efficacy of this method.

In the next place, he thought a political party the
most expensive, wasteful, and least efficacious of all
instrumentalities for moral agitation and the enlightenment of the people.

In assuming, as a body, a partisan attitude, and
nominating each other for office, Abolitionists would

close the ears of multitudes to their appeals, and
expose themselves to strong temptations to lower their
standard for the sake of political success. The purity
of the movement would thus be sullied by the ambition for office, its moral tone depressed, and the day
of its final triumph deferred. As a moral and relig-
ous movement, its disinterestedness was acknowledged
and respected even by its enemies; as a political
organization, it would be distrusted not only by its
avowed opponents, but by many of those friendly to
its object. The machinery of politics, he thought,
was far more costly than that of moral and religious
movements, and far more liable to abuse. The men
engaged in working that machinery would be liable to
undervalue and neglect moral instrumentalities, and
thus the movement would be liable to degenerate into
a mere scramble for power and place.

Moreover, he insisted that a political anti-slavery
party would be subject to the limitations and hampered
by the compromises of the Constitution. It could not
represent the cause in all its length and breadth, its
height and depth. It could only propose to itself such
measures as the Constitution sanctioned, and these
would fall far short of fulfilling all the purposes of the
anti-slavery movement. When the National Government had exhausted its whole power in relation to
slavery, the system itself would remain intact. Hence
the moral movement should be kept in vigorous operation, and its power augmented by every rightful
means. In doing this the Abolitionists would be taking
the course most likely to secure every political object
which they had in view, and that at the earliest possible day. Politicians would be quick to discover when
public opinion demanded anti-slavery action by the
Government, and glad enough to avail themselves of
a popular issue; while as a means of forming such a
public sentiment a political party was the poorest of

instrumentalities. Meanwhile anti-slavery voters, without nominating candidates of their own, should exercise their right of suffrage in conformity with their principles. The Abolitionists of Great Britain had pursued this course with great success.

On this subject Mr. Garrison remained of the same opinion to his dying day. He always believed that the cause would have triumphed sooner, in a political sense, if the Abolitionists had continued to act as one body, never yielding to the temptation of forming a political party, but pressing forward in the use of the same instrumentalities which were so potent from 1831 to 1840. He was confirmed in this opinion by watching the course of the Liberty party, which receded in part from its original anti-slavery principles. to support that political trickster, Martin Van Buren, and again in suffering .itself to be absorbed by the Republican party upon the single issue of the non-extension of slavery to new territory. He thought there was no necessity for Abolitionists to take a downward course to reach that point. If they had remained firm in demanding of the government all that it had power to do for the overthrow of slavery, the political parties would all the sooner have come up to the ground of non-extension. In other words, if the money expended in organizing and running a political party had been employed in the work of moral agitation and in the fearless and impartial application of anti-slavery principles to sects and parties, vastly more would have been accomplished, and political action against slavery the sooner secured.

In saying this let me not be understood to question the motives of those who originated the Liberty party, or to speak in a controversial spirit upon the subject. My sole object is to make clear to my readers the position held by Mr. Garrison and his associates. Whether that position was justified or not by the facts

in the case, every reader must judge for himself. Nor
let it be for a moment supposed that I undervalue the
results of political action, or would detract from the
praise due to the noble men who fought the Slave
Power by this means. On the contrary, my heart
swells with gratitude when I think of the courage and
devotion of Slade and Giddings, Gates and Hale, Wilson and Sumner, Morris and Chase, and scores of
others, who exhausted all the powers of the Constitution in their efforts to resist the encroachments of
slavery; and, above all, when I think of Abraham
Lincoln, patient, conscientious, firm, waiting for the
hour when, as Commander-in-Chief of the Military
and Naval forces of the United States, he could rightfully strike off the fetters of the slaves, and then, by
a single stroke of his pen, lifting four millions of
human beings from the condition of chattels to that of
men, and delivering the Republic forever from the
guilt and shame of slavery. Still, I cannot forget
that it was the madness of the Slave Power alone that
opened the way to this glorious consummation. I
cannot forget that the political party which went into
power in 1861, and which had absorbed into itself the
anti-slavery voters of the country, contemplated nothing more than keeping slavery within its then present
limits, and that Abraham Lincoln, during the first
month of his administration, diligently enforced the
infamous Fugitive Slave law, in order to convince the
slaveholders that neither he nor his party contemplated
any infraction of their constitutional rights, and that
they could remain in the Union with the perfect assurance that their diabolical system would be preserved
from harm. I cannot forget that the great mass of the
Northern people, including the ministers and churches
of nearly every denomination, were not only willing,
but anxious to have the South remain in the Union,
with all their slaves, and ready to fulfil, for the protec-

tion of slavery, all the obligations imposed by the Constitution. And if the South had listened to the persuasions of the North, in all probability slavery, with all its indescribable atrocities, would be existing to-day, and the Northern ministry and church, perhaps, as indifferent as ever to the wrongs and woes of its victims. The Northern people should not take too much credit to themselves for an event which was made possible and necessary, not by any virtue of their own, but by a madness which they earnestly deprecated, and which, by the proffered renewal of unholy compromises, they sought to subdue. God, who looketh on the heart, is not mocked. He holds men responsible not alone for iniquity consummated, but for that which they were willing to do if opportunity had not failed.

Some of the best friends of Mr. Garrison—men who had no part or sympathy in the efforts to oust him from his rightful place in deference to sectarian prejudices—were in favor of the Liberty party. It will be enough to mention among these the names of Samuel E. Sewall and John G. Whittier, for whose conscientious convictions Mr. Garrison cherished the utmost respect. But he could not avoid seeing that a very large proportion of the leaders and members of that party were men who had taken an active part in dividing the anti-slavery host on sectarian grounds, and whose minds and hearts were full of enmity to the old organization. It was to him a very instructive spectacle to observe a score or two of clergymen aroused all at once to a pitch of high enthusiasm for political purity, and willing at the same time to wink at the impurity of the church; too conscientious to vote at the polls for a slaveholder or a pro-slavery man, but quite willing to remain connected with religious denominations that were in open complicity with slavery and wholly indifferent to the wrongs of the slaves. These preachers, who turned their backs upon the anti-slavery movement as originally organized, had come to the conclusion that it was time for judgment to begin, not at the house of God, but in the political parties! It did not matter so much that slaveholders had access to the Northern pulpits and communion-tables, as it did that they had places of honor in the political parties, and held office under the government. These men had labored for years to elevate the standard of morality in the churches, and had found the task so hard of accomplishment, and entailing such unpleasant consequences upon themselves, that now they resolved to turn their attention to the political field, and give the churches a rest. Perhaps in this way they might recover their ecclesiastical standing, while keeping up the pretence of being just as much opposed to slavery as ever ; and then perhaps the clergy and the churches, after being let alone for a time, and no longer angered by anti-slavery rebukes, or worried by Garrison's "infidelity," would be able, without any expense to their pride, to work their way round to some sort of anti-slavery position. All this was just as plain as if written out in so many words, and emblazoned on the sky, for all men to read. Mr. Garrison and his friends must have been blind not to see it, and unfaithful to the slave not to expose and denounce it.

Moreover, this new political zeal sought to justify itself by arguments which Mr. Garrison regarded as a disparagement of the moral agitation against slavery, and well calculated to bring it into contempt. Slavery, it was said, was the creature of law, and could only be abolished by statute ; therefore, the great duty of every Abolitionist was to cast an anti-slavery vote. The ballot-box was the cure-all, the end-all of the whole matter. Of what use was it to talk against slavery? To vote against it was "the end of the law for righteousness." Who ever knew any good thing to be ac-

complished by talk alone? Now, in the first place, it
was not true that slavery was the creature of law; on
the contrary, the slave laws, in letter as well as spirit,
were the creatures of slavery, born of the public
sentiment which that vile system had first created;
and the first thing to be done, therefore, was to form
a public sentiment amid which slavery itself could not
live. The mere act of changing the laws, after that,
would be the easiest of all possible tasks; it would
follow as a matter of course. The one thing to be
done, therefore, Mr. Garrison insisted, was to change
public sentiment; and for this moral agitation, in
other words, "the opposition of moral purity to
moral corruption, the destruction of error by the
potency of truth, the overthrow of prejudice by the
power of love," was the chief instrumentality. The
best weapons of the anti-slavery warfare were "spiritual, and mighty through God to the pulling down of
strongholds." With the example of Jesus, the prophets
and the apostles before them, not one of whom ever
cast a ballot, it was not becoming in men to sneer at
"the foolishness of preaching," or to doubt the wisdom of proclaiming the truth in the ears of a sinful
nation.

Such were the views of Mr. Garrison. Whether they
were wise or foolish posterity will judge. He and his
friends believed with all their hearts that they were
sound, and they acted upon them with an energy, a
fidelity that overcame all obstacles, and that yielded
neither to obloquy nor persecution. Frederick Douglass, after the organization of the Free Soil party, with
the instinct of one who had worn the fetters of a slave,
set the subject in a clear light. "We declare," he said,
"that the Free Soil movement ought not to be considered as the real anti-slavery movement of the country, and our further belief, that so far from regarding
our movement in the light of a political one, we should

strive by every means in our power to keep it mainly
a moral movement. The facts, arguments and principles with which the Free Soilers so powerfully assail the
ramparts of slavery have been drawn chiefly from the
repositories prepared to their hands. The ground has
been deeply ploughed for them, and they find it comparatively mellow, requiring little effort to cultivate
it. The party came into operation, not by its own
impulse, but by invitation, and a state of preparation
which made it easy to operate. Pride and self-glory
may conceal it, but time will reveal that to the earnest,
unwearying, and faithful toil of William Lloyd Garrison
and the American Anti-Slavery Society with its auxiliaries, we are indebted for the Free Soil movement."
The Liberty party set itself up in business upon
capital created for it by ten years of moral agitation,
and the anti-slavery parties that followed profited by
the same and other similar accumulations of moral
power, the fruit of the agitation which some of them
affected to despise. Mr. Garrison himself did not
hesitate to claim for the movement with which he was
identified the credit which so many others have given
it. "If," he said, "the Garrisonian Abolitionists had
been supplanted or driven from the field, what would
have become of the anti-slavery movement? Assur-
edly, a collapse would have followed more disastrous
than that which followed the Missouri struggle in 1820,
and neither a Giddings nor a Sumner, neither a Wilson nor a Julian would have been seen as a political
representative of the movement in Congress." Possibly there may be some to whom this will read like an
idle boast, but those who know how to trace important
public events to their original causes, and to weigh the
influences — not always those which first challenge
attention — that shape the character and mould the
destiny of nations, will not doubt its truth.

XIX.

Explanatory and Apologetic — The Moral Agitation, its Instru-
ments, Agents and Resources — Bad Effects of the Secession —
The Garrisonians "Hold the Fort" — The Movement Still Formidable — Pennsylvania — The Western Society — Anti-Slavery
Papers — Annexation of Texas — Theodore Parker — The Lecturing Agents — Rev. Samuel May — Stephen S. Foster — Parker
Pillsbury.

I HAVE now completed my sketches of the anti-
slavery movement up to and including the divisions of
1839–40, treating the subject with only such a degree
of fullness as it seemed absolutely to require.. I must
remind my readers that I have not undertaken to
write a complete history, but only to present an outline of the principal events embraced in this period.
Many interesting occurrences have either not been
mentioned at all, or referred to only in the briefest
terms. I trust I have not wholly failed in my design
to give a true account of the origin and early growth
of one of the grandest moral and philanthropic movements that the world has ever witnessed. It was my
cherished hope for many years that one far more com-
petent than myself would perform this task; and I
consented to undertake it at last only because no one
else appeared, or seemed likely to appear, on the field.
I believe I have not erred in thinking that it was
above all things important to take such a proportion
of the space at my command as might be required to
describe the origin and foundation of the anti-slavery
movement, to show what mighty efforts were made to
crush it in its earliest years, and to depict the persecu-

tions endured by its first advocates. The remainder of the history, though crowded with events of thrilling interest, will yet, in view of the strong light cast upon it from the foundation period already described, bear to be treated with the brevity made imperative by the limits of this volume. The origin of the movement, the fundamental principles upon which it rested, the methods by which its ends were sought, and the resistance it met with, having been already made clear, there is the less need of a close attention to details in what remains to be written. And yet I will frankly confess my regret, for the reader's sake, that I cannot now avail myself fully of the rich materials gleaned from a survey of the later period of the history. The broadest outline is all that I can attempt.

I must also ask my readers to remember that I have not undertaken to write a history, however brief, of either of the three political parties which, at different periods before emancipation, represented in a certain sense the anti-slavery sentiment of the country, or of the discussions in Congress that preceded and followed the Rebellion. And this not because I do not appreciate the immense importance of this branch of the subject, but because it has already been treated with more or less fulness by William Goodell in his "Slavery and Anti-Slavery" (1855), by Horace Greeley in his "Great American Conflict," and by Vice-President Wilson in his "History of the Rise and Fall of the Slave Power." It is my ambition to do a work which they neglected, but which is certainly not less important than that which they so well performed. The portion of anti-slavery history which received their attention is in no danger of being thrown into the shade, nor is the world likely to overlook its indebtedness to the heroes who fought on that conspicuous stage. But the fresh mountain-springs of moral influence, by which the life of the anti-slavery

political parties was constantly renewed and their
blood kept from degenerating, have not been appreciated as they deserve. Men indeed who live in the
excitement and turmoil of political life; are often utterly oblivious of the moral influences which, having no
organic connection with the machinery of parties, are
yet its chief propelling force. So true is this that multitudes of otherwise well-informed people conceive of
the anti-slavery movement in this country as having
begun either with the formation of the Liberty party
or with the Fremont campaign, and as having been
carried forward almost entirely by political instrumentalities. For this reason it has seemed to me important, for the instruction of the present and coming
generations, to bring out into full view the self-sacrificing labors of men who neither sought office for
themselves or others, who worked no political wires
and entered no caucuses, but devoted themselves
steadily and persistently, year after year for three
decades, to the work of enlightening the people as to
the character of slavery, the wrongs and woes of the
slaves, the duty and safety of immediate emancipation,
and the terrible guilt of those who, whether in church
or state, lent themselves to the support of so atrocious a system. But for the public sentiment originally created by this means, no anti-slavery political
party could ever have been formed; nor could such a
party have succeeded in its struggle with the Slave
Power, if that public sentiment had not been constantly fed and sustained by moral agitation, outside
and independent of itself. There was more than one
crisis in the history of parties, when the political agitation, but for the moral influences that lay behind it,
and that were beyond the reach of politicians, would
in all probability have been overcome. Such men as
Giddings and Slade and Sumner and Wilson were perfectly aware of this, and often confessed it in private

if not in public. Hundreds of Republicans knew it, and gladly contributed of their means to sustain the anti-slavery societies in their work. Some of them were even glad to take part occasionally in the moral agitation, by means of which the veins of their party were constantly infused with fresh blood.

I do not belittle the evil effects of the secession when I say that, in spite of that untoward and ever to be lamented event, the anti-slavery societies and other agencies controlled by the Garrisonians were still powerful enough to alarm the slaveholders for the safety of their cherished institution, and to keep the pro-slavery party at the North in a constant fever of excitement. The American Society was indeed left at first in a condition like that of a ship dismantled in a hurricane. The seceding directors of that society were men of great influence, and when they set up a new organization, the abolition forces in some quarters were thrown into a state of bewilderment, which was like a paralysis in its sudden effects. Some of the State societies, and numbers of smaller ones, never recovered from that condition. They did nothing either for the old or the new organization, adopting the policy of keeping out of a controversy, of which they were not prepared to take either side. At the time of the secession there were in the country nearly or quite two thousand anti-slavery societies, representing a vast body of public sentiment in opposition to slavery; and if the National Society had not been divided, there is every reason to believe that the cause would have made very rapid progress in the next two or three years. As it was, the anti-slavery army, which had stood in serried ranks before the enemy, prepared to give battle at every point, was thrown into sudden confusion, one division straggling in this direction, another in that, and altogether presenting the appearance of a rout rather than of an impending battle. What shouts of exulta-

tion went up from the enemy's camp! The pro-slavery
party on every hand assumed that the Abolitionists
had at last done for their own movement what mobs,
the denunciations of the press, and ecclesiastical and
social proscription had utterly failed to do, viz:—PUT
IT DOWN, beyond the hope of resuscitation. "We
shall not," said the New York "Journal of Commerce,"
one of the most virulent of pro-slavery papers, "have
occasion to write the word 'abolition' many times
more." But these exultations were premature. It
was an over-intensity of life rather than a diminution
of vital force that divided our ranks. Although the
different divisions of the anti-slavery army no longer
obeyed the voice of any single leader, every one of
them was full of fight, and confident of its power to
win a victory in every contest. The division was
more external than internal. The abolition of slavery,
by one means or another, was the animating purpose
of all. The power of the movement, though impaired
for lack of unity, was not destroyed. It still had its
"quarrel just," and therefore was more than a match
for enemies "whose consciences with injustice were
corrupt."

The position of Mr. Garrison and his friends in this
crisis was not doubtful. They were still at the head
of the moral movement. It was theirs to "hold the
fort;" to stand firmly on the ground marked out by
the Declaration of 1833; to apply anti-slavery principles impartially to every party and sect, and to
every institution and society in the land that stood
in the way of the slave's redemption; to send forth
anti-slavery lecturers as extensively as they were
able; to distribute anti-slavery papers, pamphlets
and tracts in every accessible quarter; to prepare
and circulate petitions to Congress and the State
Legislatures; to hold anniversaries and conventions;
in short to carry on the work of moral agitation, by

every legitimate means, enlightening the people as to
the character of slavery and their duties, political as
well as moral, social and ecclesiastical, concerning it;
thus hastening the formation of a PUBLIC SENTIMENT,
in whose atmosphere slavery could not live. If others
had either wholly or partially forsaken this work for
less onerous or more agreeable tasks, then their duty
was all the more imperative. Nor were they in the
least discouraged by anything that had happened.
Their spirit and purpose are indicated by the words
of Mr. Garrison on another occasion. " Our cause,"
said he, "is of God. It has been so from the beginning. Why did this nation tremble at the outset?
Why were the slaveholders smitten as with the fear
of death? Who were the Abolitionists? Confessedly,
in a numerical sense, not to be counted. They had
no influence, no station, no wealth. Ah, but they had
the truth of God, and therefore God himself was on
their side; and hence the guilty nation quaked with
fear when that truth was uttered and applied. We
have fought a good fight, and we yet shall conquer,
God helping us. All the spirits of the just are with
us; all the good of earth are with us; and we need
not fear as to the result of the conflict." It was
this invincible trust in God, under all circumstances,
that drew to Mr. Garrison's side the men and women
who were best fitted to carry on a moral warfare.
The attempt of a recreant church and a time-serving
pulpit to fasten upon him the opprobrious name of
infidel did not disturb their equanimity. They knew
that they were enlisted in a pre-eminently Christian
work, and that if Jesus himself should appear again
on the earth, it would be to give them his blessing and
lead them to victory. If they were called fanatics
and infidels, so had Jesus been called a blasphemer,
while his apostles were denounced as "movers of sedi-
tion." It was not for them to complain that they were

41

treated as other reformers had been in all ages of the world. To be called infidels by a church that stopped its ears to the cry of the poor, while paying tithes of mint, annis and cummin, and forgetting the weighty matters of the law, was only a compliment to their Christian fidelity, for which they should feel not shame but pride.

So far as the National Society was concerned, it was a new departure, though not by any means a change of position. The management, for greater efficiency, was transferred from New York to Boston, but the society was still represented at the old headquarters by the "National Anti-Slavery Standard," no expense being spared to make it a worthy expositor of the cause. The pecuniary resources of the society were seriously diminished by the secession, and the diversion of so many Abolitionists from the moral to the political field. The Massachusetts society remained true to its former allegiance; the great body of the Abolitionists in that State rallying around Mr. Garrison with renewed confidence and affection. *They* knew, as many good friends of the cause in other States did not, how utterly false were the accusations brought against their leader by busy and not over-scrupulous sectarians. The New Hampshire society also stood firmly by the old organization, and so also did the Pennsylvania society, embracing in its membership a large body of most intelligent and clear-sighted friends of the cause, among whom were noble women not a few. The Quaker atmosphere was not anywhere congenial to the new organization, being but slightly if at all infused with the sectarian spirit that led to the secession. The Liberty party, however, was not without a few zealous friends among the Quakers, the influence of John G. Whittier in this direction being powerfully felt. But a large majority of the Abolitionists in Pennsylvania remained in hearty sympathy with the old organization. The Secretary and General Agent of the State Society was that "prudent rash man," James Miller McKim, who combined an earnest zeal with great wisdom in administration. Fitted by his intellectual gifts as well as by education for any place of influence and power to which he might have chosen to aspire, he devoted himself unreservedly for a generation to the cause of the slave, rendering it service of the very highest character by his pen and his voice, as well as by his wisdom in counsel. The Pennsylvania Society was for years under the management, to a large extent, of women. Lucretia Mott, Mary Grew, Sarah Pugh and Abby Kimber were for many years valued members of the Executive Committee, furnishing in their own persons an illustration of the wisdom of the Divine arrangement in fitting women for equal co-operation with men in all the important concerns of life. Whatever the anti-slavery societies may have lost by the secession, which had its cause in the admission of women to full membership, they gained vastly more by the acquisition of many such women as those above named, who remained true to the cause in every emergency. Mrs. Mott and Miss Grew took high rank as speakers, in which capacity they were great favorites in the anti-slavery meetings. Miss Grew also rendered the cause valuable service with her pen, not only in the annual reports of the Philadelphia Female Anti-Slavery Society, but as the editor, at different times, of the "Pennsylvania Freeman." C. C. Burleigh had done noble work as a lecturer in Eastern Pennsylvania, before the division. He was succeeded in that field by his younger brother, Cyrus M. Burleigh, who gave himself to the cause in his earliest manhood. He was a young man of the very highest character, a forcible speaker and a vigorous writer. He did excellent service both as a lecturer

and editor of the "Pennsylvania Freeman," and his
early death — which was no doubt caused by his unreserved devotion to his work — deprived the cause of a
champion whose place could never be filled. The
cause in Eastern Pennsylvania was also greatly indebted to the wise liberality and the indefatigable
labors of Edward M. Davis, whose mind was as fertile
in planning as his hand was in executing anti-slavery
measures. Another power that wrought mightily for
the cause in that region, and especially in Philadelphia, was the pulpit of the Rev. William H. Furness,
D. D., of the Unitarian denomination. In every
crisis of the cause his voice rang out in clear tones, in
vindication of outraged right, and in rebuke of popular
wrong. He occupied in Philadelphia a position like
that of Theodore Parker in Boston, who surpassed
him neither in clearness of vision nor boldness of
utterance. His pulpit was a great light amid the
darkness of the time, and to it the Abolitionists constantly turned for words of cheer and hope.

After the separation, the Western Anti-Slavery
Society was organized in North-eastern Ohio, Western
Pennsylvania being included in the field of its operations. "The Anti-Slavery Bugle" was also founded at
Salem, Ohio, Benjamin S. and Jane Elizabeth Jones
being its editors until 1849, when I took charge of it
for two years, being followed at the end of that time
by Marius R. Robinson. Mrs. Jones, as Jane Elizabeth Hitchcock, was the first woman, I believe, to
follow the example of Abby Kelley in entering the
lecture field. She was admirably fitted for the work,
being an excellent speaker as well as a forcible writer.
Her labors in the State of New York and in the field
occupied by the Western Anti-Slavery Society won
for her the esteem and affection of her associates and
the respect of the community. The Western Society
was largely indebted for its efficiency to the labors of

Our Country is the World, our Countrymen are all Mankind.

REDUCED FAC-SIMILE OF THE HEADING OF "THE LIBERATOR."

James W. Walker, for many years its indefatigable lecturing agent. He was, I believe, when he first entered the field, a preacher of the new anti-slavery denomination of Wesleyans. His heart was thoroughly enlisted in the work, and his life was no doubt shortened by a zeal which would not permit him to rest, but constantly impelled him to overtax his strength.

It will be seen, therefore, that the Garrisonians, besides preserving the National Society, had the support, during much of the time after 1840, of not less than four State auxiliaries — one of them, that of Massachusetts, having been the most efficient of all from the first — and of five weekly papers, viz., "The Liberator," in Boston; the "National Anti-Slavery Standard," in New York; the "Pennsylvania Freeman," in Philadelphia; the "Anti-Slavery Bugle," in Salem, Ohio; and the "Herald of Freedom," in Concord, N. H. The last-mentioned paper was discontinued in 1846, or thereabout; while the "Freeman" was united with the "Standard" in 1855. The "Bugle" was not discontinued till near the day of emancipation. "The Liberator" and the "Standard" continued in the field long enough to record not only Lincoln's decree of emancipation, but the adoption of those amendments to the Constitution which dissolved forever that "covenant with death" and that "agreement with hell" which they had done so much to make odious in the eyes of the people. Mr. Garrison and his supporters were not indeed formidable in respect of numbers, or wealth, or social position; but theirs was a warfare of the kind in which one is able to chase a thousand, and two to put ten thousand to flight; nay, in which one, with God, is a majority. Their movement was like a great revolving light on a headland, whose rays penetrate far out into the darkness, warning the navigator of the breakers to be

shunned, and revealing the course to a safe harbor.
Careful navigators on the sea of politics watched for
that light and laid their course by it in times of
danger. Such men as Sumner and Wilson, if they
did not always agree with Mr. Garrison, took note of
his warnings, which they knew were never given
without cause. They read "The Liberator" and the
"Standard," and were not ashamed to acknowledge
their indebtedness to them for wise suggestions and a
wholesome moral stimulus, such as they rarely found
in their party journals. Mr. Sumner, during the
twelve years that I was connected with the "Standard," never failed to call at the Anti-Slavery Office,
on his way to and from Washington, to consult those
whom he found there in regard to the issues of the
time. If he was more clear-sighted than many others,
and less inclined to adopt half-way measures, or to
relax his hold upon great principles, it was in part
because from the first he was a diligent reader of
"The Liberator" and the "Standard," and often in
close consultation with Mr. Garrison. That so many
others in the Republican ranks occasionally faltered in
their allegiance to the cause, and were ready sometimes to enter into specious compromises with the
enemy, may be accounted for by the fact, that not
having read the Abolition journals, nor become
acquainted with non-political Abolitionists, they did
not set their compass by the eternal stars, but were
governed by the shifting rules of expediency. Again
and again, as Mr. Sumner himself sadly admitted, the
cause was well-nigh shipwrecked on this account.
Daniel Webster, after his apostasy, spoke with bitter
contempt of "the rubadub of abolition;" but the
power which he would fain have persuaded himself
was only a fanatical din, was sufficient to defeat his
carefully-laid schemes for the humiliation of New
England, and send him to his grave under an unen-

durable load of shame and self-reproach. If he had availed himself of the instruction of "The Liberator" at as early a day as Mr. Sumner did, he might have spared Massachusetts the pain of discarding him as one who had betrayed her in the hour of her extremity.

The uppermost question in politics at the time of the division in the anti-slavery ranks and for some years afterwards, was the annexation of Texas. Mr. Garrison was one of the first to discern and expose the plot of the slaveholders in that quarter. As early as 1837 he began to agitate the subject, and it was largely owing to his influence that Massachusetts was roused to make a stubborn though unsuccessful resistance to the annexation scheme. Lecturing agents took up the theme, diffusing light and stirring the people to action. The subject of slavery in the District of Columbia was also extensively discussed, and the doors of Faneuil Hall were opened for a meeting on that subject, at which Mr. Garrison presided. In short, whatever it was possible to do to keep the subject of slavery in all its aspects, political, economical and religious, before the people of the whole country, was done by the Garrisonians, through their newspapers, lecturers and tracts. Members of Congress, wishing to speak upon the subject, turned to the anti-slavery papers for facts and arguments, and those papers in turn spread their speeches before the people. Thus there was a genuine reciprocity of labor between those in the moral and those in the political field. This was so to the very end of the conflict, Mr. Garrison and his friends always recognizing and commending every act of genuine hostility to slavery, on whatever field it might be witnessed. If they felt, as they undoubtedly did, that their own position was more favorable than any other for efficient action against slavery, and if they sought by every means in their

power to bring others to their ground, they did not
forget that many of those who differed very widely
from them upon some important points, were yet as
conscientious as themselves, and as earnestly bent
upon destroying slavery by the means which seemed to
them right and feasible.   The moral platform, indeed,
was broad enough for all earnest workers, and all
were invited to stand upon it and speak the word that
was in their hearts.   There was hardly ever an anniversary or other public occasion, when one or more of
the invited speakers did not differ on some important
points from the majority.   No offence was taken if one
speaker, out of his regard for the cause, criticised
another.   Indeed, it was one of the peculiarities of the
Garrisonian movement that it kept its platform free,
not only to dissenting friends, but even to the avowed
enemies of the cause, if they would consent to substitute arguments for brickbats and rotten eggs.

Any account of the moral agitation of the slavery
question from 1846 to 1858 would be sadly defective,
which did not recognize the powerful presence of Theodore Parker.   He did not accept the Garrisonian
view of the Constitution, but on every other point he
was in close affinity with us.   He loved to speak from
our platform, and never once declined to do so if it
was in his power to answer our summons.   He was at
home there, and set a very high value upon the influence of the Garrisonian movement.   He knew that
the discussions of our platform contributed mightily
to the formation of that sound public sentiment, without which no measures in opposition to slavery could be
effective.   In his own pulpit he never failed to improve
an opportunity to bring the question of slavery before
his hearers.   His name was a terror to the ecclesiastical and political trimmers of his time, but a star of
hope to the oppressed, especially to fugitive slaves,
harried by official kidnappers and in danger of being

seized under the shadows of Faneuil Hall or of the stee-
ples of numberless fashionable churches, and doomed
once more to wear the chain and feel the lash of slavery.
The brave words spoken by him were a part of the
very soul of the time, and his name will be reverently
cherished when the moral dwarfs of the Boston pulpit,
Orthodox and Liberal, who droned over their creeds
and formalities while the nation was sinking into the
embrace of the Slave Power, will be remembered no
more.

Three other young preachers of the time, kindred
in spirit to Mr. Parker, and equally bold in their
sphere, deserve to be mentioned for the help they gave
to our struggling cause. One of these, Thomas Went-
worth Higginson, first in Newburyport, then in
Worcester, made his pulpit a centre of light and
power; the other, O. B. Frothingham, standing in
one of the most conservative pulpits in the State,
dared to plead for the oppressed when most of the
ministers around him were silent. Mr. Higginson
often, Mr. Frothingham occasionally, gave us valuable
aid on the platform upon anniversary occasions. Mr.
Higginson, in the dark days of the Fugitive Slave law,
was foremost among those who organized resistance
to that infamous statute ; and soon after the war broke
out he entered the army, and was subsequently made
commander of the first regiment of colored soldiers
called into the service. Samuel Johnson, for many
years pastor of the Free Church in Lynn, bore weighty
testimony in every crisis of the cause. There is
yet another man, who, though he never made a public
address, deserves honorable mention for long and
valuable service of the cause with his pen. I allude
to Charles K. Whipple, whose faithful exposures, in
tracts and newspaper articles, of the subterfuges and
false pretences of the pro-slavery clergy and churches
were always timely and effective.

42

As my memory runs back over the thirty years and more of the anti-slavery conflict, a long procession of anti-slavery lecturers passes before me, with many of whom I was more or less closely acquainted, while others were known to me only by name or through such information respecting their labors as could be gleaned from the anti-slavery papers. This phalanx was the advance-guard of the anti-slavery army — its pioneers, scouts, sappers and miners, foragers, etc. — each of whom had to encounter the foe single-handed and take many a hard blow. Or, to change the military for an industrial figure, they were the "field hands," who bore the heat and burden of the day, and endured hardships and toils, especially in the mob days, which put their pluck and endurance to the proof. On the head of each one of these faithful soldiers, were it in my power, I would place the chaplet he so richly deserves; but these pages are all too scant for the bestowment of such honors. Of some of them I have spoken in previous chapters. A few others only will it be possible for me to mention here.

And first, let me speak of one who for eighteen years filled the responsible post of general agent of the Massachusetts Anti-Slavery Society, and a part of the time that of the American Society as well, — the Rev. Samuel May, to whose sound judgment, unwearied patience, and unselfish devotion the cause was most deeply indebted. In him gentleness is most happily combined with firmness, and a courage that knows no fear. He relinquished a pulpit because he could not consent to wear a chain, and cheerfully took up the cross of Abolitionism amid the scoffs and frowns of misguided but influential men. The agents who labored under his wise direction loved him as a brother. His contributions to the anti-slavery press, especially to "The Liberator," were of much practical value. No man stood higher than he did in the con-

fidence of Mr. Garrison, and, when the great leader
died, he was fitly selected to conduct the funeral
services.

Stephen S. Foster, if I mistake not, was in full
career for the pulpit when the slave's cry of anguish
broke upon his ear, and touched his warm heart.
That cry was for him a summons to another field, and
to that summons he paid instant heed, not doubting
that it was from the Master to whom he had consecrated his powers. A more guileless and ingenuous
man I have never known. No saint of the middle
ages ever surrendered himself more completely than
he did to what he understood to be the service of God
and humanity. His faith in moral principles was
absolute, and he could not knowingly or consciously
swerve from them in his conduct. He felt the wrongs
of the slave as if they were inflicted upon himself;
and such was his courage that he could face a mob,
withstand a friend, or go into a minority of one without flinching. Neither his hatred of wrong nor his
rebukes of wrong-doers were mixed with any dross of
passion. Sometimes those who best loved him dissented from his opinions and criticised his acts; but
no one ever questioned his honesty or doubted his
perfect candor. His rare earnestness and sincerity
gave him great power over an audience, and made him
popular with many as a speaker. His coolness in
facing a mob was phenomenal. He was one of the
"sappers and miners" of the anti-slavery army, and
ready at all times to attack the enemy's fortifications.
His old friends will enjoy this humorous description
of him by James Russell Lowell : —

> "Hard by, as calm as summer even,
> Smiles the reviled and pelted Stephen,
> The unappeasable Boanerges
> To all the churches and the clergies;
> The grim *savant*, who, to complete
> His own peculiar cabinet,

Contrived to label with his kicks
One from the followers of Elias Hicks;
Who studied mineralogy,
Not with soft book upon the knee,
But learned the properties of stones
By contact sharp of flesh and bones,
And made the *experimentum crucis*
With his own body's vital juices;
A man with caoutchouc endurance,
A perfect gem for life insurance;
A kind of maddened John the Baptist,
To whom the harshest word comes aptest,
Who, struck by stone or brick ill-starred,
Hurls back an epithet as hard,
Which, deadlier than stone or brick,
Has a propensity to stick.
His oratory is like the scream
Of the iron horse's frenzied steam,
Which warns the world to leave a space
For the black engine's swerveless race."

Another member of the "sappers and miners' corps" was Parker Pillsbury, who got clear into the pulpit before the cause laid hold of him, but who, notwithstanding, came into our ranks at an early day, in time to see hard service. He carried the gospel of freedom into many a dark place. Endowed with a vivid imagination, he could set the enormities of the slave system and the guilt of its supporters in their true light. His speeches were strong in argument, earnest and solemn in the manner of delivery, and adorned with an imagery which to many was exceedingly fascinating. In many places, both in New England and the West, he was a great favorite. His labors in many fields were abundant and valuable. He also did excellent service for a time as editor of the "Herald of Freedom." I must again draw upon James Russell Lowell for a bit of genial description, the accuracy of which will be generally acknowledged : —

" Beyond, a crater in each eye,
Sways brown, broad-shouldered Pillsbury;
Who tears up words, like trees, by the roots —
A Theseus in stout cowhide boots.

A terrible denouncer he!
Old Sinai burns unquenchably
Upon his lips; he well might be a
Hot-blazing soul from fierce Judea,
Habakkuk, Ezra, or Hosea.
His words burn as with iron searers,
And, nightmare-like, he mounts his hearers,
Spurring them like avenging fate; or
As Waterton his alligator."

As I lay down my pen, the procession moves on before me, and I see the faces of C. L. Remond, Frederick Douglass, James Munroe, A. T. Foss, William Wells Brown, Sallie Holley, Henry C. Wright (fighting "on his own hook," but always at the front), Dr. E. D. Hudson, Aaron M. Powell, George Bradburn, Lucy Stone, Edwin Thompson, Nathaniel H. Whiting, Sumner Lincoln, James Boyle, Giles B. Stebbins, Thomas T. Stone, George W. Putnam, Joseph A. Howland, Anna E. Dickinson, Susan B. Anthony, Frances E. Watkins, Loring Moody, Adin Ballou, W. H. Fish, Daniel Foster, A. J. Grover, James N. Buffum, and scores beside, — some of them in the spirit-land, others still lingering amid the scenes of earth, — to whom I can only give from my heart a passing salute of recognition. Blessings on them all, and upon each one of the unknown and innumerable host that fought to redeem the Republic and break the fetters of the slave !

XX.

The Question of Disunion — The Declaration of 1833 — The Ameri-
can Idol — The "Covenant with Death," and the "Agreement with.
Hell " — Dr. Channing's Opinion — "No Union with Slavehold-
ers " — The Demoralizing Influence of the Constitution — The
Claim that it was Anti-Slavery — John Quincy Adams's Opinion
— Judge Jay in Favor of Disunion — Need of a Sound Ethical
Basis — Political Effects of the Agitation — The Rebellion
Changes the Issue — Mr. Garrison Vindicated.

As early as 1843, Mr. Garrison began to discuss in
"The Liberator." the question whether it was not the
duty of the people of the free States, on account of
the inherent wickedness of those provisions of the
Constitution which related to slavery, to dissolve their
political relations with the South.   It was a startling
proposition, from which many Abolitionists while
acknowledging the strength of the arguments urged in
its behalf, shrank back appalled.   It seems strange
now that Mr. Garrison's mind did not sooner arrive
at this point, and that for so long a time the Abolitionists habitually claimed that their movement had a
tendency to preserve the Union.   Turning to the
Declaration of Sentiments — our Magna Charta —
adopted in 1833, I find this passage :—

"They [the people of the free States] are now living
under a pledge of their tremendous physical force, to fasten
the galling fetters of tyranny upon the limbs of millions in
the Southern States ; they are liable to be called at any
moment to suppress a general insurrection of the slaves ;
they authorize the slave-owner to vote for three-fifths of his
slaves as property, and thus enable him to perpetuate his

oppression ; and they seize the slave, who has escaped into
their territories, and send him back to be tortured by an
enraged master or a brutal driver. This relation to slavery
is criminal, and full of danger: IT MUST BE BROKEN UP."

That Mr. Garrison could write this passage with
care and deliberation, and read it many times in the
course of ten years, without being aware that it was a
specific argument for disunion, only shows how near
even a clear-headed man can sometimes come to a new
thought without quite discovering it. If the relation
of the people of the free States to slavery, as defined
in the provisions of the Constitution, was " criminal
and full of danger," how could it be innocently
tolerated for an hour? And how could it " be broken
up," without at the same time breaking the bonds of
the Union? The Constitution could not be changed
without the consent of the slave States, or a considerable portion of them; and certainly that consent was
not likely to be given. And yet, it is to be presumed
that, for ten years, Mr. Garrison regarded this striking
paragraph from his own pen only as defining an obligation " resting upon the people of the free States to
remove slavery by moral and political action, as prescribed in the Constitution of the United States."
And it would seem that the Abolitionists, as a body,
cherished the conviction that the measures sanctioned
by the Constitution were adequate to the complete
overthrow of the slave system; although from the
beginning they confessed that, " under the present
national compact, Congress has no right to interfere
with any of the States, in relation to this momentous
subject." However this apparent blindness may be
explained, it now passed away from the mind of Mr.
Garrison, who thenceforth saw clearly that the obligations imposed by the Constitution upon the people of
the non-slaveholding States in relation to slavery were
immoral in their nature, and therefore not to be inno-

cently acknowledged by them, on any plea of interest
or necessity, for a single day. Of course, when this
became clear to his mind, he did not lack courage to
declare the truth. No man knew better than he that
the Union was the idol of the American people, and
worshipped by them as the source of every national
blessing, the glory of the past and the present, and
the foundation of every hope for the future. The
Jewish nation hardly had a deeper reverence for the
ark, which they supposed to be the very dwelling-place
of Jehovah, than the people of the United States had
for their national compact; and when Mr. Garrison,
finding in the words of the prophet Isaiah a phrase
happily suited to his purpose, denounced it as a
"covenant with death" and an "agreement with hell"
(Is. xxviii. 18), they lifted up their hands as if they had
heard the most awful blasphemy. Even the religious
press chose to seem unaware that the words were borrowed from Scripture, and went on prating of Mr.
Garrison's "harsh and vituperative language." If any
one imagines that the Hebrew prophet had any more
provocation for the use of such words than Mr. Garrison had, he is advised to study the record. If the
Jews acknowledged any covenant more deadly, or any
agreement more characteristic of hell than that by
which the Northern people bound themselves in respect to slavery in the National Constitution, the eye
of no commentator upon the Scriptures has ever pointed
it out. Mr. Garrison found his models of style in dealing with popular systems of iniquity in the Jewish
prophets, and in Jesus and his Apostles; which accounts at once for his "hard language" and his great
power as a reformer. Dr. Channing, though he did
not follow Isaiah so closely as Mr. Garrison did, yet
saw clearly the character of the national compact.
" The free States," he said, "are guardians and essential supports of slavery. We are the jailers and con-

stables of the institution. . . . On this subject our
fathers, in framing the Constitution, swerved from the
right. We, their children, at the end of half a century, see the path of duty more clearly than they, and
must walk in it. No blessings of the Union can be a
compensation for taking part in the enslaving of our
fellow-creatures. And to this conviction they must
speedily come, or the power of self-recovery will be
lost forever, and their damnation made sure." If Dr.
Channing had not died so soon after writing these
words, perhaps he and Mr. Garrison would have struck
hands in the effort to induce the people of the free
States to repudiate the unrighteous promises made by
the fathers, and refuse to be the jailers and constables
of the slave system. Who knows?

Mr. Garrison, as soon as the truth became clear to
his own mind, set himself to the task of bringing his
associates up to the same high ground, and to the
exhibition of the same courage that he had himself
displayed. There must be no faltering at such a
crisis; the truth must be proclaimed, whether men
would hear or forbear. The right, and the right
alone, was his pole-star, to be followed in every emergency and at every hazard. Henceforth it must be
his chief business to convict the Northern people of
sin in consenting to be "the guardians and essential
supports" of slavery, and to bring them to a heartfelt
and speedy repentance. Their dangerous and criminal
relation to the slave system must soon "be broken
up," or, in the words of Channing, "the power of self-
recovery would be lost forever." There were, there
could be, no questions of expediency worth a moment's
consideration, or that could offer any excuse for delay.
He began with the Massachusetts Society in January,
1844; but even that body was not then quite ready to
follow his lead. He brought the subject before the
American Society in May, and, after a long and very

43

exciting discussion, that society, by a vote of 59 to
21, put itself squarely on the ground of disunion.
The New England Convention followed, two weeks
later, voting the same way, — 250 to 24. Then the
whole Garrisonian phalanx swung solidly round to
the same position, and the movement thenceforth carried aloft the banner, "No Union with Slaveholders."

Not for a moment did Mr. Garrison stop to consider
what would be the consequences, near or remote, of
taking this ground. Whether a multitude would rally
around him, or half his old friends turn sorrowfully
away, he could not, nor did he even seek to know.
He saw the truth, and instantly obeyed its voice,
sure, if he considered the matter at all, that the consequences could not be otherwise than good; and the
result justified his confidence. If there was no flock-
ing of great numbers to the standard, the moral power
of the movement was augmented by being placed upon
a sound and consistent ethical basis, where its friends
could stand without dodging or wavering, and which
made all weapons formed against it harmless. The
time had come when it was absolutely necessary to
destroy the idolatrous reverence for the Constitution
which had so long been the shield and buckler of
slavery, and a covert for tricksters and hucksters of
every sort. Nothing could more surely promote the
demoralization of a people than the "exaltation above
all that is called God, or that is worshipped," of a
Constitution of government defiled by slavery, and
made the chief fortress for its protection. In any
point of view, therefore, it was a high service rendered to the people of this country when the anti-
slavery movement assailed this fortress, and showed it
to be full of dead men's bones and all uncleanness.
In the early days of the cause, we used to wonder why
Northern members of Congress who were anti-slavery
at home found it so hard to keep their footing in

Washington. The simple truth was that, between what the Constitution forbade them to do in opposition to slavery and required them to do for its support, there was hardly an inch of ground on which they could stand; and so, one after another, smitten by the popular idolatry of the instrument, they found no place for the soles of their feet save in the slippery ways of compromise, where they were utterly powerless to help the slave. Year after year, the Abolitionists had seen this farce played before their eyes without half understanding it; but now their eyes were opened, and everything was clear to their vision. How could men be true to the slave, and at the same time obey an oath to sustain a pro-slavery Constitution? Under such conditions, Congress became a sepulchre, where free souls could hardly draw the breath of life. If Sumner and Wilson and Hale and Chase *did* breathe and do noble work there, it was only because they found a way to break through the web which the Constitution wove about them, and thus maintain their allegiance to the Higher Law. That they were able to do this may have been owing very largely to the influence of the Garrisonian movement in diminishing the popular reverence for the Constitution as it had so long been interpreted, and in forming a public opinion which would pardon a breach of sinful compromises, but would *not* pardon a want of fealty to the cause of freedom.

There was a considerable body of men, some of them eminent for ability and worth as well as for long service in the cause of freedom, who strenuously held that there was not a clause or word in the Constitution that was not, upon a fair and right construction, in accordance with sound principles of law and rigid rules of philology, anti-slavery. William Goodell, Gerrit Smith, George B. Cheever, and Frederick Douglass also in the later years of the struggle, were of this

party. Their reasoning was ingenious and plausible,
and sometimes quite effective, like that of the man
who has a logical way of showing that you have no
nose on your face. If there is no mirror present and
your hands are tied behind your back, he can convince
you for the moment; but the very next time you confront a looking-glass you find your nose in the same
old place. It was easy to show, if a man could only
be made to forget the facts of history, that the Constitution was as pure as if made in heaven, instead of
being the work of a nation with hundreds of thousands
of slaves, and of politicians bent not only upon guarding
the system of slavery from national encroachment, but
even upon gaining for it positive protection. The fact
that for twenty years that Constitution lent the national
flag for the protection of the foreign slave-trade, and
that during that long period the shores of Africa were
invaded by American man-hunters, employed by New
England capital to pillage, murder, burn and kidnap
at their will, without the least fear of being called to
account for their crimes, settles the character of the
old Constitution so far as slavery was concerned; and
when to this was added the provision allowing the
slaveholders to count three-fifths of their slaves in the
basis of representation, the clause providing for the
suppression of slave insurrections by the national
forces, and the article making provision for the return
of fugitive slaves, its character became so black that
the phrases "covenant with death" and "agreement
with hell" seemed a label all too mild. The interpre-
tations by which the instrument was made to wear an
anti-slavery character had, however, some value as an
honest protest against the wickedness of slavery, and
as a method of relieving some troubled consciences.
An association, called the American Abolition Society,
was organized upon this basis, but it was short-lived.
In comparison with this, the doctrine of disunion,

revolting as it was to many, seemed reasonable and
practical, for it was in perfect accordance with the
facts in the case, and rested upon a basis of moral
principle which everybody could comprehend. "There
are some very worthy men," said Mr. Garrison, "who
are gravely trying to convince this slaveholding and
slave-trading nation that it has an anti-slavery Constitution, if it did but know it—always has had it since
it was a nation—and so designed to be from the
beginning. Hence, all slaveholding under it is illegal,
and ought forthwith to be abolished by act of Congress.
As rationally attempt to convince the American people
that they inhabit the moon and 'run upon all fours,'
as that they have not intelligently, deliberately and
purposely entered into a covenant by which three
millions of slaves are now held securely in bondage.
They are not to be let off so easily, either by indignant
Heaven or outraged earth. To tell them that for three-
score years they have misunderstood and misinter-
preted their own Constitution, in a manner gross and
distorted beyond anything known in human history;
that Washington, Jefferson, Adams, all who framed
that Constitution — the Supreme Court of the United
States and all its branches and all other courts, the
National Congress and all State Legislatures — have
utterly perverted its scope and meaning, is the coolest
and absurdest thing ever heard of beneath the stars.
. . . . The people of this country have bound
themselves by an oath to have no other God before them
but a CONSTITUTIONAL GOD, which their own hands have
made, and to which they demand homage of every one
born or resident on the American soil, on peril of imprisonment or death. His fiat is 'the supreme law of
the land.' . . . Three millions of the American
people are crushed under the American Union. They
are held as slaves, trafficked as merchandise, registered
as goods and chattels. The government gives them

no protection, the government is their enemy, the government keeps them in chains. Where they lie bleeding, we are prostrated by their side; in their sorrows and sufferings we participate; their stripes are inflicted on our bodies; their shackles are fastened on our limbs; their cause is ours. The Union which grinds them to the dust rests upon us, and with them we will struggle to overthrow it. The Constitution which subjects them to hopeless bondage we cannot . swear to support. Our motto is, 'No Union with Slaveholders,' either religious or political. They are the fiercest enemies of mankind, and the bitterest foes of God. - We separate from them, not in anger, not in malice, not for a selfish purpose, not to do them an injury, not to cease warning, exhorting, reproving them for their crimes, not to leave the perishing bond-man to his fate — Oh, no. But to clear our skirts of innocent blood — to give the oppressor no countenance — and to hasten the downfall of slavery in America and throughout the world."

In his estimate of the character of the American Union, Mr. Garrison was supported by John Quincy Adams, who said: "The bargain between Freedom and Slavery, contained in the Constitution of the United States, is morally and politically vicious, inconsistent with the principles on which alone our Revolution can be justified, cruel and oppressive by riveting the chains of slavery, and by pledging the faith of freedom to maintain and perpetuate the tyranny of the master." The doctrine of disunion, too, found strong backing in influential quarters. "Should the slaveholders succeed," — said the Hon. William Jay, in a letter to Edward M. Davis of Philadelphia, — "in their design of annexing Texas, then indeed would I not merely discuss, but with all my powers would I advocate an immediate dissolution. I love my children, my friends, my country too well to leave them a prey to

the accursed government which would be sure to follow." Again, writing to Mr. Henry I. Bowditch of
Boston, March 19, 1845, he said: "Dissolution must
take place, and the sooner the better. It is far more
probable that a continuance of our present connection
will enslave the North than that it will free the South.
A separation will be more easily effected *now* than
when the relative strength of the South shall have
been greatly augmented. Hereafter we shall be as
serfs rebelling against their bonds. *Now*, if the North
pleases, we may dissolve the Union without spilling a
drop of blood." Thus it looked to Judge Jay after
the annexation of Texas. But he, no more than the
rest of us, foresaw that, after gaining Texas, the
South would bring disaster upon herself by wrenching
from Mexico a still larger domain, on the shores of
the Pacific, upon which she would find it impossible to
plant her hateful system, but which would restore the
balance of power to the North. In principle, however,
his words are a complete justification and endorsement
of the course pursued by Mr. Garrison.

A working hypothesis is not more indispensable to
the scientific investigator than is a sound ethical basis
of action to the moral reformer. The latter, indeed,
dooms himself to inevitable defeat if he substitutes
expediency for principle, or fails to declare the ultimate and fundamental truth. Mr. Garrison did not
concern himself with the modes of political action by
which the Northern people might escape from the toils
of the Slave Power; he fabricated no scheme of government to supersede that of the Union. He knew
that, in their individual capacity, they could at once
peaceably repudiate the immoral compromises of the
Constitution and cease to give support to slavery; and
he knew equally well that when a majority of their
number should be brought to take this high ground,
they would find a way to organize such a government

as their needs required. As emancipation must pre-
cede all effective effort to uplift the slave, so the people of the North must first dissolve their guilty relation
with the Slave Power before they could establish for
themselves a pure government. The path of duty for
him was clear. He must cry aloud, spare not, and lift
up his voice like a trumpet, showing the people their
transgression, the citizens of the Republic their sins.
Called of God, as he believed, to this work, he obeyed
the heavenly voice with no concern for the consequences, knowing that they could only be such as naturally follow right-doing. "Do you ask," he said,
"what can be done if you abandon the ballot-box?
What did the crucified Nazarene do without the elec-
tive franchise? What did the Apostles do? What
did the glorious army of martyrs and confessors do?
What did Luther. and his intrepid associates do?

'If thou must stand alone, what then? The honor shall be more!
But thou canst never stand alone while heaven still arches o'er—
While there's a God to worship, a devil to be denied—
The good and true of every age stand with thee, side by side!'

The form of government that shall succeed the present
government of the United States, let time determine.
It would be a waste of time to argue that question
until the people are regenerated and turned from their
iniquity. Ours is no anarchical movement, but one of
order and obedience. In ceasing from oppression, we
establish liberty. What is now fragmentary shall in
due time be crystallized, and shine like a gem set in
the heavens, for a light to all coming ages."
    From 1844 to 1861, the Garrisonian agitation pro-
ceeded upon this ground of the inherent defilement of
the Constitution—" the saturation of the parchment," as
John Quincy Adams said, " with the infection of slavery,
which no fumigation could purify, no quarantine could
extinguish." The truth was proclaimed in the anti-

slavery journals, in pamphlets and tracts, in conventions innumerable, and by the voices of a phalanx of lecturers, with Garrison and Phillips at their head. But while all discussion led in one way or another to this point, no aspect of the slavery question was neglected. The movements in Congress and the State Legislatures were watched and stimulated by every means in our power. The action of the political parties and ecclesiastical bodies was carefully scrutinized, and wherever any honest voice was heard pleading the cause of the slave, no matter under what limitations, it was welcomed and cheered. The bruised reed was not broken, nor the smoking flax quenched. Timidity was encouraged to be brave, despair was taught to be hopeful. Tricksters and trimmers, men of false pretences, were alone repelled and scourged. The Garrisonian movement quickened and elevated every other. It helped to make the Republican party firm in purpose, quick in action, and proof against compromise. Our meetings in New York and Boston—sometimes in Faneuil Hall—were watched with intense eagerness and constantly increasing respect by men of all parties and sects. However far public sentiment might at any time fall short of our ground, the politicians knew that it was constantly advancing, and would ultimately reach the highest mark. Garrison led the great chorus of voices that swelled up to heaven from every part of the country, from people of every variety of opinions upon other subjects, but united in proclaiming slavery to be a sin and crime, and in demanding its immediate extinction. Grumblers, forced by public opinion out of the pro-slavery ranks, and compelled to do half-hearted service in the cause, kept up their denunciations of the founder of the movement; but those who, in whatever way, in good faith and with their whole hearts, fought slavery, recognized his power and honored him for his heroic adherence to principle.

41

And he, on his part, honored them, while fighting in
their own way, and whether they approved of all his
measures or not.

There can be no doubt that in the sixteen years immediately preceding the Rebellion, the Garrisonian
movement did much to prepare the Northern people
for the crisis through which they were called to pass.
It taught them the folly of that superstitious reverence
for the Constitution which was so long a main depend-
ence of the Slave Power. It made further compromise
impossible, and nerved the arm of the North to do
and dare in the cause of liberty. If the moral influence that stood behind the Republican party in that
trying hour, and which was very largely represented
by the Garrisonian movement, had been withdrawn,
who knows into what new depth of humiliation the
North might have been dragged? If Abraham Lincoln, in the hope of thereby averting a civil war, could
execute the infamous Fugitive Slave law, what might
not have been expected of smaller men, if they had
not felt the influence of that moral power, which, independent of any party influence, was working in the
hearts of their constituents? We needed in that
awful hour all the strength which a whole generation
of MORAL AGITATION had developed. No whit of it
could have been safely spared—least of all that which
came from the faithful founder and leader of the
movement.

The madness of the Rebellion changed all the conditions of the problem, and worked out the deliverance of the North as well as of the slaves by a
process which no one had contemplated. But if the
South had submitted to the election of Lincoln, and
gone on demanding her "pound of flesh" under the
Constitution, the Garrisonian movement would have
brought victory by another process. It was simply
impossible that the North could much longer endure

the domination of the Slave Power. She must have found a way to annul the "covenant with death," and overthrow the "agreement with hell." All the signs pointed to that result. It was not in vain that the true character of the American Union, as affected by what John Quincy Adams called "the deadly venom of slavery," had been faithfully depicted for sixteen successive years by men whom no bribes could seduce and no terrors frighten from the field.

When Abraham Lincoln accepted the task of suppressing the Rebellion, and the whole North rose up to sustain him, Mr. Garrison saw at once that the days of slavery were numbered; that the restoration of the Union under the old conditions was impossible; that the slaveholders themselves had discarded their main defence. There was no longer any need of inculcating the duty of disunion at the North. He at once removed from "The Liberator," as an anachronism, his motto of "No Union with Slaveholders," and set himself to work to develop that public opinion for which President Lincoln so long waited, and which at last made it safe for him to decree the emancipation of the slaves. To those who questioned his consistency in taking this course, he said, substantially: As Benedick, when he said he would die a bachelor, did not think he should live till he were married, so he (Mr. Garrison), when he pledged himself to fight while life lasted against the "covenant with death" and the "agreement with hell," did not think that he should live to see death and hell secede from the Union. As they had done so, however, he thought his consistency might be safely left to take care of itself. As one who accepted the principle of non-resistance as taught and exemplified by Jesus, he could not himself bear arms even in the cause of liberty and humanity; but he felt it right to judge the people of the North by their own standard, and to tell them that, as they believed in war, they would be poltroons if they did not fight. Upon this point, also, he was willing to leave his consistency without defence. His own conscience was clear. He had tried to persuade the people to abolish slavery by peaceful means, warning them the while that, if they should refuse to do so, the judgments of God might come upon them in a war from which there would be no escape. The day of retribution had come, and the Northern people were shut up to the necessity of either sacrificing their own liberty or fighting for the freedom of the slave.

After the war was over, and when the work of reconstruction was before the country, did any one not an apologist for slavery dream of restoring the Union under the Constitution as it then stood? Did not every loyal citizen see clearly that the instrument must be so amended that death and hell could never again find protection in it? In the amendments which were then adopted, and by which slavery was forever debarred from the soil of the Republic, Mr. Garrison's doctrine of disunion was completely vindicated. The Constitution under which we are now living is not that which he publicly burned on a certain Fourth of July in Framingham; nor is the Union which he sought to dissolve any longer in existence. The Union of to-day is a Union "redeemed, regenerated, and disenthralled by the Genius of Universal Emancipation."

XXI.

Mr. Garrison's Visits Abroad — The London Conference of 1840 — American Women Excluded — Mr. Garrison Refuses to be a Member — Excitement in England — O'Connell and Bowring — The Visit of 1846 — The Free Church of Scotland — The Visit of 1867 — The London Breakfast — John Bright — The Duke of Argyll — John Stuart Mill — Goldwin Smith — George Thompson — Speech of Mr. Garrison — The Visit of 1877 — Sightseeing — Visits to Old Friends — Delectable Days — Farewells.

OF Mr. Garrison's first visit to England (1833) I have already given an account. He went a second time as a delegate to the London Anti-Slavery Conference of 1840. The friends of New Organization had the ear of the British and Foreign Society at that time, and care was taken, on this side the water, to guard the Conference against the intrusion of women from America. The Garrisonian anti-slavery societies, having admitted women to membership, were bound in honor to respect their rights in the appointment of delegates to the Conference. The women commissioned as delegates by the different societies were: Lucretia Mott, Mrs. Wendell Phillips, Sarah Pugh, Mary Grew, Elizabeth J. Neall (now Mrs. Sydney Howard Gay), and Emily Winslow (now Mrs. Taylor). I venture to say that these were as well qualified for the service as any equal number of the other sex, sent to the Conference from this or any other country. But the committee of the British and Foreign Society, which assumed the right to frame rules for the Conference, excluded them, on the ground that their admission would be contrary to "British usage." Wendell Phillips made a strenuous effort to induce the Conference to repeal this rule and admit the women delegates, but in vain. He spoke eloquently, but to men whose minds were made up and impatient of argument. The Conference had been in session about a week when Mr. Garrison, with N. P. Rogers, Charles L. Remond and William Adams, all delegates, arrived in London. When Mr. Garrison learned that the credentials of the women delegates had been dishonored, he at once determined not to enter the Conference, but to take his place in the gallery as a spectator. His example was followed by the other gentlemen who arrived at the same time with himself. Seven other American delegates, who had entered the Conference before Mr. Garrison's arrival, framed a protest against the exclusion. These were Prof. W. Adam, James Mott, C. E. Lester, Isaac Winslow, Wendell Phillips, Jonathan P. Miller and George Bradburn.

Of course, these occurrences made no little stir among British Abolitionists. The excluded women were treated with the highest respect socially, save by a few of the more bigoted sort. The question of their exclusion was warmly discussed in private, and many of those who made their acquaintance were not a little mortified that "British usage" had found such an illustration. Daniel O'Connell was among those who expressed regret in view of their exclusion, and who showed them marked attentions. So also was Sir John Bowring, who said, "The coming of those women will form an era in the future history of philanthropy. They made a deep impression, and have created apostles, if as yet they have not multitudes of followers." Mr. Garrison won universal respect by his course in refusing to be a member of the Conference. As the recognized founder of the movement in the United States, he became all the more conspicuous

from his outside position; and the gallery where he
sat, surrounded by the excluded delegates, was a point
of interest hardly inferior to the Conference itself.
The head of the table, by a fore-ordained necessity,
must be where McGreggor sits! Some (not all) of
the friends of New Organization from America made
desperate efforts to discredit Mr. Garrison with the
Abolitionists of England, but succeeded only in dis-
crediting themselves. He was treated with the utmost
respect and consideration on every side, and invited to
unfold, in private, all those dreadful heresies of opinion
which had been the cause of so much disturbance in
his own country. The Abolitionists of Great Britain
liked him not a whit the less, but all the more, after
listening to his frank statements and explanations.
He afterwards said: "If there is any one act of my
life of which I am particularly proud, it is in refusing
to join such a body [the London Conference] on terms
which were manifestly reproachful to my constituents,
and unjust to the cause of liberty."

Mr. Garrison crossed the Atlantic for the third time
in 1846, at the special invitation of the Glasgow
Emancipation Society, and by advice of the Executive
Committee of the American Society, to take part in
the arraignment before the people of Scotland of the
agents sent by the Free Church of that country to collect
funds for church purposes among the slaveholders of
the South. Scotland was deeply moved by the action
of those agents. Meetings were held in all the principal towns, and the cry, "Send Back the Money!"
rang out from the lips of thousands and tens of thousands of people. The Free Church, however, held on
to the gains of oppression. Henry C. Wright, and, if
I mistake not, Charles L. Remond and James N.
Buffum were already in Scotland when the agents
returned from the United States. They, with Mr.
Garrison and George Thompson, took part in the

meetings called to protest against the scandalous endorsement of slavery by Scottish Christians.   The
conduct of the agents of the Free Church excited
universal indignation among the Abolitionists.   The
Executive Committee of the American and Foreign
Society sent an eloquent protest, in the form of a letter
to the Free Church, from the pen of Judge Jay.   How
much money the church obtained at the South, as a
reward for the silence of its agents in regard to the
atrocities of slavery, I do not remember, but it was a
considerable sum.   Mr. Garrison spoke on the subject
in many places in Scotland, with his usual eloquence
and power; but he might as well have tried to unlock
the grasp of a miser on his hoard as to force out of a
church treasury, under such circumstances, the gains
of unrighteousness.

In 1867, two years after the close of the civil war,
Mr. Garrison, partly on account of impaired health
and partly to make what he then supposed would be
his farewell visit to his English, Scotch and Irish
friends, crossed the ocean for the fourth time.   As
two of his children were then in Paris, he embraced
the opportunity of visiting the Continent for the first
time.   Crossing the Atlantic in May, in company with
George Thompson, who was returning to England
from America for the last time, he immediately joined
his children in Paris, where he remained, enjoying the
Exposition, till June 15, and then, in company with his
son Frank and his daughter, Mrs. Villard, he went to
London.   During the next two weeks he was the
recipient of marked attentions from the Duke and
Duchess of Argyll, and the latter's mother, the Duchess of Sutherland, who sent for him to come and see
her in the sick-chamber to which she was confined by
what proved to be her last illness.   Then followed, on
June 20th, the great public breakfast held in his
honor, in St. James's Hall, London.   It was a re-

markable gathering, and one scarcely paralleled. Hon.
John Bright occupied the chair. F. W. Chesson,
Esq., and Richard Moore, Esq., were the Secretaries.
The Committee of Arrangements embraced, among
others, Lord Houghton, Sir Thomas Fowell Buxton,
John Bright, M. P., John Stuart Mill, M. P., Thomas
Hughes, M. P., T. B. Potter, M. P., Prof. Maurice,
P. A. Taylor, M. P., Prof. Huxley, Goldwin Smith,
William Howitt, and others not less distinguished.
Among the guests were Prof. Huxley, Herbert Spen-
cer, Prof. Maurice, Lady Trevelyan, Victor Schoel-
cher, and many others of equal distinction; also a
considerable body of ladies, some of them from the
United States, and a large number of ministers of the
gospel, of various denominations. The American
Minister, Hon. Charles Francis Adams, sent a note
alluding to Mr. Garrison's "long and arduous services
in the cause of philanthropy," and expressing his
regret that he was unable, from the pressure of important engagements, to be present. Mr. F. H. Morse,
the American Consul in London, was present, as was
also the Rev. W. H. Channing. The Comte de Paris
sent an eloquent letter, in which he said : "In receiving
a man whose character honors America, I thank you,
sir, for having thought of me, and for having counted
on my sympathy for all that is great and noble in that
country, which I have seen in the midst of such a terrible crisis."

The first speaker on the occasion was John Bright,
whose address was pronounced by those accustomed to
hearing him to have been one of the finest efforts of
his life. It was a most generous tribute, not to Mr.
Garrison alone, but to American Abolitionists in general. "To Mr. Garrison," he said, "more than to any
other man this is due ; his is the creation of that opinion which has made slavery hateful, and which has made
freedom possible in America. His name is venerated
45

in his own country — venerated where not long ago it
was a name of obloquy and reproach.   His name is
venerated in this country and in Europe, wheresoever
Christianity softens the hearts and lessens the sorrows
of men ;   and I venture to say that in time to come,
near or remote I know not, his name will become the
herald and the synonym of good to millions of men
who will dwell on the now almost unknown continent
of Africa. . . . To him it has been given, in a manner not often permitted to those who do great things of
this kind, to see the ripe fruit of his vast labors.   Over
a territory large enough to make many realms, he has
seen hopeless toil supplanted by compensated industry, and where the bondman dragged his chain, there
freedom is established forever.   We now welcome
him among us as a friend whom some of us have
known long ;   for I have watched his career with no
common interest, even when I was too young to take
much part in public affairs ;   and I have kept within
my heart his name and the names of those who have
been associated with him in every step which he has
taken ;   and in public debate in the halls of peace, and
even on the blood-soiled fields of war, my heart has
always been with those who were the friends of freedom.   We welcome him, then, with a cordiality which
knows no stint and no limits for him and his noble
associates, both men and women ;   and we venture to
speak a verdict which, I believe, will be sanctioned by
all mankind, not only those who live now, but those
who shall come after, to whom their perseverance and
their success shall be a lesson and a help in the future
struggles which remain for men to make.   One of our
oldest and greatest poets has furnished me with a line
that well expresses that verdict.   Are not William
Lloyd Garrison and his fellow-laborers in that world's
work — are they not

'On Fame's eternal bead-roll worthy to be filed' !"

An official address to Mr. Garrison, from the pen of Prof. Goldwin Smith, embodying the sentiments and feelings of the distinguished company in respect to him and his labors, was next moved by the Duke of Argyll, who, in the performance of this duty, made a most eloquent and felicitous speech. After declaring that "the cause of negro emancipation in the United States of America has been the greatest cause which, in ancient or modern times, has been pleaded at the bar of the moral judgment of mankind," and justifying the interest felt in it by the people of England, he said : "If such be the cause, what are we to say of the man and of the services which he has rendered to that cause? We honor Mr. Garrison, in the first place, for the immense pluck and courage he displayed. . . . In attacking slavery at its headquarters in the United States, he had to encounter the fiercest passions which could be roused. That is, indeed a tremendous sea which runs upon the surface of the human mind when the storms of passion and self-interest run counter to the secret currents of conscience and the sense of right. Such was the stormy sea on which Mr. Garrison embarked at first — if I may use the simile — almost in a one-oared boat. He stood alone. And so in our reception this day we are entitled to think of him as representing the increased power and force which is exerted in our own times by the moral opinions of mankind. . . . We can all understand the joy of him, who, like our distinguished friend, after years of obloquy and oppression, and being denounced as the fanatical supporter of extreme opinions, finds himself acknowledged at last by his countrymen and the world as the prophet and apostle of a triumphant and accepted cause."

The official address, prepared by Prof. Goldwin Smith, was appropriately phrased, in the true spirit of the occasion, and was very warmly endorsed, being

seconded by Earl Russell, who had privately solicited
an invitation to the breakfast, that he might, as then
appeared, make the *amende honorable*, in the most
public and significant manner, for his unfriendly attitude toward the United States during the Rebellion.
He did this in terms most honorable to himself, receiving the hearty acknowledgment of the guest of
the occasion, who upon this point certainly spoke for
his country. The Earl, in his brief address, avowed
himself a sincere admirer and warm friend of Mr.
Garrison, whom he reckoned among the deliverers of
mankind.

John Stuart Mill made an exceedingly happy address, in which he enforced some of the lessons of Mr.
Garrison's career. The first was, "Aim at something
great; aim at things which are difficult." The second
was, "If you aim at something noble, and succeed in
it, you will generally find that you have not succeeded
in that alone." The mind of America had been emancipated by the anti-slavery movement. The whole
intellect of the country had been set thinking about
the fundamental questions of society and government,
and great good must be the result.

The official address having been adopted by a unani-
mous show of hands, Mr. Garrison rose to reply. He
was received with an enthusiastic burst of cheering,
hats and handkerchiefs being waved by nearly all present. His address was marked by the speaker's usually
direct and simple style. He began with offering his
grateful acknowledgments for this marked expression
of personal respect and appreciation of his labors in
the anti-slavery cause, by the formidable array of rank,
genius, intellect, scholarship, and moral and religious
worth, which he saw before him, and by which he was
profoundly impressed. He then drew a striking contrast between the encomiums of which he was now the
subject, and the odium under which he so long rested

in his own country for pleading the cause of the slave. He always found in America that a shower of brickbats had a remarkably tonic effect, materially strengthening the back-bone. But the shower of compliments · and applause that had greeted him on this occasion would have caused his heart to fail him, were it not that this generous reception was only incidentally personal to himself. They were met to celebrate the triumph of humanity over its most brutal foes; to rejoice that universal emancipation had at last been proclaimed throughout the United States, and to express sentiments of good-will toward the American Republic. "I must here disclaim," he said, "with all sincerity of soul, any special praise for anything that I have done. I have simply tried to maintain the integrity of my soul before God, and to do my duty. I have refused to go with the multitude to do evil. I have endeavored to save my country from ruin. I have sought to liberate such as were held captive in the house of bondage. But all this I ought to have done." . . . "I made the slave's case from the start, and always, my own—thus: Did I want to be a slave? No. Did God make me to be a slave? No. But I am only a man—only one of the human race; and if not created to be a slave, then no other human being was made for that purpose. My wife and children—dearer to me than my heart's blood —were they made for the auction-block? Never! And so it was all very easily settled here (pointing to his breast). I could not help being an uncompromising Abolitionist." Having shown over what tremendous obstacles the anti-slavery movement had triumphed, he said : "Henceforth, through all coming time, advocates of justice and friends of reform, be not discouraged; for you will and you must succeed, if you have a righteous cause. No matter at the outset how few may be disposed to rally round the standard you

have raised—if you battle unflinchingly and without
compromise—if yours be the faith that cannot be
shaken, because it is linked to the Eternal Throne—
it is only a question of time when victory shall come to
reward your toils. Seemingly, no system of iniquity
was ever more strongly entrenched, or more sure and
absolute in its sway, than that of American slavery;
yet it has perished.

> 'In the earthquake God has spoken;
> He has smitten with his thunder
> The iron walls asunder,
> And the gates of brass are broken.'

So it has been, so it is, so it ever will be throughout
the earth, in every conflict for the right." Mr. Garrison spoke of the cause of woman, paying a tribute
to Lucretia Mott and John Stuart Mill for their advocacy of that cause; referred to his visit to Fort Sumter; uttered a warm eulogium upon George Thompson, and returned thanks to other British Abolitionists
for help given to the cause in America; and finally
expressed the pleasure with which he had listened to
Earl Russell's ingenuous confession of fault in the
position he took in relation to the slaveholders' Rebellion.

George Thompson followed in a most appropriate
speech, — the last, perhaps, that he ever delivered.
There were brief addresses, also, by Mr. Stansfeld,
M. P., Mr. W. Vernon Harcourt, Q. C., and by the
Hon. E. L. Stanley; after which the proceedings were
closed with another brief address by the chairman.

This breakfast struck the key-note for the kingdom,
and other cities hastened to follow London's example.
Contrary to any wish or expectation on his part, Mr.
Garrison found himself compelled to accept a dinner,
on the Fourth of July, at Manchester; a supper at
Newcastle-on-Tyne; another at Edinburgh, where the
freedom of the city was conferred upon him, — the

only American, except George Peabody, who had ever
received it ; a breakfast, and later a public meeting, at
Glasgow.   Then Mr.   Garrison, with his son and
daughter, returned to the Continent to attend the Anti-
Slavery Conference, to which he had been accredited
as a delegate by the Freedmen's Aid Commission, of
which he was one of the vice-presidents.   From Paris
they went to Switzerland, revelling for a time in the
grand and beautiful scenery of that country.   Richard
D. Webb, of Dublin, was with them there.   They
just touched the edge of Germany, at Frankfort, and
came back through Belgium, enjoying a day at Brus-
sels.   Mr. Garrison was sorely tried while on the
Continent by his inability to speak the language and
converse with the people, and constantly expatiated
on the need of a universal language for all the nations
of the earth.

Two or three weeks more were spent in England
before returning to America.   Birmingham gave him
a breakfast, and honored him by a public meeting.
At Manchester he attended a grand temperance gathering, where he had a hearty reception by an audience
of five thousand people.   He had two or three delightful interviews, meanwhile, with Mazzini ; and, just
before sailing for home, he was honored with a private
breakfast by a distinguished merchant of Liverpool, at
which he met some fifty other guests.

Ten years later, in 1877, in company with his son
Frank, Mr. Garrison crossed the Atlantic again, and
for the last time.   His engagements, during his previous trip, confined him pretty closely to the large,
smoky cities, affording him little opportunity for sightseeing.   But now, for imperative reasons, and under
the instructions of his physician, he refused public
meetings, receptions, and the breakfasts of which the
English are so fond, and was able to take a great deal
of recreation amid the lovely rural scenery of England.

At Liverpool, on landing, he quietly made the acquaintance of Mrs. Josephine E. Butler, the lady who
has labored so persistently to procure the repeal of
the iniquitous Contagious Diseases acts.   He became
deeply interested in this cause, and bore his emphatic
testimony in its favor as he found opportunity.
Wherever he went, he was received with honor, love,
and reverence, and found troops of friends who listened to his words with breathless attention and
interest.   And his private discourse was most noble,
inspiring, and uplifting.   Whether he spoke of slavery
or war, of intemperance or impurity, of the cause of
woman, or the question of non-resistance and the in-
violability of human life, he enunciated the broad and
fundamental principles on which are based all rights
and all duties, and with a clearness and axiomatic force
that can never be forgotten by those who heard him.
"For three days," said a very distinguished lady,
after being with him for that time, "we have heard
the gospel preached."   And one who met him then for
the first time, writing since his death, says : "He came
among us like a perfected spirit, bearing testimony."
The social enjoyment of that visit was very great, as
he moved about among the lovely and hospitable homes
which everywhere opened wide their doors to welcome
him.   Delectable days were spent amid the charming
scenery of Derbyshire ; Oxford, the fine old University town, was visited ; a rare fortnight was spent in
London in meeting scores of old friends, and having
two tender and long-to-be-remembered interviews with
John Bright.   He went to Somersetshire to see Mr.
Bright's daughter, Mrs. Clark ; visited Bristol, War-
wick and Kenilworth castles, Birmingham, Leeds (to
take a final leave of George Thompson), Scarborough
(where Sir Harcourt Johnstone, Bart., M. P., gave
him a supper), Newcastle-on-Tyne, Edinburgh, and
Glasgow, and finally took a delightful trip through the

Highlands and the English Lake District, winding up
with a little run into Wales. After twelve weeks of
unalloyed enjoyment, he turned his face homeward.
As he parted with dear friends, one after another, he
said, tenderly, as if feeling that he should never see
them again in this life, "If we do not meet again in
this world, we surely shall in a better."

American Abolitionists will linger with pride and
delight over the record of the honors bestowed upon
their beloved and venerated leader by the good and
great of the Old World, reading therein the verdict of
posterity, and thanking God that they were permitted
to bear a part in the great struggle which his illustrious
name will forever recall. One thought impresses
itself upon my own mind whenever I look at this
record. Mr. Garrison, in the course of his visits to
Great Britain, spoke many times to great audiences,
embracing all classes of the people, from the nobility
to the toilers for their daily bread. He was heard by
Churchmen and Dissenters, by eminent ministers and
laymen of all denominations, by statesmen of every
party and philanthropists of every school. On these
occasions he spoke just as he was in the habit of speaking at home, never suppressing a truth which he
thought should be uttered, or withholding an epithet
which he thought needful to characterize slavery
or the conduct of its champions and apologists.
And yet it seems never to have occurred to his British
hearers that he was a man of a bitter spirit, or that his
language was "harsh and vituperative." They thought
his vocabulary exactly suited to awaken in the minds
of Christian and humane men just feelings toward
slavery and slaveholders, and heard him always with
delight, as a man under the sway of the noblest convictions and purposes that could animate the human
soul. If any one chooses to compare the unbounded
sympathy of Mr. Garrison's English audiences with

46

the carping and grumbling of those which he sometimes addressed at home, and to seek for the cause of the difference, he has only to remember that England had no slaves, no slaveholders, and no apologists for slavery; while in almost every American audience there were always some, oftentimes many, who, if not consciously pro-slavery themselves, were yet sensitive to epithets which they thought might hit some kinsman, friend or acquaintance, whose reputation they were concerned to defend. But the faithful champion of the slave could not consent to tip his arrow with wax and draw his bow with only an infant's strength, lest some apologist for oppression should be hurt.

XXII.

I AM not aware that Mr. Garrison ever made any systematic statement of his religious opinions. His mind was too much absorbed in the application of moral principles to the conduct of life to permit him to pay much attention to the theological speculations which are so fascinating to many. Those words of the Master, "Seek ye *first* the kingdom of God, and HIS RIGHTEOUSNESS," seem to have been always in his mind and heart as a rule of life. He was Orthodox at first by inheritance and through the influence of his noble Baptist mother; and he would perhaps have remained so to the end of life, if the attitude of the ministers and churches upon the slavery question had not forced him to investigate certain points which he had supposed were settled beyond controversy. The first of these was the Sabbath question. He was a very strict Sabbatarian in early life, but he thought it eminently proper, in accordance with Christ's humane example, to plead the cause of the enslaved on the Sabbath day. When the pro-slavery clergy availed themselves of the popular superstition to prevent anti-slavery lecturers from gaining a hearing upon that day, he was set to thinking and reading upon the subject, and the result was a conviction that the views

of the Friends in relation to Sunday were sound and
scriptural. When the great lights of the American
Church — Stuart, Hodge, Fisk and others — boldly
asserted that the Bible sanctioned slaveholding, he
was naturally led to consider the question of the
inspiration of that book, and its authority over the
consciences of men. His investigations resulted in the
conviction that on this subject also the Friends were
substantially right; that the revelation of God in man
was older and more authoritative than that inscribed
upon any parchment, however ancient, or by whatever
miracles authenticated; and that if, as Stuart and
other professors of theology affirmed, the Bible sanctioned slavery, then the passages containing such
sanction could not be from God, but must be from the
devil. His mind thenceforth became settled in such
views of inspiration as are now quite common in
Orthodox pulpits. In early life he reverenced the
Church and the Ministry; but when the effort was
made to strangle the anti-slavery movement by their
authority, alleged to be derived directly from Heaven,
and therefore binding upon men, he was set upon
another course of investigation, and was not long in
coming to the conclusion that this claim of authority
was neither reasonable nor scriptural, but in its
nature superstitious and hurtful; that churches, no
more than anti-slavery societies, had any organic relations with God, and that preachers, no more than anti-
slavery lecturers, were commissioned by Him.

These changes of opinion, however, worked not the
least disturbance of his faith in God, and in those
principles of righteousness, justice and truth which are
the foundation of his throne. On the contrary, his
faith was clarified and confirmed, as any one may see
who studies his later writings. The questions raised
by modern scientific investigation had no terrors for
him. He believed in the spiritual nature of man, in

the presence of God in the human soul, dissuading
from sin and kindling aspirations for purity and holiness of life ; and he was no more afraid that this faith
would die out of the heart of man than he was that the
sun would cease to shine, or that the law of gravitation
would break down and the universe be thrown into
chaos. The Bible was to him still "the Book of
books," not by virtue of any theory concerning its
authorship as a whole or in its several parts, but on
account of the primordial truths that illuminate its
pages, and that will forever authenticate themselves to
the minds and hearts of men. He did not think the
injunction to love God and man, and to do unto others
what we wish them to do unto us, could derive any
additional weight or authority from the most brilliant
display of fireworks, or even from any miraculous
manifestation whatever. He read the Bible more diligently than any other book, and let its grand truths
search him through and through, and feed him as with
the bread of eternal life, careless of all the fine-spun
theories of the theological schools. "I have lost," he
said, "my traditional and educational notions of the
holiness of the Bible ; but I have gained greatly, I
think, in my estimation of it. As a divine book, I
never could understand it ; as a human composition, I
can fathom it to the bottom. Whosoever receives it as
his master will necessarily be in bondage to it ; but he
who makes it his servant, under the guidance of truth,
will find it truly serviceable. It must be examined,
criticised, accepted or rejected, like any other book,
without fear and without favor. Whatever excellence
there is in it will be fire-proof ; and if any portion of
it be obsolete or spurious, let that portion be treated
accordingly. . . . . I am fully aware how grievously the priesthood have perverted the Bible, and
wielded it both as an instrument of spiritual despotism,
and in opposition to the sacred cause of humanity.

Still, to no other volume do I turn with so much interest; no other do I consult or refer to so frequently;
to no other am I so indebted for light and strength;
no other is so identified with the growth of human
freedom and progress; no other have I appealed to so
effectively in aid of the various reformatory movements which I have espoused; and it embodies an
amount of excellence so great as to make it, in my
estimation, the BOOK OF BOOKS."

For a whole generation Mr. Garrison was denounced by the pro-slavery ministry and church as
an infidel. It was so much easier to hurl that epithet
at his head than to answer his arguments against slavery! Some professed Abolitionists, in order to pro-
pitiate their pro-slavery brethren, joined in circulating
this calumny. The New York "Independent," on one
occasion, stigmatized him as "an infidel of the most
degraded sort;" and the reluctant apology it afterwards made for the outrage did not by any means
indicate the presence of that "godly sorrow" that
"worketh repentance to salvation." If the men who
are so fond of applying the epithet infidel to those
who dare to do their own thinking are not careful,
they will shortly succeed in changing the word from a
term of obloquy to one of honor. Indeed, it has
almost come to this already. Wendell Phillips once
said, in Faneuil Hall, that he only wished two words
written on his tombstone — "Infidel and Traitor: Infidel to a Church that could be at peace in the presence
of sin; Traitor to a Government that was a magnificent
conspiracy against justice." But in truth, nothing could
be more unjust and preposterous than the application of
the term infidel to a man like Garrison. There are men
in the church, and even in the pulpit, who see and
acknowledge this. Several years since, a clergyman,
bearing a name of great eminence throughout the Chris-

tian world, said to me, in substance: "I should not
dare to call Mr. Garrison an infidel, for fear of bringing
Christianity itself into reproach. For, if a man can
live such a life as he has lived and do what he has
done — if he can stand up for God's law of purity and
justice in the face of a frowning world, and when even
the professed ministers of Christ are recreant — if he
can devote himself to the redemption of an outraged
and plundered race and be pelted with the vilest
epithets for a whole generation, without flinching or
faltering, and yet be an infidel, men may well ask
what is the value of Christianity? No, no; I must
believe that Mr. Garrison is a Christian, who has his
walk with God, or he never could have had strength
and courage to go through the fiery trials to which he
has been exposed." It is due to Mr. Garrison to let
him speak for himself upon this point. On one occasion, replying (in 1841) to a most virulent attack made
upon him, in a letter to England, by an American
clergyman, one of the seceders from the American
Anti-Slavery Society, he said: —

" I am as strongly opposed to infidelity as I am to priest-
craft and slavery. My religious sentiments (excepting as
they relate to certain outward forms and observances, and
respecting these I entertain the views of Friends), are as
rigid and uncompromising as those promulgated by Christ
himself. The standard which he has erected is one that I
reverence and advocate. In a true estimate of the Divine
authority of the Scriptures no one can go beyond me. They
are my text-book, and worth all the other books in the universe. My trust is in God, my aim to walk in the footsteps
of his Son, my rejoicing to be crucified to the world, and the
world to me. . . . I stand upon the Bible, and the Bible
alone, in regard to my views of the Sabbath, the church,
and the ministry. If I cannot stand triumphantly on that
foundation, I can stand nowhere in the universe."

Ten years later, replying to a similar attack, from another quarter, he said : —

"I claim to be a Christian ; why do you persist in representing me as an infidel? I am a lover of Christian institutions ; why do you accuse me of seeking their overthrow? I have engaged in no reform, I have promulgated no doctrines, which I have not vindicated by an appeal to the Bible — an appeal more frequent than to all other books in the world beside ; why do you insist that my religious views are not in harmony with Divine revelation?"

He adds : —

"Technically I think very little of the Christian name or profession at the present day ; it has long since ceased to be odious — it has become reputable and popular. Eighteen hundred years ago it was a badge of infamy, and decisive evidence of heresy, and cost those who assumed it reputation, ease, wealth, personal safety and life itself. Then it was a test of character ; now it is a fashionable appendage."

The same charge of infidelity was brought against the anti-slavery movement as led by Mr. Garrison, though no one ever heard an infidel sentiment uttered on its platform. True, the ministry and church were arraigned and condemned ; but they were always criticised by a Christian standard, and condemned because they were false to Christ. The Abolitionists made a broad discrimination between the Church of Christ and the pro-slavery churches of the United States. They reverenced the former, they denounced and repudiated the latter. They discriminated also between *Christ*ianity and *church*ianity, between piety and "piosity," between sincerity and cant. When they saw on the one hand the slave clanking his chains, and on the other the great body of the church and clergy indifferent to his wrongs, full of sympathy for the master, and pleading for slavery in the name of Christ and the Bible, they did not mince their words, but said with heart and lip, "Out upon such pretenders! their professions of Christianity are a mockery — their use of the name of Christ to sanction 'robbery and crime and blood,' a hideous blasphemy!" And of this they will repent when it can be shown that it is a sin to call things by their right names.

As to the infidelity of the anti-slavery movement, let Mr. Garrison himself speak:—

"If abolitionism be an infidel movement, it is so only in the same sense in which Jesus was a blasphemer, and the apostles were 'pestilent and seditious fellows, seeking to turn the world upside down.' It is infidel to Satan, the enslaver; it is loyal to Christ, the redeemer. It is infidel to a gospel which makes man the property of man; it is bound up with the Gospel which requires us to love our neighbor as ourselves, and to call no man master. It is infidel to a Church which receives to its communion the 'traffickers in slaves and souls of men'; it is loyal to the Church which is not stained with blood, nor polluted by oppression. It is infidel to the Bible, interpreted as a pro-slavery volume; it is faithful to it as construed on the side of justice and humanity. It is infidel to a Sabbath, on which it is hypocritically pronounced unlawful to extricate the millions who lie bound and bleeding in the pit of slavery; it is true to the Sabbath on which it is well-pleasing to God to bind up the broken-hearted and to let the oppressed go free. It is infidel to all blood-stained compromises, sinful concessions, unholy compacts, respecting the system of slavery; it is devotedly attached to whatever is honest, straight-forward, invincible for the right. No reformatory struggle has ever erected a higher moral standard, or more disinterestedly pursued its object, or more unfalteringly walked by faith, or more confidingly trusted in the living God for succor in every extremity, and for a glorious victory at last. At the jubilee its vindication shall be triumphant and universal."

47

If Jesus may be presumed to have understood and
taught his own religion, and if he was right when he
declared that all the law and the prophets were summed
up in the two commandments which require us to
love God with all our hearts, and our neighbor as ourselves, then Mr. Garrison was as Orthodox a Christian,
both in theory and practice, as ever lived in this world.
Moreover, if to accept Christ as a leader and guide,
to imbibe his spirit and follow in his steps, at whatever cost or hazard, is to entitle one's self to the name
of Christian, then there are few men to whom that
name may be more appropriately applied than to him.
His writings, open them where we may, throb with
Christian vitality.   His doctrine of non-resistance,
which has been so much caricatured and ridiculed, and
on account of which some narrow-minded bigots
thought him unworthy to be a member of the anti-
slavery societies which he himself had created, was
always presented by him as a Christian doctrine.
Here is an extract from the Declaration of Sentiments,
written by him, and adopted by the Peace Convention
of 1838.   See how it breathes the very spirit of
Christ :—

"The Prince of Peace, under whose stainless banner we
rally, came not to destroy, but to save, even the worst of
enemies.   He has left us an example, that we should follow
his steps. 'God commendeth his love toward us, in that
while we were yet sinners, Christ died for us.' . . .   We
advocate no jacobinical doctrines.   The spirit of jacobinism
is the spirit of retaliation, violence and murder.   It neither
fears God, nor regards man.   We would be filled with the
spirit of Christ.   If we abide by our principles, it is impossible for us to be disorderly, or plot treason, or participate
in any evil work ; we shall submit to every ordinance of
man for the Lord's sake ; obey all the requirements of
government, except such as we deem contrary to the commands of the gospel ; and in no wise resist the operation of
law, except by meekly submitting to the penalty of dis-

obedience. . . . In entering upon the great work before us, we are not unmindful that, in its prosecution, we may be called to test our sincerity even as in a fiery ordeal. . . . We shall not think it strange concerning the fiery trial which is to try us, as though some strange thing had happened unto us ; but rejoice, inasmuch as we are partakers of Christ's sufferings. Wherefore, we commit the keeping of our souls to God, as unto a faithful Creator. ' For every one that forsakes houses, or brethren, or sisters, or father, or mother, or wife or children, or lands, for Christ's sake, shall receive an hundred-fold, and shall inherit everlasting life.' "

We may well be patient with those who think Mr. Garrison misunderstood the teachings of Jesus in regard to the law of retaliation and self-defence ; but how can we feel anything but disgust and indignation toward those who coolly assert that this passage and others like it embody the spirit of jacobinism and infidelity ?

I do not hesitate to express my belief that the anti-slavery movement, while it continued, did more than anything else to elevate the tone and purify the character of American Christianity. It was not without its good influences upon the sects that hated it most. It set before them a standard of morals higher than their own, and sometimes brought blushes to the cheeks of men who affected to despise it. It emancipated thousands from the bondage of sectarianism, and taught them that Christianity does not consist in conformity to a creed, or in the observance of forms, but in purity of life and devotion to the welfare of mankind. It broke the shackles of superstition from a vast multitude of people ; and if a few, in the revulsion from detected shams, were swept away from the solid ground of truth, a much greater number were quickened to a new and higher spiritual life. The anti-slavery meetings were distinguished for their

earnest and healthful religious tone, and the anti-
slavery papers, appealing as they did at all times to
what was best and noblest in their readers, exerted a
wholesome influence. I believe that the young men
and women, who grew up in households where one or
more of these papers was a part of the family reading,
and where the questions they presented were topics of
daily discourse, will, as a rule, be found to be excep-
tionally high-toned in their views and habits. "It is a
dictate of reason," as Mr. Garrison says, " that whatever enlarges the spirit of human sympathy, opposes
tyranny in every form, inculcates love and good-will to
mankind, and seeks to reconcile a hostile world, must
be in consonance with the Divine Mind." I believe
there does not live a single reader of "The Liberator," who will not gratefully bear testimony to the
truth of every word contained in the following paragraph from the now sainted editor's pen :—

"In the long, dark struggle with national injustice
through which I have been called to pass, I have been
cheered and strengthened by the knowledge of the reformatory change which has taken place in the sentiments of
thousands through the instrumentality of 'The Liberator.'
To this they gratefully testify : that it has given them more
exalted views of God, a more just appreciation of man, a
truer conception of Christianity ; that it has emancipated
them from the bondage of party and sect, dispelled from
their minds the mists of superstition, and made them courageous in the investigation of truth ; that it has enlarged the
limits of their country, and multiplied the number of their
countrymen, so that they no longer regard geographical
boundaries, but truly esteem every one as 'a man and a
brother,' whether he be near or remote ; that, instead of
lowering the standard of moral obligation, or lessening the
sphere of human duty, it has quickened their moral sense,
and given unlimited scope to their sympathies, and supplied
them with more objects of benevolent concern than they can
readily discharge. This testimony has been borne by its

patrons on both sides of the Atlantic. Among those
patrons are some of the best intellects, the purest spirits,
the most devoted Christians, to be found in Europe or
America."

Clarkson, at the close of his "History of the Slave
Trade," has this striking passage respecting the great
conflict in which he was so long engaged, which is
equally true of the anti-slavery movement in America : —

"It [the conflict] has been useful, also, in the discrimination of moral character. In private life, it has enabled us
to distinguish the virtuous from the more vicious part of the
community. I have had occasion to know many thousand
persons in the course of my travels on this subject, and I
can truly say that the part which these took on this great
question was always a true criterion of their moral character.
It has shown the general philanthropist. It has unmasked
the vicious in spite of his pretension to virtue. It has separated the moral statesman from the wicked politician. It
has shown us who, in the legislative and executive offices of
our country, are fit to save, and who to destroy a nation."

A most striking confirmation of these words of
Clarkson, in their application to the anti-slavery
movement in America, will be found in this extract
from "The Savannah Georgian," uttered in 1853 : —

"Were the votaries of abolition base and unprincipled,
low and degraded, we should have little to fear from their
hostility. But this is not the fact. The strongholds of
abolition are not the cities, with the vice which generally
characterizes the cities; they are the rural districts, with
their sober, serious, moral and religious population. Northern abolition mobs are usually composed of the rabble of the
towns and cities. Find a community in the free States
remarkable for quiet decorum, industrious habits, and religious devotion, and the probability is that there will be
found, not perhaps anti-slavery clamor, but anti-slavery
feeling in its worst and deepest intensity. These are the
men who hate slavery because they believe it sinful."

Was it not cruel in this Southern paper thus to
remind the pro-slavery divines of the North, who had
done so much to bolster up the system of slavery, that
they had their allies, not in the intelligent, God-fearing
classes in the rural districts, but in "the rabble of the
towns and cities," the "base, unprincipled, low and
degraded," who haunted the dens of vice and crime?
But, if men will serve the devil, they should be content with their wages!

Mr. Garrison revealed the nobility of his character
and his entire confidence in the principles he held, in
the fairness with which he treated opponents and
critics in his own columns. He always gave them a
full hearing, often permitting them to use twice the
space that he claimed for himself. In turning over
the files of "The Liberator," one is reminded continually of this fact. He believed in free discussion with
all his heart, and never shrank from the scalpel of the
critic. He often allowed himself to be roundly abused
in his paper without offering a word of reply. That
he sometimes, in the heat of the struggle, misjudged
the motives of men, and so did them injustice, is
probably true. That, owing to the strength of his
moral convictions, and his intolerance of anything that
looked like a dereliction of principle, his tone was
sometimes imperious and irritating to men who were
sensitive under criticism from a man so eminent, will
be admitted by his best friends. He did not always
make due allowance for the moral obtuseness that falls
short of guilt, and that confusion of the intellect which
is compatible with sincerity. But there was not in his
heart the least shadow of ill-will, or of a desire to
wound. He struck hard blows, and expected to take
them in return. No heart was ever more generous
than his, more ready to forgive an injury, or quicker
to pardon a momentary weakness. The cause of the
slave was to him as the apple of his eye; any appear-

ance of treachery to that, however disguised, was sure to kindle his indignation. As to his treatment of opponents, he shall speak for himself: —

"Before ' The Liberator ' was established, I doubt whether, on either side of the Atlantic, there existed a newspaper or periodical that admitted its opponents to be freely and impartially heard through its columns — as freely as its friends. Without boasting, I claim to have set an example of fairness and magnanimity, in this respect, such as had never been set before; cheerfully conceding to those who were hostile to my views on any subject discussed in ' The Liberator,' not only as much space as I, or as others agreeing with me, might occupy, but even more, if they desired it. From this course I have never deviated. Nay, more; I have not waited for opponents to send in their original contributions, but, in the absence of these, have constantly transferred their articles, published in other periodicals, to my own paper, without prompting from any quarter."

His faith in free discussion is illustrated in passages such as this : —

"Let, then, the mind, and tongue, and press, be free. Let free discussion not only be tolerated, but encouraged and asserted, as indispensable to the freedom and welfare of mankind. . . . If I give my children no other precept — if I leave them no other example — it shall be a fearless, impartial, thorough investigation of every subject to which their attention may be called, and a hearty adoption of the principles which to them may seem true, whether those principles agree or conflict with my own, or with those of any other person. The best protection which I can give them is to secure the unrestricted exercise of their reason, and to inspire them with true self-reliance. I will not arbitrarily determine for them what are orthodox or what heretical sentiments. I have no wish, no right, no authority to do so. I desire them to see, hear and weigh, both sides of every question. For example: — I wish them to examine whatever may be advanced in opposition to the doctrine of the divine inspiration of the Bible, as freely as they do whatever

they find in support of it ; to hear what may be urged against
the doctrines, precepts, miracles, or life of Jesus, as readily
as they do anything in their defence ; to see what arguments
are adduced for a belief in the non-existence of God, as unreservedly as they do the evidence in favor of his existence.
I shall teach them to regard no subject as too holy for examination ; to make their own convictions paramount to all
human authority; to reject whatever conflicts with their
reason, no matter by whomsoever enforced ; and to prefer
that which is clearly demonstrative to mere theory."

It is almost needless to say that he was hospitable to
new thoughts and facts, from whatever quarter they
might come, and if they commended themselves to
him, upon examination, as true, he never lacked the
courage to avow his faith, regardless of the ridicule or
the reproaches of men. An illustration of this is found
in his treatment of the subject of modern Spiritualism.
Having given much time to an investigation of the
phenomena pertaining to the question, and being
thoroughly satisfied that he had received many com-
munications from friends in the spirit-world, he did
not hesitate to incur the odium involved in a frank
avowal and defence of his opinion. To no question
that concerned the progress of the human race in
knowledge, virtue and freedom, was he indifferent.
He was patient even with the great procession of bores
who were forever invoking his attention to their crude
and ill-digested schemes, and who consumed much
time that he would gladly have reserved for some more
useful purpose. Called a fool and a fanatic himself,
every day of his life, he had great tenderness for
weak, well-meaning people, who were victims of the
world's indifference or scorn.

XXIII.

Subjects Omitted — The Absorbing Issue in Politics — The Moral
Agitation More Intense than Ever — The Fugitive Slave Law —
Webster's Apostasy — Trial of Castner Hanway — Anniversary
of the American Anti-Slavery Society Invaded by a Mob — Driven
from New York for Two Years — A Flying Leap — Lincoln's
Administration — His Re-election — Mr. Garrison's Attitude —
Visit to Charleston — Scenes and Incidents — Withdrawal from
the American Anti-Slavery Society — Close of " The Liberator."

As I approach the end of my work, I am dismayed
in glancing at the list of topics, pertaining to the later
period of the anti-slavery movement, on which I have
not space to say even a word. The expulsion of Mr.
Hoar from Charleston; the war with Mexico in the interest of slavery extension; the annexation of Cali-
fornia; the defeat of the attempt to establish slavery
on the Pacific coast; the compromises of 1850, including the infamous Fugitive Slave law, and the apostasy
of Webster; the slave-catching era, its excitements
and convulsions, in Boston, Syracuse, Christiana, and
elsewhere; the trial of Castner Hanway for treason;
the publication of "Uncle Tom's Cabin," by Harriet
Beecher Stowe, and its wonderful effects in creating
sympathy for the slaves; the appearance of Richard
Hildreth's "White Slave," a most powerful delineation
of the workings of slavery; the repeal of the Missouri
Compromise, and the desperate attempt to force slavery
into Kansas; the Dred Scott decision; the John Brown
raid, its incidents and consequences; the first election
of Abraham Lincoln to the Presidency; the attempt
to avert secession and war by fresh compromises; the

48

attack upon Fort Sumter, and the grand uprising of
the North; the futile attempts to put down the Rebellion without destroying slavery; the war, with its
ups and down; the Decree of Emancipation; the en-
listment of negro soldiers; the re-election of Lincoln
in 1864; the final surrender at Appomattox; the
assassination of Lincoln; the process of reconstruction; the "Underground Railroad," in all its wide
ramifications, affording means of escape to thousands
of slaves, whose adventures were of the most thrilling
character; the trials and sufferings of men who aided
the fugitives in their flight,—these are some of the
subjects from which it is hard to turn away, but for
the adequate treatment of which another volume is
required.

While it is true that the slavery question, during
the period referred to above, was the all-absorbing
issue in politics, so that every successive election
hinged upon it, and the question was thereby forced
into every household in the land, it would be a great
mistake to suppose that the MORAL AGITATION was
either superseded or thrown into the shade. On the
contrary, the anti-slavery societies, if we except a
portion of the time during the war, were never more
active; the anti-slavery papers—"The Liberator," "The
Standard," etc.—were never more extensively circulated, or more weighty in their utterances; the anti-
slavery speakers were never heard by larger or more
deeply interested crowds. Mr. Garrison was in constant request at widely distant points; the words of
Phillips echoed throughout the land, criticising, rebuking, inspiring; and Theodore Parker, until death tore
him from our side, not only thundered weekly in Music
Hall, but from the lecture-platform in many States;
and our faithful agents were never more indefatigable
in the prosecution of their work. Anniversaries and
conventions were points of intense interest; being

watched by the politicians as the mariner watches for
the beacon on a stormy night. Massachusetts was thoroughly excited and roused. The most thoughtful and
serious of the Republicans, who felt how critical was
the condition of the country, and who trembled lest
their party should shirk the issue, or fail to understand
its import, looked to the moral agitators, whom the
politicians could not silence, to point out the way of
safety and success. If Northern Senators and Representatives in Congress withstood the slaveholders face
to face in hot debate, and resisted them by every constitutional means; and if soldiers on the battle-field
gave up their lives that the slave might go free; it is
none the less true that neither in legislative halls nor
on the field of bloody strife could the contest have
been carried to a successful issue without the moral
influences out of which it originally grew, and from
which its inspiration was constantly derived. That
these influences came more or less directly from the
agitation of which Garrison was the recognized leader,
there can be no doubt.

It is not too much to say that there were moments
in the struggle when, if the moral agitation had ceased,
and Garrison and his friends retired from their work,
the North would have faltered and turned back, and
the Slave Power would have held the country more
firmly than ever in its grasp. Those who remember
the dark days of 1850, when, by a combination of the
Democratic and Whig parties, a last great effort was.
made to effect "a final settlement" of the slavery
question, by giving the South substantially all that
she demanded, and to put the anti-slavery agitation
down by a tremendous display of public sentiment
and governmental authority, will not need to be reminded how dismal, for a time, was the prospect.
Fugitive slaves were hunted in cities and towns on
every hand, and ruthlessly dragged back into bondage

by the power of the National Government.   The court-
house in Boston was girded with chains, and official
kidnappers, by the aid of the military, marched their
victim down State Street, over ground hallowed by
patriot blood, and in the presence of an indignant but
helpless crowd.   It was a question for some time
whether the apostate Webster would not drag New
England down after him into the pit of infamy to
which he had himself descended.   Boston, surprised
and indignant at first in view of his defection, had
been won to his side; Andover Theological Seminary,
which for twenty years had interpreted the Bible in
the interest of the men-stealers, now made haste to
commend him, and to scoff at the idea that Conscience
had any right to sit in judgment upon "iniquity
framed by law" and sanctioned by the Constitution.
Then it was that thirty ministers of the Methodist
church made a pious pilgrimage to Marshfield, to con-
gratulate Mr. Webster upon his success in making the
land of the Pilgrims a hunting-ground for slaves.
And then it was, thank God! that Garrison and his
brave comrades, unterrified, unseduced, lifted up a
voice of power that rang out over the hills and through
the vales of New England, summoning the friends of
freedom to the rescue, and bidding them be of good
cheer, for God was still God, and the Throne of Iniquity could not prosper.   To that summons New England responded, and not New England alone, but the
Middle States and the prairies of the West, and the
Republic was saved!
    The Fugitive Slave law, and the decision of the
Supreme Court in the Dred Scott case, virtually
declaring that the negroes of the country had "no
rights which a white man was bound to respect,"—
measures which it was supposed by their inventors
would utterly crush the anti-slavery movement,—only
added fuel to the flame that was so hot before.   They

supplied Mr. Garrison and his friends with fresh arguments, and kindled in the hearts of thousands a deep
hatred of the Union that bore such accursed fruit.
The first of these measures begat a spirit of resistance
with which the minions of slavery found themselves
unable to cope. Daniel Webster, in the hope of
striking terror to the hearts of Abolitionists, set up
the doctrine that resistance to the slave-catching statute
was treason against the United States, and punishable
with death; but the effort to enforce this dictum in
the trial of Castner Hanway covered the great "ex-
pounder" with universal ridicule.

These days brought great trial and suffering to
many. The mob spirit was revived in not a few
places. In 1850, the anniversary of the American
Anti-Slavery Society, in New York, was invaded by a
band of ruffians, with Isaiah Rynders at their head.
His efforts, however, to break up the anniversary
failed. The scene was in a high degree dramatic and
amusing. Mr. Garrison's coolness and tact as chairman completely baffled the disturbers. Frederick
Douglass distinguished himself on this occasion, as on
many others, by his wit and eloquence. A subsequent
meeting of the society for business was, however,
broken up by the same crew, the authorities of the
city conniving at the outrage. In 1851 and 1852, the
society was unable to secure the use of any church or
hall in New York, and its meetings were consequently
held in Rochester and Syracuse, successively. In
1853 public sentiment had changed so that there was no
longer any fear of disturbance, and the society returned
to New York. It should be mentioned that, immediately after the Rynders mob of 1850, Mr. Phillips was
invited to speak in Plymouth Church, in Brooklyn, the
pastor appearing on the platform to vindicate freedom of
speech, and the city authorities protecting the meeting.

But I must take a flying leap from this point to the

closing days of the struggle. During the first two
years of the war, Mr. Garrison, in common with all
other friends of freedom, was exceedingly impatient
with what seemed to be the uncertain, shilly-shally
policy of President Lincoln. If they could have
known all that was passing in his mind, and how fixed
was his determination to free the slaves the instant
that he believed he could do so rightfully, and with
the certainty that the Northern people would stand by
him, I have no doubt their patience would have been
equal to the crisis; but they had seen so many men in
high station falter and fail, that they were in constant
terror lest he should be tempted to take some fatal
step. He seemed to them like a turtle for slowness,
and they piled hot coals upon his back to quicken
his movements. But, when at last he issued his
Proclamation of Emancipation and committed himself
fully to the work of exterminating slavery, Mr. Garrison distrusted him no longer, and took the most
charitable view of such of his acts as he could not
wholly approve. When combinations were formed to
prevent his renomination in 1864, Mr. Garrison gave
them no countenance, believing that his re-election
was absolutely necessary to keep the North united,
and to defeat the schemes of those who were in sympathy with the Rebellion. Mr. Lincoln set a high
value upon Mr. Garrison's support, not only as a
tribute to his own fidelity, but on account of his great
influence among the honest enemies of slavery of
every class; and, when the arrangements were made
to raise again the Flag of the Union on the walls of
Fort Sumter, Mr. Garrison was invited, as a guest of
the Government, to witness the imposing spectacle,
and informed that his son, George Thompson Garrison, then an officer in the Fifty-fifth Massachusetts
(colored) Regiment in South Carolina, would be fur-
loughed in order that he might meet him there. At

EMANCIPATION GROUP.

PRESENTED TO THE CITY OF BOSTON,

By HON. MOSES KIMBALL.

Dedicated Dec. 6, 1879.

the suggestion of the Hon. Henry Wilson, a similar invitation was extended to the Hon. George Thompson, the English champion of emancipation, who was then in the country. It was a most happy circumstance that these two men, so long and so intimately associated in the cause of the slave, and who had endured together the fiercest persecution from the minions of slavery, were permitted to mingle their exultations in this grand celebration. The company, including the orator of the occasion, the Rev. Henry Ward Beecher, went from New York to Charleston in the United States steamer "Arago." Mr. Thompson, in a note written on board the steamer as she was leaving the harbor, said: "In former years, the question was often put to me, 'Why don't you go to the South?' To-day I answer, 'I am going; going to celebrate the triumph of Garrisonian abolitionism in Charleston; going in company with Garrison himself.'"

Mr. Garrison's arrival in Charleston created a great stir among the freedmen, who thronged the streets, rending the air with their shouts, or singing their songs of triumph, whenever he made his appearance. The flag-raising at the fort on Friday, April 14, was a scene of deepest interest, which cannot be described here. On the following day, meetings of the freedmen to do honor to Mr. Garrison, Mr. Thompson, and other distinguished friends of emancipation, were held in "Citadel Square," and "Zion's Church." At an early hour the colored people began to assemble in the square. The colored children from the public schools met at the school-houses and marched to the meeting in procession, led by Superintendent Redpath. While waiting for the speakers to arrive, the crowd was addressed by Major Delaney (colored) of Gen. Saxton's staff. The arrival of Mr. Garrison was announced by the surging and cheering of the vast crowd, whose enthusiasm was irrepressible. Cheering did not sufficiently express their joy; they pressed toward the great leader of the anti-slavery cause, and bore him on their shoulders to the speaker's stand. Senator Wilson, being unable to speak in the open air, it was concluded to adjourn the meeting to "Zion's Church." Three thousand freedmen were packed within the walls of that edifice. Mr. Garrison, Mr. Thompson, the Hon. Henry Wilson, the Rev. Joshua Leavitt, D.D., Judge Kelly of Pennsylvania and others, crowded the platform, while a large number of officers of the army and navy, and a number of ladies, occupied the space in front. Then followed a scene which angels and men might contemplate with equal satisfaction. Samuel Dickerson, one of the men whose shackles were broken by Lincoln's proclamation, rose to perform a duty which had been assigned to him by his emancipated brethren. Accompanied by his two daughters, bearing a beautiful wreath of flowers, he advanced to the pulpit, and, addressing Mr. Garrison, spoke as follows : —

Sir — It is with pleasure that is inexpressible that I welcome you here among us, the long, the steadfast friend of the poor, down-trodden slave. Sir, I have read of you, I have read of the mighty labors you have had for the consummation of this glorious object. Here you see stand before you your handiwork. Three children were robbed from me and I stood desolate. Many a night I pressed a sleepless pillow from the time I retired to my couch until the close of the morning. I lost a dear wife, and after her death that little one, who is the counterpart of her mother's countenance, was taken from me. I appealed for her with all the love and reason of a father. The rejection came forth in these words : " Annoy me not, or I will sell them off to another State." I thank God that through your instrumentality, under the folds of that glorious flag which treason tried to triumph, you have restored them to me. And I tell you it is not this heart alone, but there are mothers, there are fathers, there are sisters, and there are brothers, the pulsations of whose hearts are unimaginable. The greeting that they would give you, sir, it is almost impossible for me to express; but simply, sir, we welcome and look upon you as our saviour. We thank you for what you have done for us. Take this wreath from these children, and when you go home, never mind how faded they may be, preserve them, encase them, and keep them as a token of affection from one who has loved and lived.

Mr. GARRISON, in reply, spoke as follows: —

MY DEAR FRIEND — I have no language to express the feelings of my heart in listening to your kind and strengthening words, in receiving these beautiful tokens of your gratitude, and in looking into the faces of this vast multitude, now happily delivered from the galling fetters of slavery. Let me say at the outset: " Not unto us, not unto us, but unto God be all the glory" for what has been done in regard to your emancipation. I have been actively engaged in this work for almost forty years — for I began when I was quite young to plead the cause of the enslaved in this country. But I never expected to look you in the face, never supposed you would hear of anything I might do in your behalf. I knew only one thing — all that I wanted to know — that you were a grievously oppressed people, and that, on every consideration of justice, humanity and right, you were entitled to immediate and unconditional freedom.

I hate slavery as I hate nothing else in this world. It is not only a crime, but the sum of all criminality; not only a sin, but the sin of sins against Almighty God. I cannot be at peace with it at any time, to any extent, under any circumstances. That I have been permitted to witness its overthrow calls for expressions of devout thanksgiving to Heaven. It was not on account of your complexion or race, as a people, that I espoused your cause, but because you were the children of a common Father, created in the same divine image, having the same inalienable rights, and as much entitled to liberty as the proudest slaveholder that ever walked the earth.

For many a year I have been an outlaw at the South for your sakes, and a large price was set upon my head, simply

because I endeavored to remember those in bonds as bound
with them.   Yes — God is my witness ! — I have faithfully
tried, in the face of the fiercest opposition, and under the
most depressing circumstances, to make your cause my
cause ; my wife and children your wives and children, subjected to the same outrage and degradation ; myself on the
same auction-block, to be sold to the highest bidder.   Thank
God, this day you are free !   And be resolved that, once
free, you will be free forever.   No, not one of you ever will,
ever can consent again to become a bondman.   Liberty or
death, but never slavery.

It gives me joy to assure you that the American Government will stand by you to establish your freedom against
whatever claims your masters may bring.   The time was
when it gave you no protection, but was on the side of the
oppressor, where there was power.   Now all is changed!
Once, I could not feel any gladness at the sight of the
American flag, because it was stained with your blood, and
under it four millions of slaves were daily driven to unre-
quited labor.   Now it floats, purged of its gory stain ; it
symbolizes freedom for all, without distinction of race or
color.   The Government has its hold upon the throat of the
-monster Slavery, and is strangling the life out of it.

In conclusion, I thank you, my friend, for your affecting
and grateful address, and for these handsome tokens of our
Heavenly Father's wisdom and goodness, and will try to
preserve them in accordance with your wishes.   Oh, be
assured, I never doubted that I had the gratitude and affection of the entire colored population of the United States,
even though personally unknown to so many of them ; because I knew that upon me heavily rested the wrath and
hatred of your cruel oppressors.   I was sure, therefore, if I
had them against me, I had you with me.   I close with saying, that, long as I have labored in your behalf, while God
gives me reason and strength I shall demand for you everything I claim for the whitest of the white in this country.

Gen. Saxton having introduced Senator Wilson,
Mr. Garrison asked leave, before he spoke, to pay
him a tribute for his faithful labors in the cause.   I
copy his words in part, as a reply to those who have

thoughtlessly charged him with a lack of appreciation of the work done outside of the Garrisonian fold. "Mr. Wilson's life," he said, "(as well as Mr. Sumner's), has been constantly imperilled at the National Capital ; so that, from session to session, it has been uncertain whether he would be permitted to see his family and constituents again. He has fought a good fight, and deserves to be crowned with laurels." Eloquent addresses followed from Mr. Wilson and Judge Kelly, and then Mr. Garrison rose to introduce George Thompson, of whom he spoke in terms of warm and affectionate appreciation, for his agency in giving freedom to the slaves in the West Indies, and for his self-sacrificing labors in behalf of the bondmen of America. Mr. Thompson made an exceedingly felicitous address, and was loudly cheered. At every mention of the name of Abraham Lincoln the cheering was like the roaring of the sea in a storm. Mr. Redpath told them of Wendell Phillips, when it was voted, with an emphasis almost loud enough to be heard in Boston, that he be invited to come and address them on the Fourth of July. Other speeches followed, outside as well as inside the church, and the occasion was fraught with an interest hardly inferior to the flag-raising at Sumter.

Mr. Garrison, while remaining in Charleston, was the recipient of many other attentions from the freedmen, expressive of their deep gratitude to him for what he had done to break their chains.

The anniversary of the American Anti-Slavery Society occurred shortly after Mr. Garrison's return from Charleston. He declared in "The Liberator," in advance of the meeting, that, in his judgment, the time for the dissolution of the society had arrived. Slavery being dead, there was no longer any need of anti-slavery societies. There were, however, some members of the society who had not concurred with

"The Liberator" and "The Anti-Slavery Standard" in the support they gave to the re-election of Lincoln, and who felt that those papers had exhibited a partisanship hardly consistent with perfect fidelity to the cause. Wendell Phillips was avowedly of this opinion, and he and those agreeing with him were in favor of continuing the society and "The Standard." The subject was earnestly debated in the annual meeting, Mr. Garrison persisting in saying, "My vocation as an Abolitionist, thank God! is ended," and refusing to be any longer an officer or a member of the society. He thought the work remaining to be done for the enfranchisement, protection and elevation of the people of color could be best performed by new associations, formed for that purpose, and composed, not exclusively of Abolitionists, but of all those friendly to the object. Mr. Quincy concurred with Mr. Garrison, and said:

" Slavery being practically abolished, wanting nothing of technical abolition but certain formalities, as sure to be performed as the world is to endure, it seems to me that anti-slavery is, *ipso facto*, abolished also. It is an anomaly, a solecism, an absurdity, to maintain an *anti-slavery* society after slavery is killed."

Other prominent friends of the cause took the same view. My own opinion was expressed in "The Standard," in these words:—

" Why run the mill after the grist is out? What if the Constitutional Amendment forever prohibiting the re-establishment of slavery is not yet tied up in the official red tape? There is nothing that Abolitionists can do to make its ratification more certain. Society action is no more needful to this end than to ensure the vernal equinox or the next eclipse, to make fire burn, or water run down hill. The Abolitionists, who have borne the heat and burden of the anti-slavery struggle, have now no distinct function. They should not, it seems to me, persist in occupying an isolated position, but rejoice to mingle with others in the great work of giving to the emancipated people of color the rights and immunities of citizens, and aiding them to rise above all the degrading influences of slavery and caste. It would be absurd to ask that the new wine of this day should be put into our old bottles."

Mr. Phillips and others argued that, as the Constitutional Amendment forbidding the re-establishment of slavery was not yet actually ratified, as the spirit of slavery was still rampant, as the negro was not yet assured of the ballot, and as the people of color were still suffering from many disabilities, the society had an important work to do. Many Abolitionists were reluctant to discontinue the holding of meetings from which they had derived so much enjoyment in the past, and were therefore strongly inclined to vote for their continuance. The vote stood 118 for continuance, 48 for dissolution. It is simple justice to say that among those who voted with the majority were a considerable number who had never acted with the society before, and some who had long been alienated from it, but were suddenly smitten with a conviction of its great usefulness. I do not wish to say a single word that can give pain to anybody; above all, I would not be understood to impeach the motives of any individual. I simply desire, while doing no injustice to others, to make clear to my readers the position taken by Mr. Garrison and those who agreed with him. Among those who voted for continuance were some of the most disinterested friends of Mr. Garrison and the cause, of whose conscientiousness I have no more doubt than I have of my own. The division, however much to be lamented, was not by any means surprising. The Abolitionists had accustomed themselves to the freest exercise of their independent judgment, and this difference, of itself, could not be the cause of any

unfriendly feelings. While it has always seemed to
me that the society would have had a more dignified
ending if it had been dissolved then and there, or
at a meeting then appointed; yet I cheerfully concede that the majority did perfectly right in acting
upon their own judgment; and if the society did any
good afterwards, let it have all the credit on that
account which it deserves. But I have never been
able to see any reason for continuing it after that date
that would not have been equally good for continuing
it to the present time, and for an indefinite period in
the future.

Mr. Garrison chose to prolong the life of "The
Liberator" till the end of December, 1865, so that its
files might cover the full period of thirty-five years.
The last number contained his original Salutatory,
printed on the first of January, 1831, followed by an
impressive Valedictory, in which he says : —

"The object for which 'The Liberator' was commenced
— the extermination of chattel slavery — having been gloriously consummated, it seems to me specially appropriate to
let its existence cover the historical period of the great
struggle; leaving what remains to be done to complete the
work of emancipation to other instrumentalities (of which I
hope to avail myself), under new auspices, with more
abundant means, and with millions instead of hundreds for
allies. . . . I began 'The Liberator' without a subscriber, and I end it — it gives me unalloyed satisfaction to
say — without a farthing as the pecuniary result of the
patronage extended to it during thirty-five years of unre-
mitted labor. . . . Never had a journal to look such
opposition in the face — never was one so constantly belied
and caricatured. If it had advocated all the crimes forbidden by the moral law of God and the statutes of the State,
instead of vindicating the sacred claims of oppressed and
bleeding humanity, it could not have been more vehemently
denounced, or more indignantly repudiated."

But for this he had satisfactory compensation in the estimate formed of the paper by those who read it through the dark years of the anti-slavery struggle : —

" To me it has been unspeakably cheering, and the richest compensation for whatever of peril, suffering and defamation I have been called to encounter, that one uniform testimony has been borne, by those who have had its weekly perusal, as to the elevating and quickening influence of ' The Liberator' upon their character and aims ; and the deep grief they are expressing in view of its discontinuance is overwhelmingly affecting to my feelings."

Among the congratulatory letters from old friends in the closing number is one from Samuel E. Sewall, from which I quote a few lines, showing the estimate formed of Mr. Garrison by one of the founders of the Liberty party, who was a political Abolitionist ever afterwards. " Without intending," he says, " to detract in the least from the incalculable value of the exertions and sacrifices of the many other devoted men who have worked for the same object, still it seems to me certain that you have done more than any other person toward effecting the absolute and unconditional abolition of American slavery, the great event of the present age, and perhaps the grandest in the history of the world." Mr. Sewall was one of Mr. Garrison's earliest and most devoted friends, and their difference of opinion as to the best method of securing the political action which both desired to witness made no difference whatever in their mutual attachment. Mr. Sewall, indeed, was one of those to whom anti-slavery politics did not mean a withdrawal from moral agitation.

In the last number but one Mr. Garrison gave place to the official ratification of the Thirteenth Amendment to the Constitution, forever prohibiting slavery on the soil of the United States. After remarking that he

had put this important voucher in type with his own
hand, he subjoins this exultant paragraph : —

" Rejoice, and give praise and glory to God, ye who so
long and so untiringly participated in all the trials and
vicissitudes of the mighty conflict. Having sown in tears,
now reap in joy. Hail, redeemed, regenerated America!
Hail, North and South, East and West! Hail, the cause of
Peace, Liberty, Righteousness, thus mightily strengthened
and signally glorified! Hail, the Present, with its tran-
scendent claims, its new duties, its imperative obligations!
Hail, the Future, with its pregnant hopes, its glorious
promises, its illimitable powers of expansion and develop-
ment! Hail, ye ransomed millions, no more to be chained,
scourged, mutilated, bought and sold in the market, robbed
of all rights, hunted as partridges upon the mountain in
your flight to obtain deliverance from the house of bondage,
branded and scorned as a connecting link between the
human race and the brute creation! Hail, all nations,
tribes, kindreds and peoples, ' made of one blood,' interested
in a common redemption, heirs of the same immortal destiny !
Hail, angels in glory, and spirits of the just made perfect,
and tune your harps anew, singing, ' Great and marvellous
are thy works, Lord God Almighty ; just and true are thy
ways, thou King of saints! Who shall not fear thee, O
Lord, and glorify thy name? for thou art holy : for all the
nations shall come and worship before thee : for thy judgments are manifest.' "

When before, in the history of the world, from
Adam until this day, did any great struggle for
humanity have a better beginning or a more glorious
ending? And when before was it ever given to the
founder of so grand a movement to live to witness its
complete triumph? "This is the Lord's doing: it is
marvellous in our eyes."

XXIV.

Mr. Garrison's Last Years — Tokens of Public Respect — His Activity in Reforms — His Power as a Public Speaker — His Modesty — His Hopefulness — His Private and Domestic Life — His Last Illness and Death — The Funeral Services.

I BELIEVE I am warranted in saying that Mr. Garrison's course in counselling the dissolution of the anti-slavery societies, and refusing to be longer identified with them, after slavery was actually dead, though lamented by some of the truest friends of the cause, was regarded with strong approbation by the regenerated public sentiment of the country. "As he knew when and how to begin, so also he knew how and when to stop," was the tribute everywhere instinctively paid to his wisdom and self-abnegation. " He knows when his work is done, and resorts to no weak or unworthy expedients to keep himself in the public eye," was the spontaneous feeling of multitudes. Many of those who had called him "fanatic" all their lives were astonished at this proof of his sound judgment and right feeling. My own belief is, that his course in this particular greatly augmented his influence, and enabled him to do far more for the Southern freedmen than he could have done at the head of an anti-slavery society, " lingering superfluous on the stage." Certainly his name became a power in the land, such as it had never been before. His counsel upon public questions was widely sought, and his judgment held in the highest respect. Having been for half a century true to the negro as a slave, he did not forget him in his efforts for self-improvement, and

50

in his sufferings under other forms of tyranny ; and his
voice and pen were still potent in his defence.   His
word of indignant protest and rebuke was sure to be
heard in every instance when the Government failed
in its duty to those whose chains it had struck off, and
it was never heard in vain.

The public respect and sympathy for him was manifested in the substantial provision made for his support during the remainder of his life.   The sum of
thirty thousand dollars was raised, mostly in this
country, but partly in England, and presented to him
on the 10th of March, 1868, in a letter signed by a
committee, consisting of Samuel E. Sewall, J. Inger-
soll Bowditch, William E. Coffin, William Endicott,
Jr., Samuel May, Jr., Edmund Quincy, Thomas Russell, and Robert C. Waterston.   John A. Andrew was
the chairman of this committee at the time of his
death.   Among those who also lent their aid in promoting this testimonial, the names of Charles Sumner,
Henry Wilson, Rev. Samuel J. May, Salmon P. Chase,
Thomas D. Eliot, Ralph Waldo Emerson, John G.
Whittier, Henry W. Longfellow, James Russell
Lowell, Attorney-General Speed, Alexander H. Rice,
George S. Boutwell, Thaddeus Stevens, William D.
Kelly, E. B. Washburne, William Cullen Bryant,
Horace Greeley, and Gerrit Smith deserve to be mentioned.   An examination of these names will show,
what I have elsewhere affirmed, that those who fought
slavery in the political arena, though dissenting earnestly from some of Mr. Garrison's opinions, yet held
him in high esteem as the leader of the moral agitation
in which anti-slavery politics had their root.   Only
the small men of the Republican party, and those
least imbued with its distinctive principles, have ever
been found denying the truth which its great founders
and leaders were ever foremost to acknowledge and
affirm.

The last fourteen years of Mr. Garrison's life were filled with such reformatory and philanthropic labors as his impaired health permitted him to perform. He delivered many public addresses, and wrote not a little for the press. Every struggling enterprise of reform was sure of his sympathy and co-operation. Temperance, Peace, Moral Purity, and Woman Suffrage engaged much of his attention, and his pen and voice were always at their service when required. His presence in any public assembly where he was known was sure to elicit visible tokens of popular esteem. One of the latest productions of his pen was a letter on the Chinese question, which showed how clearly he apprehended the universal bearing and application of the principles on which the anti-slavery movement was founded, and how quickly his sympathies flowed out toward all who were oppressed.

He was not, in the usual sense of the word, an orator; nevertheless, he was one of the most impressive and forcible public speakers to whom it has ever been my good fortune to listen. In early life, he was a complete slave to his pen; he could not trust himself to make a speech without carefully writing it out beforehand. He grew tired of this sort of slavery after a while, and resolved to emancipate himself, which he did *immediately* and triumphantly. He found, upon trial, that thoughts and words on his favorite themes flowed freely. He was so thoroughly alive to his subject, and so intensely in earnest, that he never failed to command the sympathy and attention of his audience. His personal presence disarmed prejudice and inspired confidence, and his constant identification of himself, in thought, principle and feeling, with "those in bonds as bound with them," the clear moral insight that enabled him to comprehend principles and penetrate every disguise of sophistry and false pretence, and his strong appeals to reason

and conscience, gave him great power over men, both
in public speech and private intercourse. If he lacked
the resources which a classical culture alone can furnish, he possessed others of the very highest importance, and which such a culture often fails to supply.
If he did not please the imagination or tickle the fancy
of his hearers, he did what was better—he enlightened
their minds, stirred their consciences, and swayed
their judgments. No cause in his hands was ever put
to shame by any hasty or ill-considered word. In dealing with opponents, his tact was unfailing. Thoughtful people especially heard him with delight, and the
largest audiences felt the power of his logic and the
magnetism of his voice and presence.

There was about him no taint of self-seeking, no
assumption of the honors of leadership. In all my
intercourse with him, extending over a period of more
than forty years, I never heard him utter a word
implying a consciousness that he was a leader in the
cause, or that he had done or achieved anything worthy of praise. He was unfeignedly modest, with not
a touch of affected humility. He had the highest
appreciation of the services of others, and loved to
do them honor, whether they worked by his methods
or not. He never mistook a molehill for a mountain,
—never fought a battle save upon a vital issue. If
he wrote a document for which others as well as himself were to be responsible, he would allow them to
criticise, and even to pick it all to pieces, if they
chose, content if no principle were dishonored. He
thought little of himself, everything of the cause.

He was always courageous and hopeful. Never in
a single instance did I see him in a discouraged mood.
His faith in the goodness of his cause and in the overruling Providence of God was so absolute that he was
calm and cheerful alike under clear or cloudy skies.
I have seen him again and again when the expenses of

"The Liberator" were running far beyond its receipts, and he did not know whence the money was to come to supply the wants of his family; but never once did any shadow fall upon his spirits on this account. He had given himself and all his powers to a cause that he believed had the favor and support of Heaven; and he did not doubt that in some way he would be taken care of. And help always *did* come — sometimes in unexpected and surprising ways. His unselfish devotion to his work touched and opened the hearts of all who witnessed it, disposing them to stay up his hands and relieve him of pecuniary embarrassment. If in his greatest extremity he had been absolutely certain that he could make his paper profitable by the slightest dereliction of principle, by trimming a little on this side or that, or by the suppression of unpopular truth, he never would have yielded to the temptation.

Of Mr. Garrison's private, domestic and social life I hardly dare trust myself to speak. A man of more spotless excellence in every relation of life I have never known. As a husband, father and friend he was indeed a model, and his home was ever the abode of love and peace. His wife, the youngest daughter of the late Mr. George Benson, of Brooklyn, Conn., was a noble woman and a true helpmate. Mr. Garrison's devotion, as a husband and father, was one of his most beautiful characteristics. He never made his public relations an excuse for neglecting his family. Did one of the children cry in the night, it was in his arms that it was caressed and comforted. In every possible way, in the care of the children and in all household matters, he sought to lighten the cares of his wife, taking upon himself burdens which most husbands and fathers shun. In short, he made his home a heaven, into which it was a delight to enter. He was never so happy as when surrounded by his wife and children and a few favored guests. Under such

circumstances he was at his best — happy as a bird,
genial, witty and full of a generous hospitality.

In 1864 Mr. Garrison purchased the estate in Roxbury known as "Rockledge," which was his home for
the remainder of his life ; and never did the sun look
down upon a happier household than that by which he
was surrounded. Children and grandchildren rose up
to do him honor, and the gracious sweetness of his
nature was in perpetual flow. The great work of his
life done, and well done, he gave himself up very
largely to the social enjoyments which are the best
solace of age. There was but one drawback to his
happiness now, and that was the illness of his beloved
wife. With what tenderness and solicitude he watched
over her, making all his plans, so far as possible,
tributary to her welfare, only his most intimate friends
can ever know. And her unselfish thoughtfulness was
equal to his own. Invalid that she was, she cast no
shadow upon the household enjoyment, but made it
brighter by her smiles and cheerful words. Her
death in 1876 left a void in the heart of her husband,
and in the household as well, that could never be filled.
But his faith in another and a better life beyond the
grave made him cheerful to the last. By hundreds of
his dear friends "Rockledge" will ever be remembered
as the scene of hospitalities large, free and confiding ;
a home in which every virtue that adorns humanity
was exemplified.

His reverence for woman was strong, and no one
ever heard from his lips a word or a sentiment that
could bring a blush to her cheek. He had a tender
regard for the feelings of others, and was always
thoughtful for their comfort and convenience. Especially was he studious for the comfort of servants and
others in his employ, willingly inconveniencing himself for their sake. His kindness extended to the
brute creation. The household cat missed him when

LATE RESIDENCE OF WILLIAM LLOYD GARRISON, ROXBURY, MASS.

he was absent and welcomed him on his return. Once, when a boy, he came home after a protracted absence, and being awakened out of sleep by Tabby's purr, found that she had brought to his pillow her whole brood of new-born kittens, confident of his sympathy in her maternal joy.   He placed good Mr. Bergh high on the roll of benefactors for his kind intervention in behalf of the oppressed brute creation, and his face lighted up with enthusiasm in telling stories of Rarey's exploits in subduing fractious horses by kindness.   To the poor and the unfortunate his heart and his purse were ever open.   Children were drawn to him by an irresistible attraction.   His conversation, though generally serious, often sparkled with wit and fun.   In how many families is his name now spoken with a tender, tearful reverence, while the memory of his gracious presence as a guest will be fondly cherished and proudly transmitted.

Seven children were born to Mr. Garrison, two of whom—a son and daughter—died in infancy. The names of those who survive are as follows, in the order of their birth :—George Thompson, William Lloyd, Wendell Phillips, Fanny (wife of Mr. Henry Villard, at whose house the father died), and Francis Jackson.   It is understood that his sons will write the life of their father, for which the materials must be abundant.   Massachusetts will some day honor herself by erecting a monument to his memory.   But the best of all mementoes of his noble life are the broken fetters of four millions of slaves !

Of Mr. Garrison's last illness and death I can give no more satisfactory account than that contained in the pamphlet report of the funeral exercises :—

" The announcement of his critical illness, speedily followed by that of his death, while absent from home, took his friends and the public on both sides of the Atlantic by

surprise ; for though it was known that he had been infirm
in health, the vigor of his recent contributions to the public
press (the latest of which, in denunciation of the anti-
Chinese bill, and on the exodus of the freedmen of Mississippi and Louisiana to Kansas, had appeared within a few
weeks) had made it difficult to believe that his health was at
all precarious. Only his family and immediate friends knew
that those letters were written while he was suffering such
pain and discomfort that the feeling that he must lift up his
voice, and bear his testimony once more on the question of
human rights, alone enabled him to accomplish the task.
The exhaustion and prostration which followed these efforts
made it evident to himself that his forces were nearly spènt,
and gave his family much concern.

" Even from his seventy-third birthday (December 10,
1878), his private letters were marked by forebodings of his
approaching end, which he welcomed as a relief from physical infirmities. In the following April, 1879, the feeling
which he described as a giving way of the internal organism
became so strong, and his malady (a chronic affection of the
kidneys) so intolerable, that, at the solicitation of his
daughter, he went. to New York to put himself under the
care of her family physician. He arrived at the Westmore-
land Apartment House, where she resided, on Monday
afternoon, April 28th. On Wednesday the treatment began,
with immediate promise of good results ; which was, however, of necessity, soon disappointed. On Saturday, May
10th, he took to his bed, but even then those about him did
not fairly realize the gravity of his condition. At the end
of another week, however, the symptoms became unmistak-
ably alarming, and on Tuesday, May 20th, the members of
the family in Boston were summoned by telegraph. They
arrived the next day. The final changes proceeded slowly,
and the death-struggle did not set in till half-past ten o'clock
on the evening of Friday. Up to that time, though disin-
clined to talk unless spoken to, he retained all his faculties,
and recognized his children and grandchildren by voice and by
sight ; and only an hour or two before he lost this consciousness, he listened with manifest pleasure to the singing of
his favorite hymns, to which, as he lay outstretched, he beat
time both with his hands and feet. He expired peacefully

at a few minutes past 11 o'clock on the succeeding night, Saturday, May 24th. His illness had been in many respects a distressing one, even in comparison with the wretched months that preceded it; but the prevailing sense was of weariness—frequently expressed in a desire to ' go home '— rather than of acute bodily pain, though that was not wanting. His vitality was remarkably illustrated throughout.

" A post-mortem examination having been made on Monday, Mr. Garrison's remains were removed the same night to Roxbury, Mass. On Wednesday afternoon, May 28th, the funeral services were held in the neighboring church of the First Religious Society, which the trustees had kindly placed at the disposal of the family and the public."

Mr. Garrison was exceedingly fond of sacred music. He had a fine ear and an excellent voice, and loved to sing the church tunes and anthems which he learned in boyhood, whenever he could find others to sing with him. As he moved about the house or played with the children, from day to day, his voice often broke forth in his favorite hymns or songs. The following are some of the pieces which his children sang to him in his dying hours, and which evidently gave him great pleasure :—

> *Hebron.*—Thus far the Lord hath led me on,
>   Thus far His power prolongs my days,
>   And every evening shall make known
>   Some fresh memorial of His grace.

> *Christmas.*—Awake, my soul, stretch every nerve,
>   And press with vigor on;
>   A heavenly race demands thy zeal,
>   And an immortal crown.

> *Amsterdam.*—Rise, my soul, and stretch thy wings,
>   Thy better portion trace;
>   Rise from transitory things
>   To Heaven, thy native place.

> *Confidence.*—Now can my soul in God rejoice.

> *Coronation.*—All hail the power of Jesus' name.

> *Old Hundred.*—From all that dwell below the skies.

> *Portuguese Hymn.*—The Lord is my Shepherd.

51

Lenox.—Ye tribes of Adam join
With Heaven and earth and seas,
And offer notes divine
To your Creator's praise.

Mr. Garrison's funeral was remarkable for the number of his surviving friends and co-laborers in the
anti-slavery and kindred reformatory movements who
came to pay the last tribute of respect to his character
and memory.   There were also present not a few who
were formerly either indifferent or hostile to the anti-
slavery cause, but who now desired to show their respect and admiration for him on account of the great
work to which his life had been consecrated.   Many
colored people also were present.   In accordance with
Mr. Garrison's views of death, care was taken to avoid
the appearance of mourning and gloom which generally characterizes such occasions.   The blinds were
opened to admit the sweet sunlight, the pulpit was
decorated with flowers, and the hymns of cheer and
inspiration of which he was so fond were sung.   The
whole audience rose when the body was borne into the
church, followed by the pall-bearers and the family.
The pall-bearers were Wendell Phillips, Samuel May,
Samuel E. Sewall, Robert F. Wallcut, Theodore D.
Weld, Oliver Johnson, Lewis Hayden and Charles
Mitchell — the two last named being colored men.
The exercises were conducted by the Rev. Samuel
May, one of Mr. Garrison's most trusted friends, who
for nearly twenty years was the general agent of the
Massachusetts Anti-Slavery Society.   After repeat-
ing the Lord's Prayer, he read a selection from the
portions of Scripture which Mr. Garrison used fre-
quently to read in anti-slavery meetings.   Then fol-
lowed addresses of a most appropriate character from
Mr. May, Mrs. Lucy Stone, Rev. Samuel Johnson,
Theodore D. Weld and Wendell Phillips, interspersed
with music by a quartette of colored singers, composed

of Mrs. Nellie B. Mitchell, soprano; Miss Fannie A.
Washington, contralto; Mr. William Walker, tenor;
Mr. Lewis A. Fisher, basso. The pieces sung were:
"Awake, my soul, stretch every nerve;" "Ye tribes
of Adam, join;" and "Rise, my soul, and stretch thy
wings." Mr. Johnson, at the close of his address,
read portions of the poem by John G. Whittier, which
will be found in the appendix, together with the
address of Mr. Phillips.

The whole assembly availed themselves of the
opportunity to look reverently at the face of the dead,
and during the time occupied by this ceremony a great
number of Mr. Garrison's old friends embraced the
opportunity to exchange friendly greetings, and to
speak tenderly and affectionately, but not sadly, of
their departed leader.

As the last rays of the setting sun fell in serene
beauty upon the cemetery at Forest Hills, glorifying
that "city of the dead," the remains of the great
philanthropist were laid, with tender and reverent
hands, in the grave, by the side of his departed wife,
in the presence of his children and grandchildren and
many of his old associates in the anti-slavery struggle.
Before the grave was filled, the quartette of colored
singers, that had rendered such acceptable service at
the church, sang a hymn, commencing, "I cannot
always trace the way," after which the company retired, leaving all that was mortal of WILLIAM LLOYD
GARRISON to its rest.

THE END.

APPENDIX.

REMARKS OF WENDELL PHILLIPS

AT THE

FUNERAL OF WILLIAM LLOYD GARRISON,

Boston, May 28, 1879.

It has been well said that we are not here to weep, and neither are we here to praise. No life closes without sadness. Death, after all, no matter what hope or what memories surround it, is terrible and a mystery. We never part hands that have been clasped life-long in loving tenderness but the hour is sad; still, we do not come here to weep. In other moments, elsewhere, we can offer tender and loving sympathy to those whose roof-tree is so sadly bereaved. But in the spirit of the great life which we commemorate, this hour is for the utterance of a lesson; this hour is given to contemplate a grand example, a rich inheritance, a noble life worthily ended. You come together, not to pay tribute, even loving tribute, to the friend you have lost, whose features you will miss from daily life, but to remember the grand lesson of that career; to speak to each other, and to emphasize what that life teaches,—especially in the hearing of these young listeners, who did not see that marvellous career ; in their hearing to construe the meaning of the great name which is borne world-wide, and tell them why on both sides the ocean, the news of his death is a matter of interest to every lover of his race. As my friend said, we have no right to be silent. Those of us who stood near him, who witnessed the secret springs of his action, the consistent inward and outward life, have no right to be silent. The largest contribution that will ever be made by any single man's life to the knowledge of the working of our institutions will be the picture of his career. He sounded the depths of the weakness, he proved the ultimate strength, of republican institutions ; he gave us to know the perils that confront us ; he taught us to rally the strength that lies hid.

To my mind there are three remarkable elements in his career. One is rare even among great men. It was his own moral nature, unaided, uninfluenced from outside, that consecrated him to a great idea. Other men ripen gradually. The youngest of the great American names that will be compared with his was between thirty and forty when his first anti-slavery word was uttered. Luther was thirty-four years old when an infamous enterprise woke him to indignation, and it then took two years more to reveal to him the mission God designed for him. This man was in jail for his opinions when he was just twenty-four. He had confronted a nation in the very bloom of his youth. It could be said of him more than of any other American in our day, and more than of any great leader that I chance now to remember in any epoch, that he did not need circumstances, outside influence, some great pregnant event to press him into service, to provoke him to thought, to kindle him into enthusiasm. His moral nature was as marvellous as was the intellect of Pascal. It seemed to be born fully equipped, "finely touched." Think of the mere dates ; think that at some twenty-four years old, while Christianity and statesmanship, the experience, the genius of the land, were wandering in the desert, aghast, amazed, and confounded over a frightful evil, a great sin, this boy sounded, found, invented the talisman, "Immediate, unconditional emancipation on the soil." You may say he borrowed it —true enough — from the lips of a woman on the other side of the Atlantic; but he was the only American whose moral nature seemed, just on the edge of life, so perfectly open to duty and truth that it answered to the far-off bugle-note, and proclaimed it instantly as a complete solution of the problem.

Young men, you have no conception of the miracle of that insight; for it is not given to you to remember with any vividness the blackness of the darkness of ignorance and indifference which then brooded over what was called the moral and religious element of the American people. When I think of him, as Melancthon said of Luther, "day by day grows the wonder fresh" at the ripeness of the moral and intellectual life that God gave him at the very opening.

You hear that boy's lips announcing the statesmanlike solution which startled politicians and angered church and people. A year afterwards, with equally single-hearted devotion, in words that have been so often quoted, with those dungeon doors behind him, he enters on his career. In January, 1831, then twenty-five years old, he starts the publication of "The Liberator," advocating the immediate abolition of slavery; and, with the sublime pledge, "I will be as harsh as truth and as uncompromising as justice. On this subject I do not wish to speak or write with moderation. I will not equivocate — I will not excuse — I will not retreat a single inch — AND I WILL BE HEARD."

Then began an agitation which for the marvel of its origin, the majesty of its purpose, the earnestness, unselfishness and ability of its appeals, the vigor of its assault, the deep national convulsion it caused, the vast and benefi- cent changes it wrought, and its wide-spread, indirect in- fluence on all kindred moral questions, is without a parallel in history since Luther. This boy created and marshalled it. His converts held it up and carried it on. Before this, all through the preceding century, there had been among us scattered and single abolitionists, earnest and able men; sometimes, like Wythe of Virginia, in high places. The Quakers and Covenanters had never intermitted their testi- mony against slavery. But Garrison was the first man to begin a *movement* designed to annihilate slavery. He an- nounced the principle, arranged the method, gathered the forces, enkindled the zeal, started the argument, and finally marshalled the nation for and against the system in a con- flict that came near rending the Union.

I marvel again at the instinctive sagacity which discerned the hidden forces fit for such a movement, called them forth, and wielded them to such prompt results. Archimedes said, "Give me a spot and I will move the world." O'Connell leaned back on three millions of Irishmen, all on fire with sympathy. Cobden's hands were held up by the whole manufacturing interest of Great Britain; his treasury was the wealth of the middle classes of the country, and behind him also, in fair proportion, stood the religious convictions of England. Marvellous was their agitation; as you gaze upon it in its successive stages and analyze it, you are as- tonished at what they invented for tools. But this boy stood alone; utterly alone, at first. There was no sympathy anywhere; his hands were empty; one single penniless comrade was his only helper. Starving on bread and water, he could command the use of types, that was all. Trade endeavored to crush him; the intellectual life of America disowned him.

My friend Weld has said the church was a thick bank of black cloud looming over him. Yes. But no sooner did the church discern the impetuous boy's purpose than out of that dead, sluggish cloud thundered and lightened a malignity which could not find words to express its hate. The very pulpit where I stand saw this apostle of liberty and justice sore beset, always in great need, and often in deadly peril; yet it never gave him one word of approval or sympathy. During all his weary struggle, Mr. Garrison felt its weight in the scale against him. In those years it led the sect which arrogates to itself the name of Liberal. If this was the bearing of so-called Liberals, what bitterness of opposition, judge ye, did not the others show? A mere boy confronts church, commerce, and college; a boy with neither training nor experience! Almost at once the assault tells; the whole country is hotly interested. What created such life under those ribs of death? Whence came that instinctive knowledge? Where did he get that sound common-sense? Whence did he summon that almost unerring sagacity which, starting agitation on an untried field, never committed an error, provoking year by year additional enthusiasm; gathering, as he advanced, helper after helper to his side! I marvel at the miraculous boy. He had no means. Where he got, whence he summoned, how he created, the elements which changed 1830 into 1835 — 1830 apathy, indifference, ignorance, icebergs, into 1835, every man intelligently hating him, and mobs assaulting him in every city — is a marvel which none but older men than I can adequately analyze and explain. He said to a friend who remonstrated with him on the heat and severity of his language, "Brother, I have need to be all on fire, for I have mountains of ice about me to melt." Well, that dungeon of 1830, that universal apathy, that deadness of soul, that contempt of what called itself intellect, in ten years he changed into the whole country aflame. He made every single home, press, pulpit, and senate-chamber a debating society, with *his* right and wrong for the subject. And as was said of Luther, " God honored him by making all the worst men his enemies."

Fastened on that daily life was a malignant attention and criticism such as no American has ever endured. I will not call it a criticism of hate; that word is not strong enough. Malignity searched him with candles from the moment he uttered that God-given solution of the problem to the moment when he took the hand of the nation and wrote out the statute which made it law. Malignity searched those forty years with candles, and yet even malignity has never lisped a suspicion, much less a charge — never lisped a suspicion of anything mean, dishonorable, dishonest. No man, however mad with hate, however fierce in assault, ever dared to hint that there was anything low in motive, false in assertion, selfish in purpose, dishonest in method — never a stain on the thought, the word, or the deed.

Now contemplate this boy entering such an arena, confronting a nation and all its forces, utterly poor, with no sympathy from any quarter, conducting an angry, widespread, and profound agitation for ten, twenty, forty years, amid the hate of everything strong in American life, and the contempt of everything influential, and no stain, not the slightest shadow of one, rests on his escutcheon ! Summon me the public men, the men who have put their hands to the helm of the vessel of state since 1789, of whom that can be said, although love and admiration, which almost culminated in worship, attended the steps of some of them.

Then look at the work he did. My friends have spoken of his influence. · What American ever held his hand so long and so powerfully on the helm of social, intellectual, and moral America? There have been giants in our day. Great men God has granted in widely different spheres; earnest men, men whom public admiration lifted early into power. I shall venture to name some of them. Perhaps you will say it is not usual on an occasion like this, but long-waiting truth needs to be uttered in an hour when this great example is still absolutely indispensable to inspire the effort, to guide the steps, to cheer the hope, of the nation not yet arrived in the promised land. I want to show you the vast breadth and depth that this man's name signifies. We have had Webster in the Senate; we have had Lyman Beecher in the pulpit; we have had Calhoun at the head of a section; we have had a philosopher at Concord with his inspiration penetrating the young mind of the Northern States. They are the four men that history, perhaps, will mention somewhere near the great force whose closing in this scene we commemorate to-day. Remember now not merely the inadequate means at this man's control, not simply the bitter hate that he confronted, not the vast work that he must be allowed to have done, — surely vast, when measured by the opposition he encountered and the strength he held in his hands, — but dismissing all those considerations, measuring nothing but the breadth and depth of his hold, his grasp on American character, social change, and general progress, what man's signet has been set so deep, planted so forever on the thoughts of his epoch? Trace home intelligently, trace home to their sources, the changes social, political, intellectual and religious, that have come over us during the last fifty years, — the volcanic convulsions, the stormy waves which have tossed and rocked our generation, — and you will find close at the sources of the Mississippi this boy with his proclamation!

The great party that put on record the statute of freedom was made up of men whose conscience he quickened and whose intellect he inspired, and they long stood the tools of a public opinion that he created. The grandest name beside his in the America of our times is that of John Brown. Brown stood on the platform that Garrison built; and Mrs. Stowe herself charmed an audience that he gathered for her, with words which he inspired, from a heart that he kindled. Sitting at his feet were leaders born of " The Liberator," the guides of public sentiment. I know whereof I affirm. It was often a pleasant boast of Charles Sumner that he read " The Liberator" two years before I did, and among the great men who followed his lead and held up his hands in Massachusetts, where is the intellect, where is the heart that does not trace to this printer-boy the first pulse that bade him serve the slave? For myself, no words can adequately tell the measureless debt I owe him, the moral and intellectual life he opened to me. I feel like the old Greek, who, taught himself by Socrates, called his own scholars " the disciples of Socrates."

This is only another instance added to the roll of the Washingtons and the Hampdens, whose root is not ability, but *character;* that influence which, like the great Master's of Judea (humanly speaking), spreading through the centuries, testifies that the world suffers its grandest changes not by genius, but by the more potent control of *character.* His was an earnestness that would take no denial, that consumed opposition in the intensity of its convictions, that knew nothing but right. As friend after friend gathered slowly, one by one, to his side, in that very meeting of a dozen heroic men, to form the New England Anti-Slavery Society, it was his compelling hand, his resolute unwillingness to temper or qualify the utterance, that finally dedicated that first organized movement to the doctrine of immediate emancipation. He seems to have understood — this boy without experience — he seems to have understood by instinct that righteousness is the only thing which will finally compel submission; that one, with God, is always a majority. He seems to have known it at the very outset, taught of God, the herald and champion, God-endowed and God-sent to arouse a nation, that only by the most absolute assertion of the uttermost truth, without qualification or compromise, can a nation be waked to conscience or strengthened for duty. No man ever understood so thoroughly — not O'Connell, nor Cobden — the nature and needs of that *agitation* which alone, in our day, reforms states. In the darkest hour he never doubted the omnipotence of conscience and the moral sentiment.

And then look at the unquailing courage with which he faced the successive obstacles that confronted him! Modest, believing at the outset that America could not be as corrupt as she seemed, he waits at the door of the churches, importunes leading clergymen, begs for a voice from the sanctuary, a consecrated protest from the pulpit. To his utter amazement, he learns, by thus probing it, that the church will give him no help, but, on the contrary, surges into the movement in opposition. Serene, though astounded by the unexpected revelation, he simply turns his footsteps, and announces that "a Christianity which keeps peace with the oppressor is no Christianity," and goes on his way to supplant the religious element which the church had allied with sin by a deeper religious faith. Yes, he sets himself to work, this stripling with his sling confronting the angry giant in complete steel, this solitary evangelist, to make Christians of twenty millions of people! I am not exaggerating. You know, older men, who can go back to that period; I know that when one, kindred to a voice that you have heard to-day, whose pathway Garrison's bloody feet had made easier for the treading, when he uttered in a pulpit in Boston only a few strong words, injected in the course of a sermon, his venerable father, between seventy and eighty years, was met the next morning and his hand shaken by a much moved friend. "Colonel, you have my sympathy. I cannot tell you how much I pity you." "What," said the brusque old man, "what is your pity?" "Well, I hear your son went crazy at 'Church Green' yesterday." Such was the utter indifference. At that time, bloody feet had smoothed the pathway for other men to tread. Still, then and for years afterwards, insanity was the only kind-hearted excuse that partial friends could find for sympathy with such a madman!

If anything strikes one more prominently than another in this career — to your astonishment, young men, you may say —it is the plain, sober common-sense, the robust English element which underlay Cromwell, which explains Hampden, which gives the color that distinguishes 1640 in England from 1790 in France. Plain, robust, well-balanced common-sense. Nothing erratic; no enthusiasm which had lost its hold on firm earth; no mistake of method; no unmeasured confidence; no miscalculation of the enemy's strength. Whoever mistook, Garrison seldom mistook. Fewer mistakes in that long agitation of fifty years can be charged to his account than to any other American. Erratic as men supposed him, intemperate in utterance, mad in judgment, an enthusiast gone crazy, the moment you sat down at his side, patient in explanation, clear in statement, sound in judgment, studying carefully every step, calculating every assault, measuring the force to meet it, never in haste, always patient, waiting until the time ripened,—fit for a great leader. Cull, if you please, from the statesmen who obeyed him, whom he either whipped into submission or summoned into existence, cull from among them the man whose career, fairly examined, exhibits fewer miscalculations and fewer mistakes than this career which is just ended.

I know what I claim. As Mr. Weld has said, I am
speaking to-day to men who judge by their ears, by rumors;
who see, not with their eyes, but with their prejudices. History, fifty years hence, dispelling your prejudices, will do
justice to the grand sweep of the orbit which, as my friend
said, to-day we are hardly in a position, or mood, to measure. As Coleridge avers, "The truth-haters of to-morrow
will give the right name to the truth-haters of to-day, for
even such men the stream of time bears onward." I do not
fear that if my words are remembered by the next generation they will be thought unsupported or extravagant,
When history seeks the sources of New England character,
when men begin to open up and examine the hidden springs
and note the convulsions and the throes of American life
within the last half century, they will remember Parker,
that Jupiter of the pulpit; they will remember the long
unheeded but measureless influence that came to us from
the seclusion of Concord; they will do justice to the masterly statesmanship which guided, during a part of his life,
the efforts of Webster, but they will recognize that there
was only one man north of Mason and Dixon's line who
met squarely, with an absolute logic, the else impregnable
position of John C. Calhoun; only one brave, far-sighted,
keen, logical intellect, which discerned that there were only
two moral points in the universe, *right* and *wrong;* that
when one was asserted, subterfuge and evasion would be
sure to end in defeat.

Here lies the brain and the heart; here lies the statesmanlike intellect, logical as Jonathan Edwards, brave as Luther, which confronted the logic of South Carolina with an
assertion direct and broad enough to make an issue and
necessitate a conflict of two civilizations. Calhoun said,
Slavery is *right.* Webster and Clay shrunk from him and
evaded his assertion. Garrison, alone at that time, met

him face to face, proclaiming slavery a sin and daring all
the inferences. It is true, as New Orleans complains to-day
in her journals, that this man brought upon America everything they call the disaster of the last twenty years; and it
is equally true that if you seek through the hidden causes
and unheeded events for the hand that wrote "emancipation" on the statute-book and on the flag, it lies still there
to-day.

· I have no time to number the many kindred reforms to which
he lent as profound an earnestness and almost as large aid.

I hardly dare enter that home. There is one other
marked, and, as it seems to me, unprecedented, element in
this career. His was the happiest life I ever saw. No
need for pity. Let no tear fall over his life. No man
gathered into his bosom a fuller sheaf of blessing, delight,
and joy. In his seventy years, there were not arrows enough
in the whole quiver of the church or state to wound him.
As Guizot once said from the tribune, "Gentlemen, you
cannot get high enough to reach the level of my contempt."
So Garrison, from the serene level of his daily life, from the
faith that never faltered, was able to say to American hate,
"You cannot reach up to the level of my home mood, my
daily existence." I have seen him intimately for thirty
years, while raining on his head was the hate of the community, when by every possible form of expression malignity let him know that it wished him all sorts of harm. I
never saw him unhappy; I never saw the moment that serene, abounding faith in the rectitude of his motive, the
soundness of his method, and the certainty of his success did
not lift him above all possibility of being reached by any
clamor about him. Every one of his near friends will agree
with me that this was the happiest life God has granted
in our day to any American standing in the foremost rank
of influence and effort.

Adjourned from the stormiest meeting, where hot debate had roused all his powers as near to anger as his nature ever let him come, the music of a dozen voices — even of those who had just opposed him — or a piano, if the house held one, changed his mood in an instant, and made the hour laugh with more than content; unless indeed, a baby and playing with it proved metal even more attractive.

To champion wearisome causes, bear with disordered intellects, to shelter the wrecks of intemperance and fugitives whose pulse trembled at every touch on the door-latch — this was his home; keenly alive to human suffering, ever prompt to help relieve it, pouring out his means for that more lavishly than he ought — all this was no burden, never clouded or depressed the inextinguishable buoyancy and gladness of his nature. God ever held over him unclouded the sunlight of his countenance.

And he never grew old. The tabernacle of flesh grew feebler and the step was less elastic. But the ability to work, the serene faith and unflagging hope suffered no change. To the day of his death he was as ready as in his boyhood to confront and defy a mad majority. The keen insight and clear judgment never failed him. His tenacity of purpose never weakened. He showed nothing either of the intellectual sluggishness or the timidity of age. The bugle-call which, last year, woke the nation to its peril and duty on the Southern question, showed all the old fitness to lead and mould a people's course. Younger men might be confused or dazed by plausible pretensions, and half the North was befooled; but the old pioneer detected the false ring as quickly as in his youth. The words his dying hand traced, welcoming the Southern exodus and foretelling its result, had all the defiant courage and prophetic solemnity of his youngest and boldest days.

Serene, fearless, marvellous man! Mortal, with so few shortcomings!

Farewell, for a very little while, noblest of Christian men! Leader, brave, tireless, unselfish! When the ear heard thee, then it blessed thée; the eye that saw thee gave witness to thee. More truly than it could ever heretofore be said since the great patriarch wrote it, " the blessing of him that was ready to perish " was thine eternal great reward.

Though the clouds rest for a moment to-day on the great work that you set your heart to accomplish, you knew, God in his love let you see, that your work was done ; that one thing, by his blessing on your efforts, is fixed beyond the possibility of change. While that ear could listen, God gave what He has so rarely given to man, the plaudits and prayers of four millions of victims, thanking you for emancipation, and through the clouds of to-day your heart, as it ceased to beat, felt certain, *certain*, that whether one flag or two shall rule this continent in time to come, one thing is settled—it never henceforth can be trodden by a slave!

To W. L. G.

CHAMPION of those who groan beneath
   Oppression's iron hand:
In view of penury, hate, and death,
   I see thee fearless stand.
Still bearing up thy lofty brow,
   In the steadfast strength of truth,
In manhood sealing well the vow
   And promise of thy youth.

Go on,—for thou hast chosen well;
   On in the strength of God!
Long as one human heart shall swell
   Beneath the tyrant's rod.

Speak in a slumbering nation's ear,
  As thou hast ever spoken,
Until the dead in sin shall hear, —
  The fetter's link be broken!

I love thee with a brother's love;
  I feel my pulses thrill,
To mark thy spirit soar above
  The cloud of human ill.
My heart hath leaped to answer thine,
  And echo back thy words,
As leaps the warrior's at the shine
  And flash of kindred swords!

They tell me thou art rash and vain, —
  A searcher after fame;
That thou art striving but to gain
  A long-enduring name;
That thou hast nerved the Afric's hand
  And steeled the Afric's heart,
To shake aloft his vengeful brand,
  And rend his chain apart.

Have I not known thee well, and read
  Thy mighty purpose long?
And watched the trials which have made
  Thy human spirit strong?
And shall the slanderer's demon breath
  Avail with one like me,
To dim the sunshine of my faith
  And earnest trust in thee?

Go on, — the dagger's point may glare
  Amid thy pathway's gloom, —
The fate which sternly threatens there
  Is glorious martyrdom!
Then onward with a martyr's zeal;
  And wait thy sure reward
When man to man no more shall kneel,
  And God alone be Lord!

                    JOHN G. WHITTIER, 1833.

GARRISON.

THE storm and peril overpast,
  The hounding hatred shamed and still,
Go, soul of freedom! take at last
  The place which thou alone canst fill.

Confirm the lesson taught of old—
  Life saved for self is lost, while they
Who lose it in His service hold
  The lease of God's eternal day.

Not for thyself, but for the slave
  Thy words of thunder shook the world;
No selfish griefs or hatred gave
  The strength wherewith thy bolts were hurled.

From lips that Sinai's trumpet blew
  We heard a tenderer undersong;
Thy very wrath from pity grew,
  From love of man thy hate of wrong.

Now past and present are as one;
  The life below is life above;
Thy mortal years have but begun
  The immortality of love.

With somewhat of thy lofty faith
  We lay thy outworn garment by,
Give death but what belongs to death,
  And life the life that cannot die!

Not for a soul like thine the calm
  Of selfish ease and joys of sense;
But duty, more than crown or palm,
  Its own exceeding recompense.

Go up and on! thy day well done,
  Its morning promise well fulfilled,
Arise to triumphs yet unwon,
  To holier tasks that God has willed.

Go, leave behind thee all that mars
    The work below of man for man;
With the white legions of the stars
    Do service such as angels can.

Wherever wrong shall right deny,
    Or suffering spirits urge their plea,
Be thine a voice to smite the lie,
    A hand to set the captive free!

                        JOHN G. WHITTIER.

MAY, 1879.

THE DAY OF SMALL THINGS.

BY JAMES RUSSELL LOWELL.

"Some time afterward, it was reported to me by the city officers that they had ferreted out the paper and its editor. His office was an obscure hole; his only visible auxiliary a negro boy; and his supporters a few very insignificant persons, of all colors."—*Letter of Hon. H. G. Otis.*

IN a small chamber, friendless and unseen,
    Toiled o'er his types one poor, unlearned young man;
The place was dark, unfurnitured and mean,
    Yet there the freedom of a race began.

Help came but slowly; surely, no man yet
    Put lever to the heavy world with less;
What need of help? He knew how types were set,
    He had a dauntless spirit and a press.

Such earnest natures are the fiery pith,
    The compact nucleus round which systems grow;
Mass after mass becomes inspired therewith,
    And whirls impregnate with the central glow.

O Truth! O Freedom! how are ye still born
    In the rude stable, in the manger nursed!
What humble hands unbar those gates of morn
    Through which the splendors of the new day burst!

What! shall one monk, scarce known beyond his cell,
    Front Rome's far-reaching bolts, and scorn her frown?
Brave Luther answered, YES!—that thunder's swell
    Rocked Europe, and discharmed the triple crown.

"Whatever can be known of Earth we know,"
    Sneered Europe's wise men, in their snail-shells curled;
"No!" said one man in Genoa; and that No
    Out of the dark created this New World.

Who is it will not dare himself to trust?
    Who is it hath not strength to stand alone?
Who is it thwarts and bilks the inward MUST?
    He and his works like sand from earth are blown.

Men of a thousand shifts and wiles, look here!
    See one straightforward conscience put in pawn
To win a world! See the obedient sphere,
    By bravery's simple gravitation drawn!

Shall we not heed the lesson taught of old,
    And by the Present's lips repeated still,
In our own single manhood to be bold,
    Fortressed in conscience and impregnable will?

We stride the river daily at its spring,
    Nor in our childish thoughtlessness foresee
What myriad vassal streams shall tribute bring,
    How like an equal it shall greet the sea.

O small beginnings, ye are great and strong,
    Based on a faithful heart and weariless brain;
Ye build the future fair, ye conquer wrong,
    Ye earn the crown, and wear it not in vain!

INDEX.

A.

Methodist Book Concern, suppress anti-slavery passages in their reprints, 185.
Methodist Episcopal Church, anti-slavery agitation in, 234–243; case of Bishop Andrew, 240; division of the church, 241.
Methodism, Whedon's defence of, 75.
Mill, John Stuart, address at the breakfast to Mr. Garrison, 356.
Ministers decline to pray in anti-slavery meetings, 72.
Mob year, 183.
Mob in Boston, 196–198.
Montpelier, Vt., mob in, 203.
Morgan, Prof. John, 168.
" Morning Star," The, Freewill Baptist organ; its influence against slavery, - 81.
Mott, Lucretia, 256.

N.

Nat Turner Insurrection, 61; debate on in Virginia legislature, 107.
" National Intelligencer, The," extract from, 63; Garrison's reply, 64.
National Anti-Slavery Society, 144; its convention in Philadelphia, 147.
" National Era," The, 295.
" National Anti-Slavery Standard," 296.
Newcomb, Stillman B., member first Anti-Slavery Society, 86.
New England Convention admits women, 271; the innovation denounced, 273.
New England Anti-Slavery Society, 86; appeal to the public, 89.
New England Non-Resistance Society, 282.
New Haven, proposed location of Colored College in, 120; strong opposition to, 123.
New Organization, The, 284; not a success, 298.
New York, headquarters Anti-Slavery Society in, 155; Dr. Cox's church attacked, 162; Lewis Tappan's house sacked, 162.
New York City Anti-Slavery Society, " Emancipator " transferred to, 288.
Newspapers, extracts from Southern, 186.
Newspapers, Garrisonian after 1840, 325.
Northfield, N. H., anti-slavery lecturer arrested in, 188.
Noyes Academy, Canaan, N. H., ruined by a mob, 188.

O.

O'Connell, Daniel, regrets exclusion of women from London Conference, 350.
Orthodox Abolitionists, they establish a new society, 284.

P.

Park St. Church, colored merchant in, 100.
Parker, Miss Mary S., 196.
Parker, Theodore, sympathizes with the Garrison movement, 329.
Parties limited by the Constitution, 309.
Pastoral Letter of Massachusetts General Association, 262.
Peace question, The, 282.
Pennsylvania Hall burned, 211.
" Pennsylvania Freemen," 323.
Phelps, Rev. Amos A., becomes an abolitionist, 73; his definition of slavery, 73; his noble service, 74; his lecture on slavery, 140; ten thousand dollars offered in New Orleans for his arrest, 187; replies to the " Clerical Appeal," 276.

Z.

www.ingramcontent.com/pod-product-compliance
Lightning Source LLC
Chambersburg PA
CBHW020859130726
47900CB00014B/1117